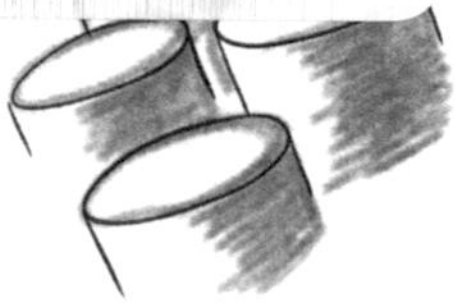

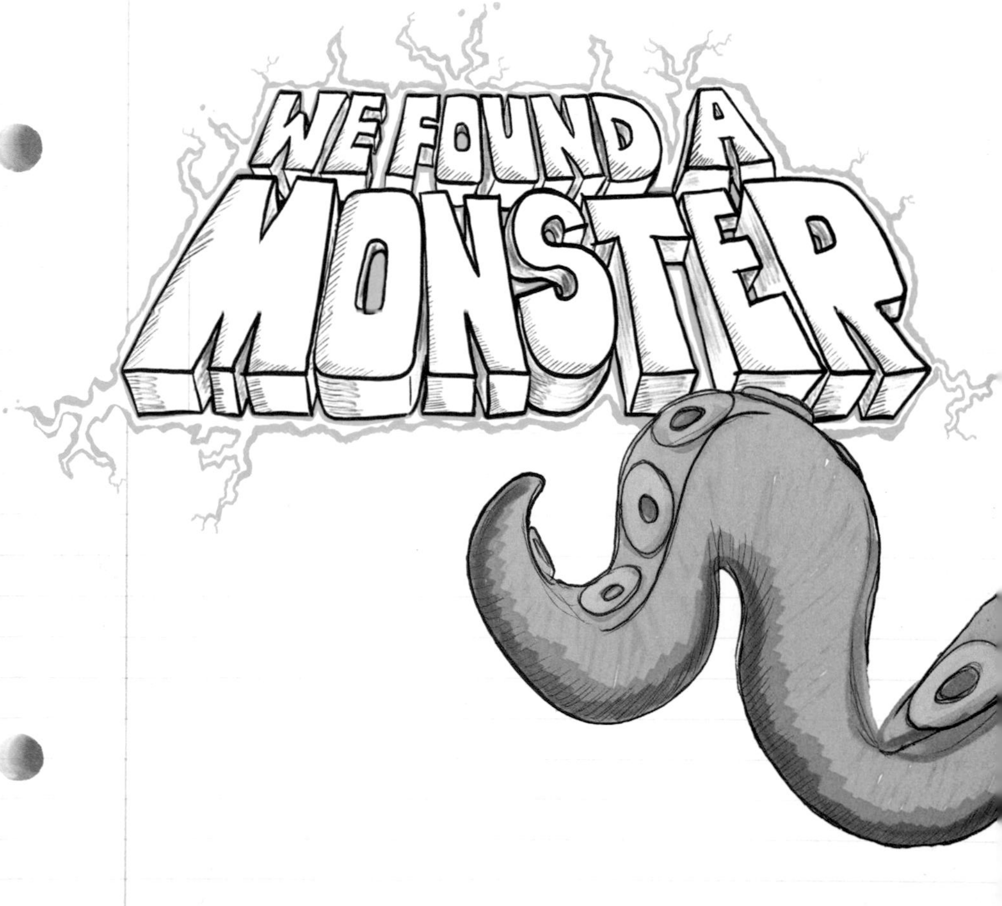
WE FOUND A
MONSTER

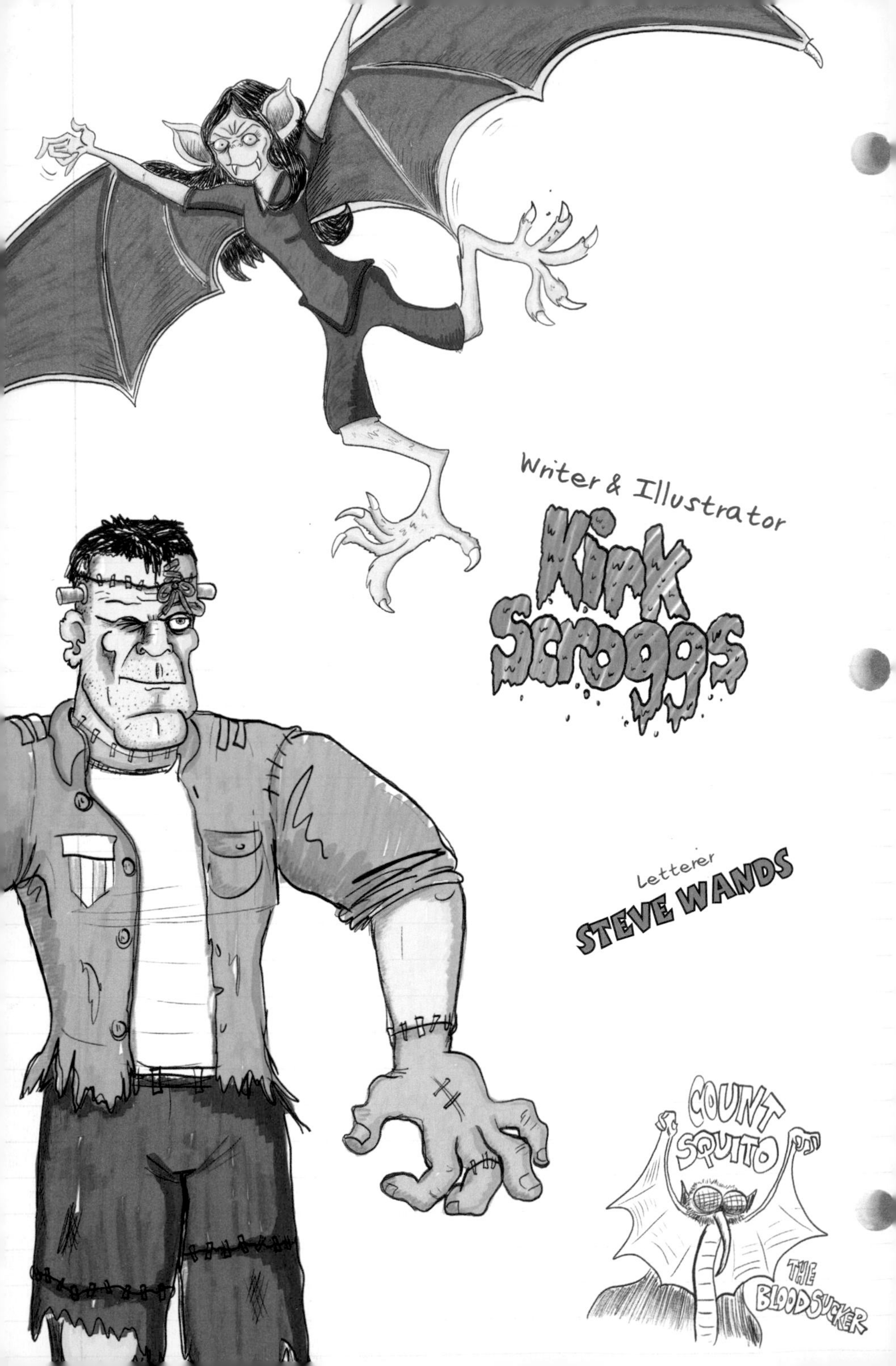
Writer & Illustrator
Kirk Scroggs
Letterer
STEVE WANDS
COUNT SQUITO
THE BLOODSUCKER

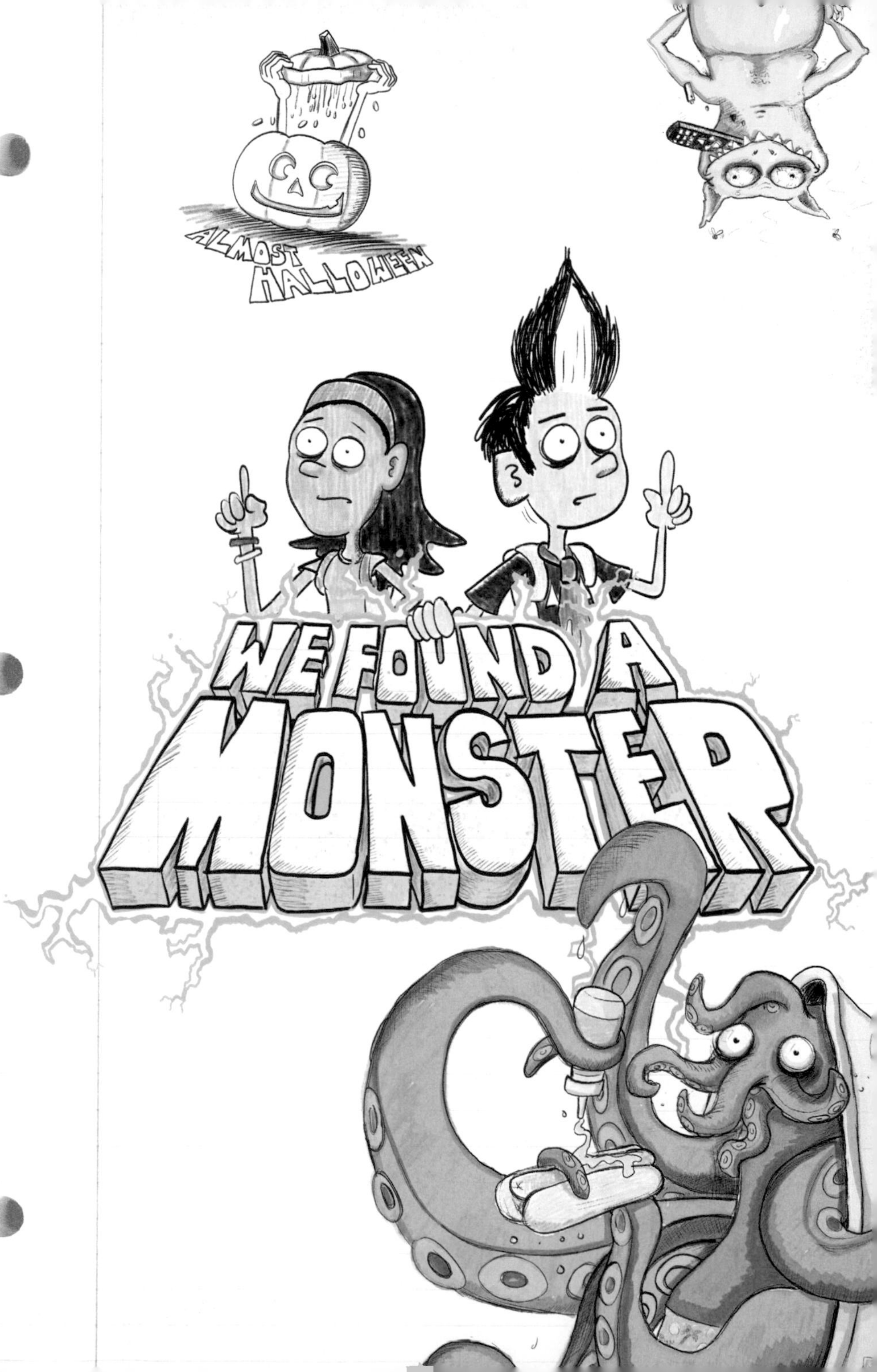
ALMOST HALLOWEEN
WE FOUND A MONSTER

DIEGO LOPEZ Editor
STEVE COOK Design Director - Books
AMIE BROCKWAY-METCALF Publication Design

BOB HARRAS Senior VP - Editor-in-Chief, DC Comics
MICHELE R. WELLS VP & Executive Editor, Young Reader

JIM LEE Publisher & Chief Creative Officer
BOBBIE CHASE VP - Global Publishing Initiatives & Digital Strategy
DON FALLETTI VP - Manufacturing Operations & Workflow Management
LAWRENCE GANEM VP - Talent Services
ALISON GILL Senior VP - Manufacturing & Operations
HANK KANALZ Senior VP - Publishing Strategy & Support Services
DAN MIRON VP - Publishing Operations
NICK J. NAPOLITANO VP - Manufacturing Administration & Design
NANCY SPEARS VP - Sales
JONAH WEILAND VP - Marketing & Creative Services

WE FOUND A MONSTER
Published by DC Comics. Copyright © 2021
DC Comics. All Rights Reserved.
All characters, their distinctive likenesses,
and related elements featured in this
publication are trademarks of DC Comics.
The stories, characters, and incidents
featured in this publication are entirely
fictional. DC Comics does not read or accept
unsolicited submissions of ideas, stories,
or artwork.
DC – a WarnerMedia Company.

DC Comics, 2900 West Alameda Ave.,
Burbank, CA 91505

Printed by LSC Communications,
Crawfordsville, IN, USA.

12/4/20.

First Printing.

ISBN: 978-1-77950-052-6

PEFC Certified
This product is from
sustainably managed
forests and controlled
sources
PEFC
PEFC/29-31-337   www.pefc.org

Library of Congress Cataloging-in-Publication Data
Names: Scroggs, Kirk, writer, illustrator. | Wands, Steve, letterer.
Title: We found a monster : a graphic novel / written & illustrated by Kirk
  Scroggs ; lettered by Steve Wands.
Description: Burbank, CA : DC Comics, [2021] | Audience: Ages 8-12 |
  Audience: Grades 4-6 | Summary: Sixth-grader and scary movie fan Casey
  Clive has been dealing with a variety of needy monsters living in his
  house, and now new girl at school, Zandra, has not only found out about
  his creature collection, she needs help with a monster she has found,
  too.
Identifiers: LCCN 2020038530 (print) | LCCN 2020038531 (ebook) | ISBN
  9781779500526 (paperback) | ISBN 9781779508553 (ebook)
Subjects: LCSH: Graphic novels. | CYAC: Graphic novels. |
  Monsters--Fiction. | Friendship--Fiction. | Humorous stories.
Classification: LCC PZ7.7.S4145 We 2021 (print) | LCC PZ7.7.S4145 (ebook)
  | DDC 741.5/973--dc23
LC record available at https://lccn.loc.gov/2020038530
LC ebook record available at https://lccn.loc.gov/2020038531

FOR CHARLOTTE AND ISAAC,
MY FAVE LITTLE MONSTERS.

—KIRK

SCRATCH
AND SNIFF!

Amazing
sticker bro.
Smells just
like a
real book!

About the author...

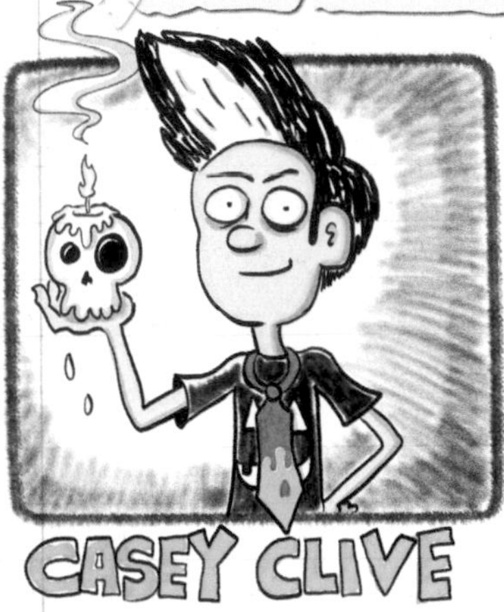
CASEY CLIVE

MOST DEFINITELY NOT TORN OUT OF DAD'S COPY OF A BRIEF HISTORY OF GOLF.

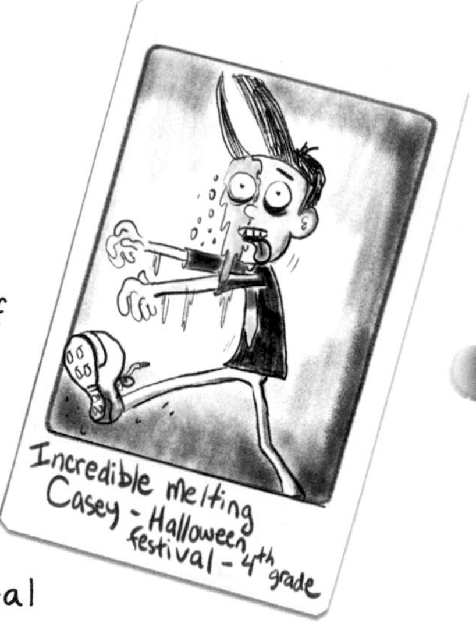

Incredible melting Casey - Halloween festival - 4th grade

Casey Clive is the New York Slimes' worst-selling author of Casey Clive's Journal volumes 1–12. He is a monster expert and has little patience for anyone who isn't. He lives in Serena Mar with his dad, a rabbit named Ygor, and several other mystery occupants.

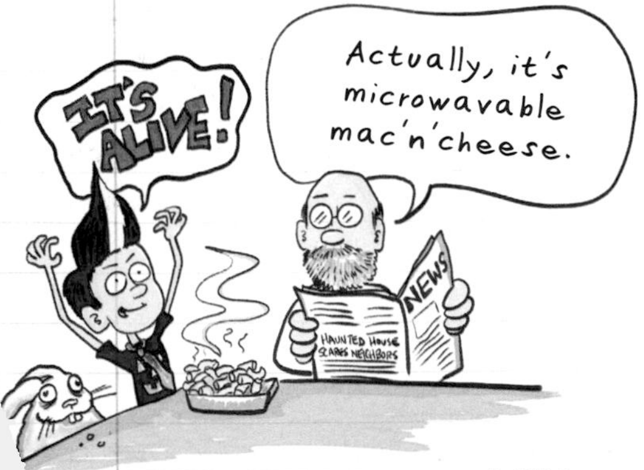
IT'S ALIVE!
Actually, it's microwavable mac'n'cheese.
NEWS
HAUNTED HOUSE SCARES NEIGHBORS

MAD SCIENTIST CASEY

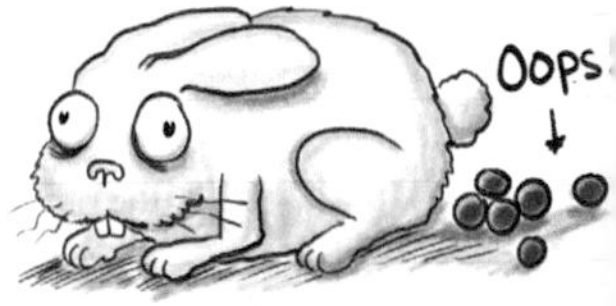
Oops

YGOR

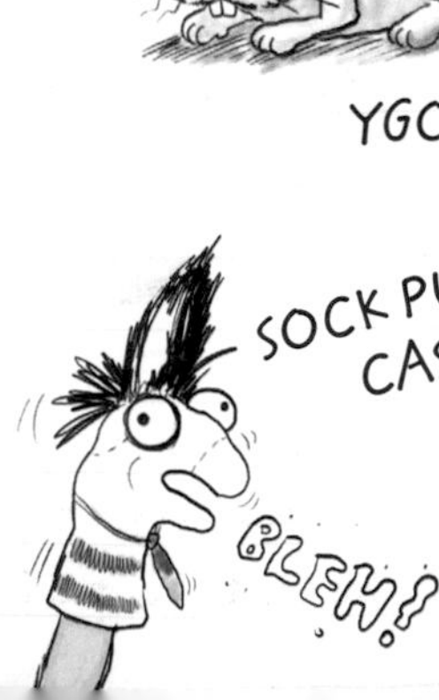
BLEH!?

SOCK PUPPET CASEY

JOURNAL 13

Here we go again!
This is my thirteenth journal. Hard to believe I've filled twelve of these notebooks with interesting facts, razor-sharp wit, thrilling ~~aneckdotes annic~~ stories—actually, they're mostly full of monster doodles.

My only rule for journaling is still in effect—NO MUSHY STUFF! This is not a sappy diary full of sorrow and whining!

Glowing eyes

getting stubby ☹

I also have an...
Important Announcement! Usually, I do all the terrifying illustrations in my journals with my trusty

COUNT FANGO PENCIL

Sadly, Count Fango has been sharpened down to barely a nub and it's bumming me out. Mom gave me Count Fango a little over a year ago, just before she... Nope! Almost broke my one rule about journals: no mushy stuff allowed! Anyway, I'm only going to use Count Fango every once in a while to preserve him.

A WORD OF WARNING!

Things have gotten really weird in my life lately! And they're bound to get weirder!

Casey Clive

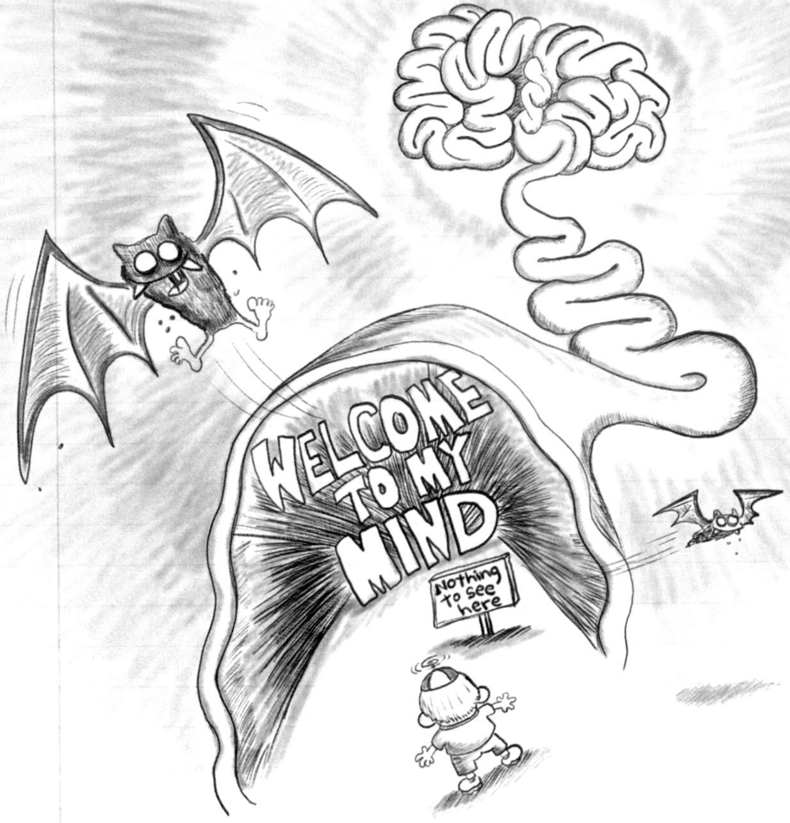
WELCOME TO MY MIND
Nothing to see here

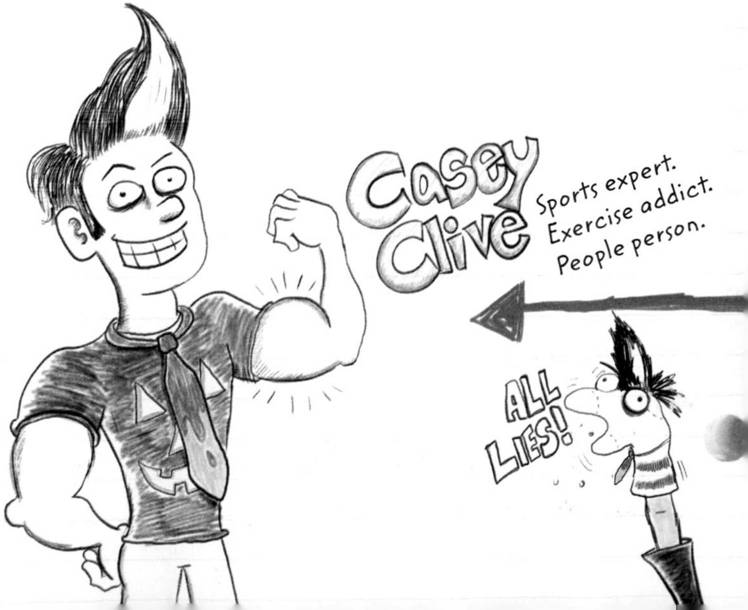
Casey Clive
Sports expert.
Exercise addict.
People person.
ALL LIES!

7:48 AM. TUES.

ON THE BUS

Oh, this day.
I have one word for it...
UGGBLARGPHARRRT!
I think that's
German for
"I'm not feelin'
it, yo."

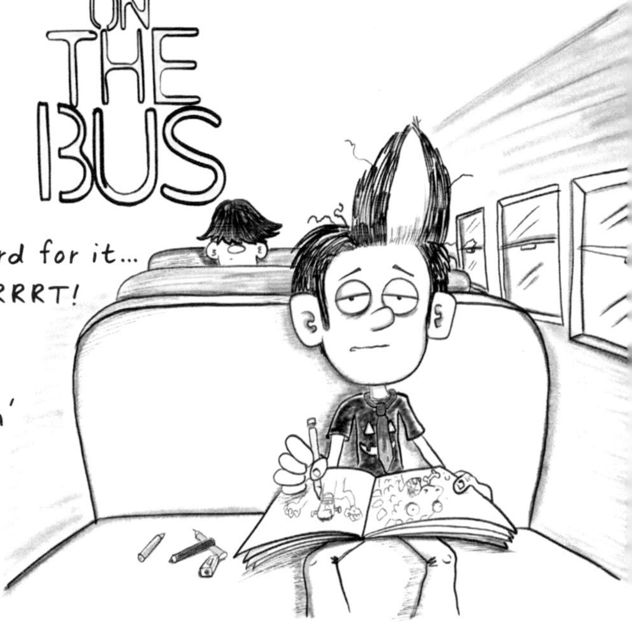

Just look at me. Does this look like the face of a well-rested, happy sixth grader?

Here's a closer look. I warn you, it ain't pretty.

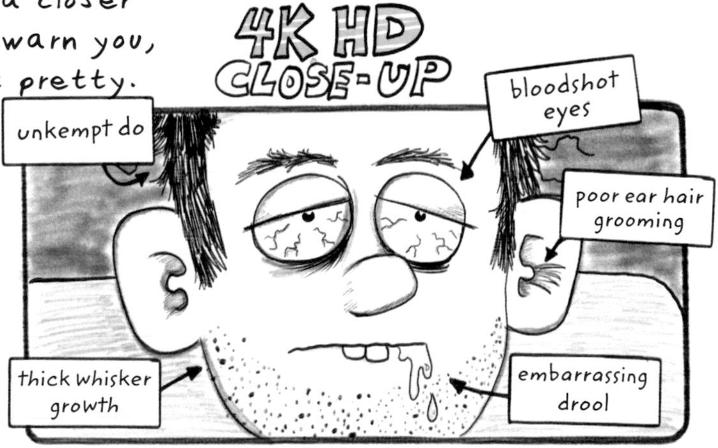

4K HD CLOSE-UP
unkempt do
bloodshot eyes
poor ear hair grooming
thick whisker growth
embarrassing drool

I don't always look this ragged. Normally, in the mornings, I look like this...
(I wish.)

Why am I so tired, you ask?
Because I DIDN'T GET ANY SLEEP LAST NIGHT!
And why didn't I get any sleep? I'll tell you why...

MONSTERS!

THAT'S WHY!

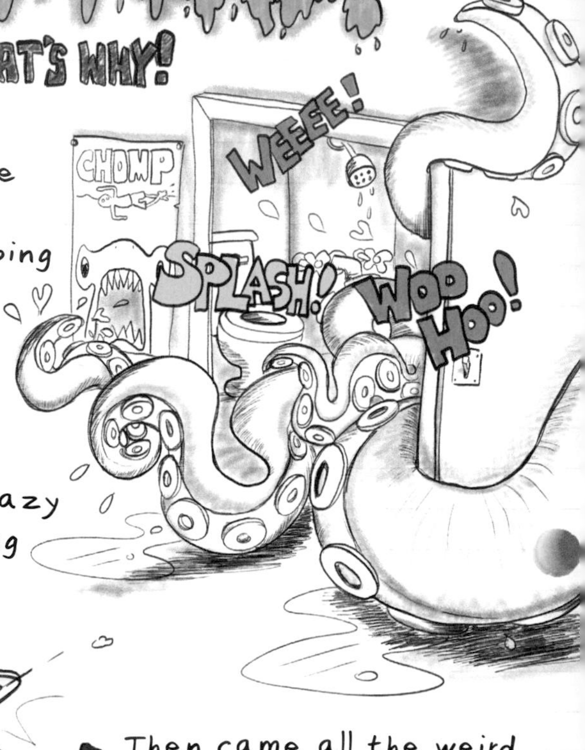

CHOMP
WEEEE!
SPLASH!
WOO HOO!

Monsters up in my house, making noise ALL NIGHT LONG! Thumping and bumping and I don't know what!

It started in the bathroom. Topo was going crazy in there, splashing and squealing.

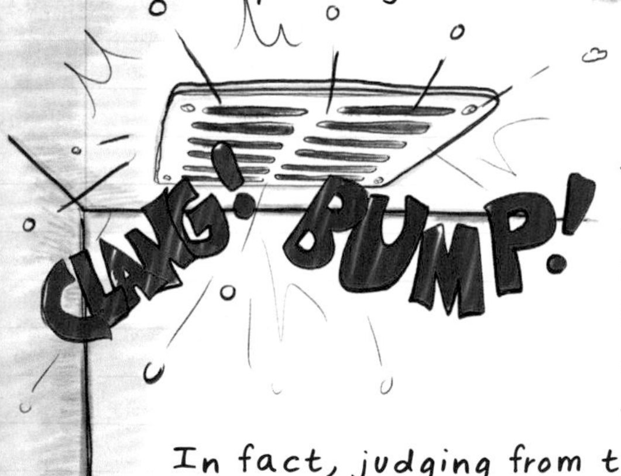

CLANG!
BUMP!

Then came all the weird sounds from the A.C. vent. I don't know what She-Bat was doing up in the attic, but it could have woken the dead...

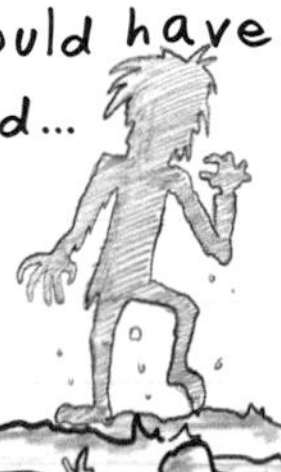

In fact, judging from the dug-up backyard, I'm pretty sure it did!

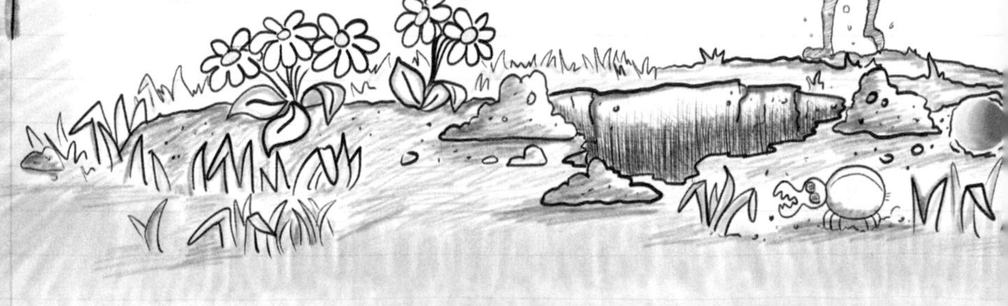

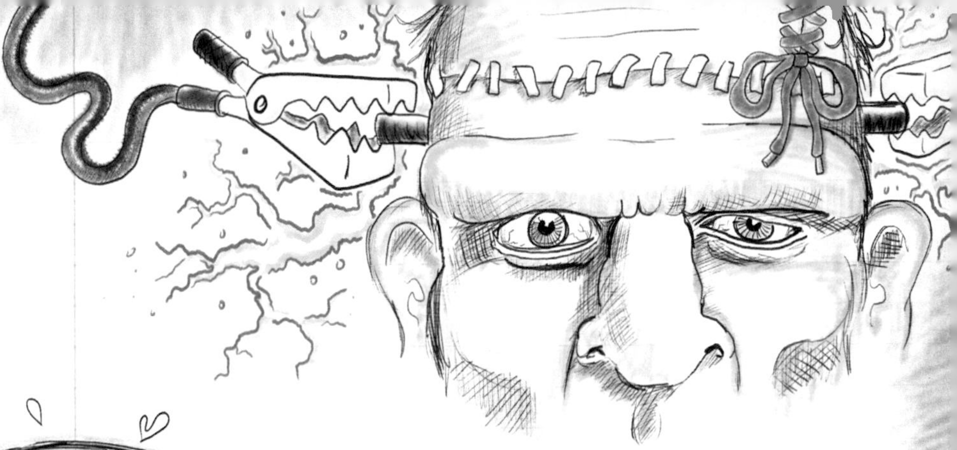

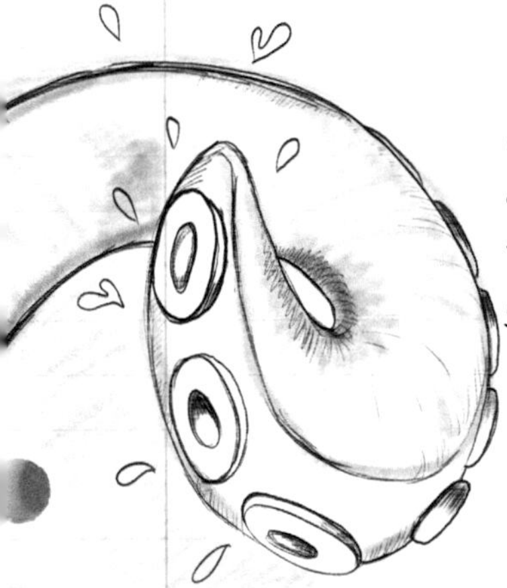

On top of everything, Frankenstein's charger was on the fritz again, and the power surge made my alarm clock go off all night!

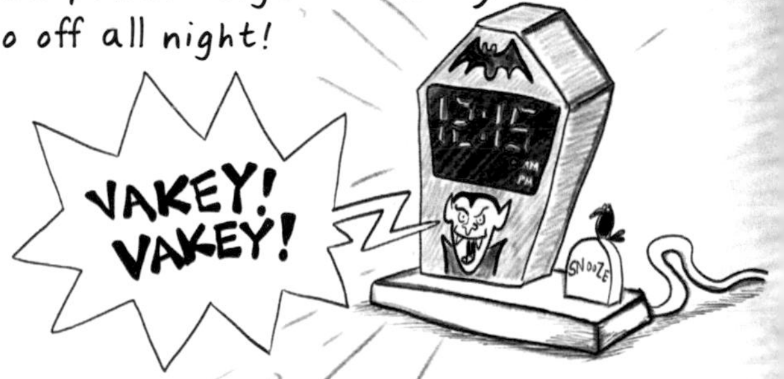

VAKEY! VAKEY!
SNOOZE

And don't get me started on the gremlins...

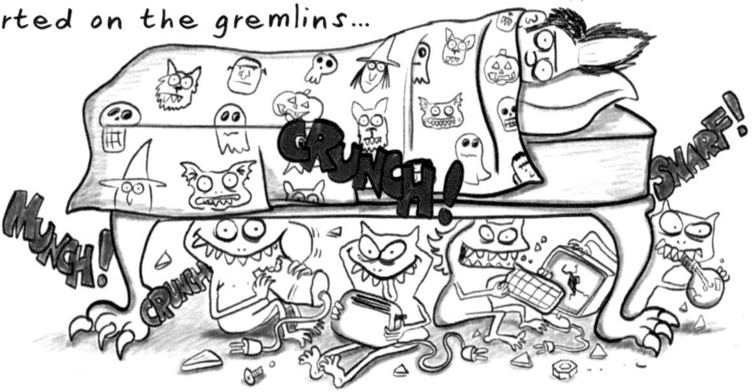

MUNCH!
CRUNCH!
CRUNCH
SNARF!

A word of advice:

NEVER! keep gremlins under your bed!

TURN SIDEWAYS

Casey's Creature Exhibit

Gremlin

HEIGHT: 2 Feet

SCIENTIFIC NAME: Eatus whateverus

HABITAT: Factories, engine rooms, anywhere with electronics

Known for causing mechanical havoc

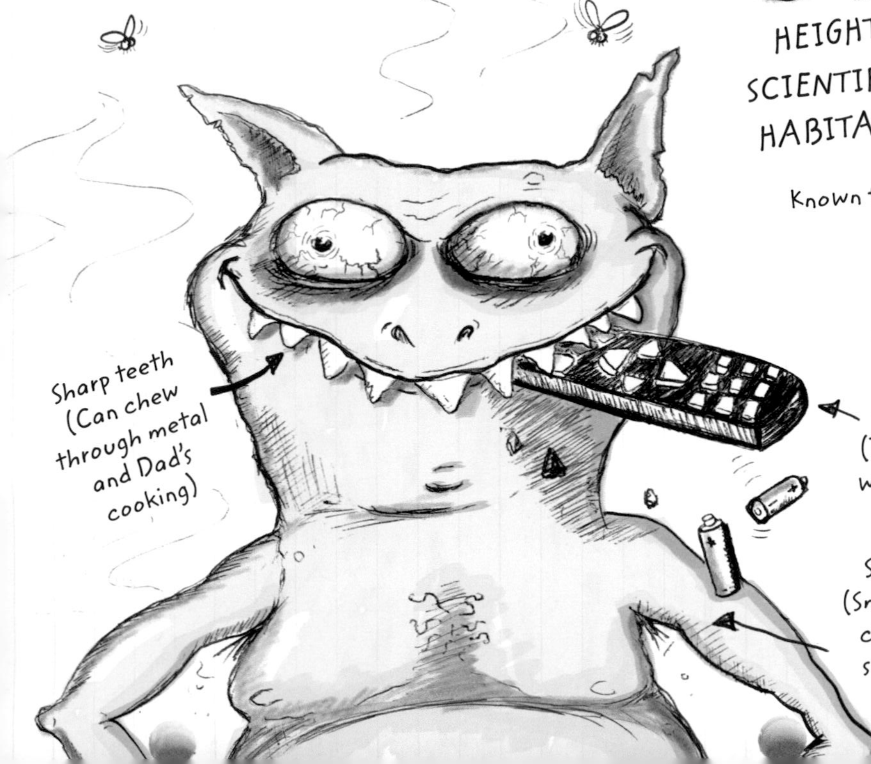
Sharp teeth (Can chew through metal and Dad's cooking)
Cable remote (I was wondering where that went.)
Scent glands (Smells like BBQ chips and dirty socks a.k.a. my bedroom)

Actual newspaper clipping from 1942!

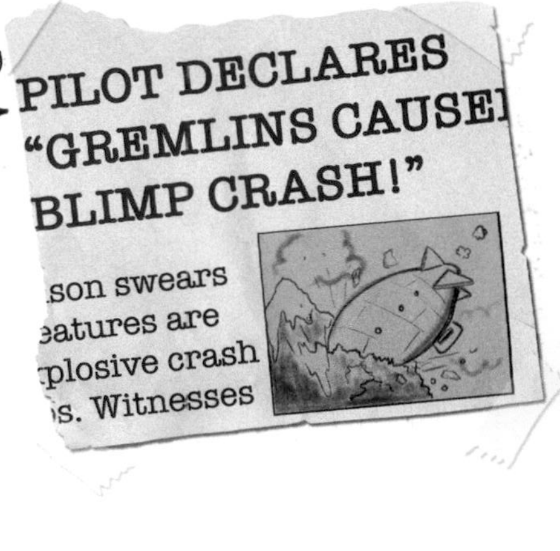
PILOT DECLARES "GREMLINS CAUSE[D] BLIMP CRASH!"

...son swears ...eatures are ...plosive crash ...s. Witnesses

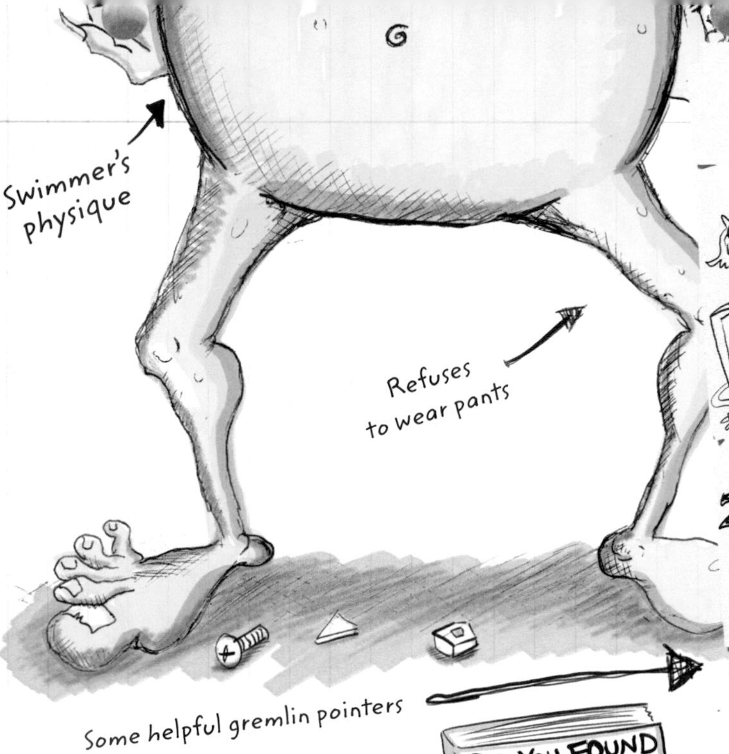
G
Swimmer's physique
Refuses to wear pants
Some helpful gremlin pointers

Someday I'm gonna compile all these expert tips into a how-to book...

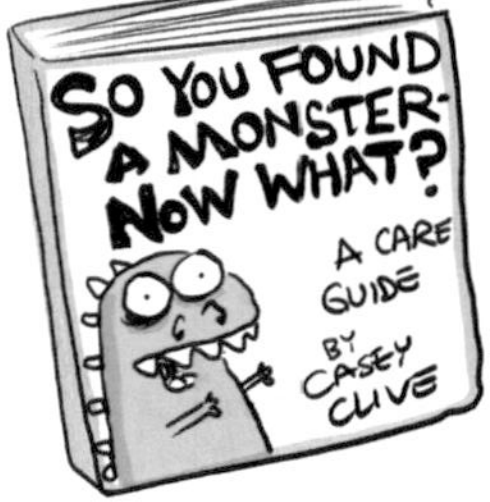
SO YOU FOUND A MONSTER- NOW WHAT?
A CARE GUIDE
BY CASEY CLIVE

Proper gremlins Care and ~~maitainense~~ ~~manten~~ Care

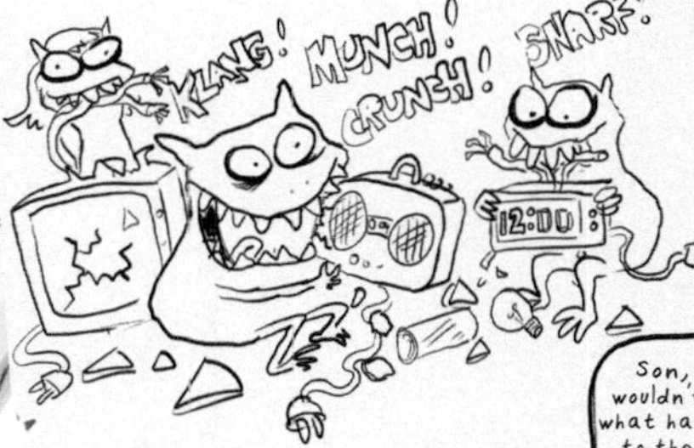
KLANG!
MUNCH!
CRUNCH!
SNARF!
12:00

1. Never sleep in the same room with snacking gremlins! Everything they eat is loud and crunchy and could release dangerous shrapnel.

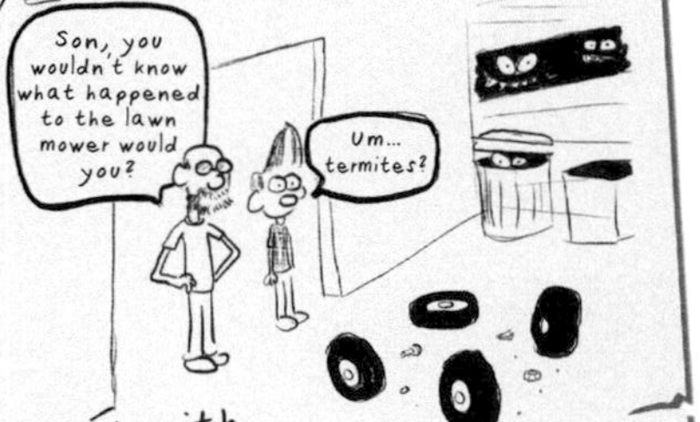
Son, you wouldn't know what happened to the lawn mower would you?
Um... termites?

2. Never keep gremlins where you store important machinery, e.g. vehicles, video game consoles, vital medical devices, etc....

3. Spice up your gremlins diet with the unexpected. Throw some old florescent bulbs, lithium batteries, and electric back massagers into their meal.

And leave old lamps plugged in. They appreciate the added zing.

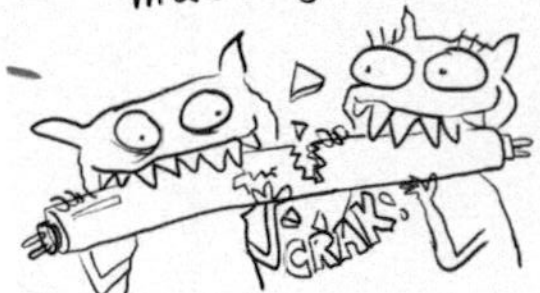
CRAK!

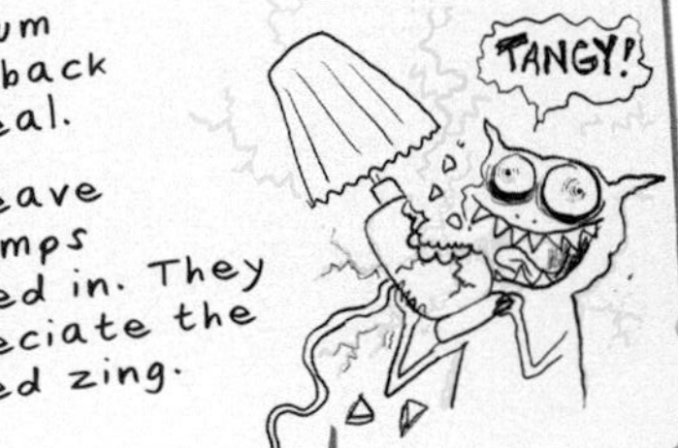
TANGY!

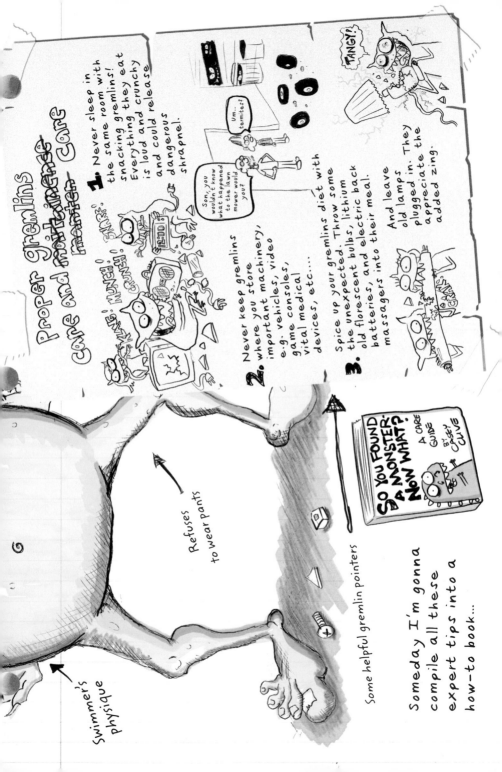

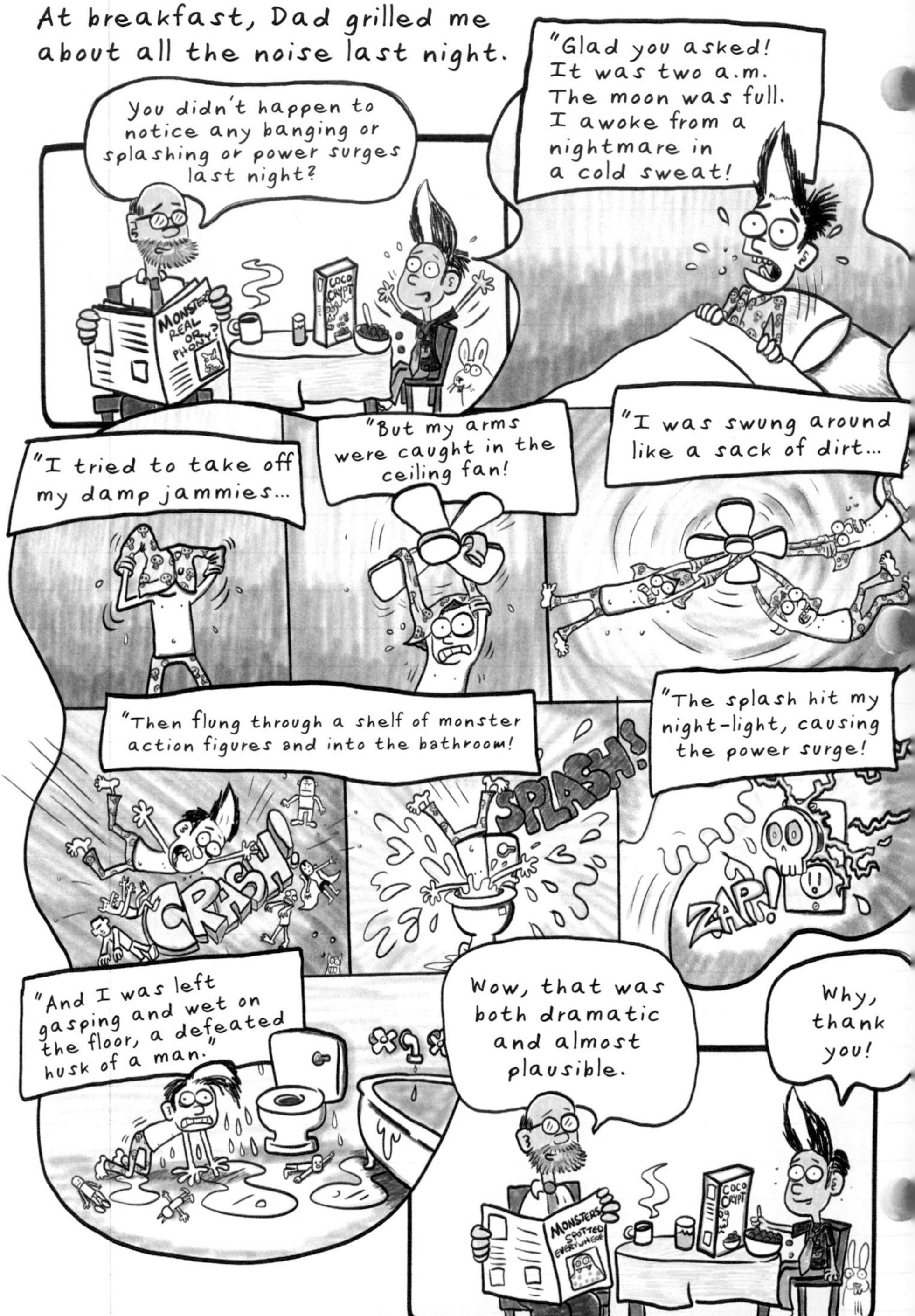
At breakfast, Dad grilled me about all the noise last night.
You didn't happen to notice any banging or splashing or power surges last night?
COCO CRYPT
MONSTERS REAL OR PHONY?
"Glad you asked! It was two a.m. The moon was full. I awoke from a nightmare in a cold sweat!
"I tried to take off my damp jammies...
"But my arms were caught in the ceiling fan!
"I was swung around like a sack of dirt...
"Then flung through a shelf of monster action figures and into the bathroom!
CRASH!
SPLASH!
"The splash hit my night-light, causing the power surge!
ZAP!
"And I was left gasping and wet on the floor, a defeated husk of a man."
Wow, that was both dramatic and almost plausible.
Why, thank you!
MONSTERS SPOTTED EVERYWHERE
COCO CRYPT

I can't hide eight monsters from Dad much longer.

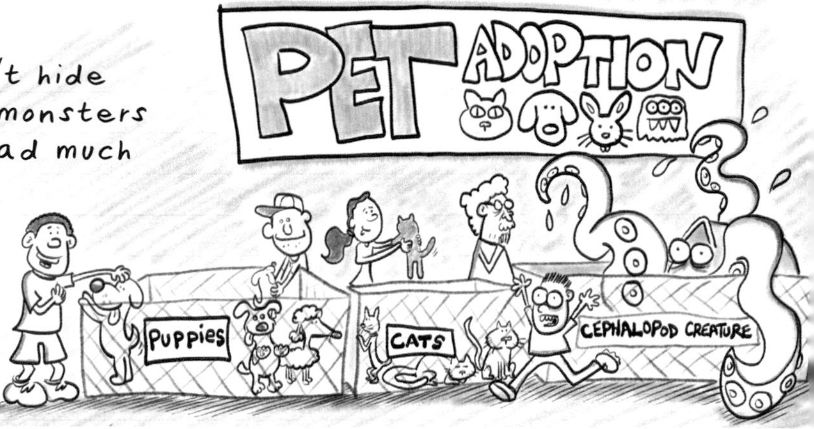
PET ADOPTION
PUPPIES
CATS
CEPHALOPOD CREATURE

And with more showing up all the time, I need to find a new housing situation A.S.A.P. But where? It's not like I can take them to the local animal shelter!

8:00 A.M. HISTORY CLASS

Oh, my beloved history class, how I love thee. I should be listening to Ms. Webber, but I usually spend most of the time drawing stuff like this.

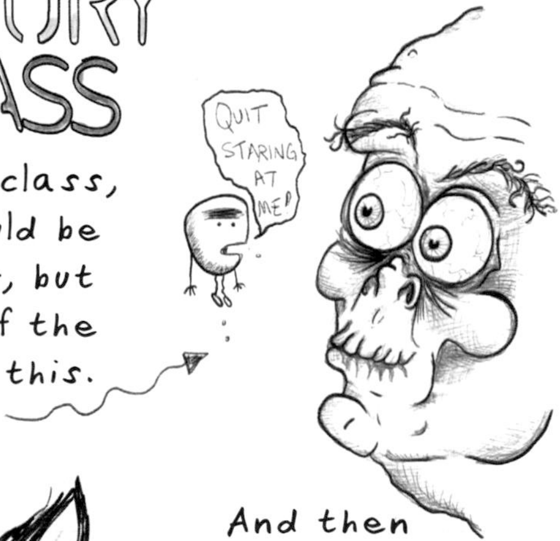
QUIT STARING AT ME!

And then there's my fave part of class— the ol' paper wad to the head I get every morning. And it always comes from you know who...

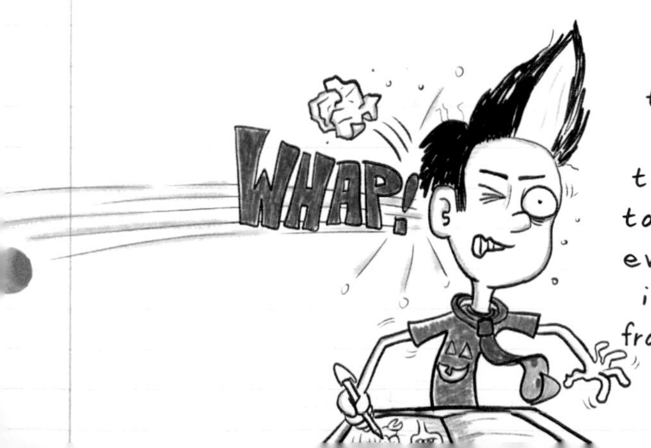
WHAP!

It's Grant, of course, my own personal motivator. (He motivates me to walk the other direction, roll my eyes, and hurl into my backpack.)

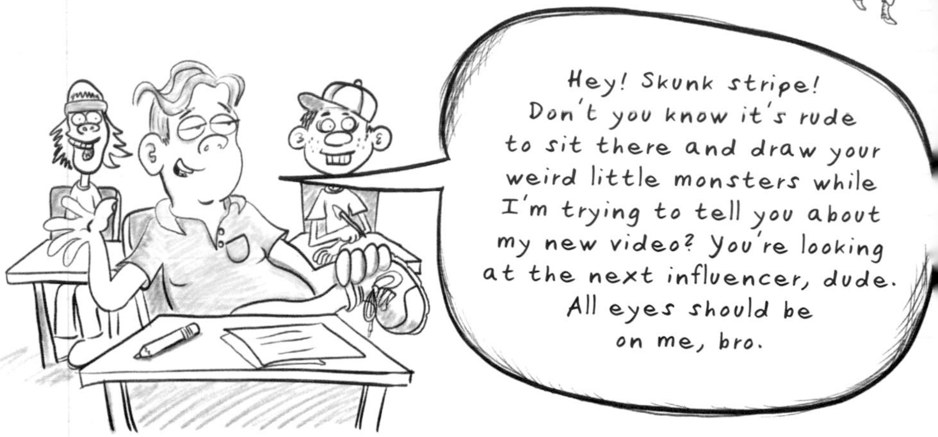
Hey! Skunk stripe! Don't you know it's rude to sit there and draw your weird little monsters while I'm trying to tell you about my new video? You're looking at the next influencer, dude. All eyes should be on me, bro.

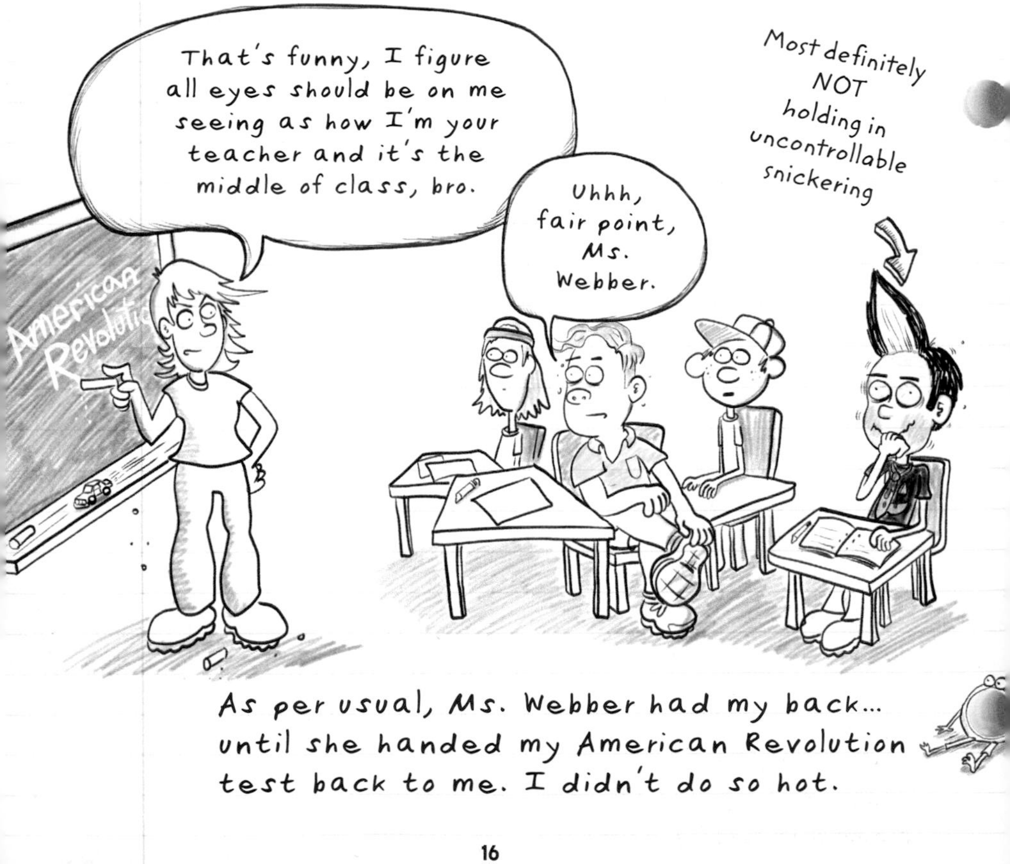
That's funny, I figure all eyes should be on me seeing as how I'm your teacher and it's the middle of class, bro.
Uhhh, fair point, Ms. Webber.
Most definitely NOT holding in uncontrollable snickering
American Revolution

As per usual, Ms. Webber had my back... until she handed my American Revolution test back to me. I didn't do so hot.

I can't believe she didn't appreciate my unique answer to the last question.

10. What did Benjamin Franklin do in Philadelphia in 1776?

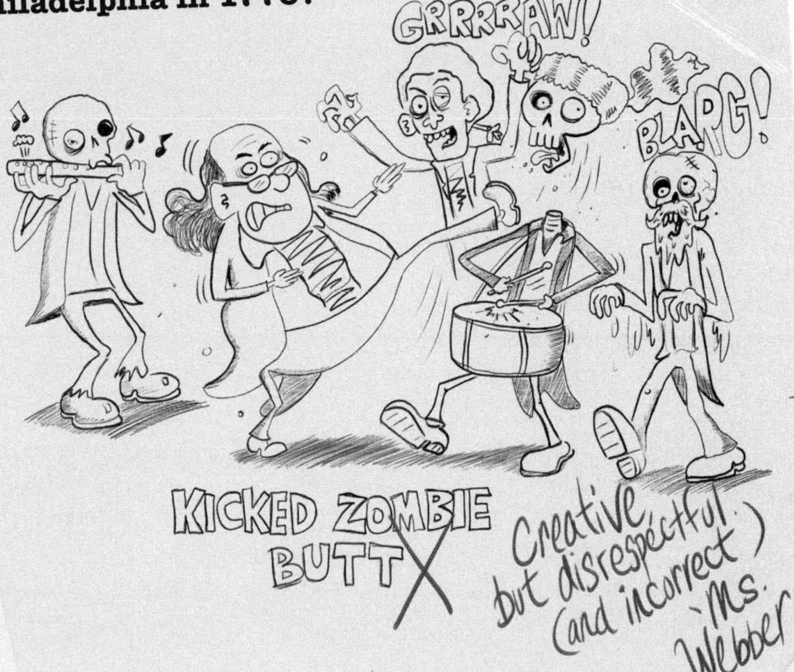
GRRRRAW!
BLARG!
KICKED ZOMBIE BUTT
Creative but disrespectful (and incorrect) -Ms. Webber

Why can't we be quizzed on some real history? Like, what's the movie where Sherlock Holmes went head-to-head with a werewolf? Or, what's the original recipe for fake blood? You know, important stuff!

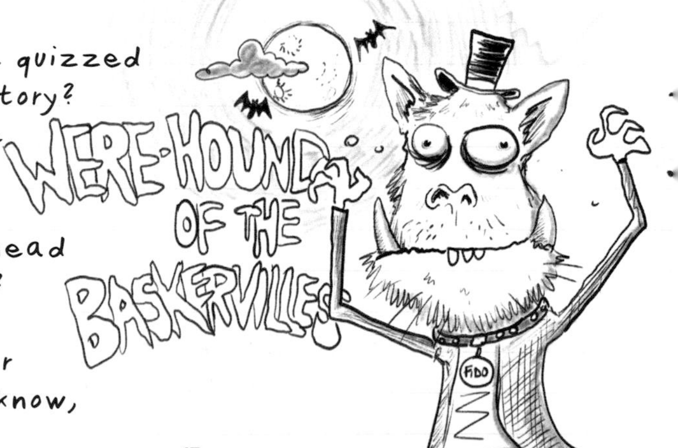
WERE-HOUND OF THE BASKERVILLES
FIDO

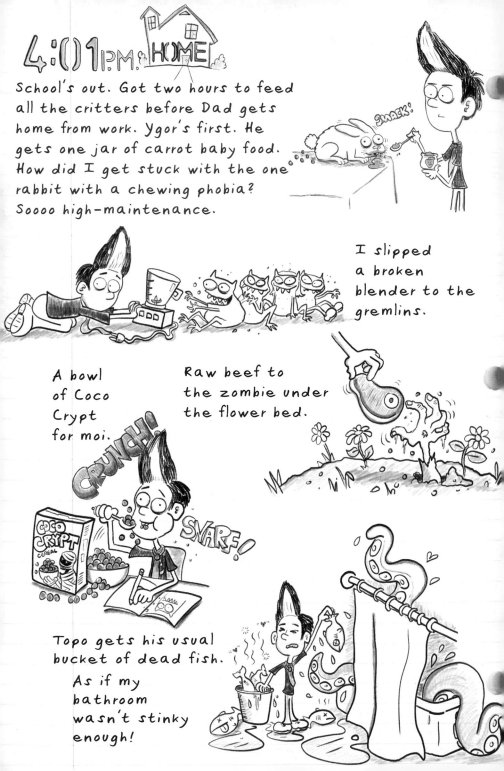

4:01 P.M. HOME

School's out. Got two hours to feed all the critters before Dad gets home from work. Ygor's first. He gets one jar of carrot baby food. How did I get stuck with the one rabbit with a chewing phobia? Soooo high-maintenance.

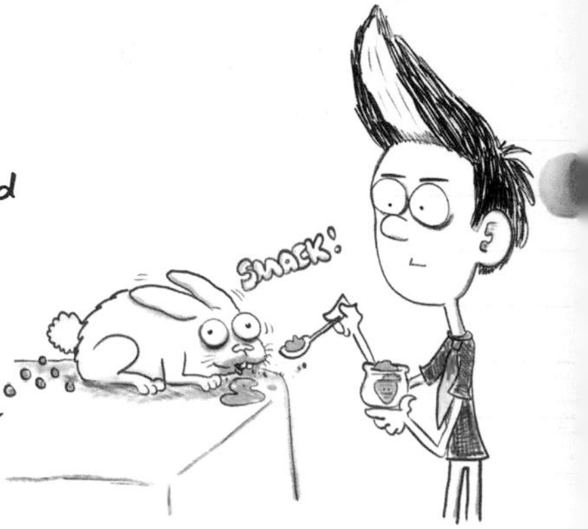
SMACK!

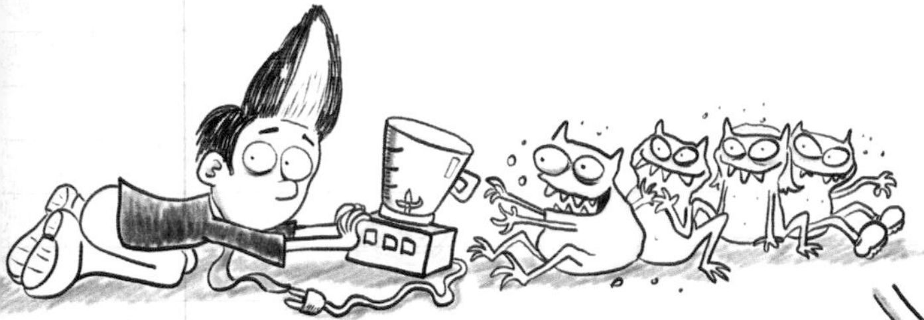

I slipped a broken blender to the gremlins.

A bowl of Coco Crypt for moi.

Raw beef to the zombie under the flower bed.

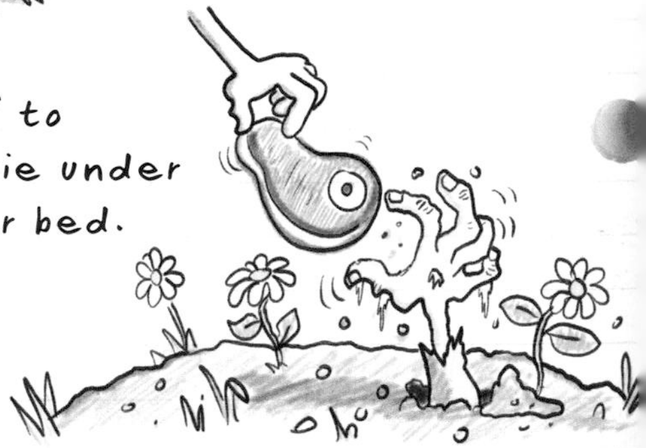

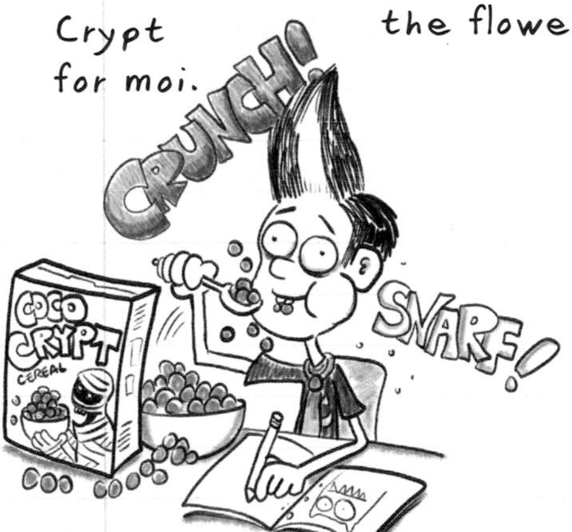
CRUNCH!
SNARF!
COCO CRYPT
CEREAL

Topo gets his usual bucket of dead fish.

As if my bathroom wasn't stinky enough!

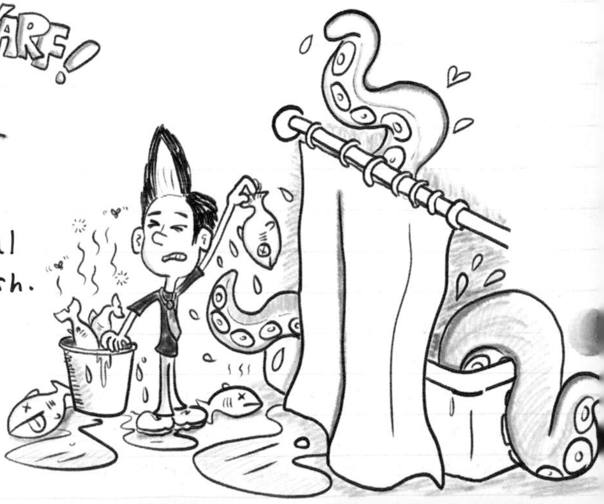

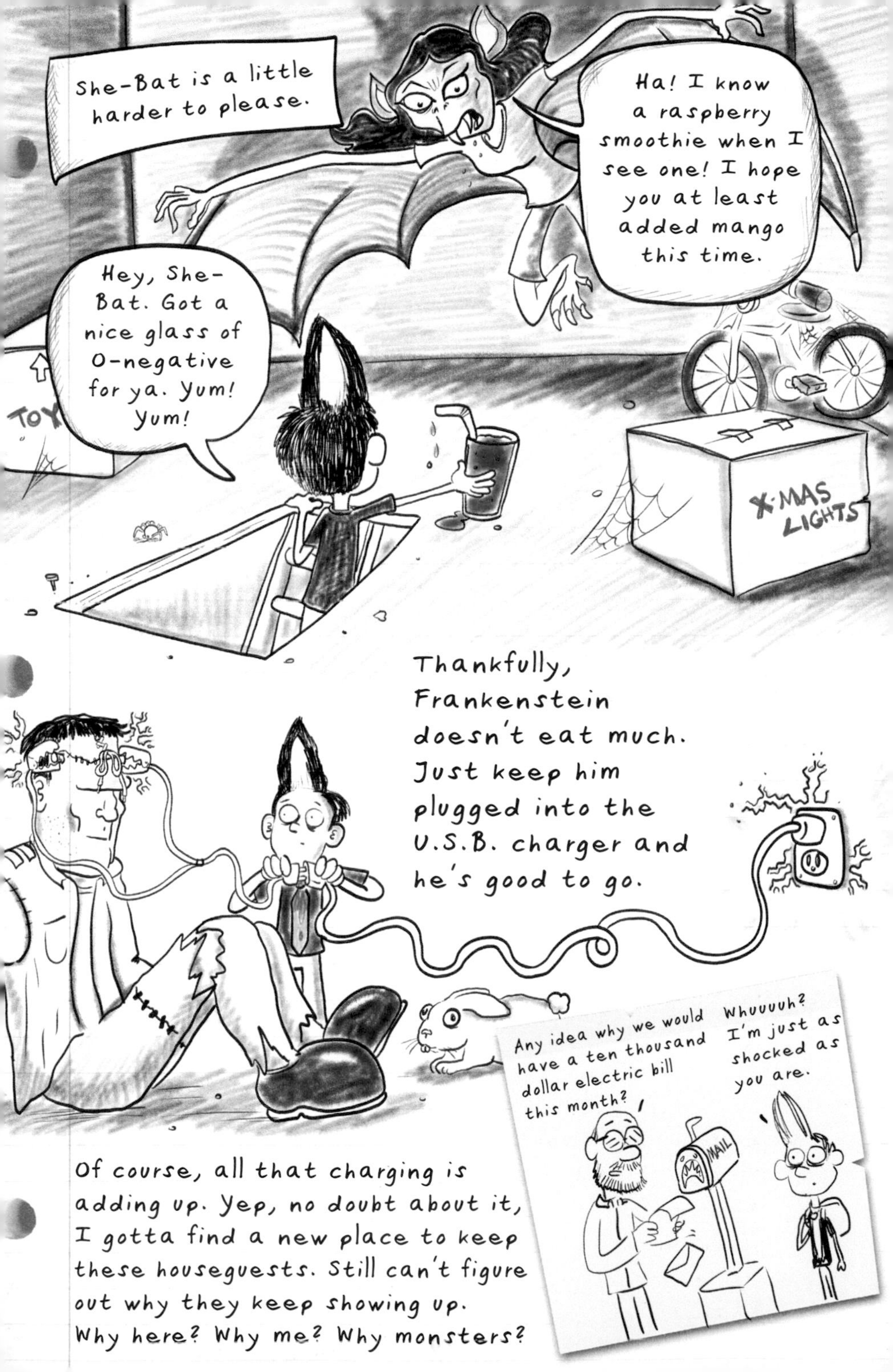
She-Bat is a little harder to please.
Hey, She-Bat. Got a nice glass of O-negative for ya. Yum! Yum!
Ha! I know a raspberry smoothie when I see one! I hope you at least added mango this time.
TOY
X-MAS LIGHTS
Thankfully, Frankenstein doesn't eat much. Just keep him plugged into the U.S.B. charger and he's good to go.
Of course, all that charging is adding up. Yep, no doubt about it, I gotta find a new place to keep these houseguests. Still can't figure out why they keep showing up. Why here? Why me? Why monsters?
Any idea why we would have a ten thousand dollar electric bill this month?
Whuuuuh? I'm just as shocked as you are.
MAIL

Casey's Creature Exhibit

Frankenstein

(Goes by Franky)

SCIENTIFIC NAME: Staggerus Droolus Groanus

ORIGIN: Spooky German castle

FAVORITE FOOD: High voltage currents

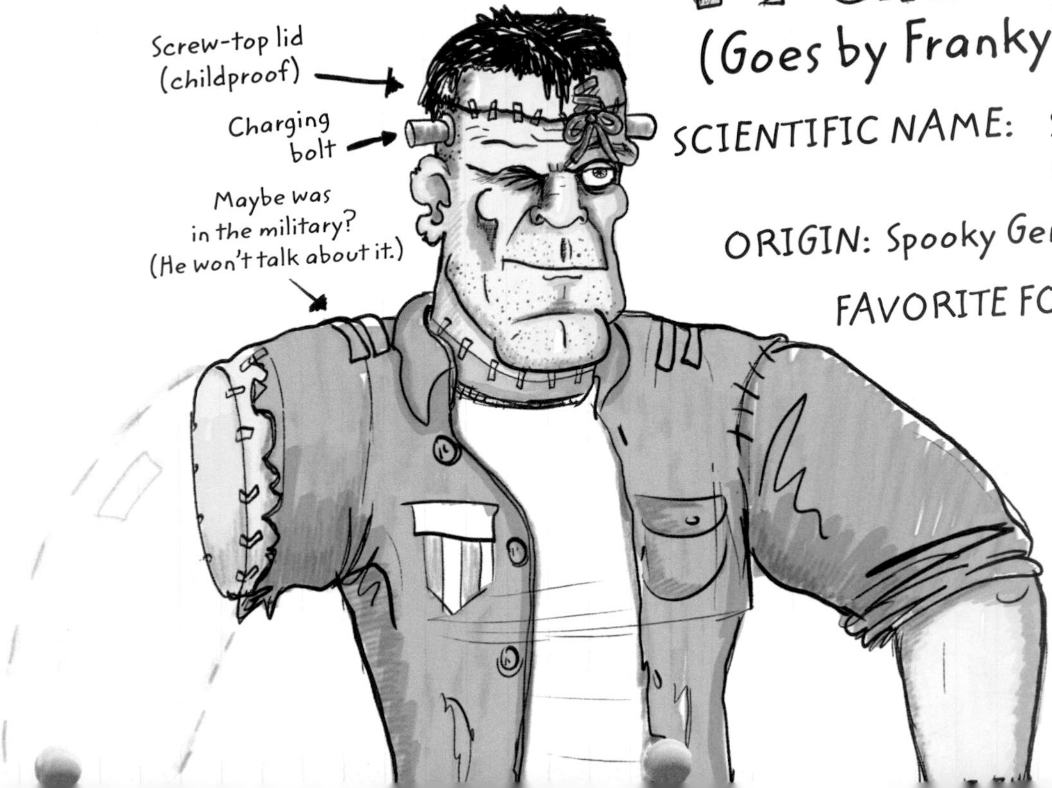
Screw-top lid (childproof)
Charging bolt
Maybe was in the military? (He won't talk about it.)

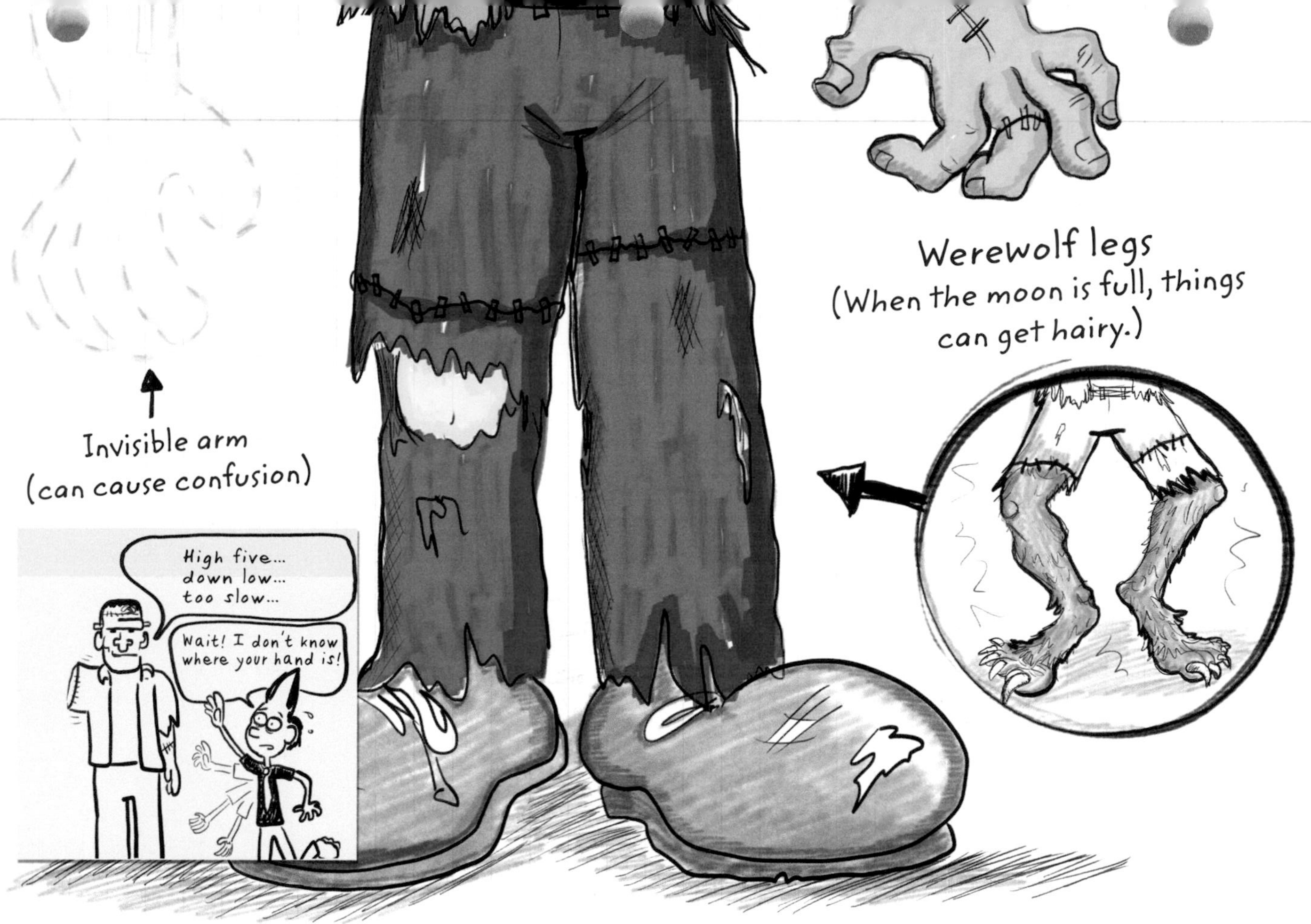
Werewolf legs
(When the moon is full, things can get hairy.)
Invisible arm
(can cause confusion)
High five... down low... too slow...
Wait! I don't know where your hand is!

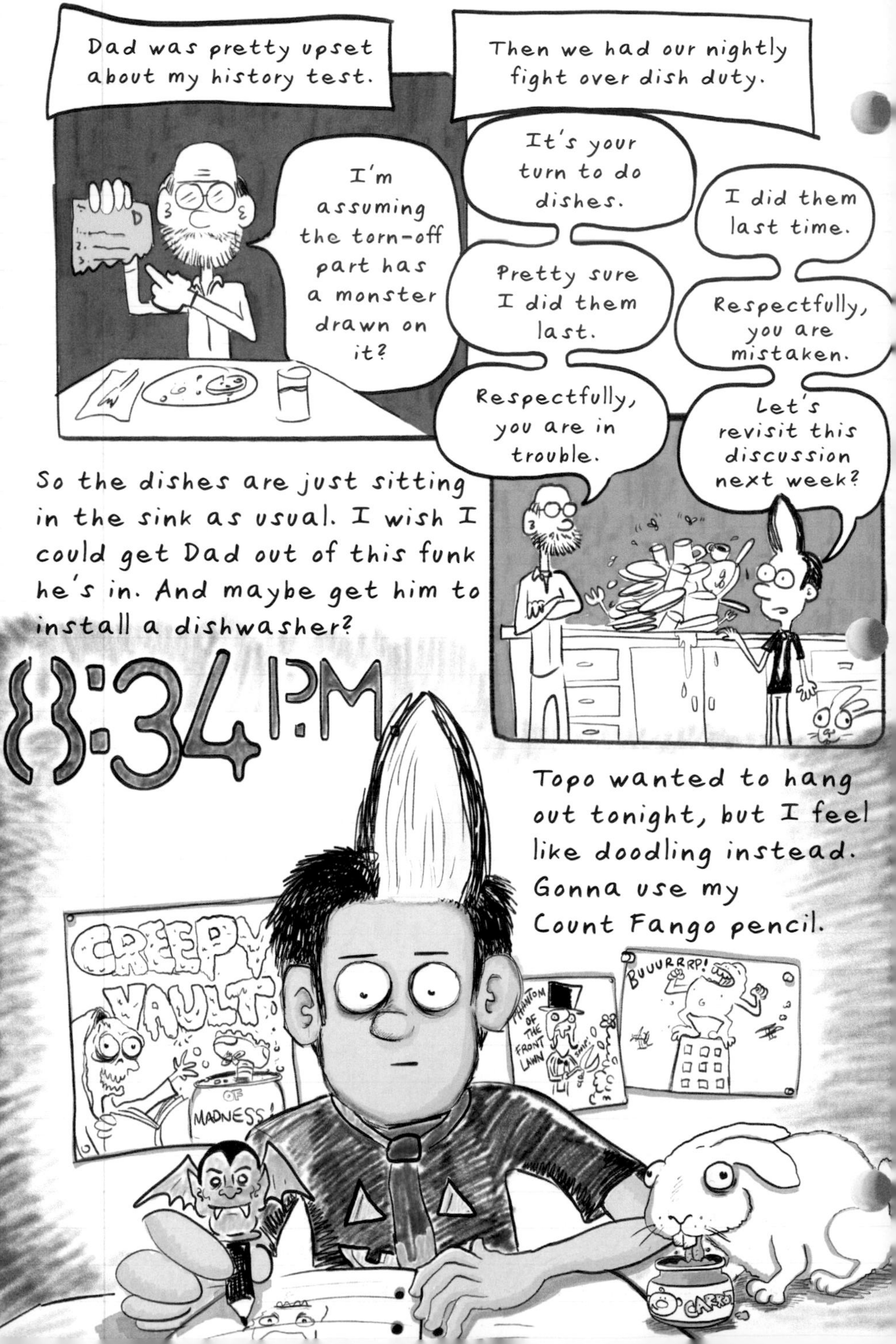
Dad was pretty upset about my history test.
I'm assuming the torn-off part has a monster drawn on it?
Then we had our nightly fight over dish duty.
It's your turn to do dishes.
I did them last time.
Pretty sure I did them last.
Respectfully, you are mistaken.
Respectfully, you are in trouble.
Let's revisit this discussion next week?
So the dishes are just sitting in the sink as usual. I wish I could get Dad out of this funk he's in. And maybe get him to install a dishwasher?
8:34 P.M
Topo wanted to hang out tonight, but I feel like doodling instead. Gonna use my Count Fango pencil.
CREEPY VAULT
OF MADNESS!
PHANTOM OF THE FRONT LAWN
BUUURRRP!

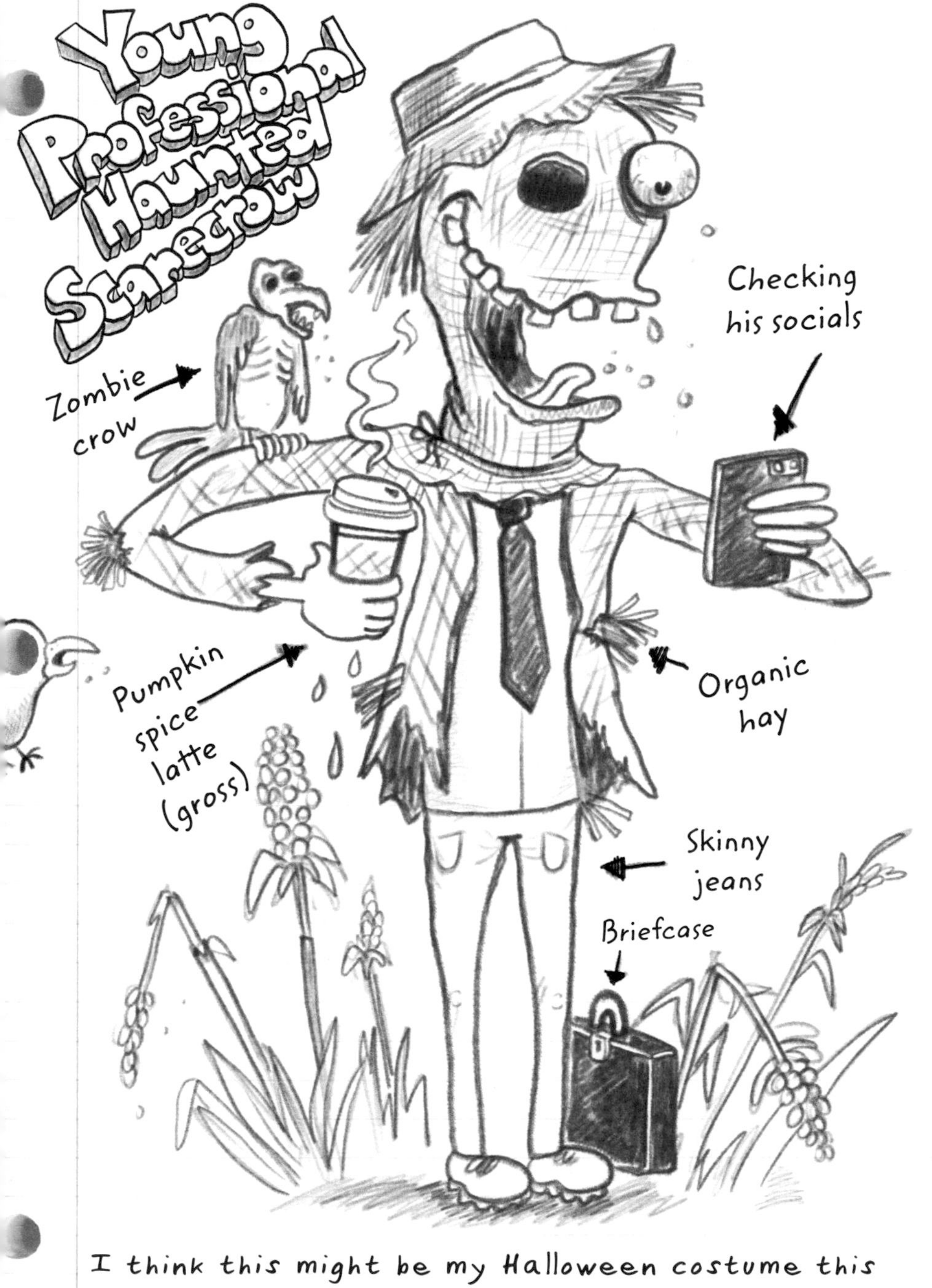
Young Professional Haunted Scarecrow
Zombie crow
Checking his socials
Pumpkin spice latte (gross)
Organic hay
Skinny jeans
Briefcase

I think this might be my Halloween costume this year. Wish Mom could help me make it like the good ol' days. I'll figure it out.

LUNCH WEDNESDAY

Hi. Back again. It's been a minute. I'm sitting out here by the school fountain on the steps. This is my fave spot for sketching.

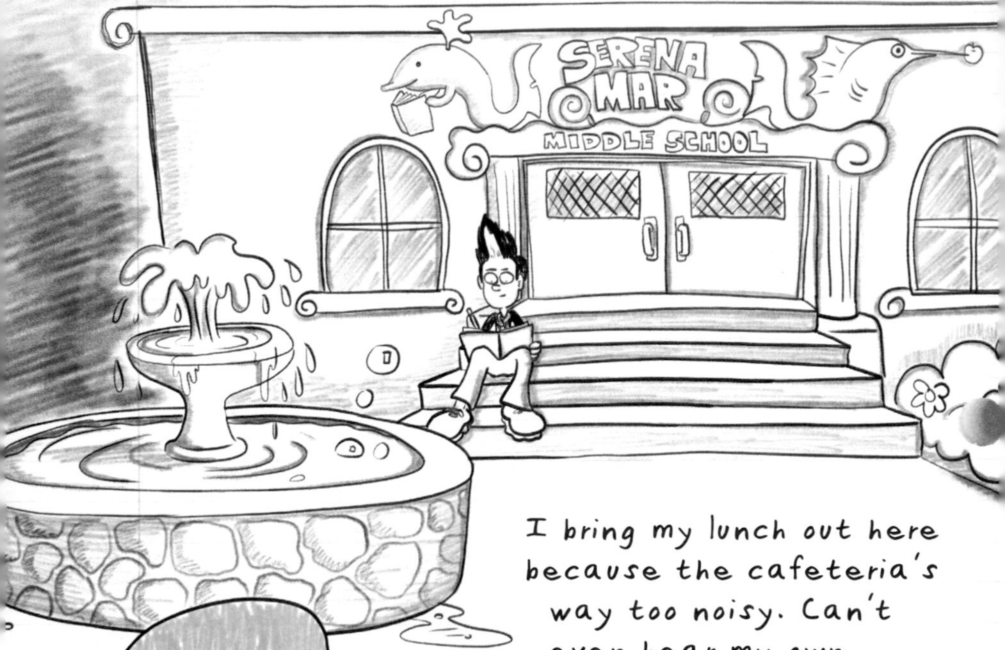
SERENA MAR
MIDDLE SCHOOL

I bring my lunch out here because the cafeteria's way too noisy. Can't even hear my own thoughts in there. Sometimes it pays to be a loner.

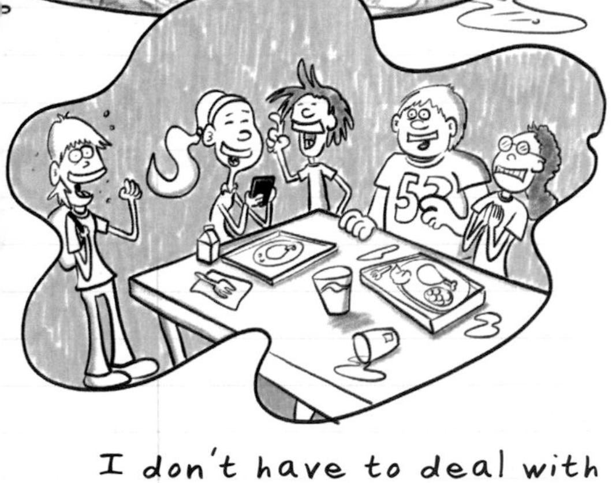

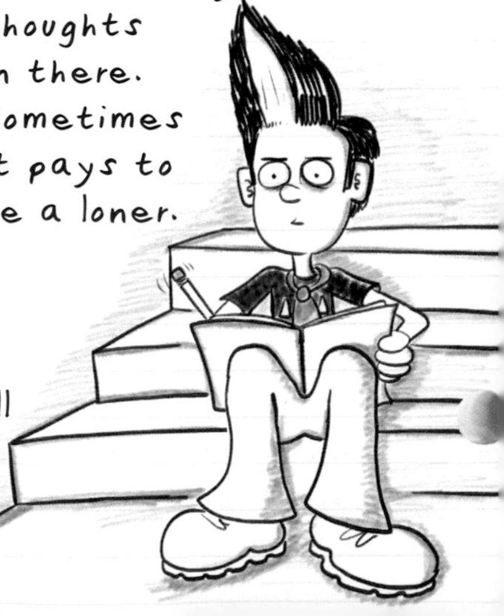

I don't have to deal with all that lunchroom nonsense. I get to sit here, in peace... by myself...sigh.

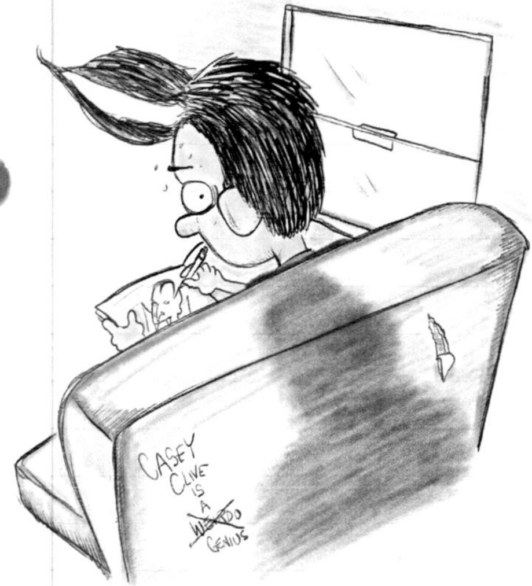
CASEY
CLIVE
IS
A
GENIUS

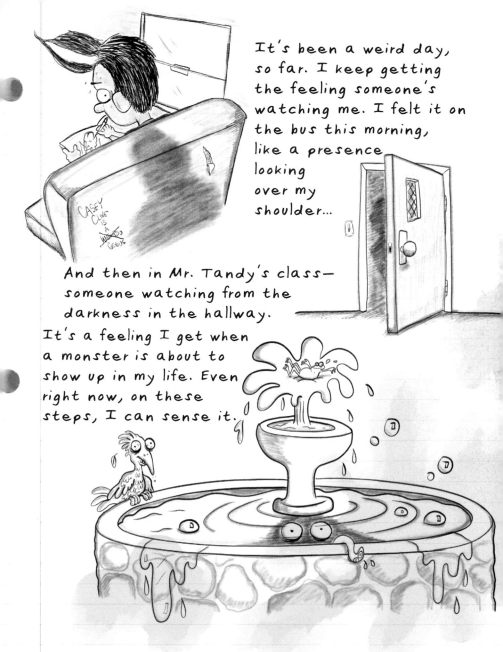

It's been a weird day, so far. I keep getting the feeling someone's watching me. I felt it on the bus this morning, like a presence looking over my shoulder...

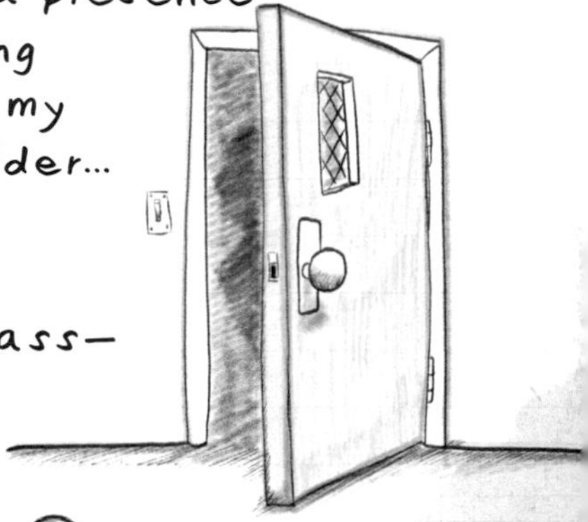

And then in Mr. Tandy's class— someone watching from the darkness in the hallway.

It's a feeling I get when a monster is about to show up in my life. Even right now, on these steps, I can sense it.

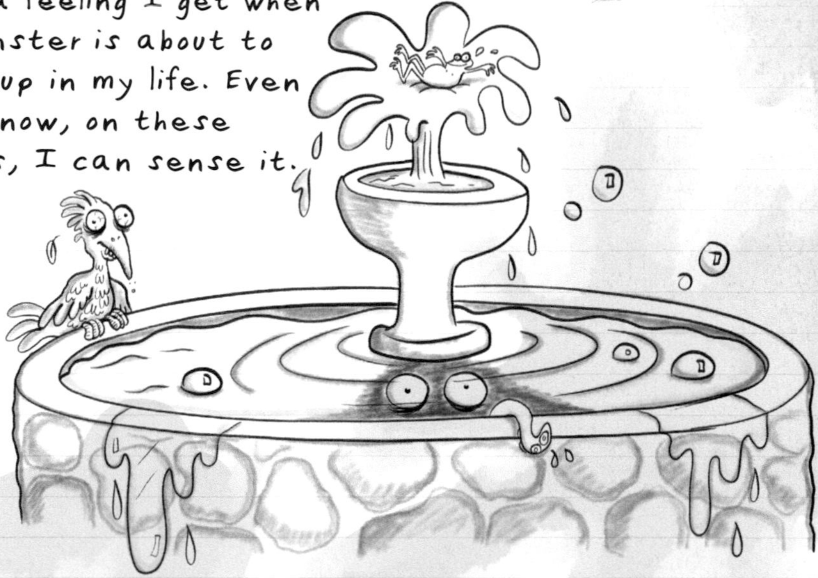

Awww man! Something just splashed me from the fountain! Now my notebook is all wet! I think I know who did it, too. I can see his beady little eyes staring at me from under the surface...

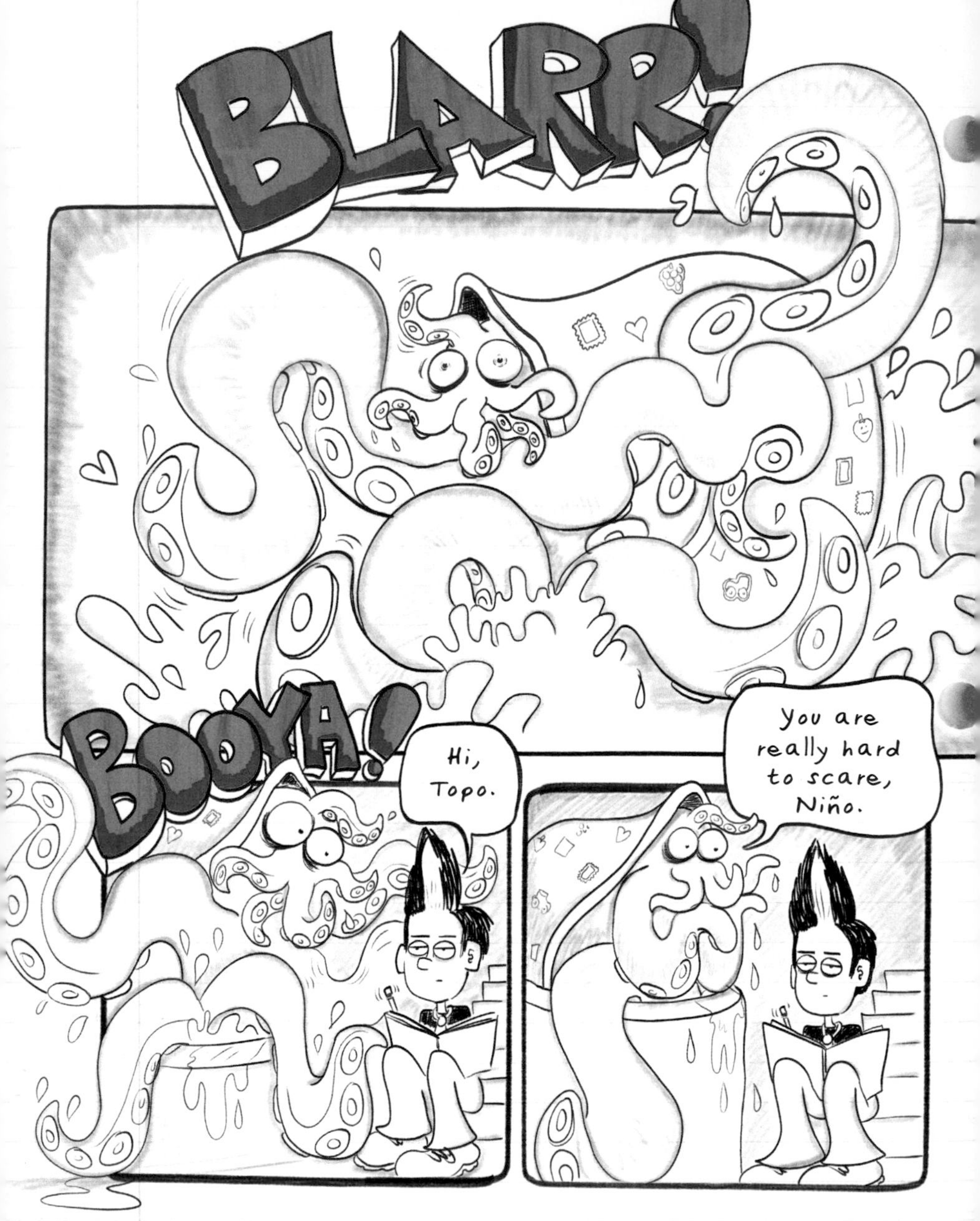
BLARR!
BOOYA!
Hi, Topo.
You are really hard to scare, Niño.

Oh Topo...the first monster to show up in my life, and the most irritating. That's the one thing you never hear about monsters—they love following kids to school.

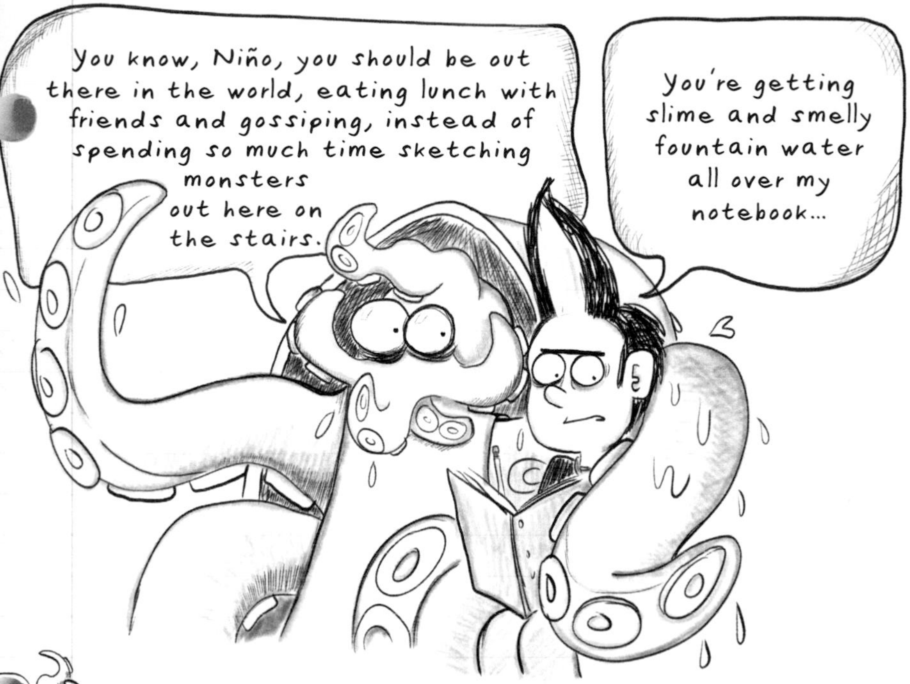
You know, Niño, you should be out there in the world, eating lunch with friends and gossiping, instead of spending so much time sketching monsters out here on the stairs.
You're getting slime and smelly fountain water all over my notebook...

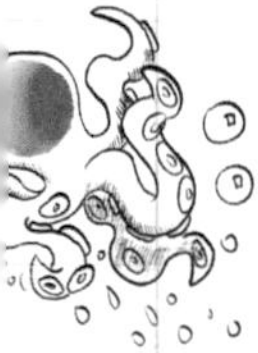

Uh-oh! I have that feeling again! We're being watched!

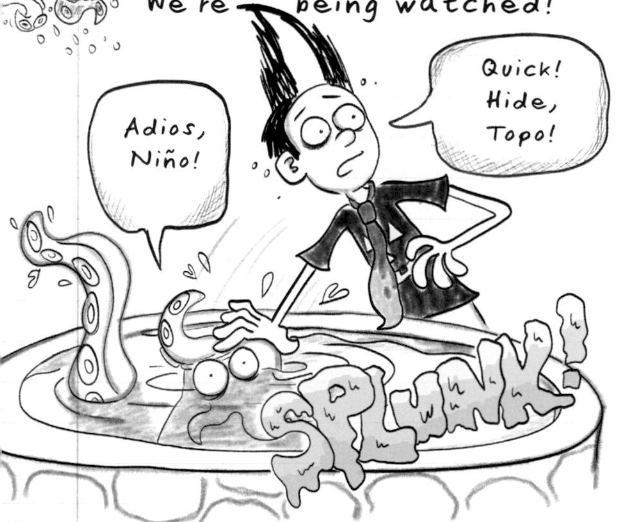
Quick! Hide, Topo!
Adios, Niño!
SPLUNK!

I was right. A girl! Spying on us from behind the trash can. Then she vanished.

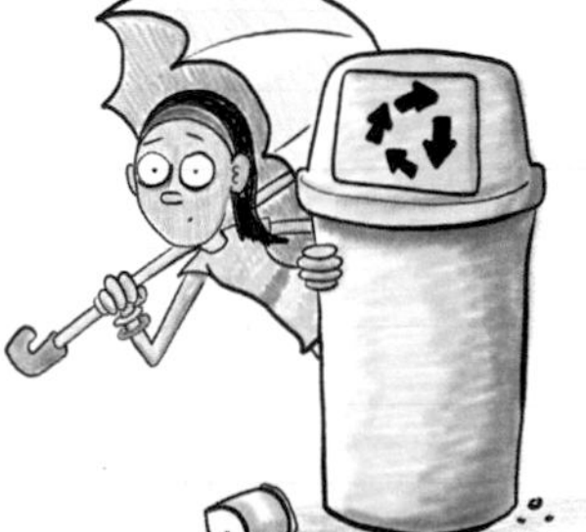

Who was she? Did she get a good look at Topo? What if she reports us? And what's with the umbrella?

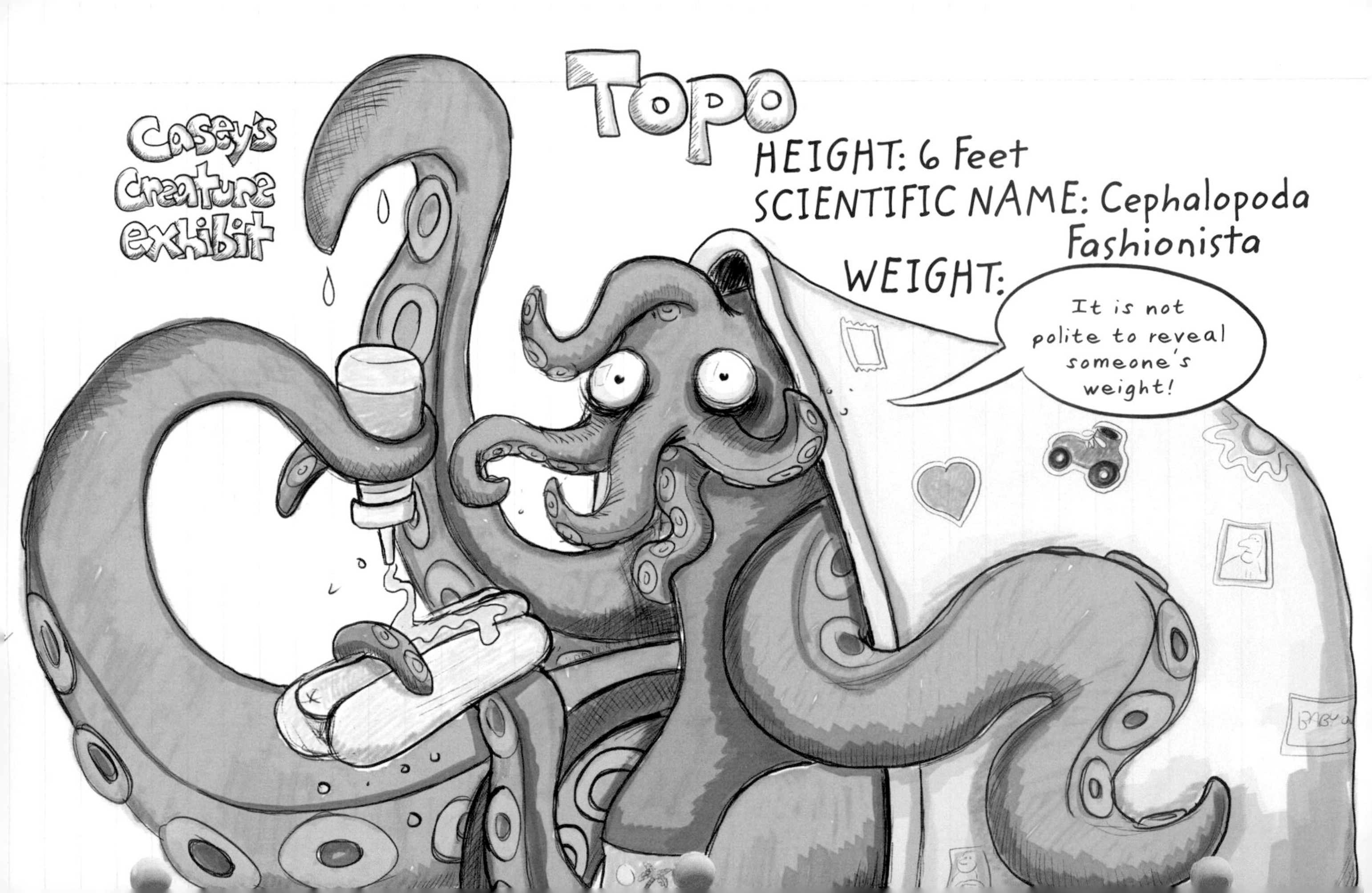
Casey's Creature exhibit
Topo
HEIGHT: 6 Feet
SCIENTIFIC NAME: Cephalopoda Fashionista
WEIGHT:
It is not polite to reveal someone's weight!

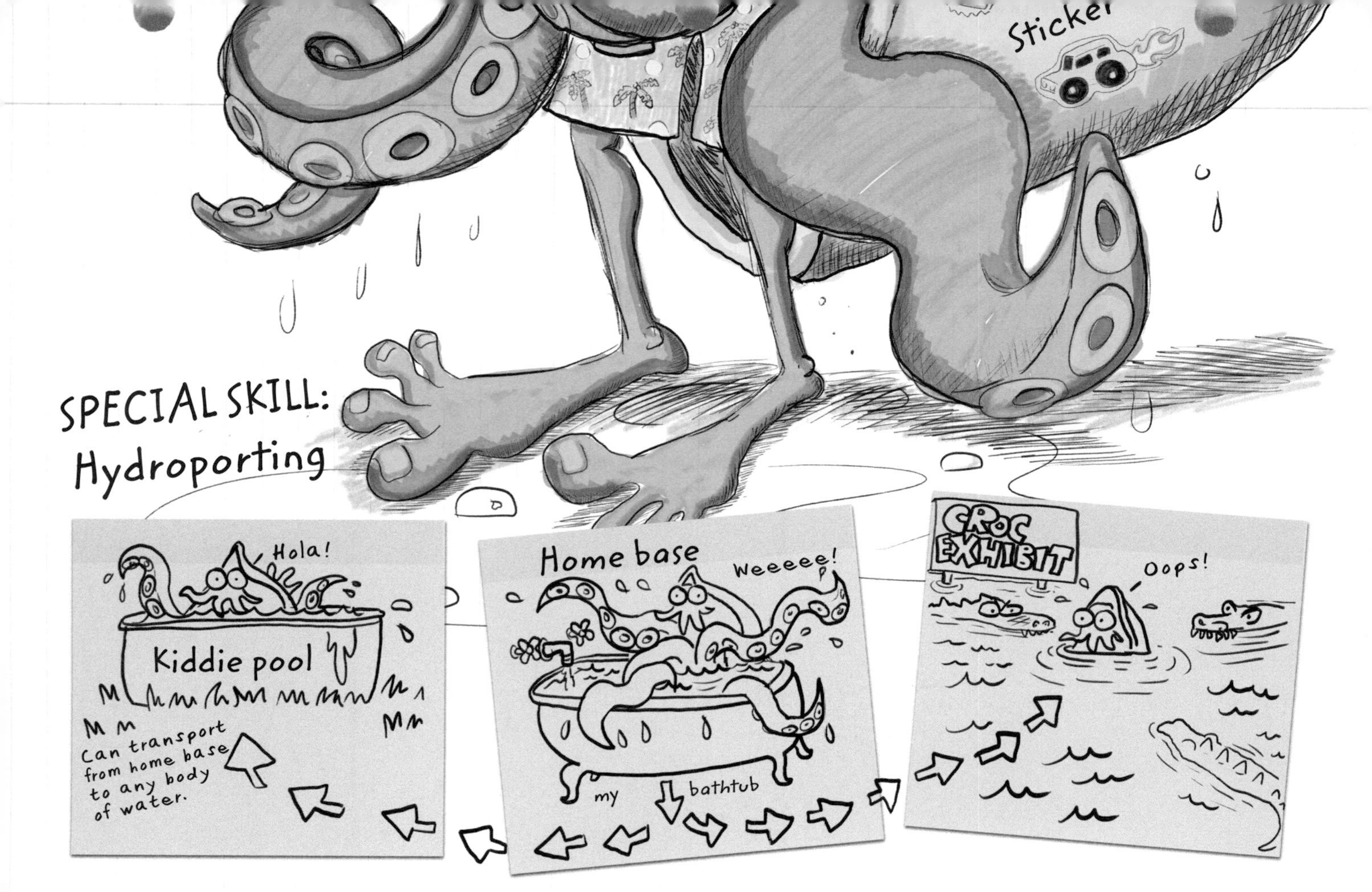
Sticker
SPECIAL SKILL:
Hydroporting
Hola!
Kiddie pool
Can transport from home base to any body of water.
Home base
Weeeeee!
my bathtub
CROC EXHIBIT
Oops!

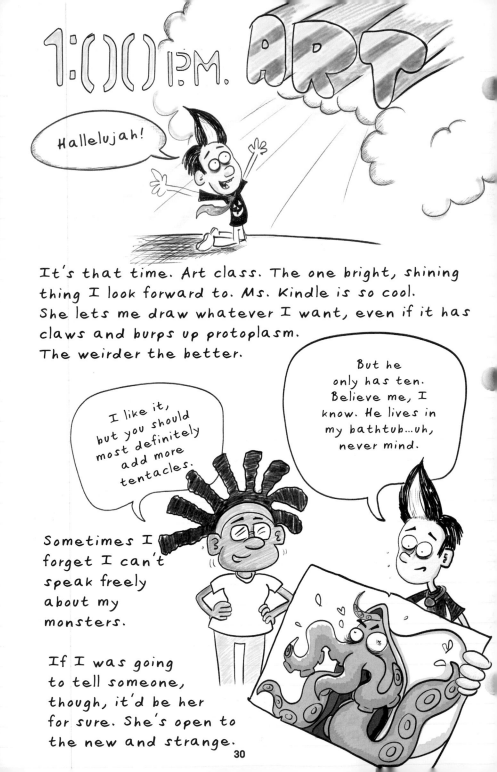

1:00 P.M. ART

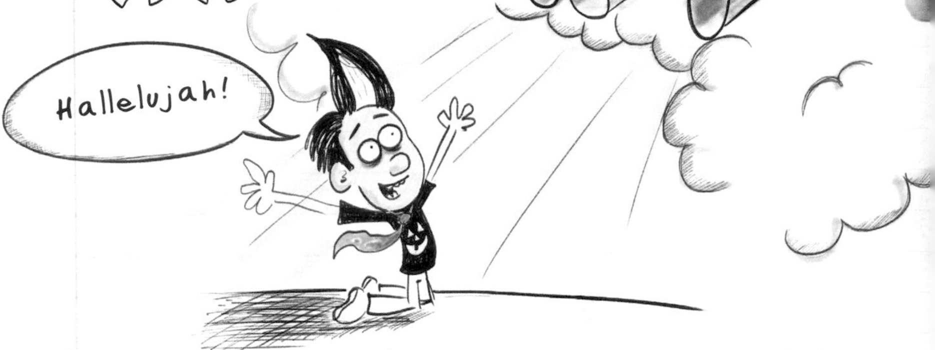
Hallelujah!

It's that time. Art class. The one bright, shining thing I look forward to. Ms. Kindle is so cool. She lets me draw whatever I want, even if it has claws and burps up protoplasm. The weirder the better.

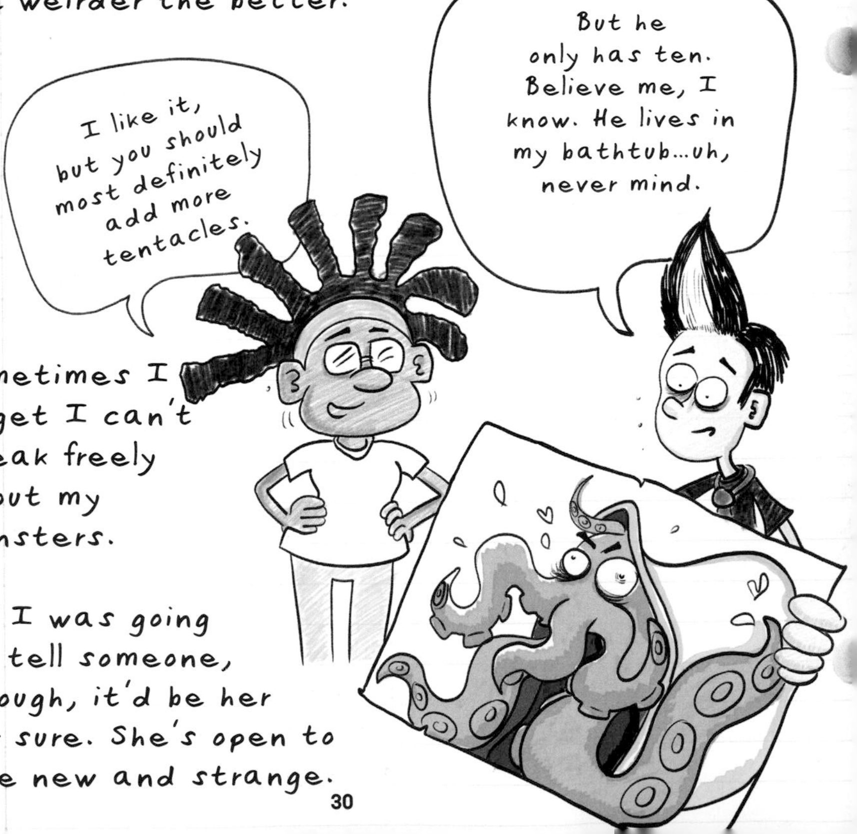
I like it, but you should most definitely add more tentacles.
But he only has ten. Believe me, I know. He lives in my bathtub...uh, never mind.

Sometimes I forget I can't speak freely about my monsters.

If I was going to tell someone, though, it'd be her for sure. She's open to the new and strange.

Speaking of new and strange—Ms. K just introduced a new kid. It's the girl I spotted behind the trash can! The one who was watching me and Topo!

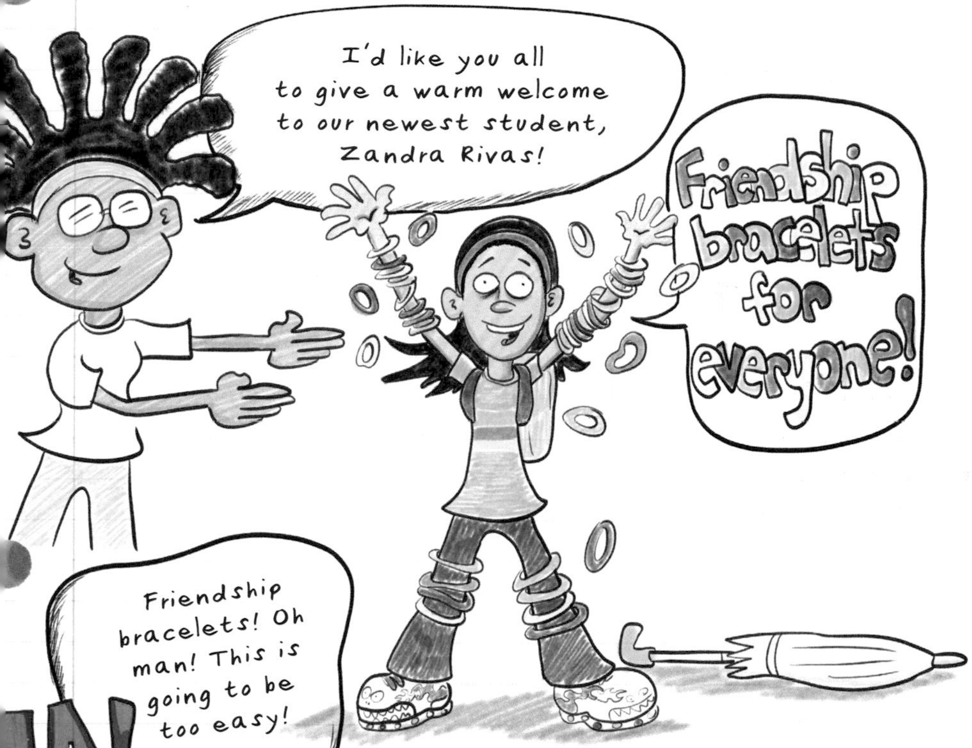

I'd like you all to give a warm welcome to our newest student, Zandra Rivas!
Friendship bracelets for everyone!

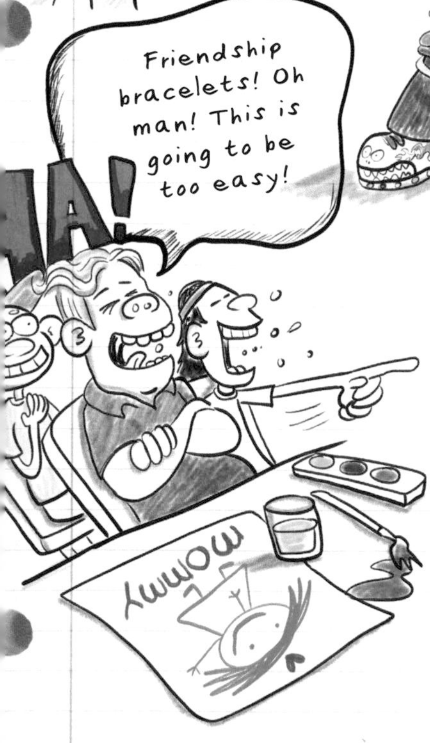

Friendship bracelets! Oh man! This is going to be too easy!
mommy

NOT the way I'd introduce myself, personally, but the other kids welcomed Zandra with open...mouths. Especially Grant and his goons. Ms. K gave them a glare that shut them up real quick.

Ugh. Zandra just sat next to me. She says she's into monsters too and loves to draw just like I do.

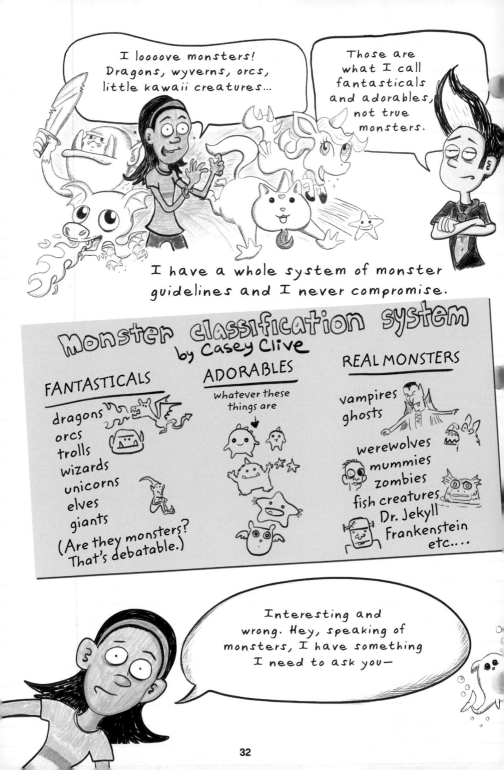

I loooove monsters! Dragons, wyverns, orcs, little kawaii creatures...

Those are what I call fantasticals and adorables, not true monsters.

I have a whole system of monster guidelines and I never compromise.

Monster classification system
by Casey Clive

FANTASTICALS
- dragons
- orcs
- trolls
- wizards
- unicorns
- elves
- giants

(Are they monsters? That's debatable.)

ADORABLES
whatever these things are

REAL MONSTERS
- vampires
- ghosts
- werewolves
- mummies
- zombies
- fish creatures
- Dr. Jekyll
- Frankenstein
- etc.....

Interesting and wrong. Hey, speaking of monsters, I have something I need to ask you—

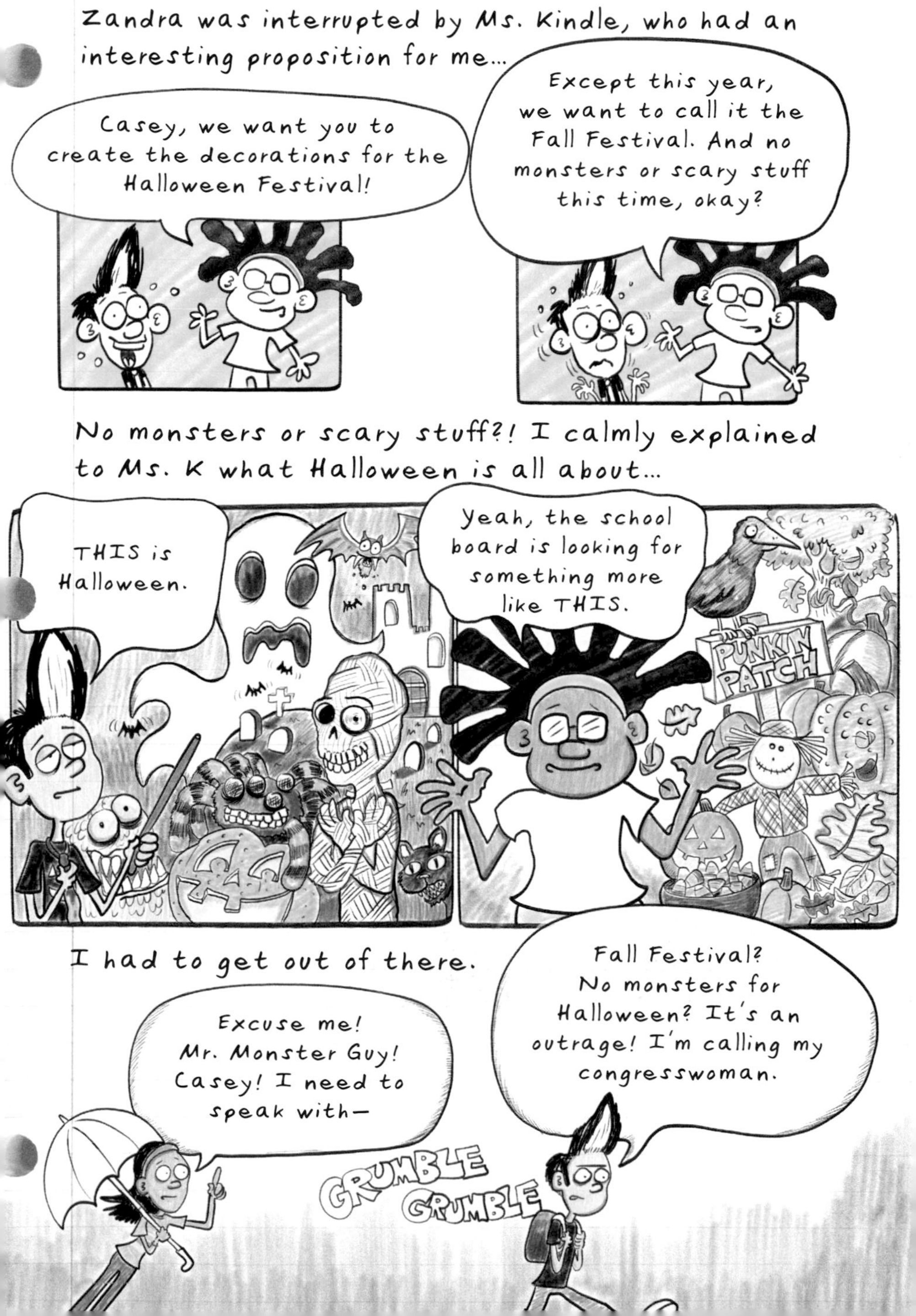
Zandra was interrupted by Ms. Kindle, who had an interesting proposition for me...
Casey, we want you to create the decorations for the Halloween Festival!
Except this year, we want to call it the Fall Festival. And no monsters or scary stuff this time, okay?
No monsters or scary stuff?! I calmly explained to Ms. K what Halloween is all about...
THIS is Halloween.
Yeah, the school board is looking for something more like THIS.
PUNKIN PATCH
I had to get out of there.
Excuse me! Mr. Monster Guy! Casey! I need to speak with—
Fall Festival? No monsters for Halloween? It's an outrage! I'm calling my congresswoman.
GRUMBLE
GRUMBLE

What's the big deal lately with making everything safe and "un-scary"? Seems like folks used to love monsters and spooky stuff. Now, it gets everyone all panicked.

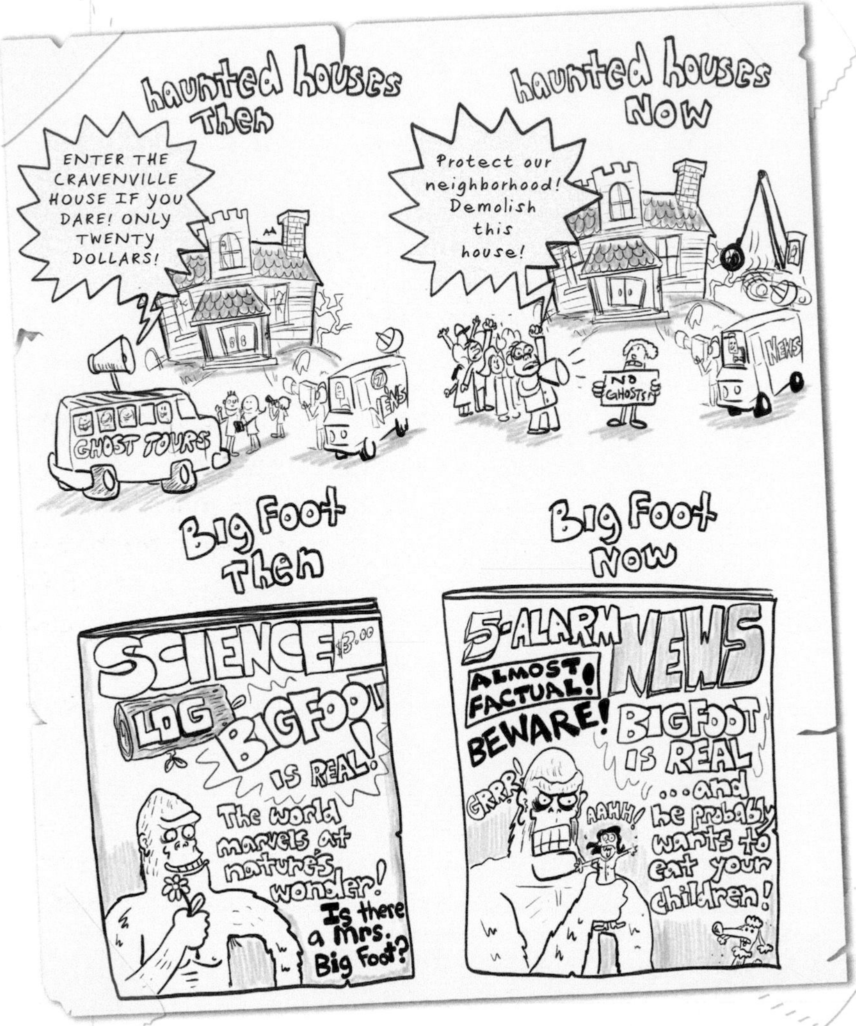
haunted houses Then
ENTER THE CRAVENVILLE HOUSE IF YOU DARE! ONLY TWENTY DOLLARS!
GHOST TOURS
NEWS
haunted houses Now
Protect our neighborhood! Demolish this house!
NO GHOSTS!
NEWS
Big Foot Then
SCIENCE LOG
$3.00
BIGFOOT IS REAL!
The world marvels at nature's wonder!
Is there a Mrs. Big Foot?
Big Foot Now
5-ALARM NEWS
ALMOST FACTUAL!
BEWARE!
BIGFOOT IS REAL
GRRR!
AAHH!
...and he probably wants to eat your children!

Calm down, people! Not all monsters are bad. I should know. I live with Frankenstein. The scariest thing about him is his snoring.

Dad thinks it's me. He even bought me some nasal anti-snoring strips!

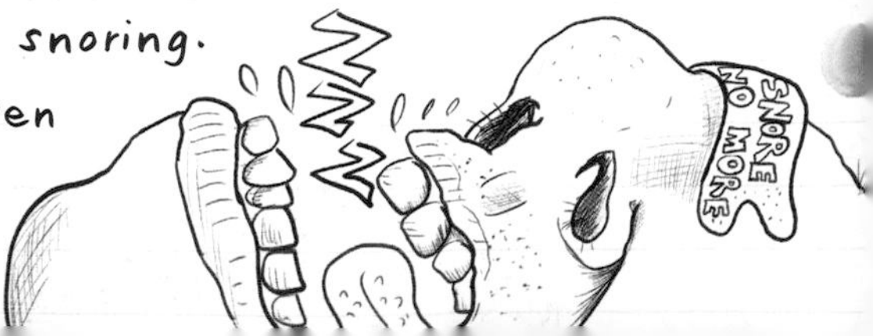
SNORE NO MORE

HOME

It's after school now. Measuring my tree house. Gotta make more space for my monsters. Maybe I can add an additional bed and a bathroom?

Apartment For Rent
1 Bed 1 Bath
No Pets or Smoking
No Nonsense
$2,300 per month

Who am I kidding? Don't think my measly allowance can afford a new apartment for them either. Maybe I can find a very open-minded person looking for a roommate...or eight roommates, some of them hungry for humans.

I vented to Dad about the school board's plan to ruin the Halloween Festival with fall colors and decorative gourds.

You know, every day is already Halloween in your brain, so this will be a nice change of pace.

Traitor!

Some comfort he is.

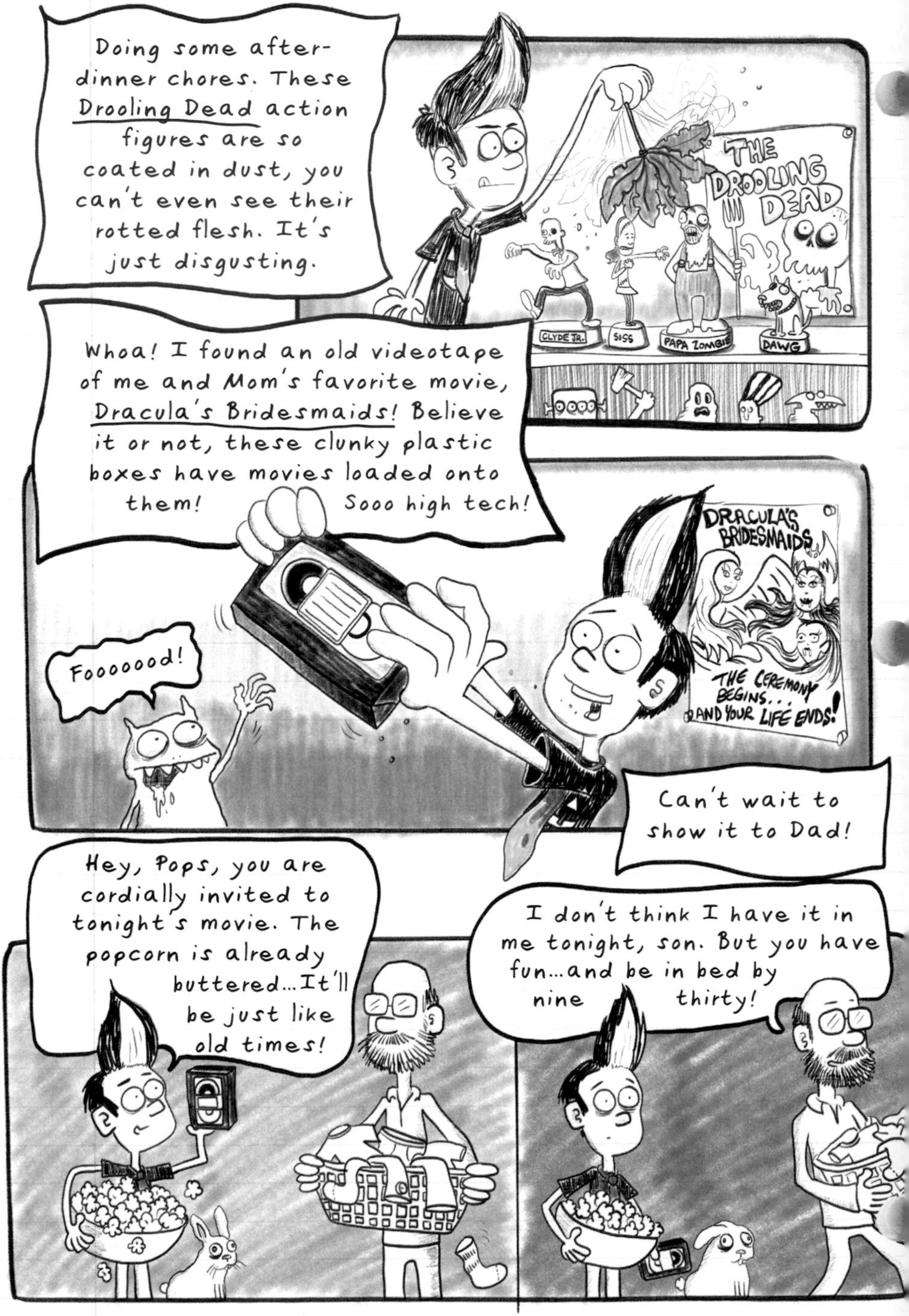
Doing some after-dinner chores. These Drooling Dead action figures are so coated in dust, you can't even see their rotted flesh. It's just disgusting.
THE DROOLING DEAD
CLYDE JR.
SISS
PAPA ZOMBIE
DAWG
Whoa! I found an old videotape of me and Mom's favorite movie, Dracula's Bridesmaids! Believe it or not, these clunky plastic boxes have movies loaded onto them! Sooo high tech!
DRACULA'S BRIDESMAIDS
THE CEREMONY BEGINS... AND YOUR LIFE ENDS!
Fooooood!
Can't wait to show it to Dad!
Hey, Pops, you are cordially invited to tonight's movie. The popcorn is already buttered... It'll be just like old times!
I don't think I have it in me tonight, son. But you have fun... and be in bed by nine thirty!

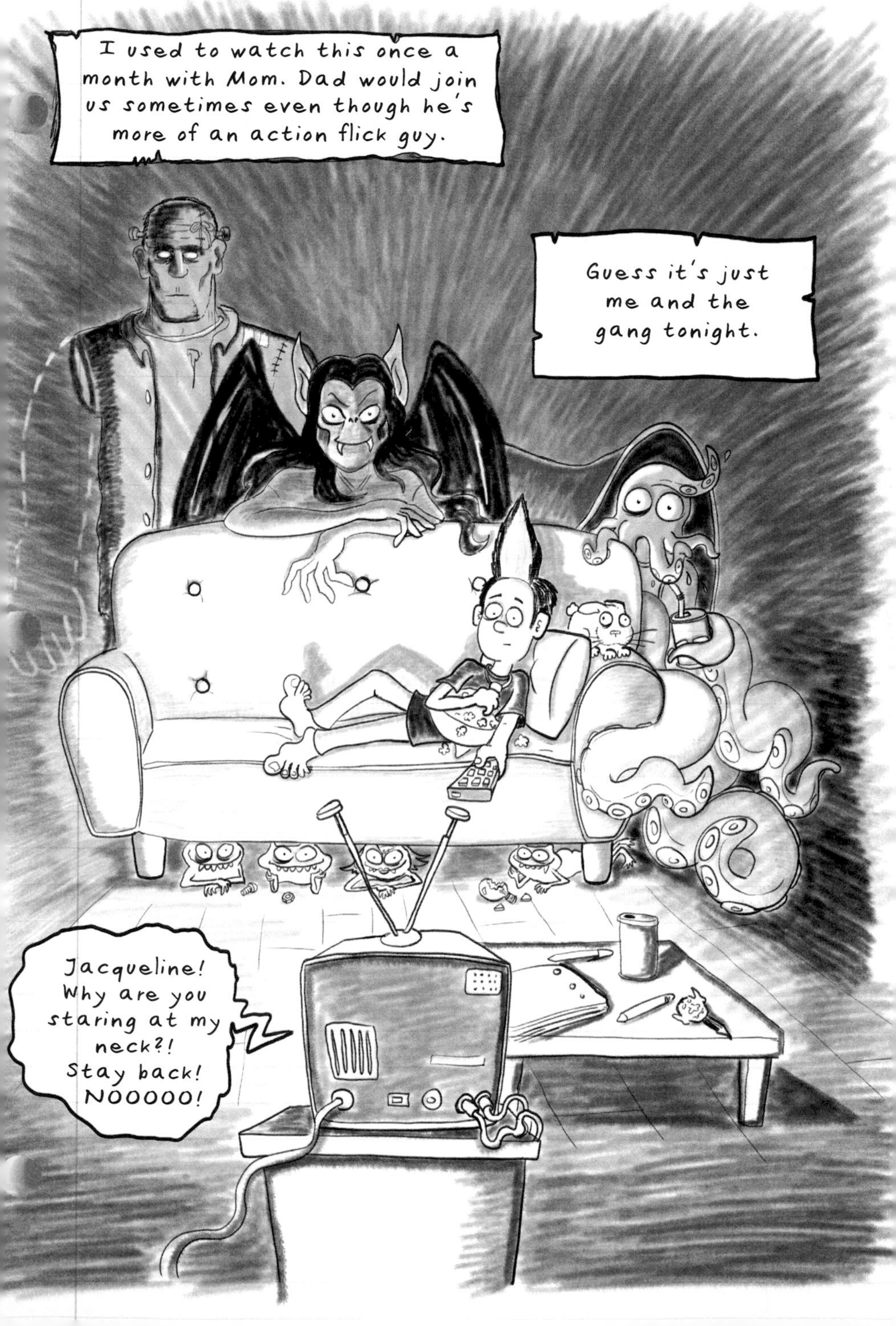
I used to watch this once a month with Mom. Dad would join us sometimes even though he's more of an action flick guy.
Guess it's just me and the gang tonight.
Jacqueline! Why are you staring at my neck?! Stay back! NOOOOO!

THUR.

Curious. This was taped to my locker when I got to school today. It's from that weird umbrella-totin' new girl. (The wizard tape is hers B.T.W.)

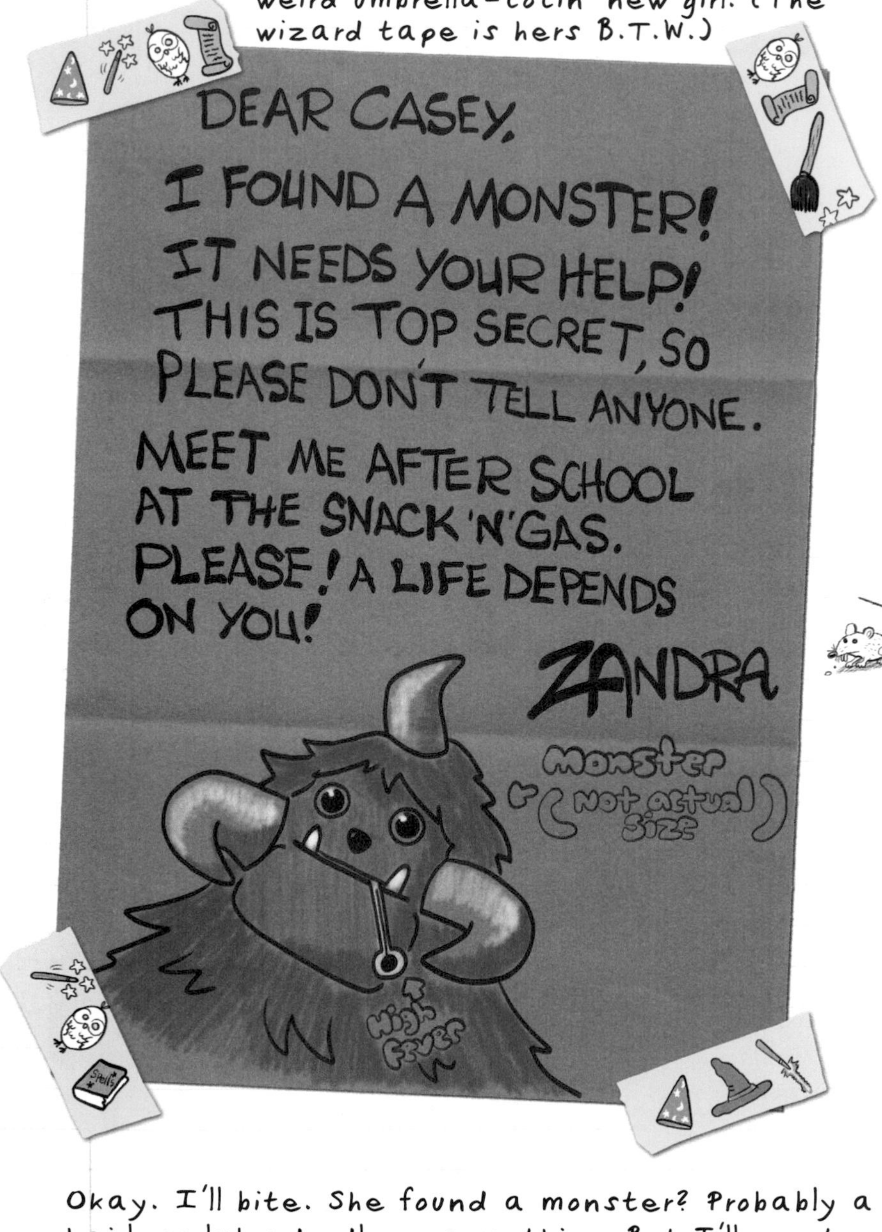
DEAR CASEY,

I FOUND A MONSTER! IT NEEDS YOUR HELP! THIS IS TOP SECRET, SO PLEASE DON'T TELL ANYONE.

MEET ME AFTER SCHOOL AT THE SNACK 'N' GAS. PLEASE! A LIFE DEPENDS ON YOU!

ZANDRA

Monster (not actual size)
High fever
Spells

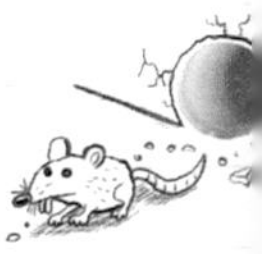

Okay. I'll bite. She found a monster? Probably a hairless labradoodle or something. But I'll meet her. Just gotta make sure it's not some kind of set up

AFTER SCHOOL

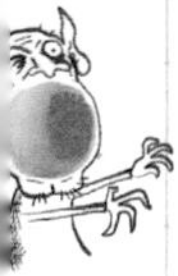

Okay, at the Snack 'N' Gas, waiting for this strange kid to show.

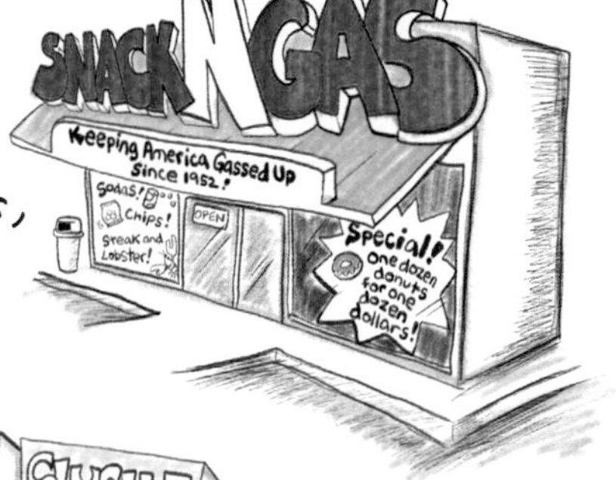

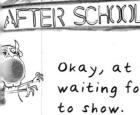

SNACK N GAS
Keeping America Gassed Up Since 1952!
Sodas!
Chips!
Steak and Lobster!
OPEN
Special! one dozen donuts for one dozen dollars!

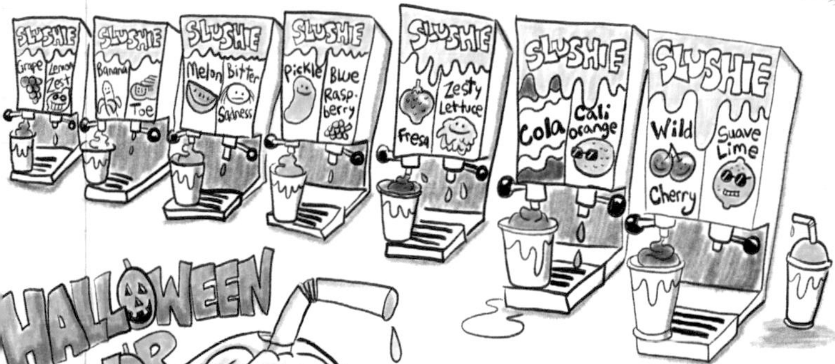

SLUSHIE
Grape
Lemon Zest
SLUSHIE
Banana
Toe
SLUSHIE
Melon
Bitter Sadness
SLUSHIE
Pickle
Blue Rasp-berry
SLUSHIE
Fresa
Zesty Lettuce
SLUSHIE
Cola
Cali orange
SLUSHIE
Wild Cherry
Suave Lime

This is where the magic happens. Twenty-two flavors of Slushies.

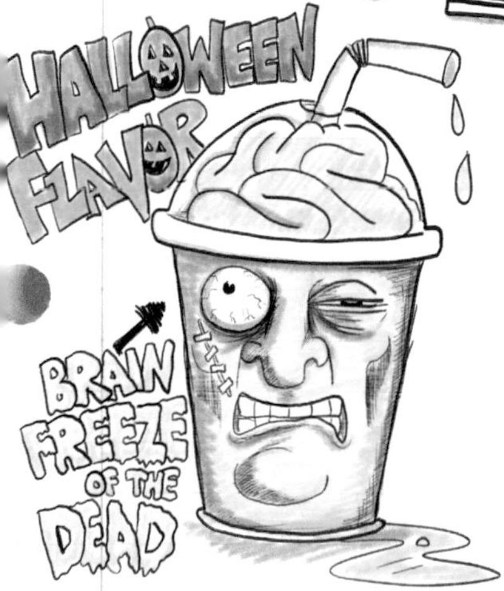

HALLOWEEN FLAVOR
BRAIN FREEZE OF THE DEAD

And it's my lucky day—they just released this year's special Halloween flavor, Brain Freeze of the Dead. It kinda tastes like a snow cone dipped in men's body wash.

Of course, I just spilled it on my journal. Smooth move.

I'm gonna bail if she doesn't show up in the next...

Oh wait! Here she comes.

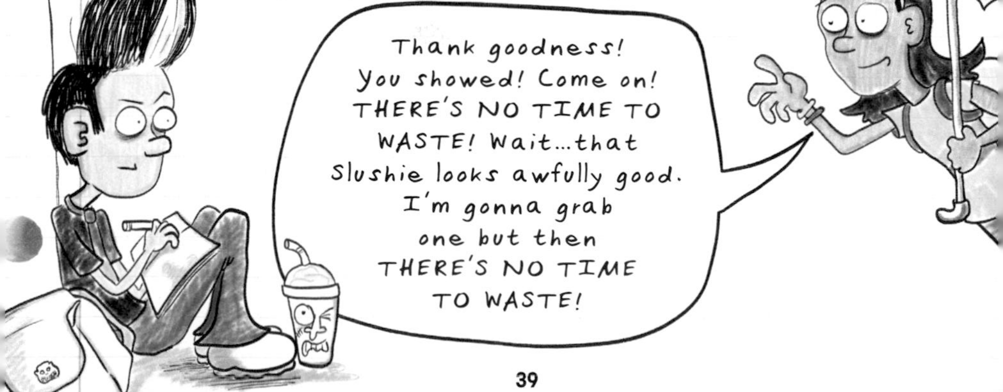

Thank goodness! You showed! Come on! THERE'S NO TIME TO WASTE! Wait...that Slushie looks awfully good. I'm gonna grab one but then THERE'S NO TIME TO WASTE!

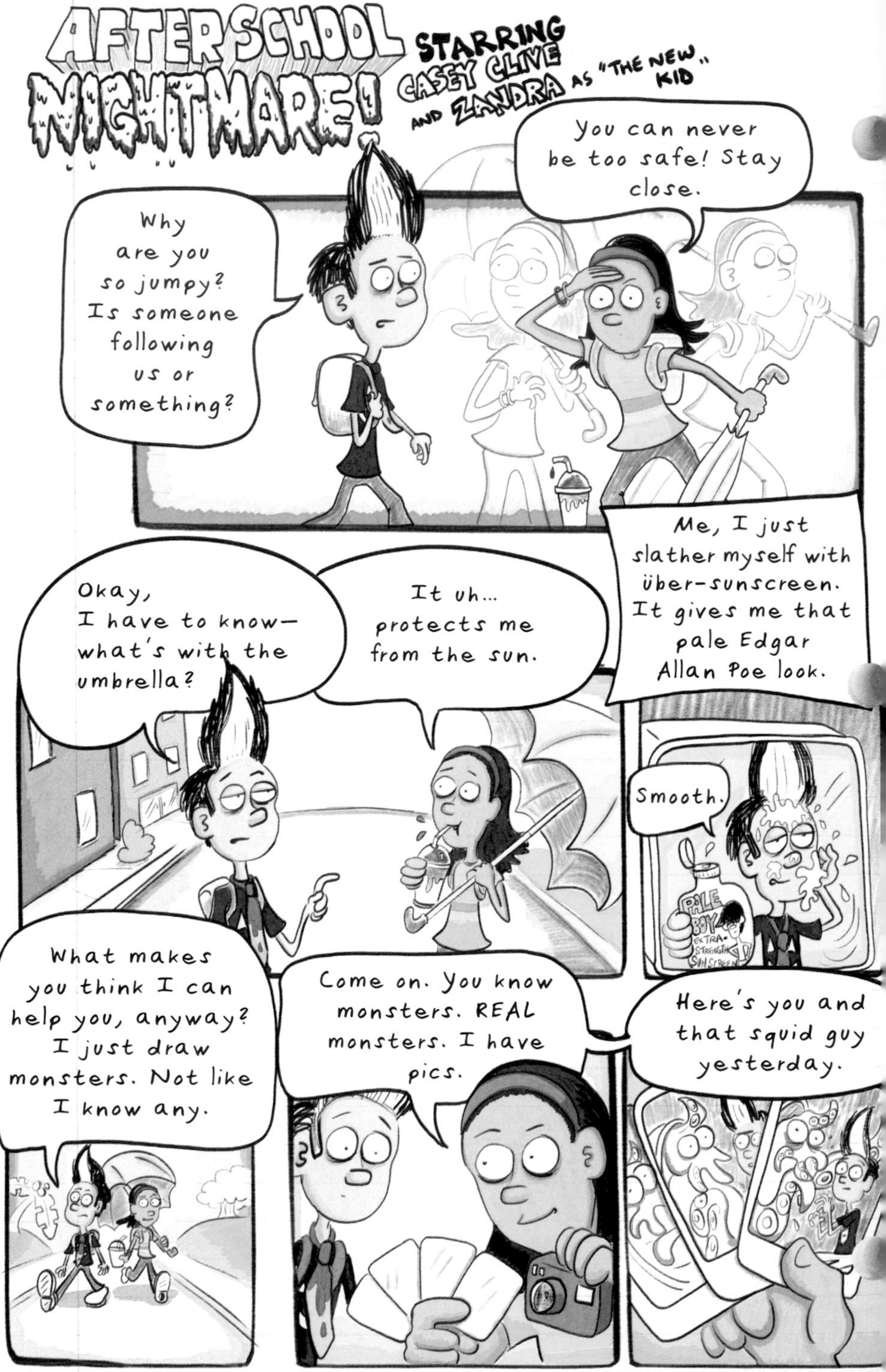
AFTER SCHOOL NIGHTMARE!
STARRING CASEY CLIVE AND ZANDRA AS "THE NEW KID"
Why are you so jumpy? Is someone following us or something?
You can never be too safe! Stay close.
Okay, I have to know—what's with the umbrella?
It uh... protects me from the sun.
Me, I just slather myself with über-sunscreen. It gives me that pale Edgar Allan Poe look.
Smooth.
PALE BOY EXTRA-STRENGTH SUNSCREEN
What makes you think I can help you, anyway? I just draw monsters. Not like I know any.
Come on. You know monsters. REAL monsters. I have pics.
Here's you and that squid guy yesterday.

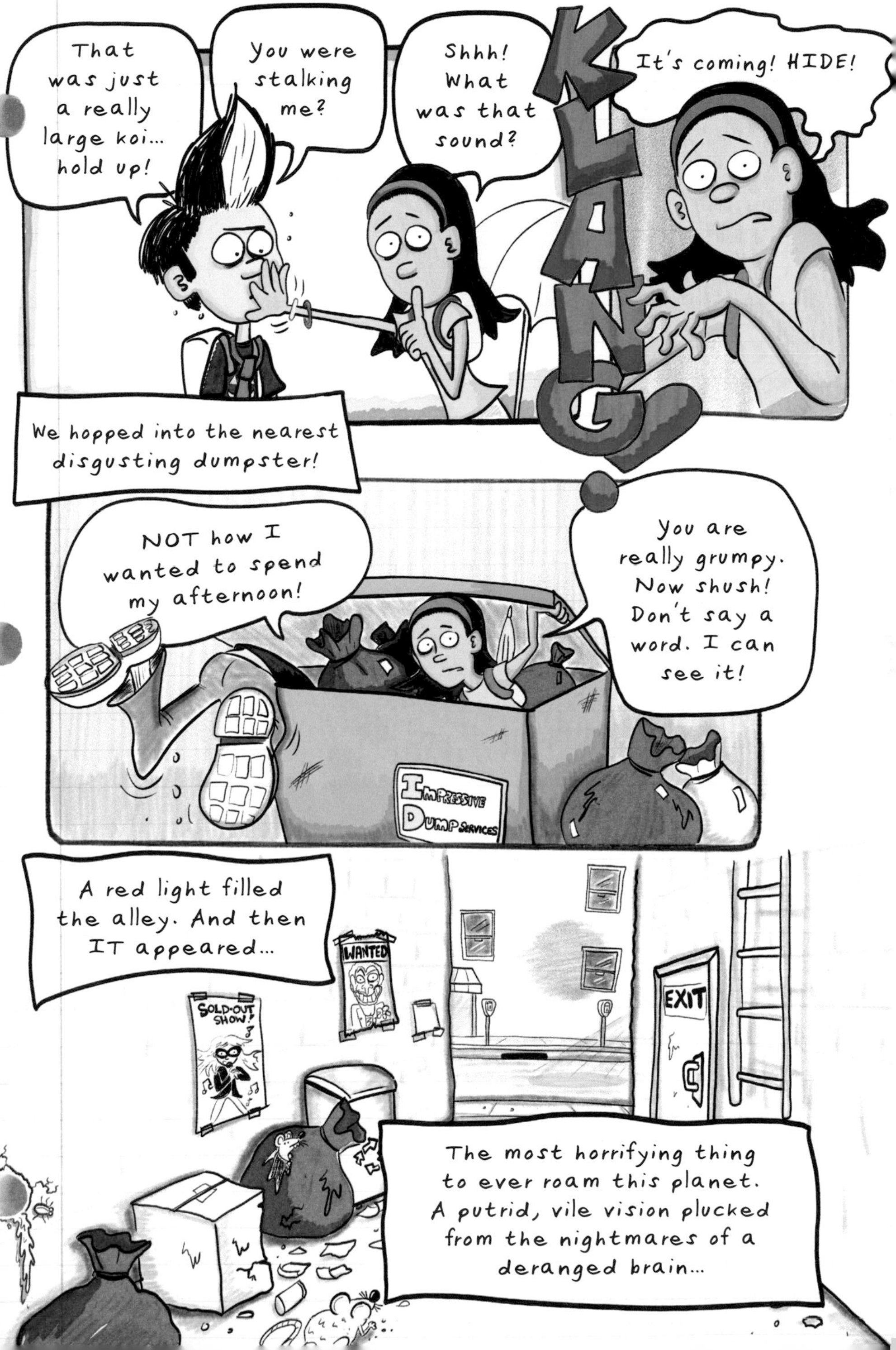
That was just a really large koi... hold up!
You were stalking me?
Shhh! What was that sound?
KLANG
It's coming! HIDE!
We hopped into the nearest disgusting dumpster!
NOT how I wanted to spend my afternoon!
You are really grumpy. Now shush! Don't say a word. I can see it!
IMPRESSIVE DUMP SERVICES
A red light filled the alley. And then IT appeared...
WANTED
SOLD-OUT SHOW!
EXIT
The most horrifying thing to ever roam this planet. A putrid, vile vision plucked from the nightmares of a deranged brain...

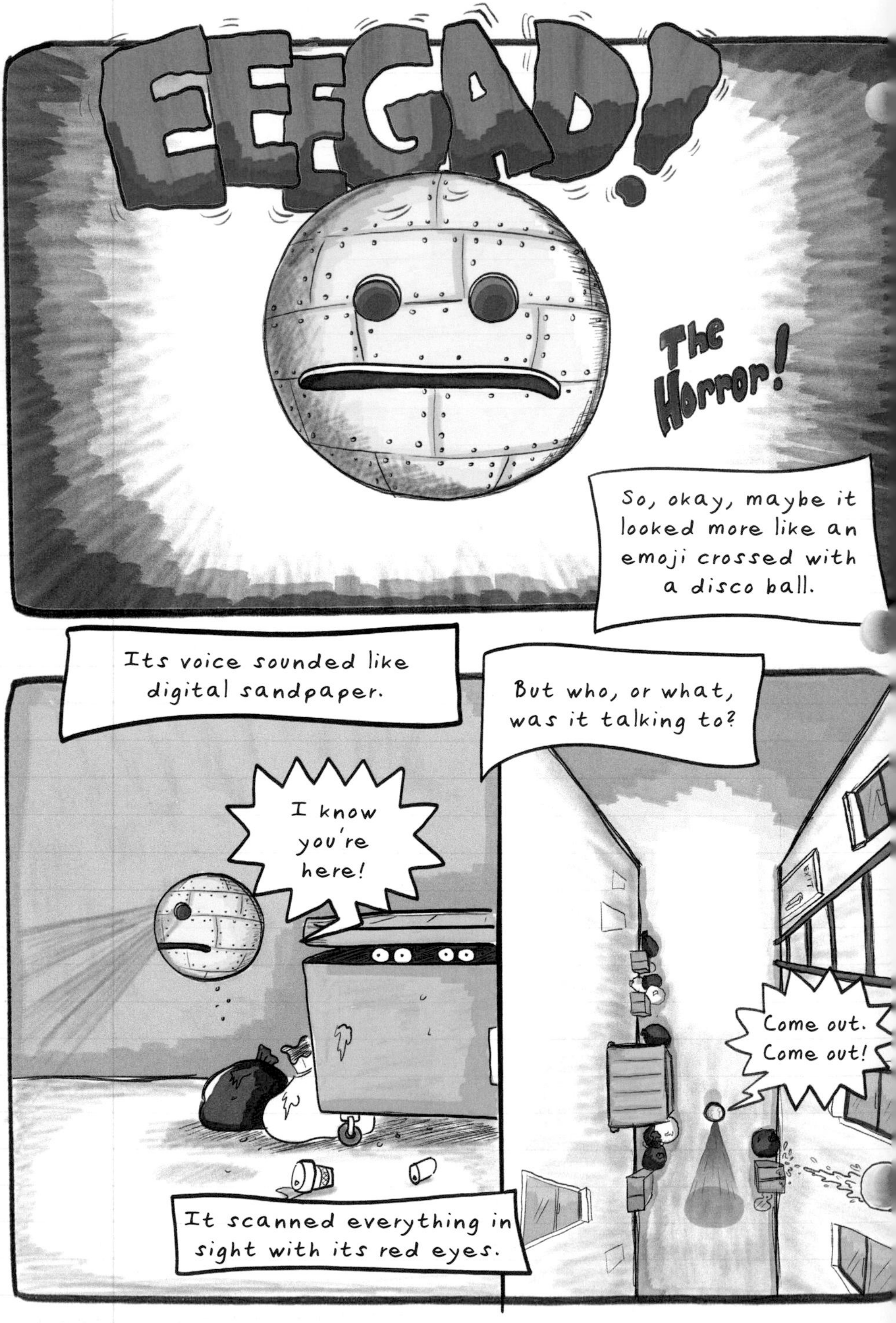
EEEGAD!
The Horror!
So, okay, maybe it looked more like an emoji crossed with a disco ball.
Its voice sounded like digital sandpaper.
I know you're here!
But who, or what, was it talking to?
Come out. Come out!
It scanned everything in sight with its red eyes.

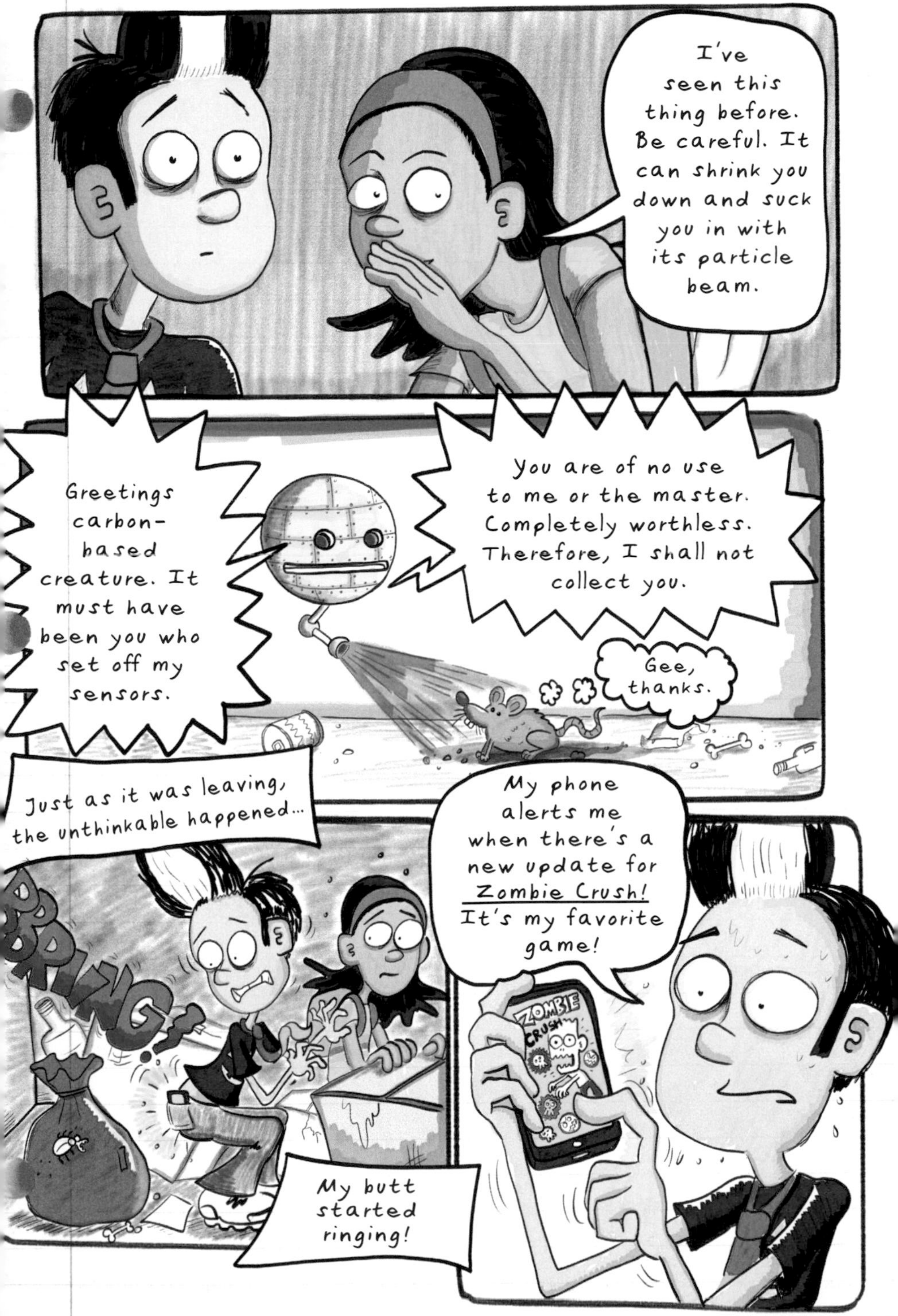
I've seen this thing before. Be careful. It can shrink you down and suck you in with its particle beam.
Greetings carbon-based creature. It must have been you who set off my sensors.
You are of no use to me or the master. Completely worthless. Therefore, I shall not collect you.
Gee, thanks.
Just as it was leaving, the unthinkable happened...
BRRING!
My butt started ringing!
My phone alerts me when there's a new update for Zombie Crush! It's my favorite game!
ZOMBIE CRUSH

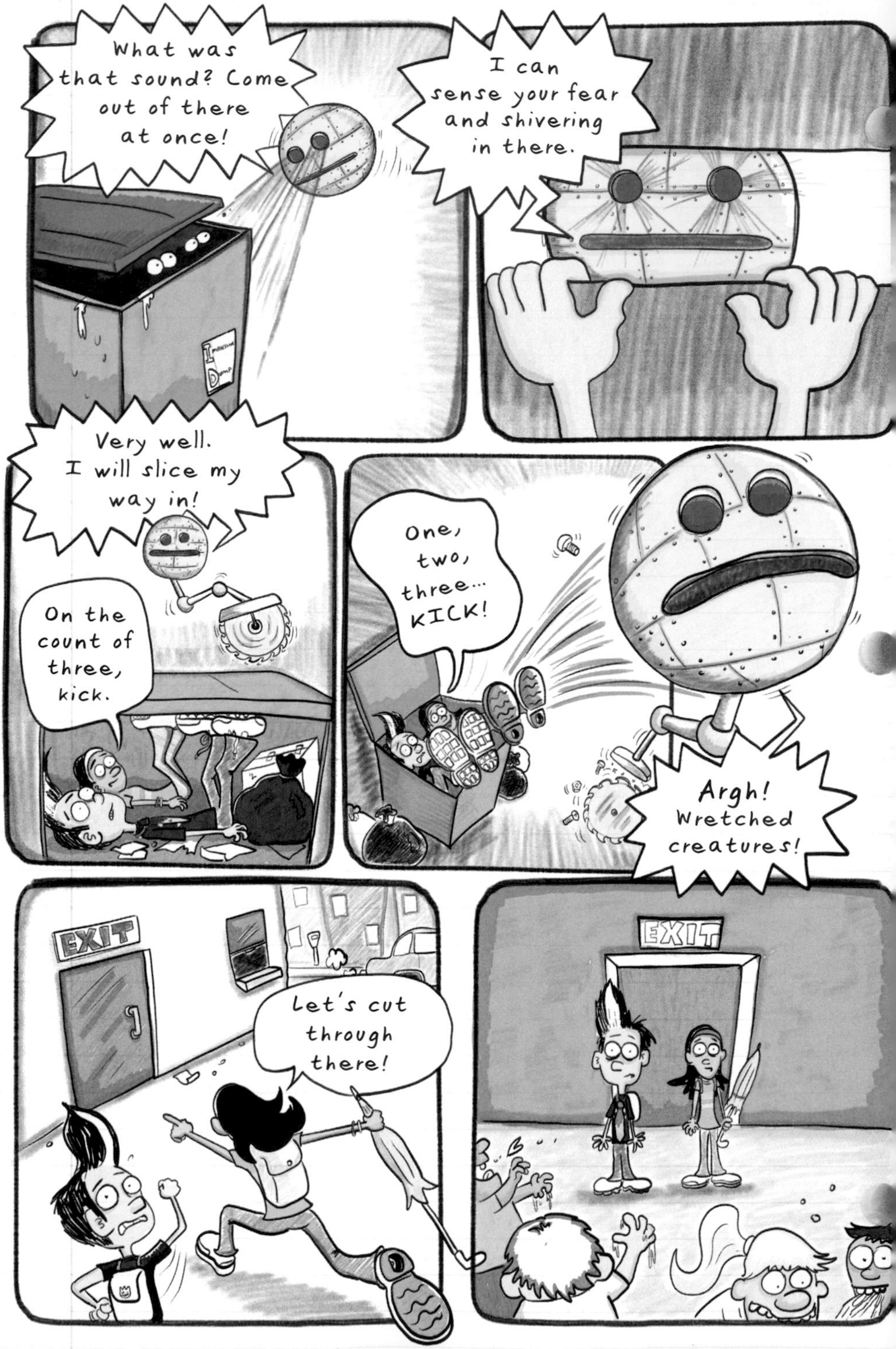
What was that sound? Come out of there at once!
I can sense your fear and shivering in there.
Very well. I will slice my way in!
On the count of three, kick.
One, two, three... KICK!
Argh! Wretched creatures!
EXIT
Let's cut through there!
EXIT

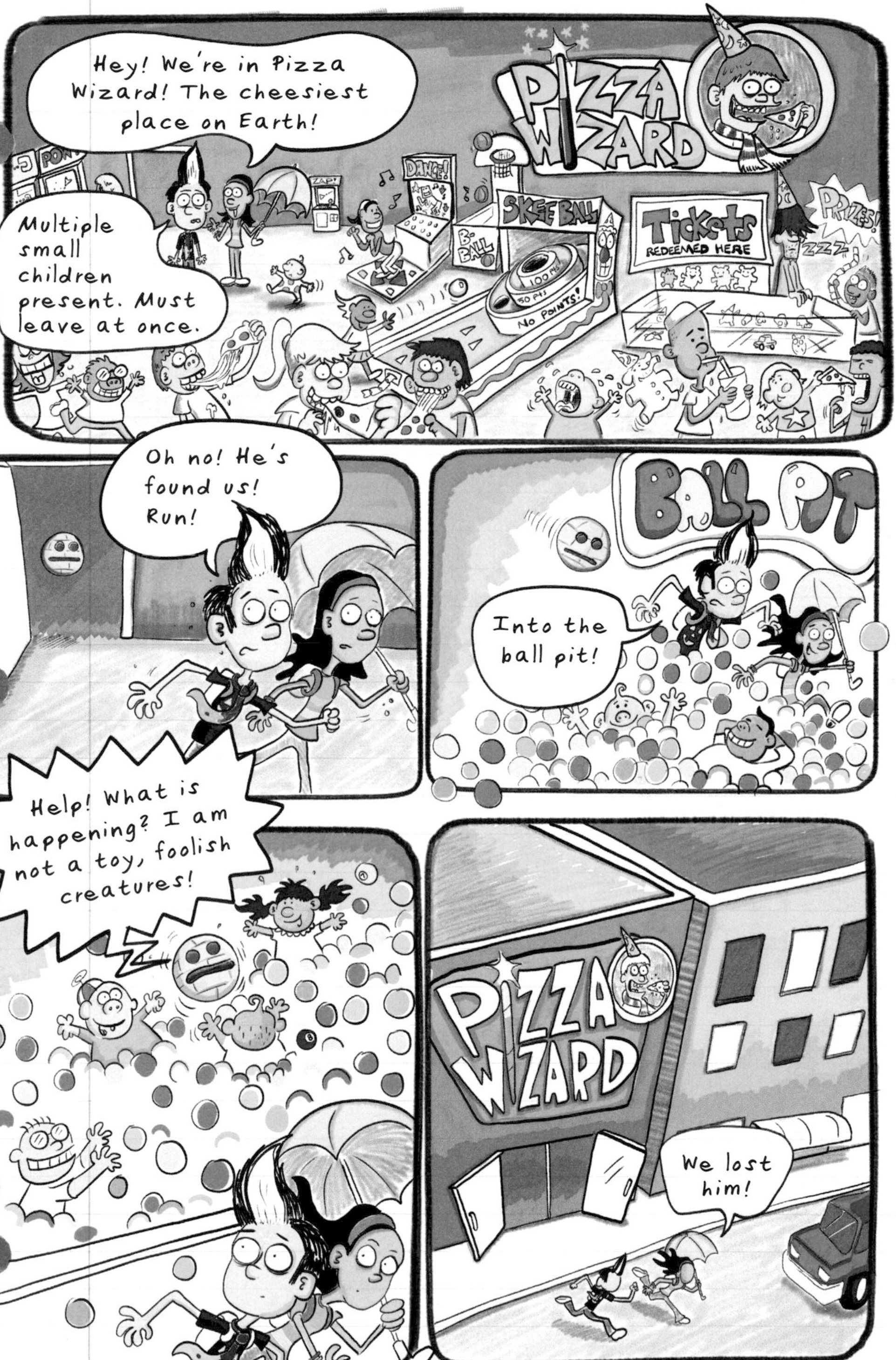

Hey! We're in Pizza Wizard! The cheesiest place on Earth!
PIZZA WIZARD
DANCE!
SKEE BALL
B-BALL
100 PTS
50 PTS
NO POINTS!
Tickets
REDEEMED HERE
PRIZES!
ZZZ
Multiple small children present. Must leave at once.
Oh no! He's found us! Run!
BALL PIT
Into the ball pit!
Help! What is happening? I am not a toy, foolish creatures!
PIZZA WIZARD
We lost him!

To make sure we had lost that angry Christmas ornament for good, Zandra took a really indirect route to her hideout. We ended up at the old pier. You know, the one that reeks of dead fish and rotten wood and has been closed down since before I was born?

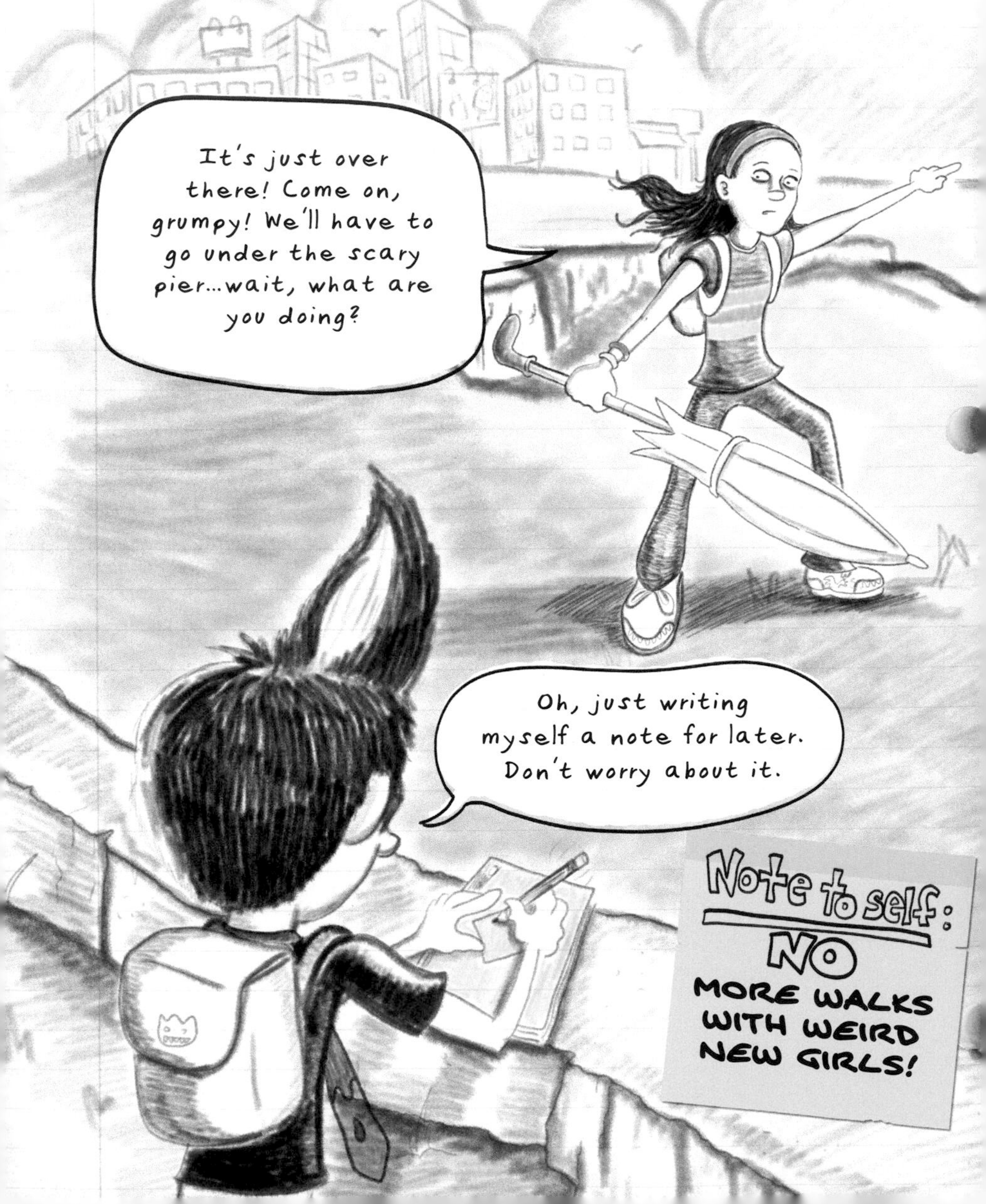
It's just over there! Come on, grumpy! We'll have to go under the scary pier...wait, what are you doing?
Oh, just writing myself a note for later. Don't worry about it.
Note to self:
NO
MORE WALKS WITH WEIRD NEW GIRLS!

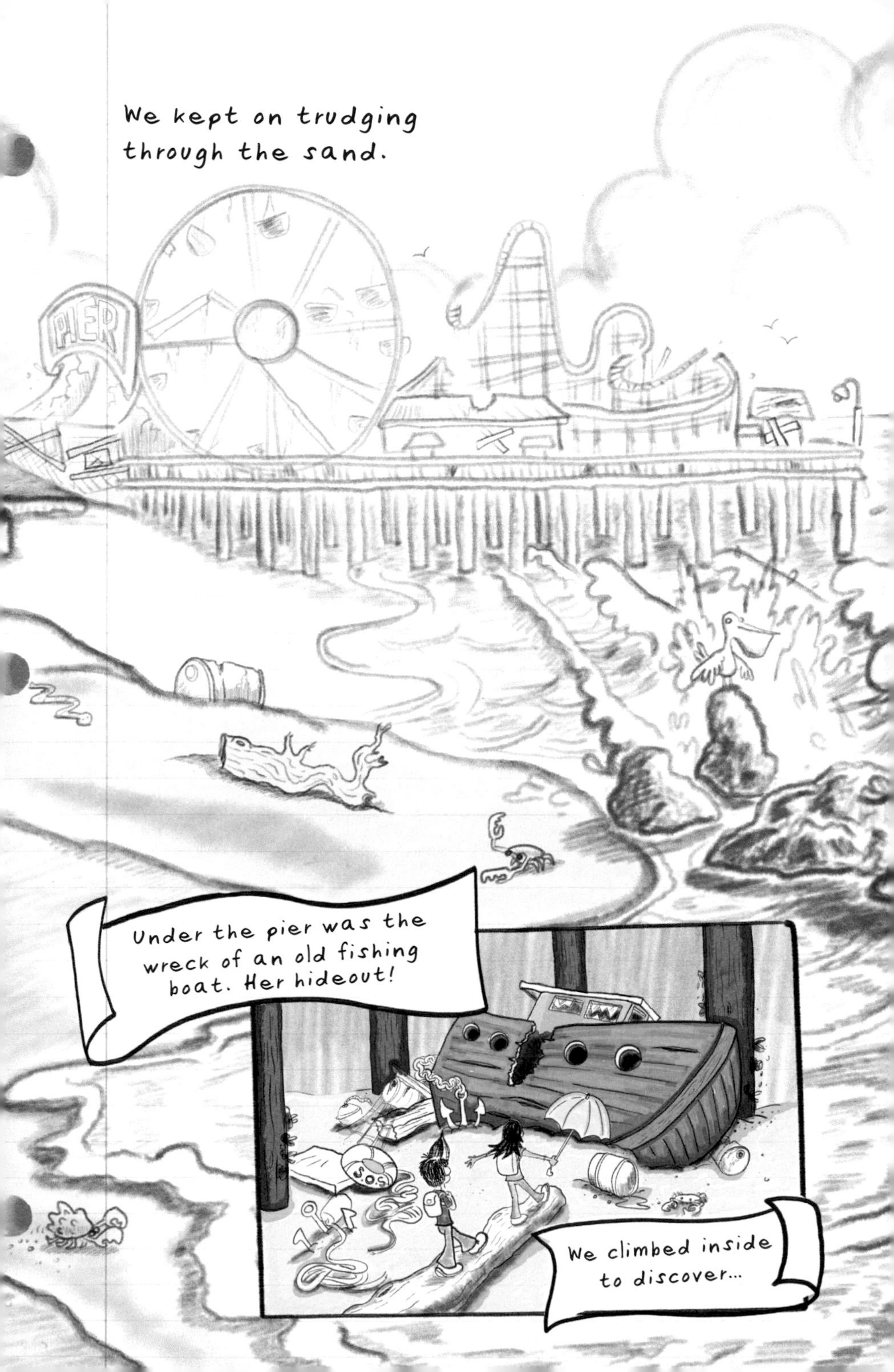
We kept on trudging through the sand.
PIER
Under the pier was the wreck of an old fishing boat. Her hideout!
S.O.S
We climbed inside to discover...

Yep! She definitely found a MONSTER!

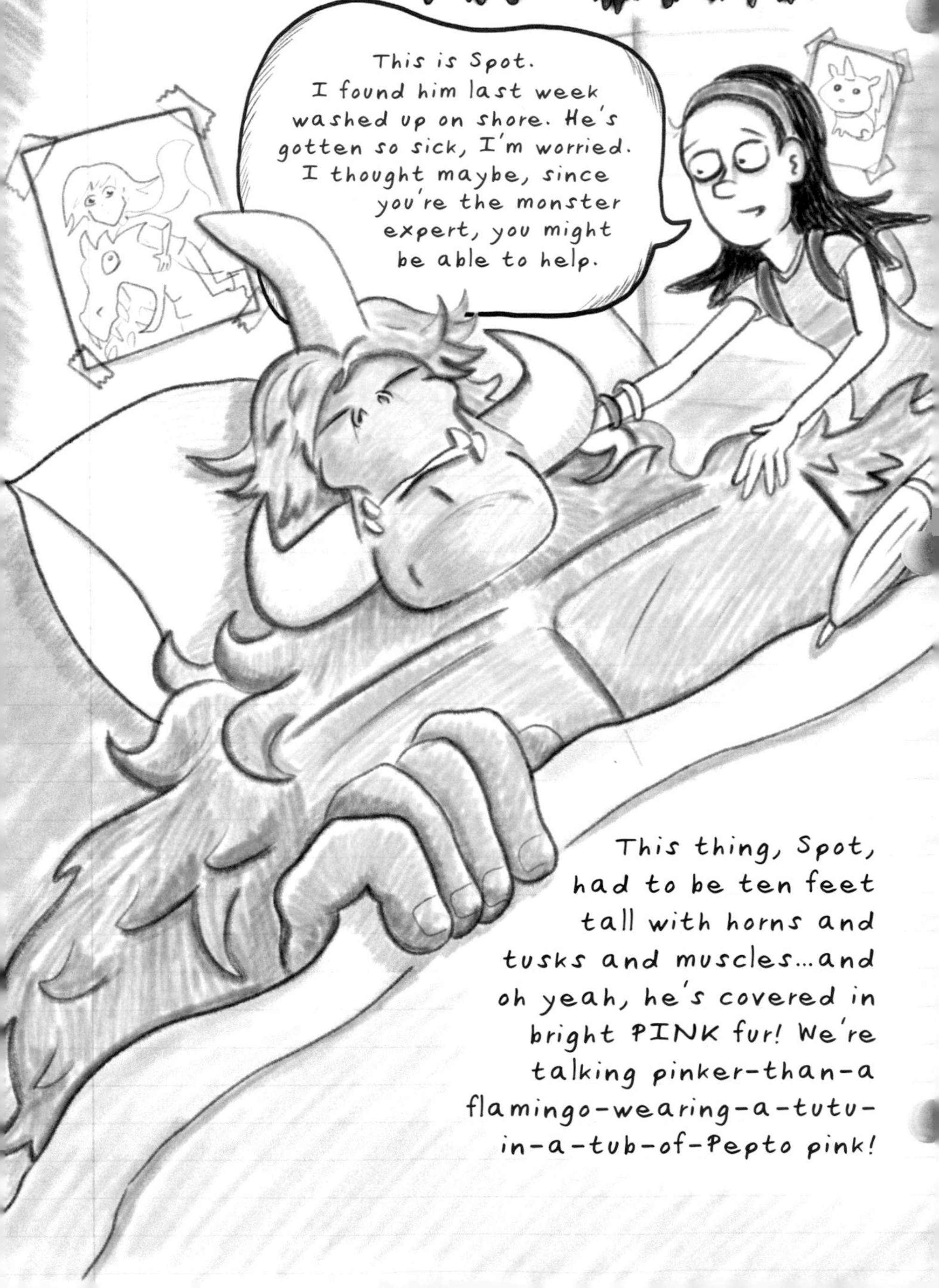
This is Spot. I found him last week washed up on shore. He's gotten so sick, I'm worried. I thought maybe, since you're the monster expert, you might be able to help.

This thing, Spot, had to be ten feet tall with horns and tusks and muscles…and oh yeah, he's covered in bright PINK fur! We're talking pinker-than-a flamingo-wearing-a-tutu-in-a-tub-of-Pepto pink!

Normally this would automatically place him in the "adorables" category, but I'm willing to make an exception, based on size alone!

Most def—a monster!

I know Zandra discovered him under the pier but why do I have a strange feeling I'm the one who was supposed to end up with him?

After all, I'm the monster magnet around here.

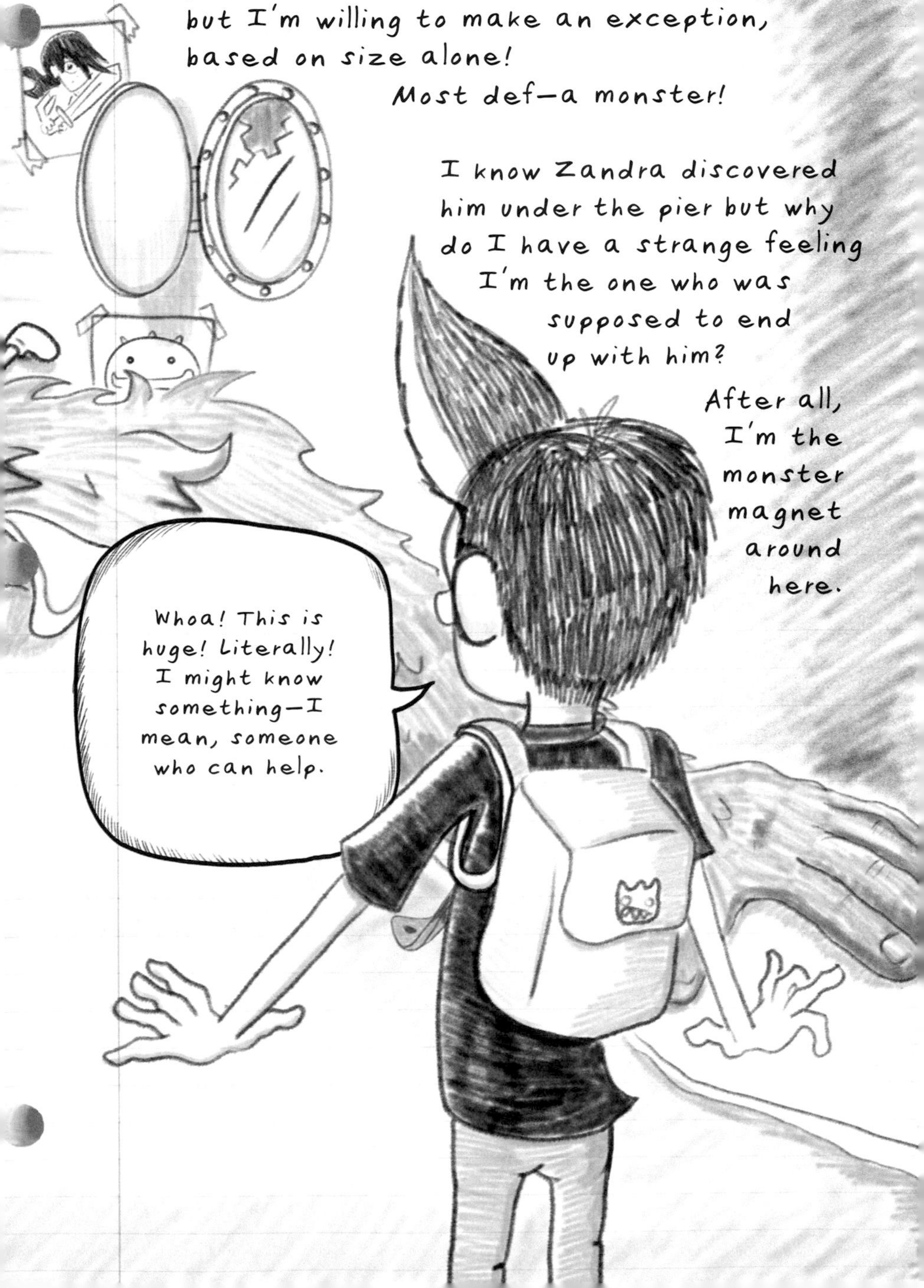
Whoa! This is huge! Literally! I might know something—I mean, someone who can help.

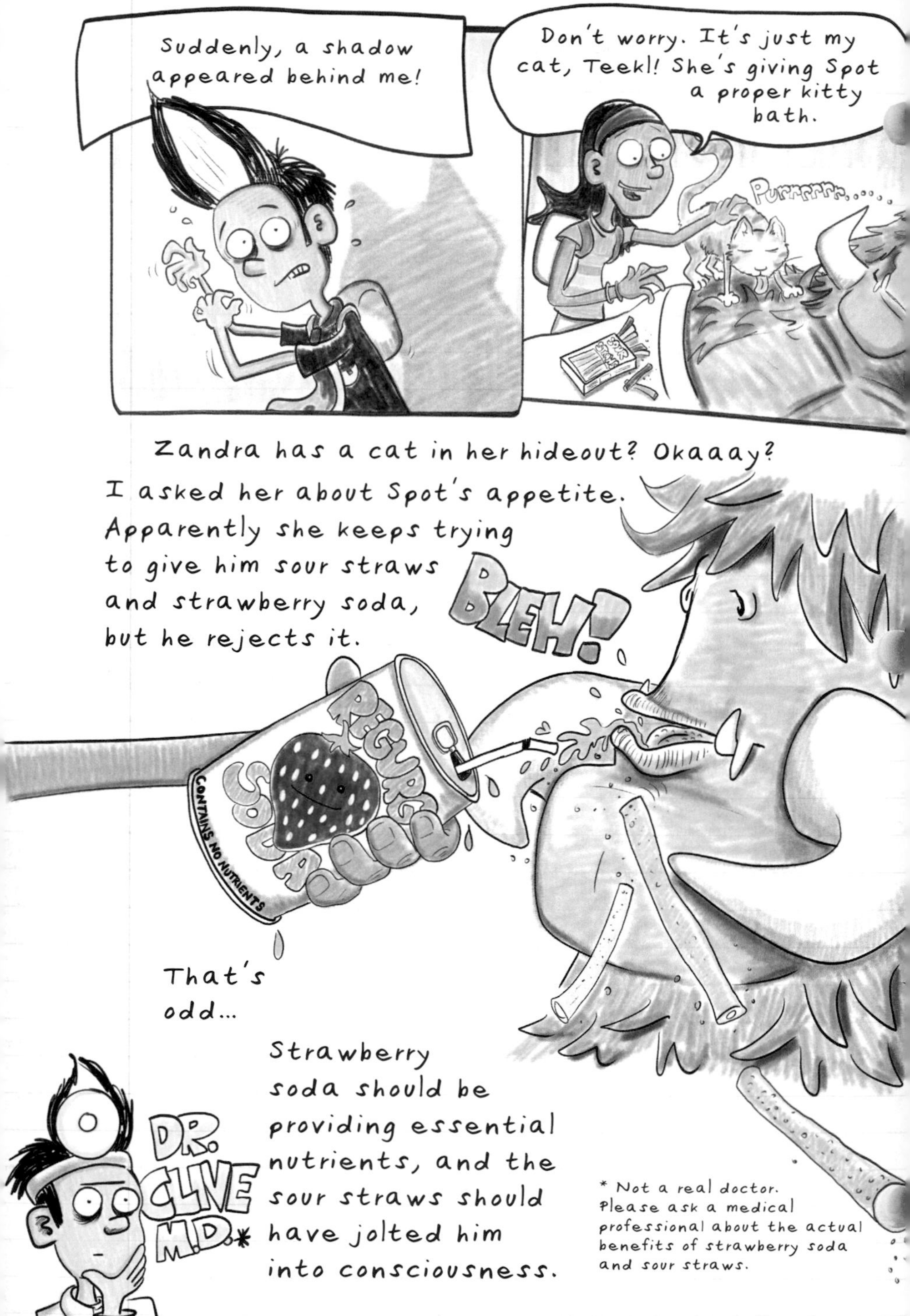

Suddenly, a shadow appeared behind me!
Don't worry. It's just my cat, Teek!! She's giving Spot a proper kitty bath.
Purrrrrr.....
Zandra has a cat in her hideout? Okaaay?
I asked her about Spot's appetite. Apparently she keeps trying to give him sour straws and strawberry soda, but he rejects it.
BLEH!
REGURG SODA
CONTAINS NO NUTRIENTS
That's odd...
Strawberry soda should be providing essential nutrients, and the sour straws should have jolted him into consciousness.
DR. CLIVE M.D.*
* Not a real doctor. Please ask a medical professional about the actual benefits of strawberry soda and sour straws.

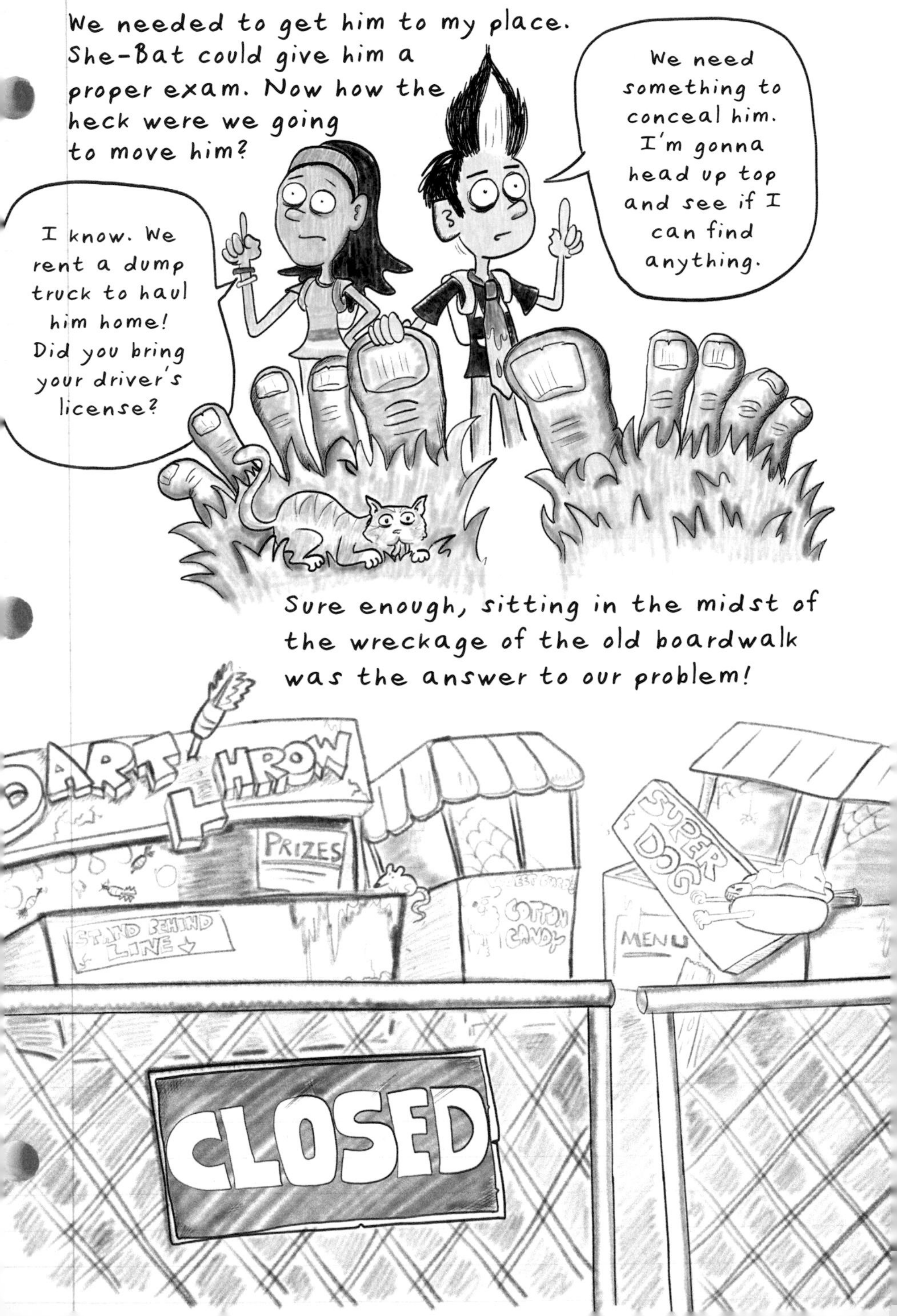
We needed to get him to my place. She-Bat could give him a proper exam. Now how the heck were we going to move him?
We need something to conceal him. I'm gonna head up top and see if I can find anything.
I know. We rent a dump truck to haul him home! Did you bring your driver's license?
Sure enough, sitting in the midst of the wreckage of the old boardwalk was the answer to our problem!
DART THROW
PRIZES
STAND BEHIND LINE
COTTON CANDY
SUPER DOG
MENU
CLOSED

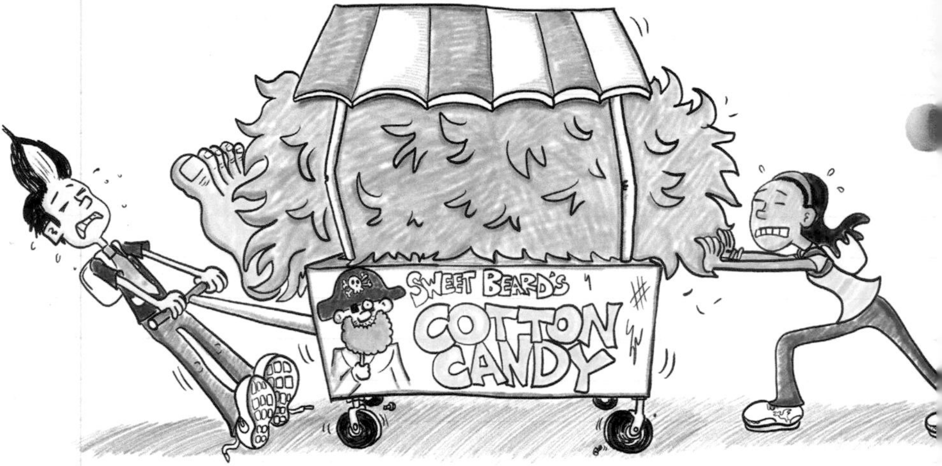
SWEET BEARD'S
COTTON CANDY

Good idea, huh? Pure genius, I'd say. Within minutes, we were rolling the big lug to my house. But I was nervous the killer sphere was going to spot us.

We managed to go five or six blocks completely unnoticed...well, almost completely unnoticed.

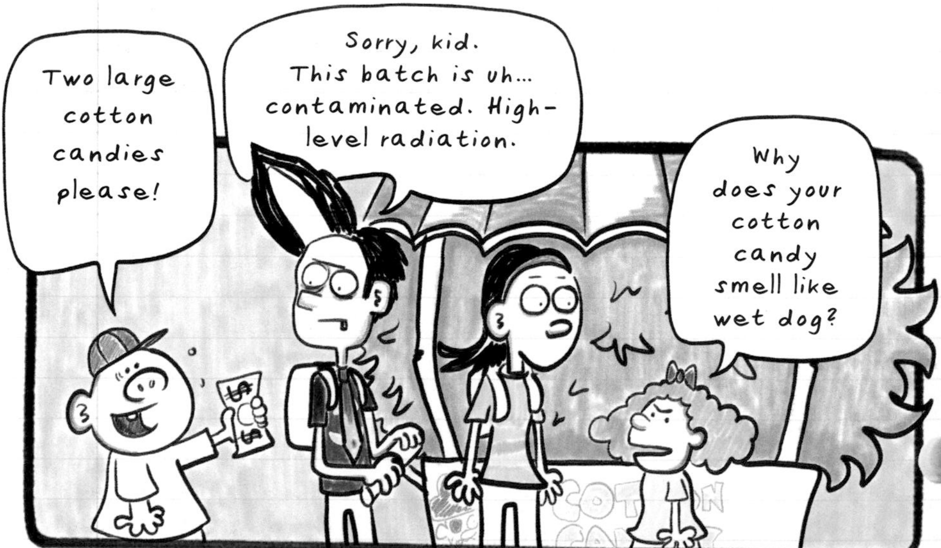
Two large cotton candies please!
Sorry, kid. This batch is uh... contaminated. High-level radiation.
Why does your cotton candy smell like wet dog?

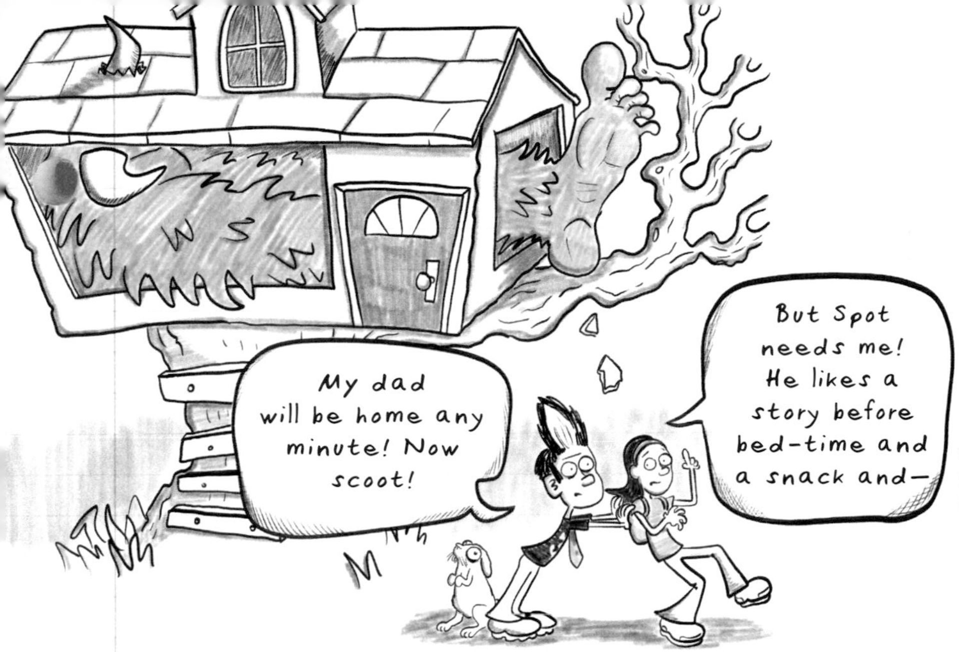
My dad will be home any minute! Now scoot!
But Spot needs me! He likes a story before bed-time and a snack and—

Once we got Spot into the tree house, Zandra wanted to meet my other monsters. But there was no time. I promised to update her later.

DINNER

Been nervous since Zandra left. Spot might be one monster too many. Dad's gonna find out for sure. Speaking of Dad—dinner was uncomfortable.

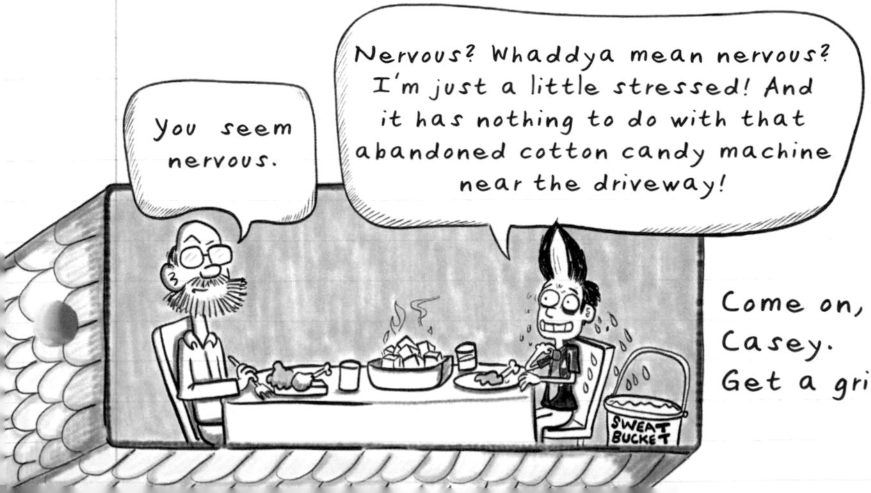
You seem nervous.
Nervous? Whaddya mean nervous? I'm just a little stressed! And it has nothing to do with that abandoned cotton candy machine near the driveway!
SWEAT BUCKET

Come on, Casey. Get a grip.

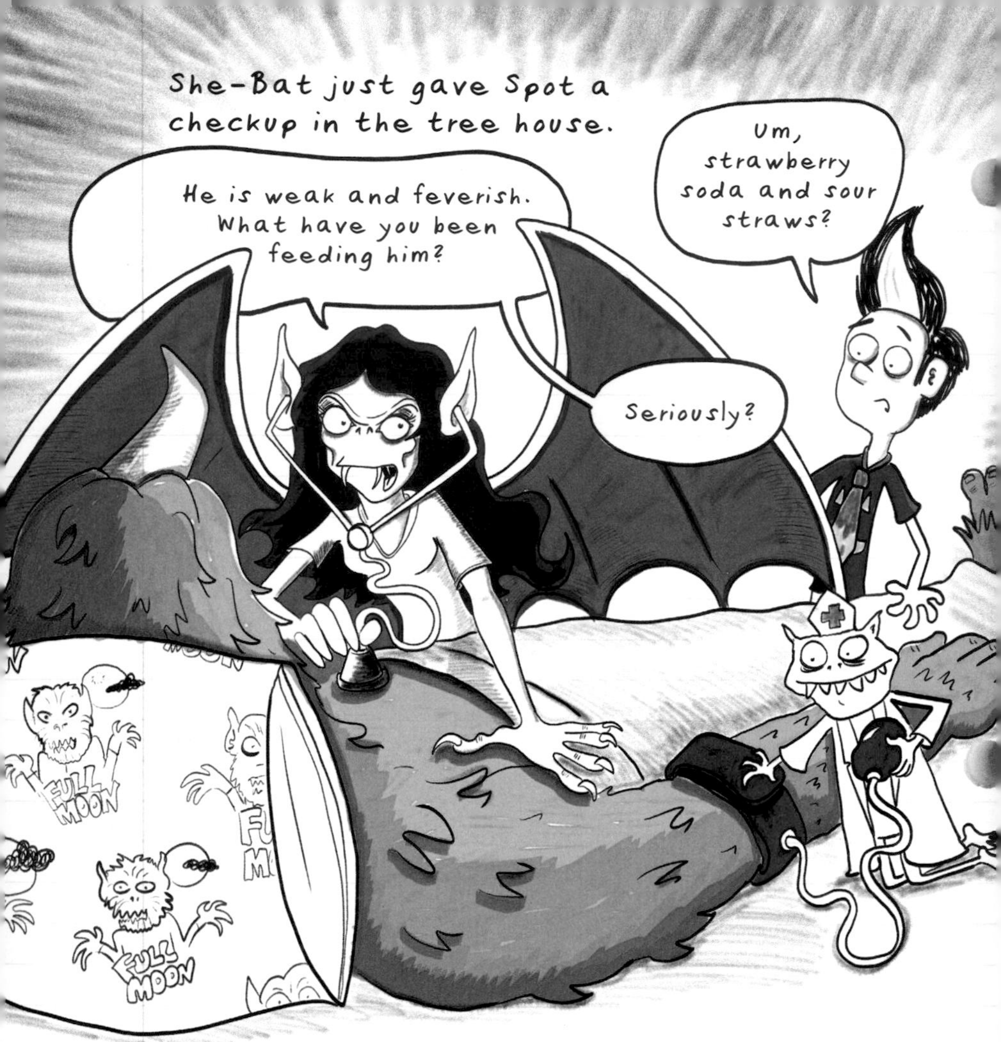
She-Bat just gave Spot a checkup in the tree house.
He is weak and feverish. What have you been feeding him?
Um, strawberry soda and sour straws?
Seriously?
FULL MOON
FULL MOON

She's trying to research Spot now.

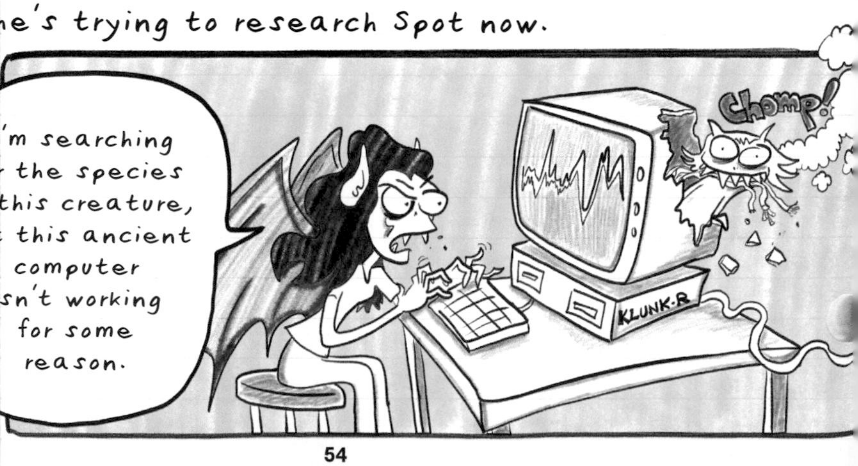
I'm searching for the species of this creature, but this ancient computer isn't working for some reason.
Chomp!
KLUNK-R

She's got a makeshift lab up in the attic and will cook up a serum to cure Spot. I just wish she'd do it more quietly. Dad's totally gonna hear.

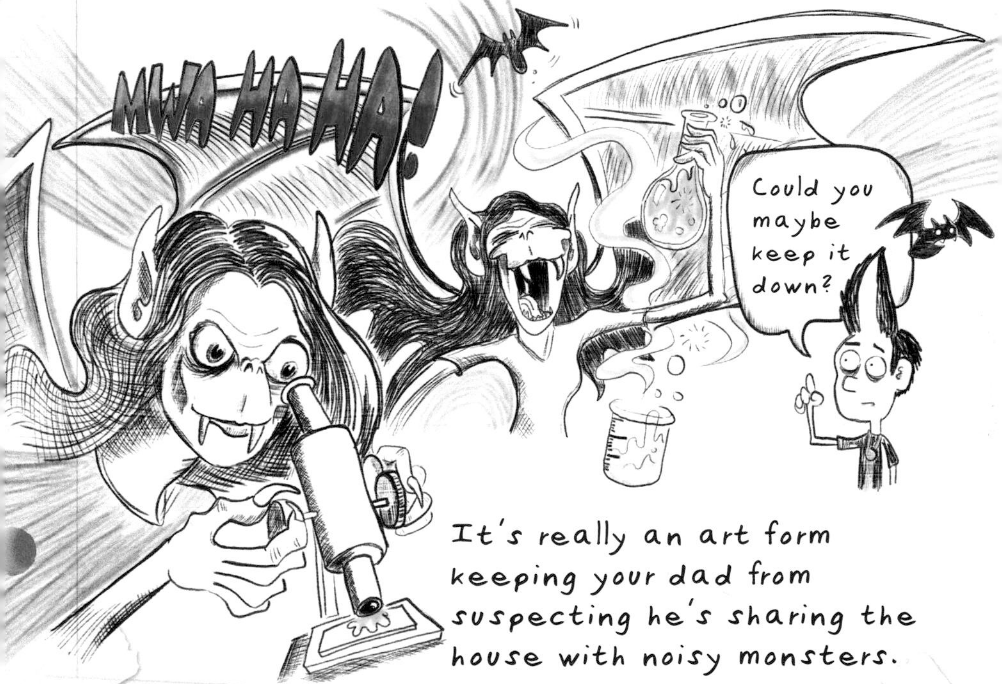
MWA HA HA!
Could you maybe keep it down?

It's really an art form keeping your dad from suspecting he's sharing the house with noisy monsters.

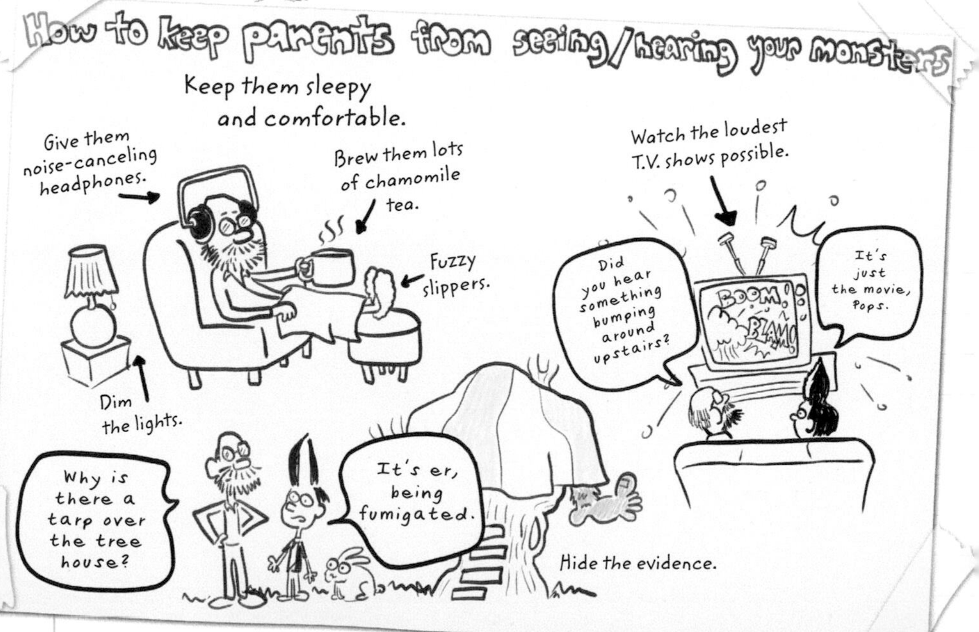
How to keep parents from seeing/hearing your monsters
Keep them sleepy and comfortable.
Give them noise-canceling headphones.
Brew them lots of chamomile tea.
Fuzzy slippers.
Dim the lights.
Watch the loudest T.V. shows possible.
Did you hear something bumping around upstairs?
BOOM! BLAM!
It's just the movie, Pops.
Why is there a tarp over the tree house?
It's er, being fumigated.
Hide the evidence.

Casey's Creature Exhibit

Still don't know a lot about She-Bat except that she frightens me...

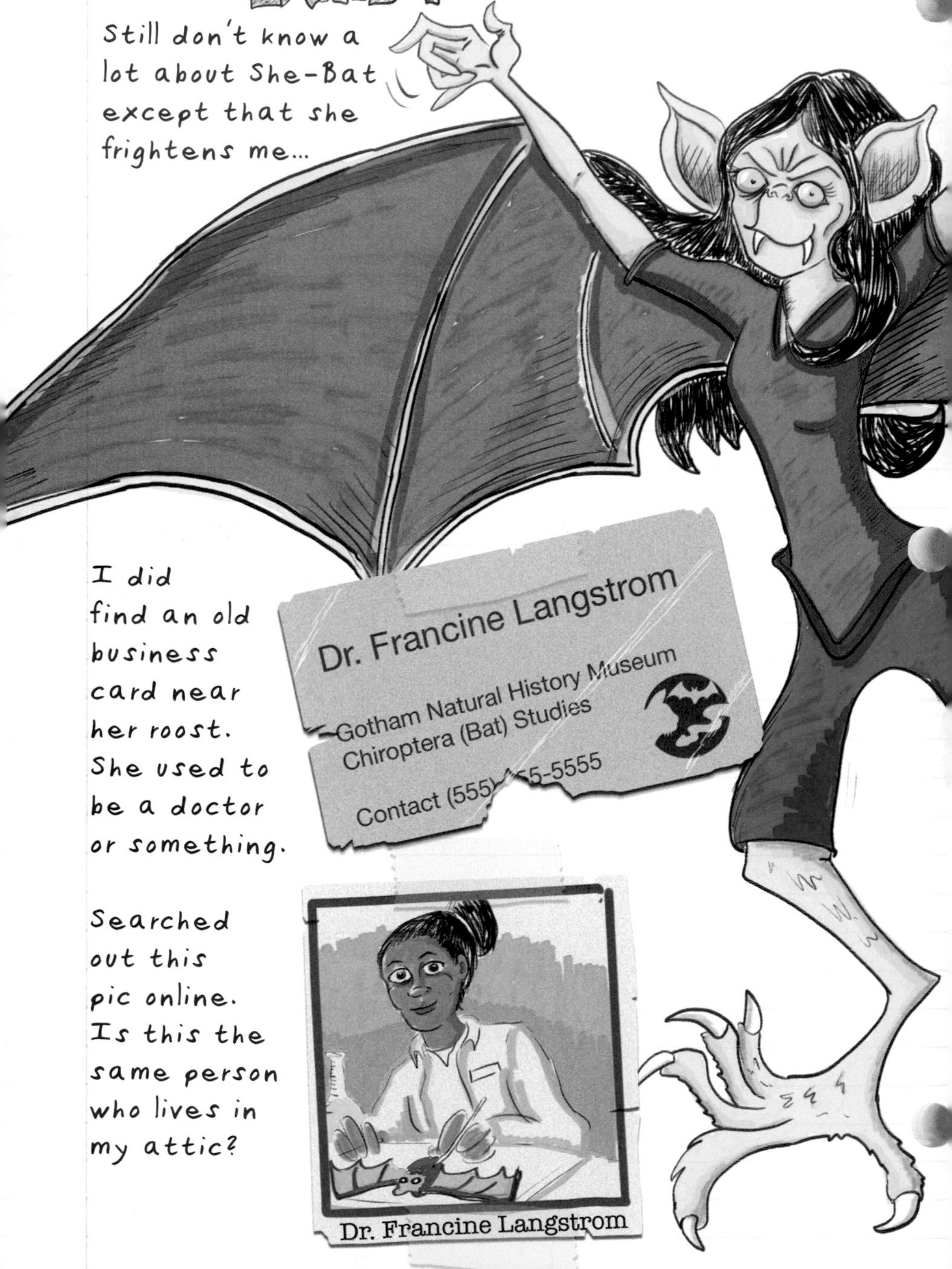

Dr. Francine Langstrom
Gotham Natural History Museum
Chiroptera (Bat) Studies
Contact (555) 55-5555
Dr. Francine Langstrom

I did find an old business card near her roost. She used to be a doctor or something.

Searched out this pic online. Is this the same person who lives in my attic?

SHE-BAT

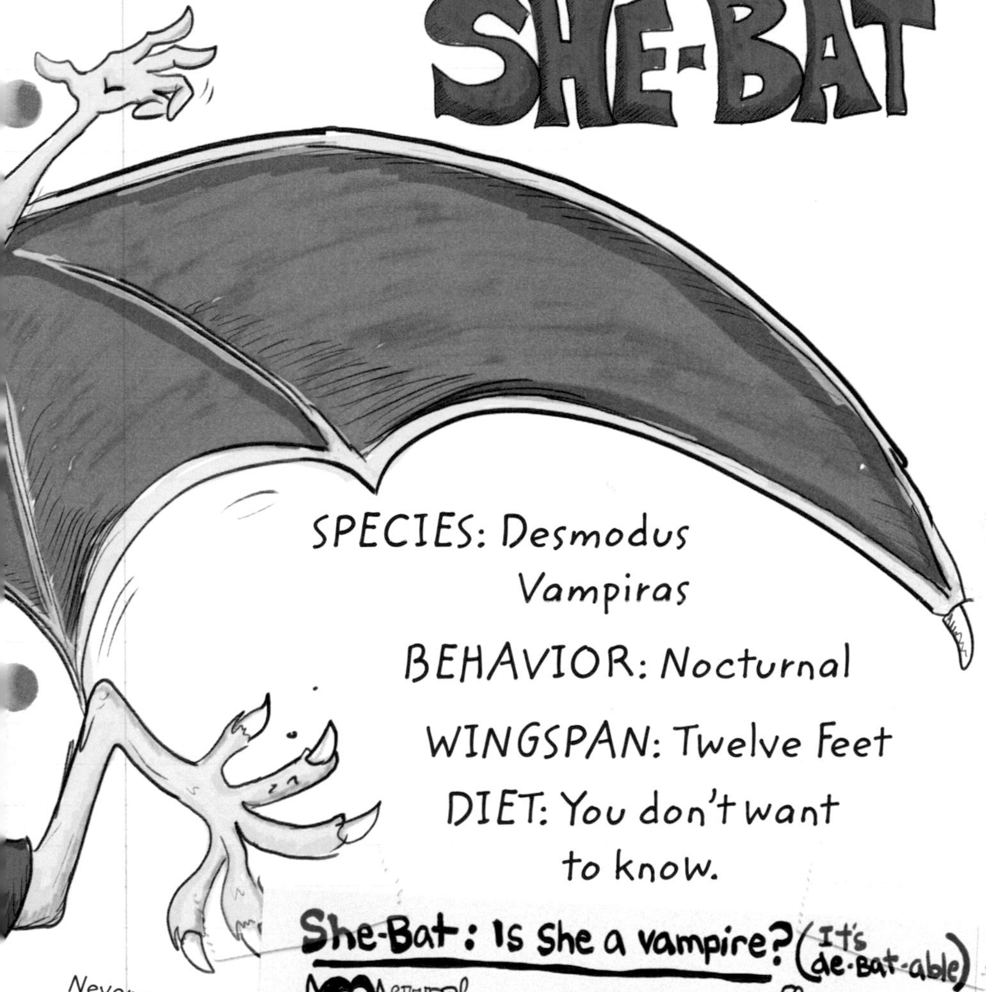

SPECIES: Desmodus Vampiras

BEHAVIOR: Nocturnal

WINGSPAN: Twelve Feet

DIET: You don't want to know.

Never comment on her feet, if you enjoy having your noggin attached to your lower body.

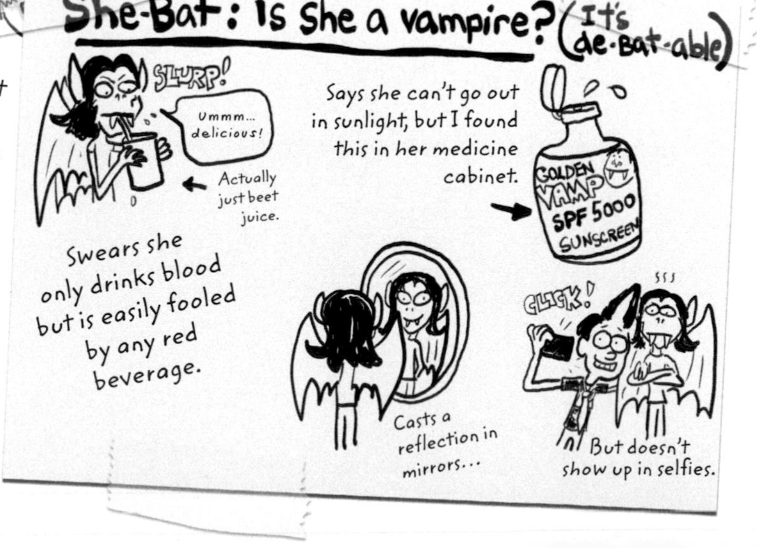

She-Bat: Is she a vampire? (It's de-Bat-able)
SLURP!
Ummm... delicious!
Actually just beet juice.
Swears she only drinks blood but is easily fooled by any red beverage.
Says she can't go out in sunlight, but I found this in her medicine cabinet.
GOLDEN VAMP SPF 5000 SUNSCREEN
Casts a reflection in mirrors...
CLICK!
But doesn't show up in selfies.

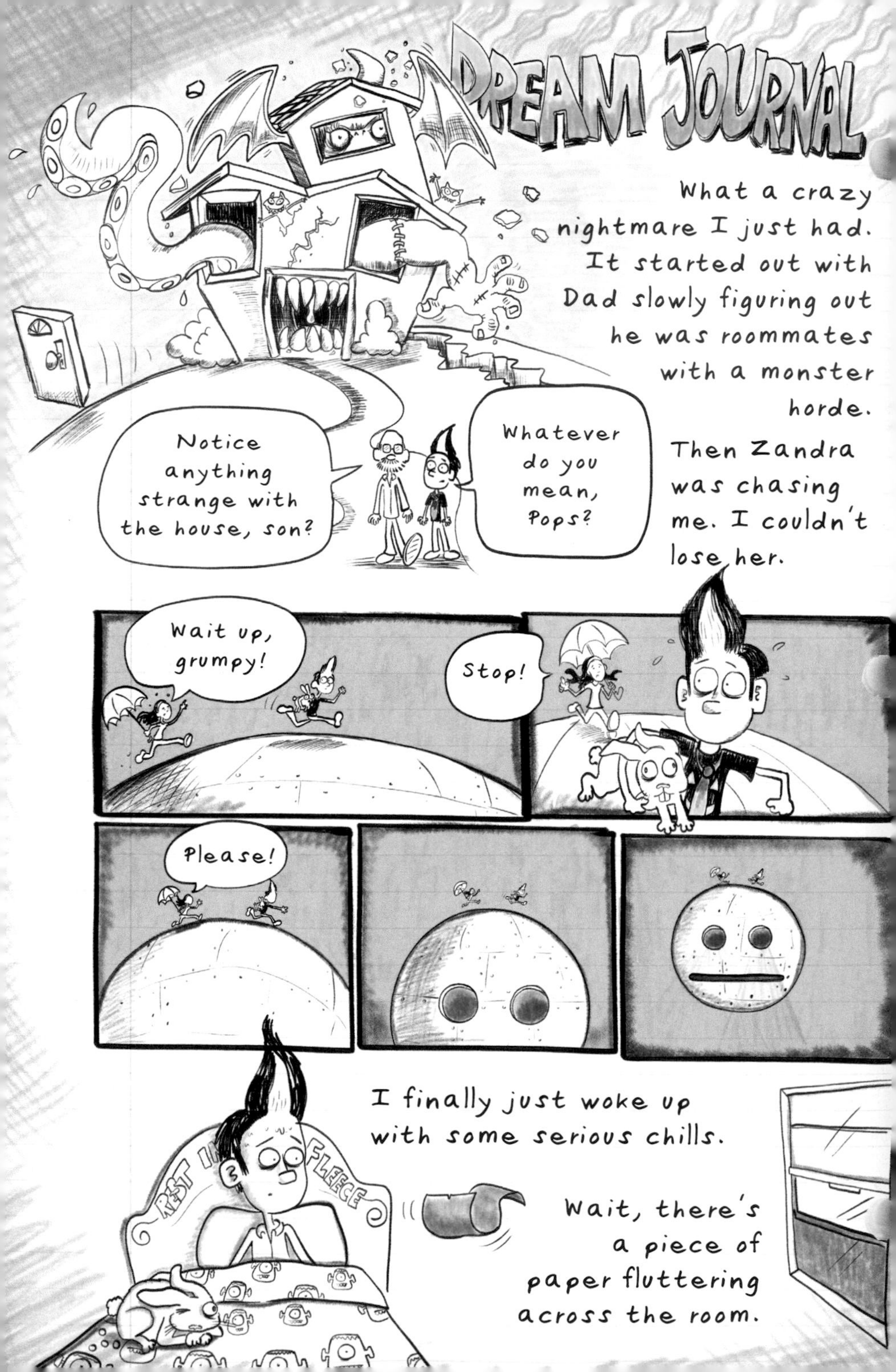

DREAM JOURNAL
What a crazy nightmare I just had. It started out with Dad slowly figuring out he was roommates with a monster horde.
Notice anything strange with the house, son?
Whatever do you mean, Pops?
Then Zandra was chasing me. I couldn't lose her.
Wait up, grumpy!
Stop!
Please!
I finally just woke up with some serious chills.
REST IN FLEECE
Wait, there's a piece of paper fluttering across the room.

It's from Zandra. An illustrated history of Spot. She's pretty good at manga-style art, by the way.

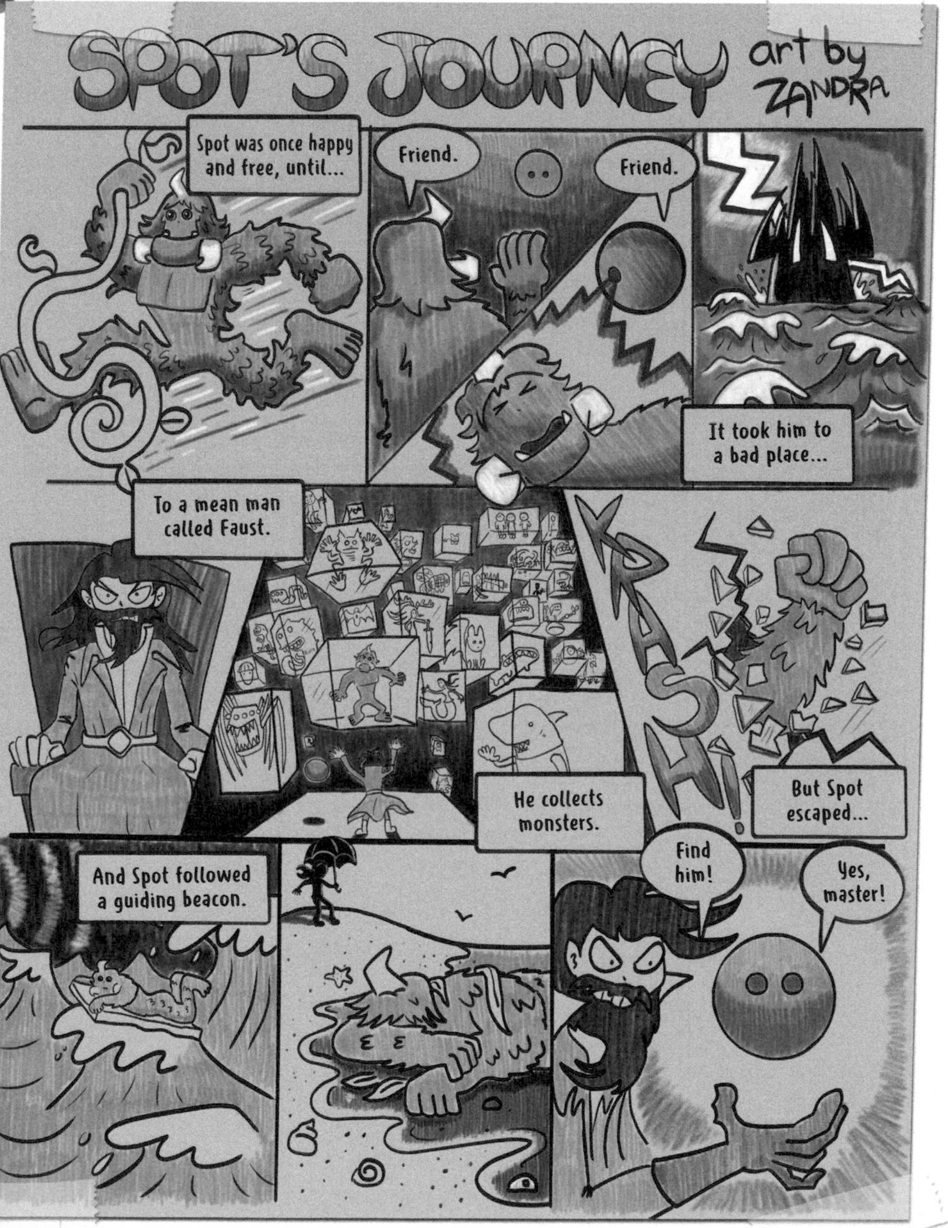
SPOT'S JOURNEY
art by ZANDRA
Spot was once happy and free, until...
Friend.
Friend.
It took him to a bad place...
To a mean man called Faust.
He collects monsters.
KRASH!
But Spot escaped...
And Spot followed a guiding beacon.
Find him!
Yes, master!

So that explains the flying orb. It's after Spot!

FRIDAY 7:23 A.M.

Whew boy. Guess I must've had nightmares all night long because I am completely exhausted this morning. Totally out of it.

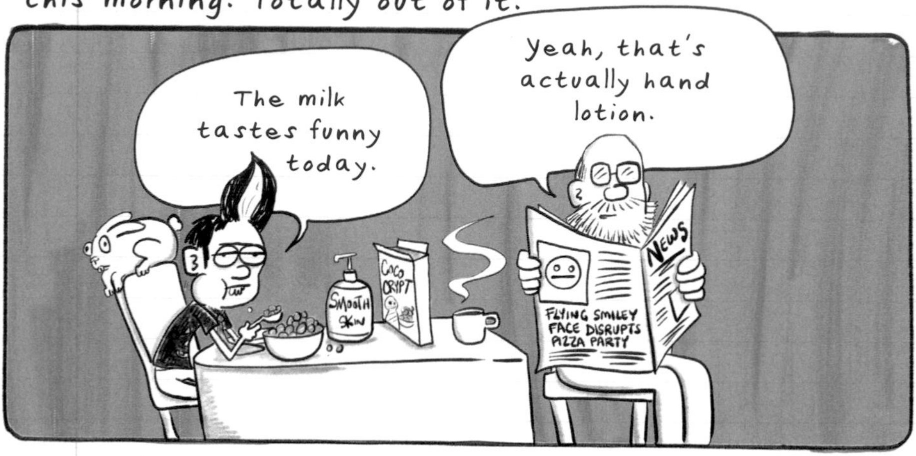
The milk tastes funny today.
Yeah, that's actually hand lotion.
SMOOTH SKIN
COCO CRYPT
NEWS
FLYING SMILEY FACE DISRUPTS PIZZA PARTY

Waited till Dad had left for work before going out to the tree house to check on Spot. When I saw him, you could have knocked me over with a gnat sneeze. The subject was not only conscious, he wasn't pink anymore.

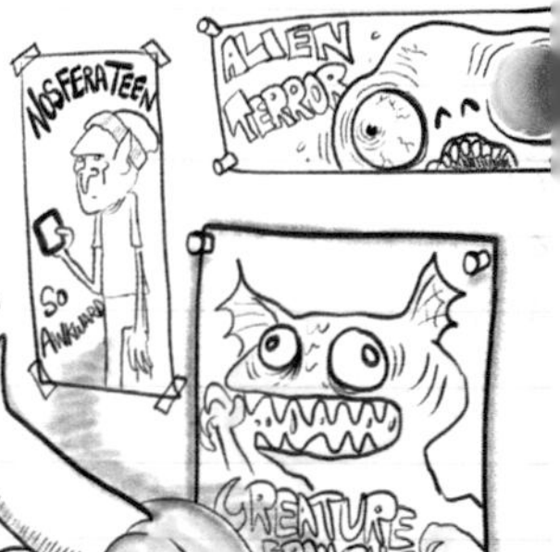
NOSFERATEEN
So Awkward
ALIEN TERROR
CREATURE FROM THE DARK DEPTHS

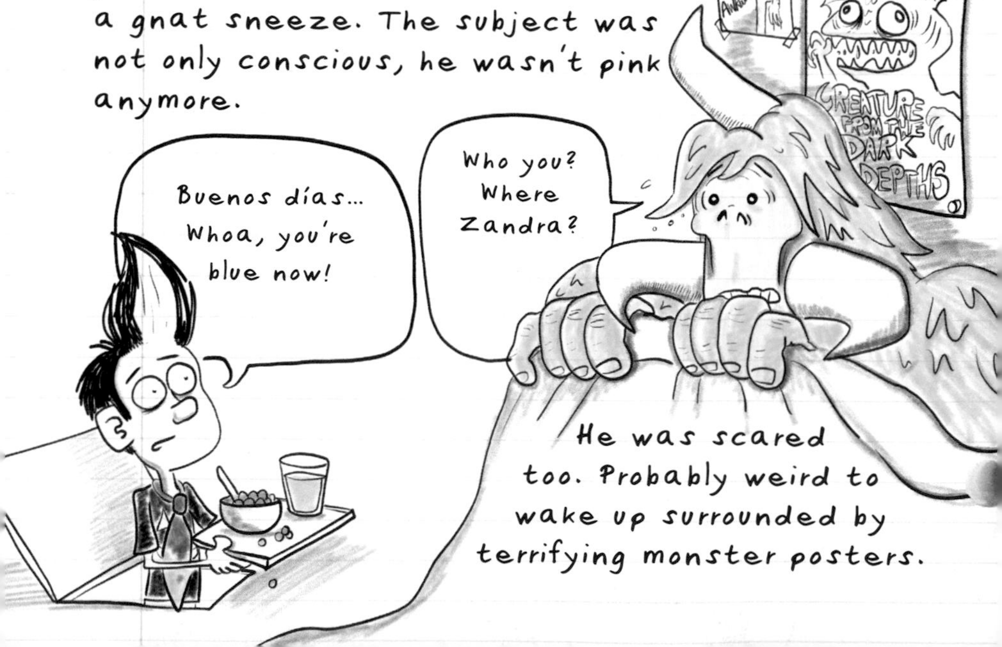
Buenos días... Whoa, you're blue now!
Who you? Where Zandra?

He was scared too. Probably weird to wake up surrounded by terrifying monster posters.

I officially introduced myself to Spot and explained why he was in a strange tree house. He seemed stressed, so I lent him Ygor for the day while I'm in class. Ygor has a soothing quality.

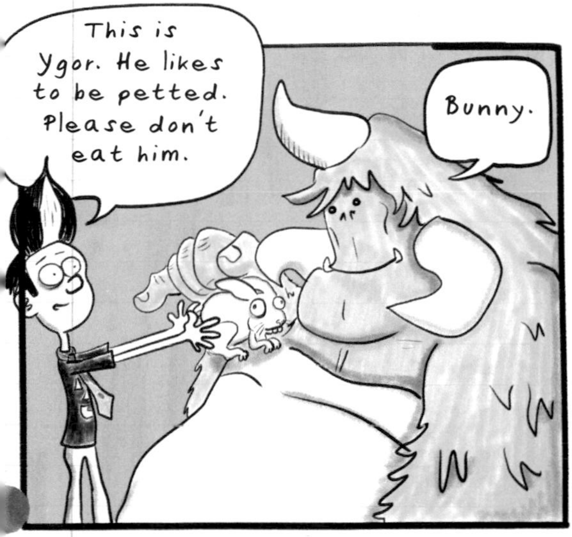

This is Ygor. He likes to be petted. Please don't eat him.
Bunny.

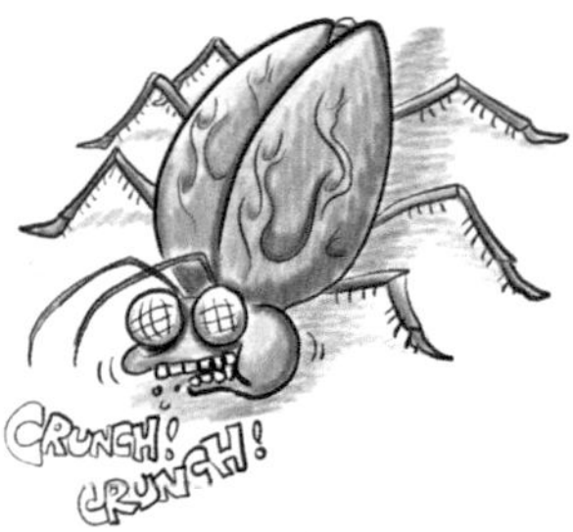

CRUNCH! CRUNCH!

Found this on the floor of my tree house—sour straw dust!

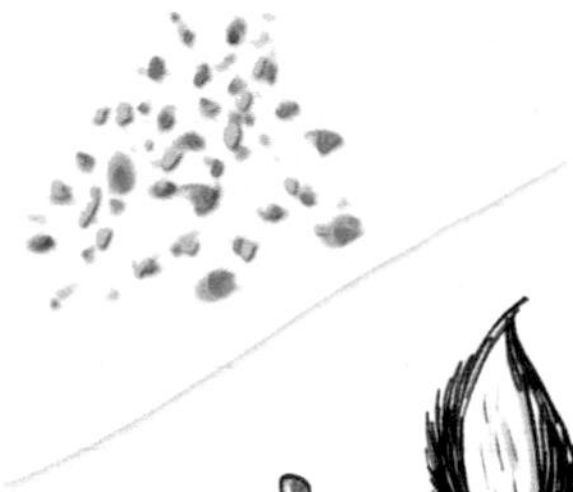

How do I know? Because I tasted it! (Don't judge me.)

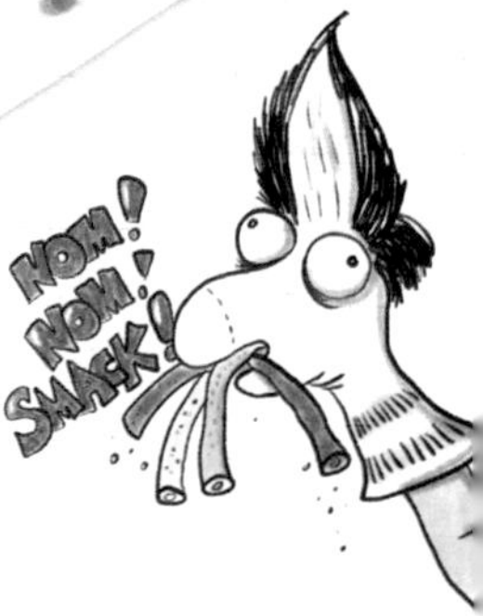

NOM! NOM! SMACK!

Zandra was eating sour straws yesterday, but these remnants seem fresh. They still have zing to them. Hmmmm.

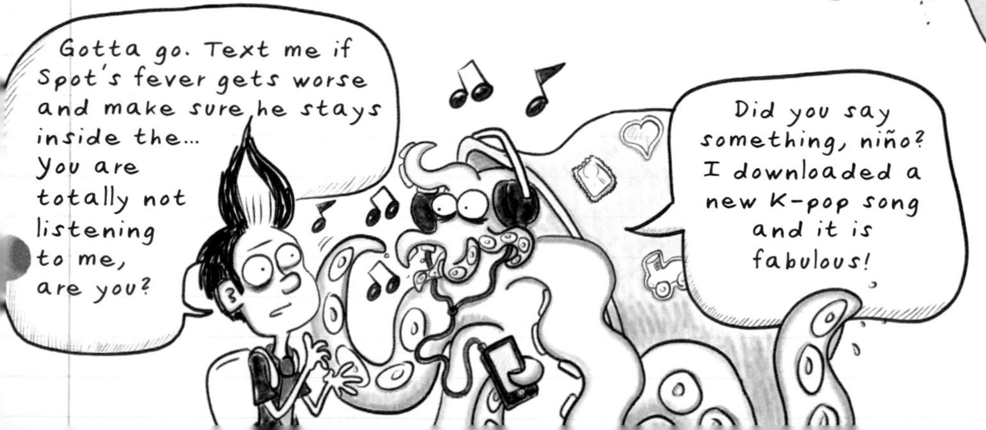

Gotta go. Text me if Spot's fever gets worse and make sure he stays inside the... You are totally not listening to me, are you?
Did you say something, niño? I downloaded a new K-pop song and it is fabulous!

8:01 A.M.

Odd way to start the morning. First thing Zandra said to me wasn't "How's Spot?" but "Do you want a donut?"

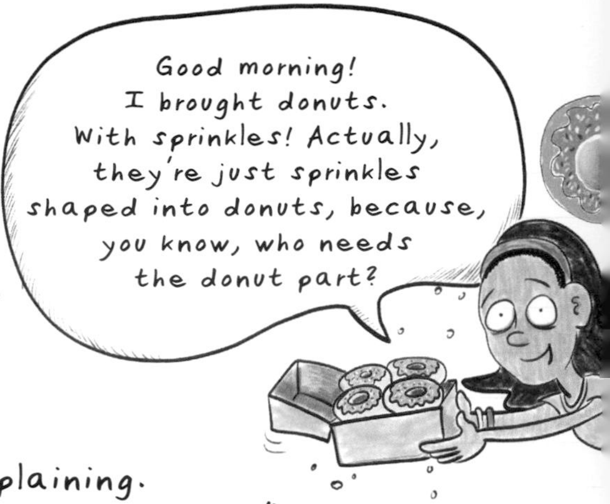
Good morning! I brought donuts. With sprinkles! Actually, they're just sprinkles shaped into donuts, because, you know, who needs the donut part?

Not that I'm complaining. I believe "Do you want a donut?" should be the universal greeting for all the nations of N.A.T.O.

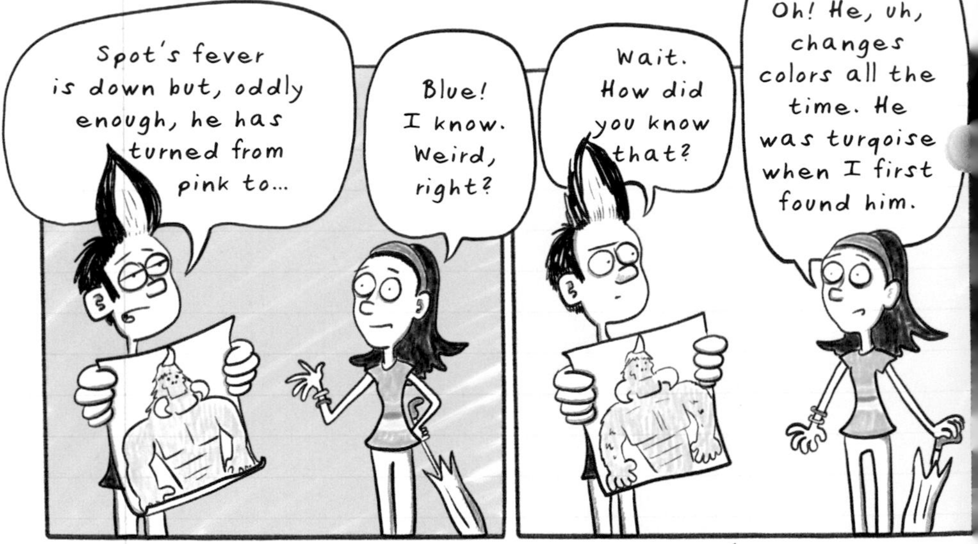
Spot's fever is down but, oddly enough, he has turned from pink to...
Blue! I know. Weird, right?
Wait. How did you know that?
Oh! He, uh, changes colors all the time. He was turqoise when I first found him.

Weird she didn't tell me about Spot's changing fur. Of course, she wears sneakers that roll, light up, AND roar like a dragon when she kicks something. So, you know, weird is relative.

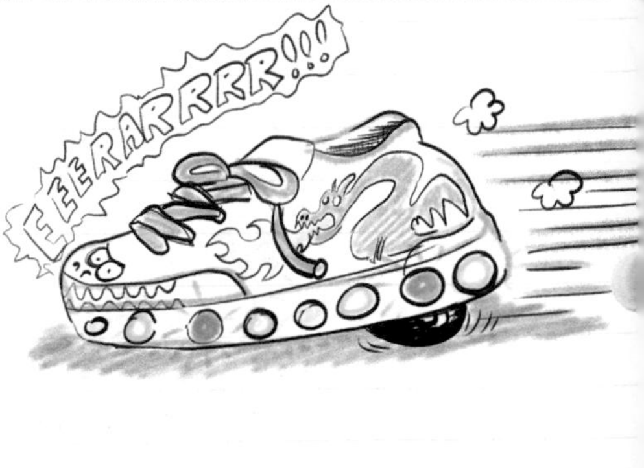
EEERARRRRR!!!

LUNCH

At lunch, Zandra finally hit me with a tsunami of questions about my monsters...

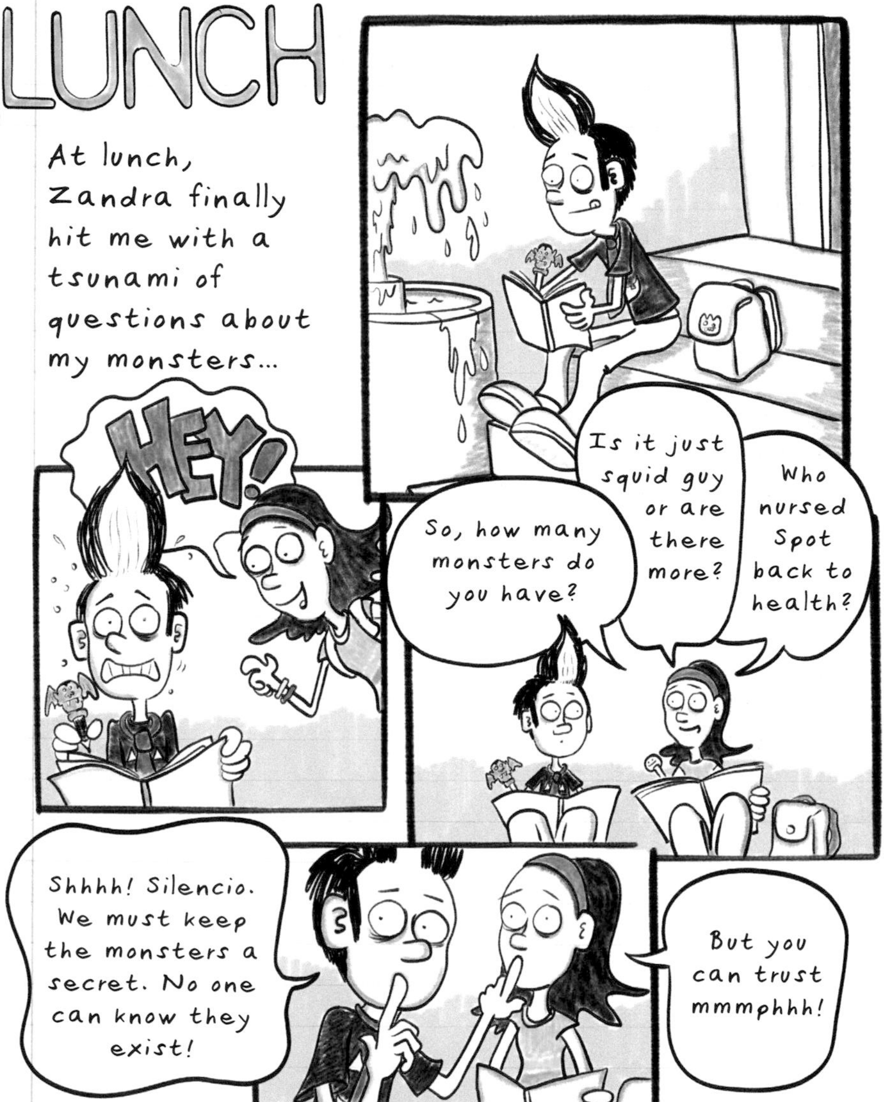

HEY!
So, how many monsters do you have?
Is it just squid guy or are there more?
Who nursed Spot back to health?
Shhhh! Silencio. We must keep the monsters a secret. No one can know they exist!
But you can trust mmmphhh!

1:01

Oh boy. I think I've got a big problem. Seems like Zandra wants to be best buds or something. Everywhere I look, there she is!

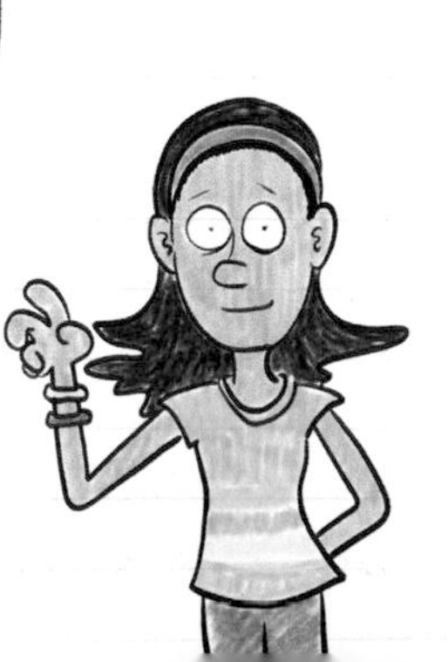

I'm going to have to level with her. This is business. She brought me a monster. I shall take care of it. We are not friends.

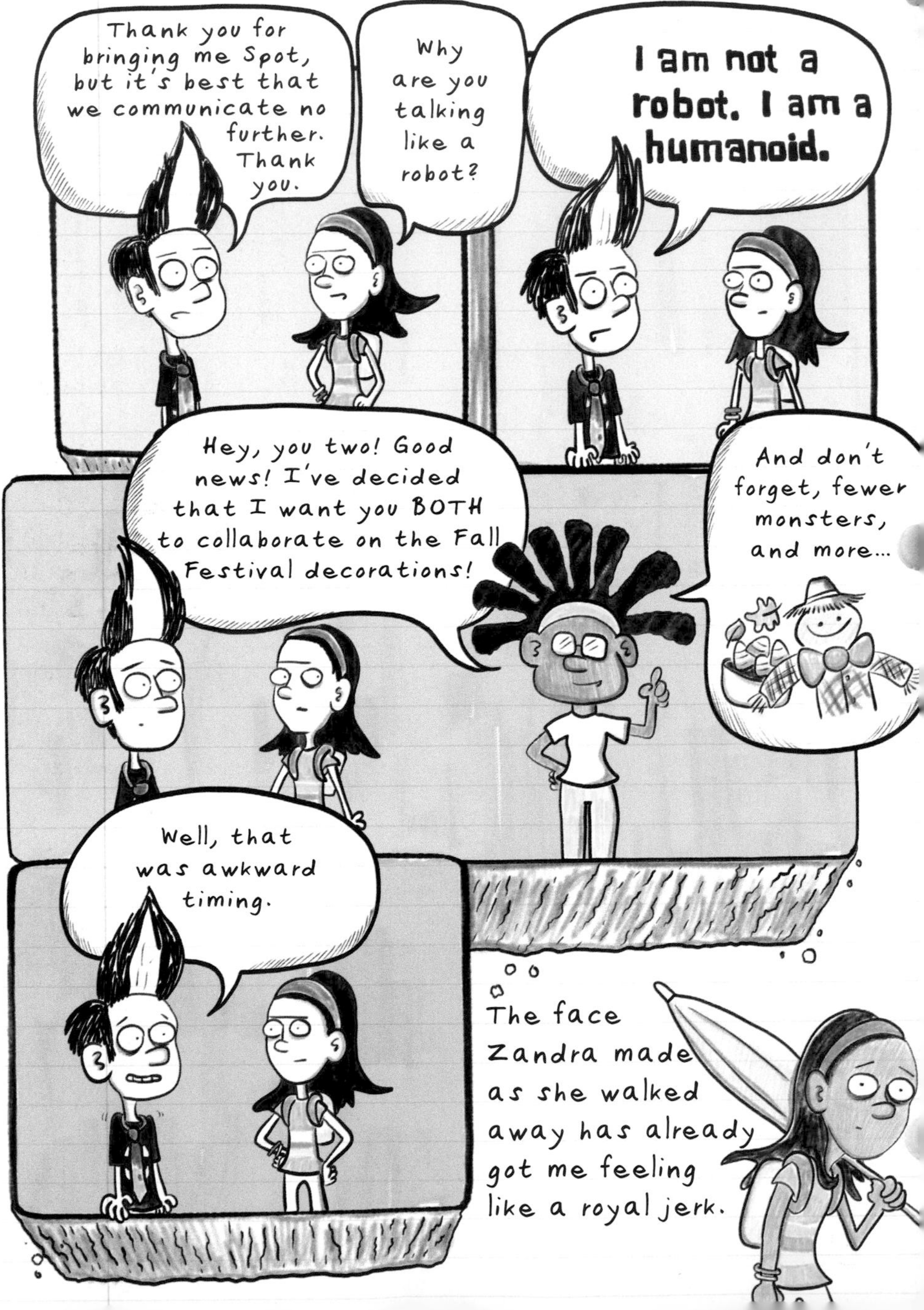
Thank you for bringing me Spot, but it's best that we communicate no further. Thank you.
Why are you talking like a robot?
I am not a robot. I am a humanoid.
Hey, you two! Good news! I've decided that I want you BOTH to collaborate on the Fall Festival decorations!
And don't forget, fewer monsters, and more...
Well, that was awkward timing.
The face Zandra made as she walked away has already got me feeling like a royal jerk.

FRI. NIGHT

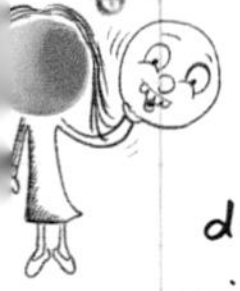

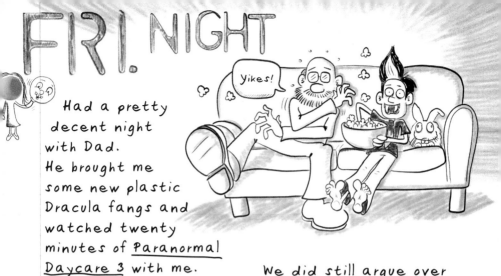

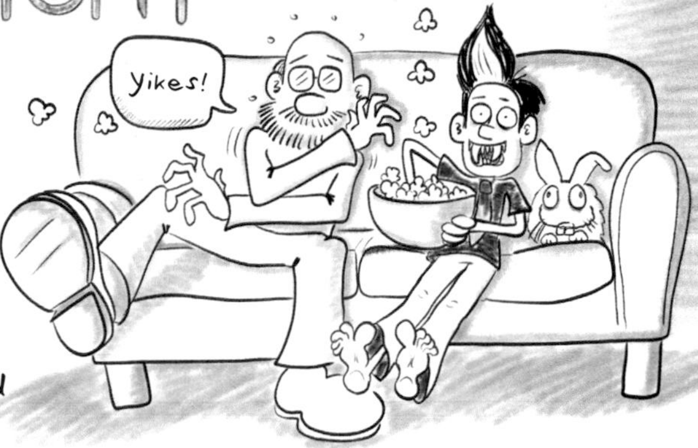
Yikes!

Had a pretty decent night with Dad. He brought me some new plastic Dracula fangs and watched twenty minutes of <u>Paranormal Daycare 3</u> with me. Hey, it's progress!

We did still argue over doing the dishes, though.

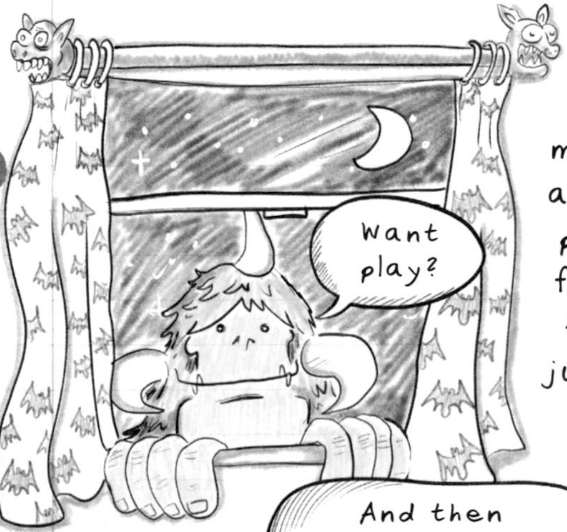
Want play?

Spot must be feeling better. It's nearly midnight and he was just at my window. He wanted pretty much two things—food and entertainment. He was ready for action just when I was ready to crash. I sure hope he's not nocturnal.

He settled for me reading him a story. I picked one Mom used to read to me when I was a kid, <u>My Alien Egg</u>.

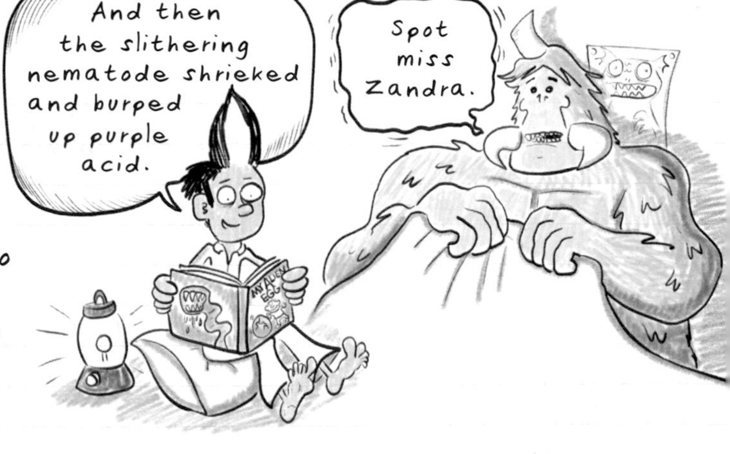
And then the slithering nematode shrieked and burped up purple acid.
Spot miss Zandra.
MY ALIEN EGG

WEEKEND MEDICAL REPORT

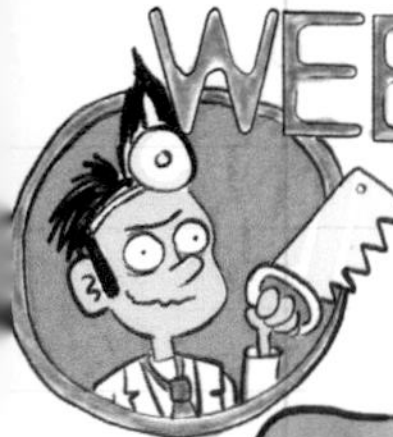

WITH DR. CLIVE M.D. (Maniacal Dissector!)

It's Saturday! Time to check on Spot!

PATIENT - SPOT

WEIGHT - Not exactly sure. I tried to weigh him this morning on the bathroom scale and this happened.

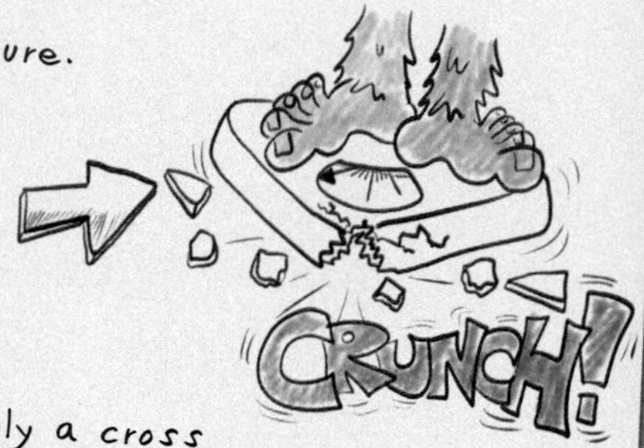
CRUNCH!

SPECIES - Unclear. Possibly a cross between Bigfoot and the Easter Bunny.

SATURDAY UPDATE

Patient is able to get out of bed. Fever is gone. Fur has changed colors again. This time purple. Reason for color change unknown but he is highly fashionable.

Patient's language skills are limited, but I believe he is trying to communicate something to me.

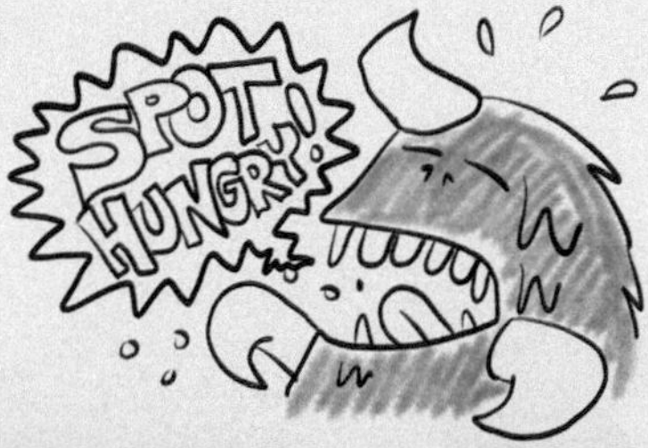
SPOT HUNGRY!

It's hard enough keeping my monsters hidden from Dad during the week, so just imagine weekends when he's lounging around the house all day watching romantic comedies! Luckily, he had somewhere exciting to be this morning.

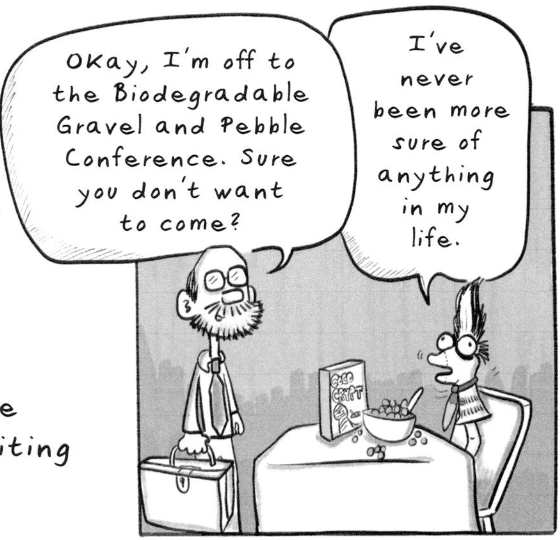
Okay, I'm off to the Biodegradable Gravel and Pebble Conference. Sure you don't want to come?
I've never been more sure of anything in my life.

With Dad gone I can finish Spot's checkup. Today I give him the last of She-Bat's special serum and make sure he gets the vital rest that he needs. He also needs essential nutrients.

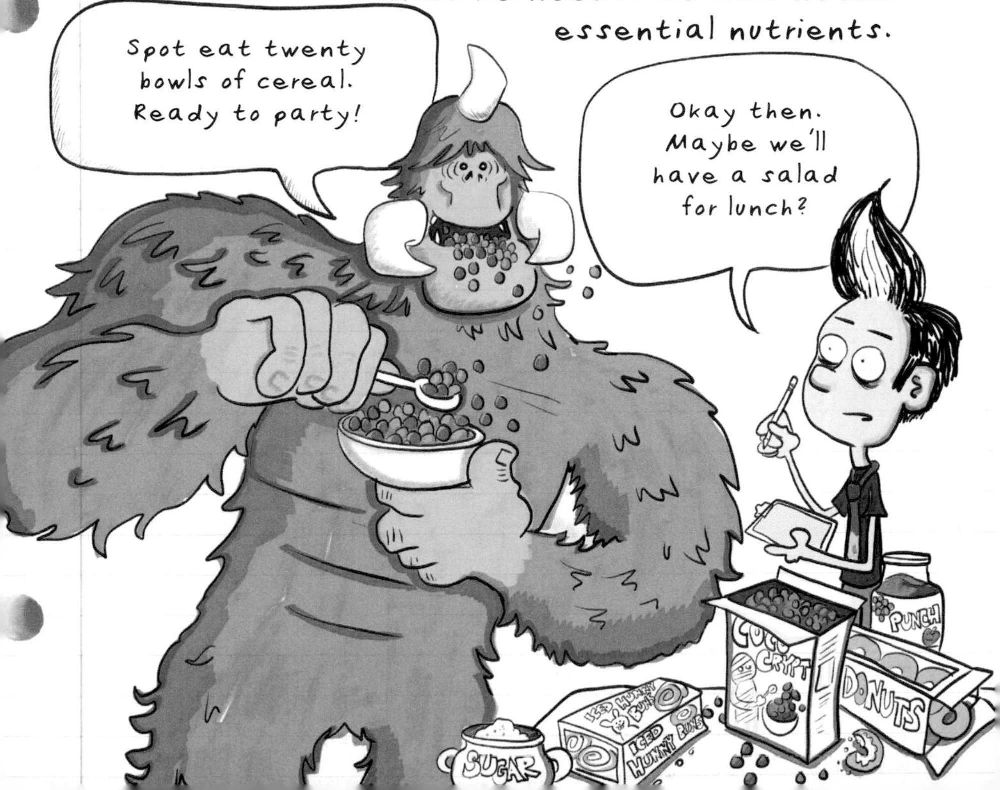
Spot eat twenty bowls of cereal. Ready to party!
Okay then. Maybe we'll have a salad for lunch?
COCO CRYPT
ICED HUNNY BUNS
DONUTS
PUNCH
SUGAR

Spot's definitely the most active of all the monsters I've met. And finding stuff to do with him is already challenging. He's just so ginormous!

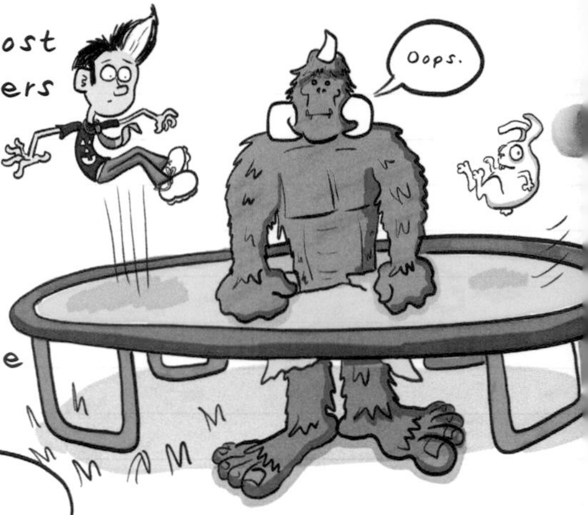
Oops.

Tried out the trampoline with him. That was a disaster.

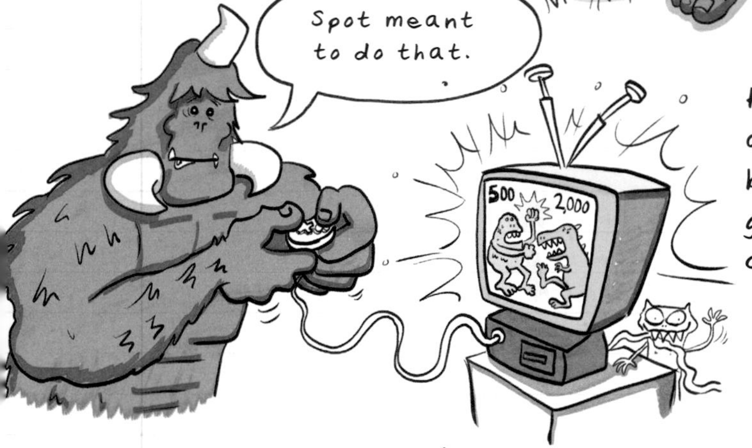
Spot meant to do that.
500
2,000

His thumbs are too darn big for video game controllers.

And a dip in Topo's pool did NOT go well.

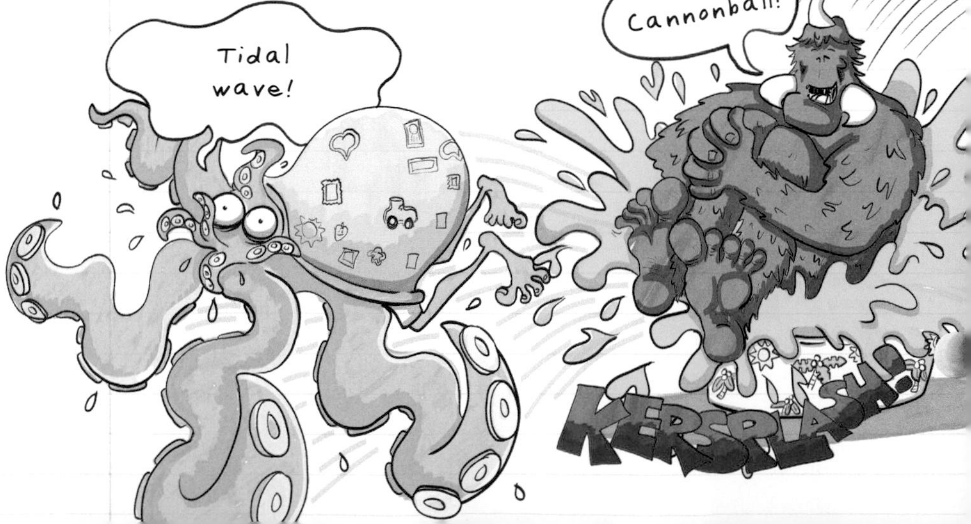
Tidal wave!
Cannonball!
KERSPLASH!

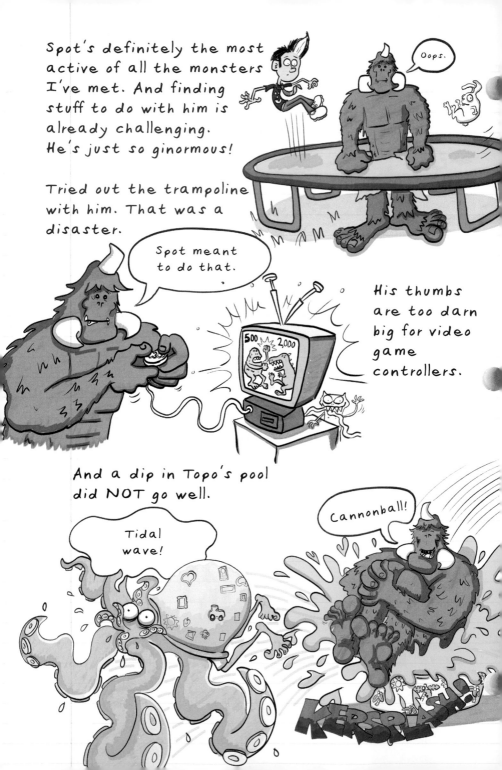

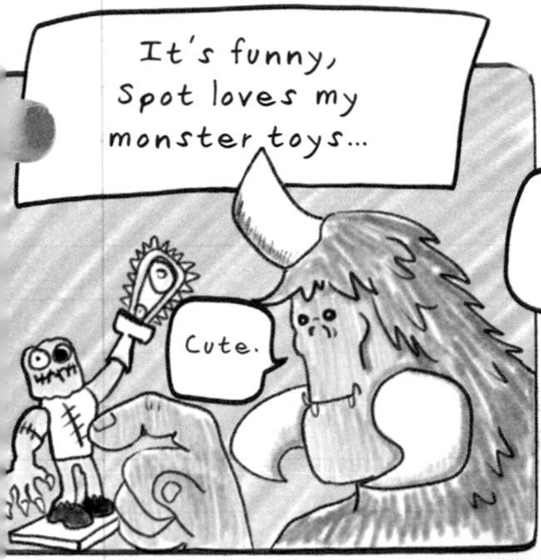
It's funny, Spot loves my monster toys...
Cute.

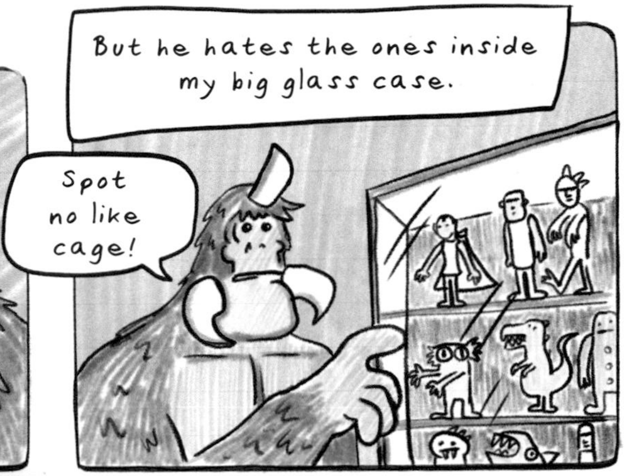
But he hates the ones inside my big glass case.
Spot no like cage!

There's some real tension between Spot and Frankenstein. I get the feeling Franky thinks there's only room enough for one gentle giant in this house.

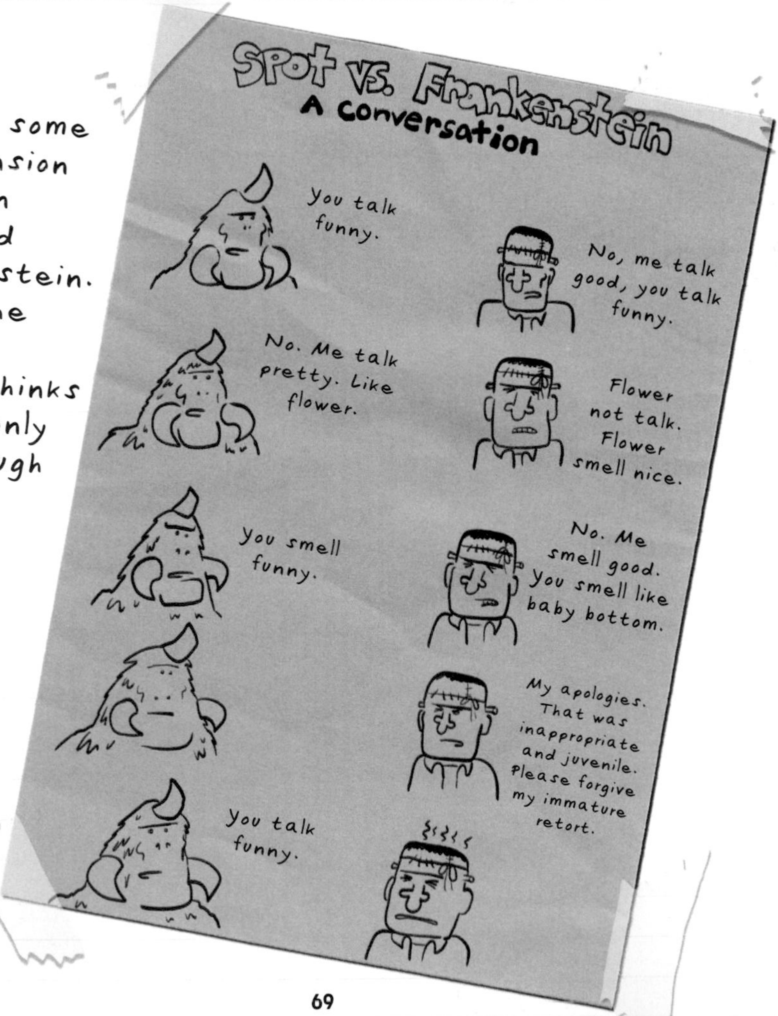
Spot vs. Frankenstein
A Conversation
You talk funny.
No, me talk good, you talk funny.
No. Me talk pretty. Like flower.
Flower not talk. Flower smell nice.
You smell funny.
No. Me smell good. You smell like baby bottom.
My apologies. That was inappropriate and juvenile. Please forgive my immature retort.
You talk funny.

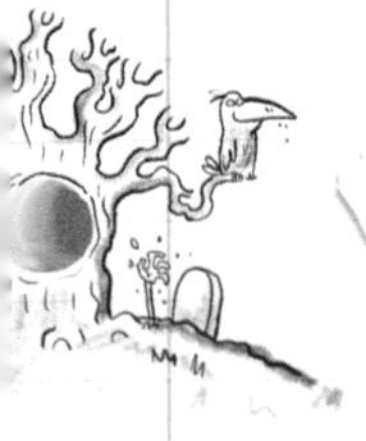

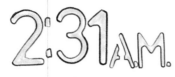

2:31 A.M.

Tonight I awoke to a disturbing sight—Ygor hovering over me, thumping my schnoz with his back foot. That's rabbit talk for DANGER! WAKE UP, FOOL!

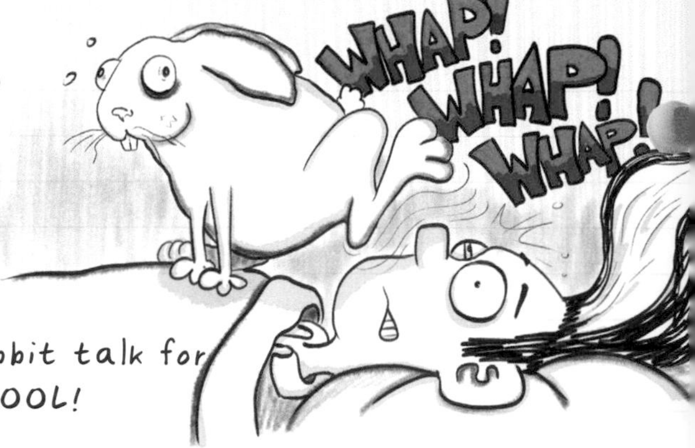
WHAP!
WHAP!
WHAP!

There was a noise coming from the backyard. Was it Spot? An intruder? I crept out the back door to find out, careful not to wake Dad.

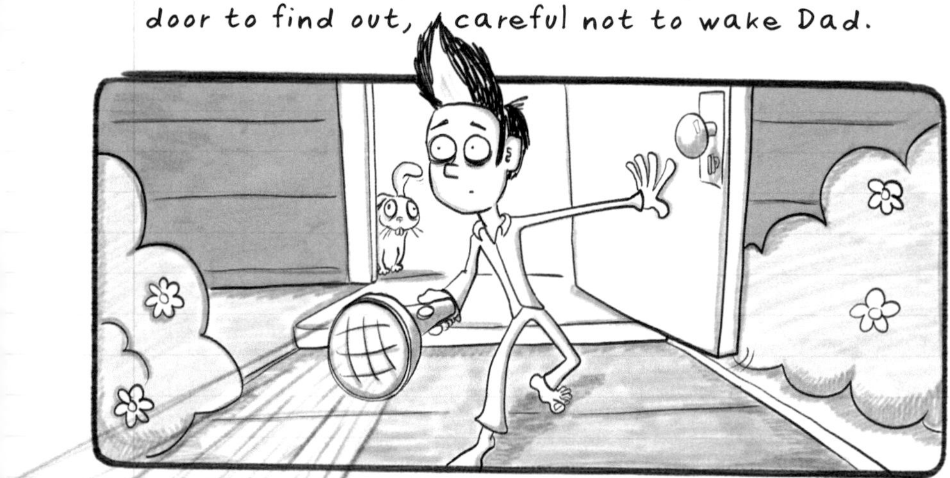

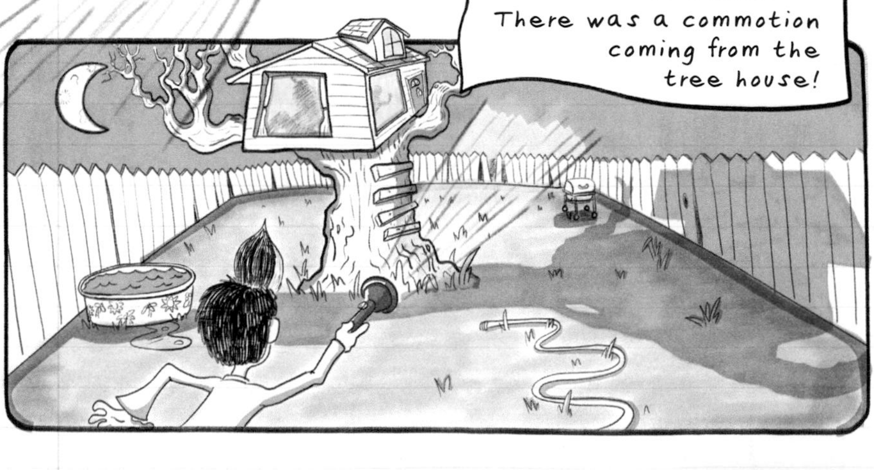
There was a commotion coming from the tree house!

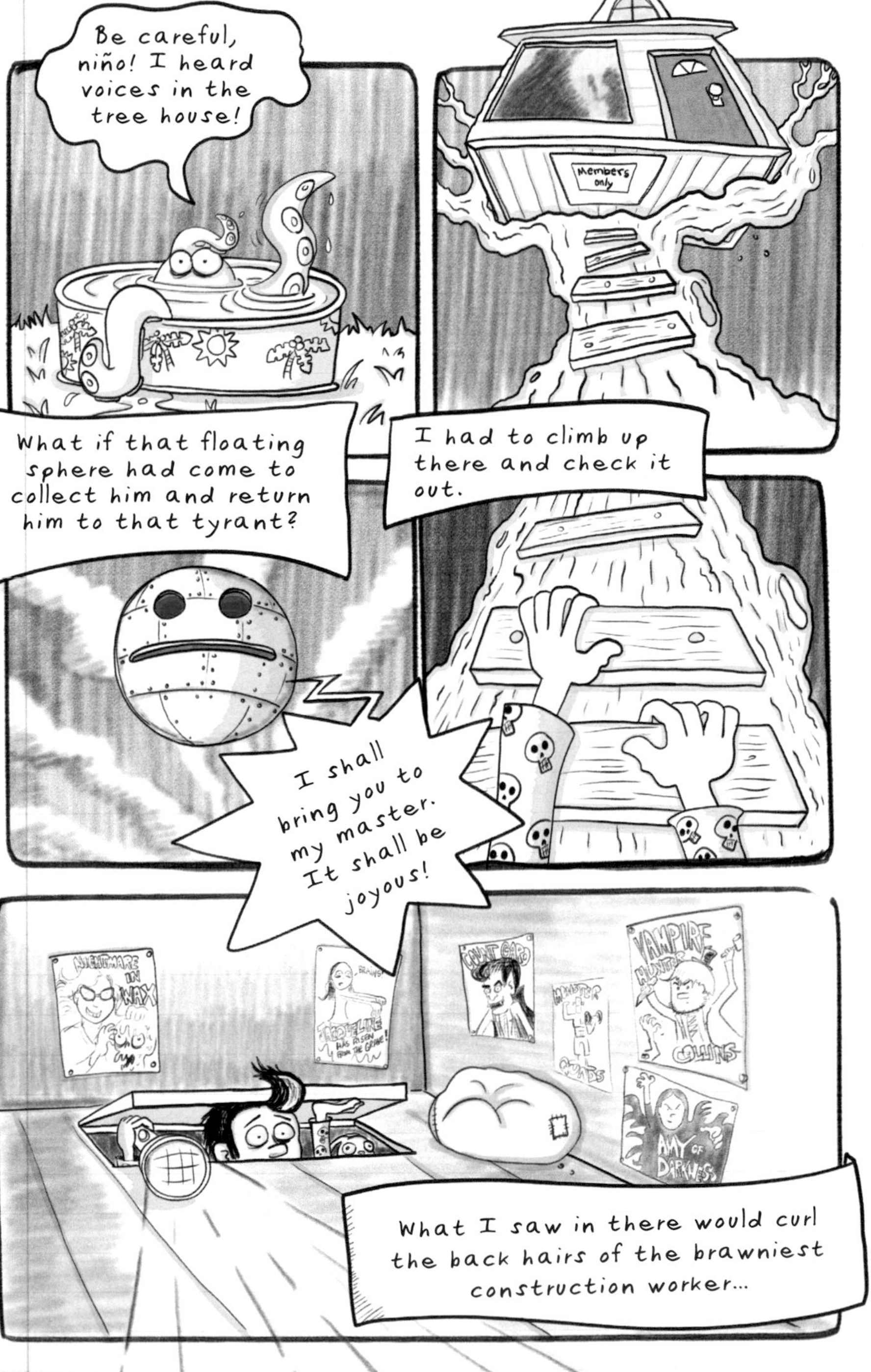

Be careful, niño! I heard voices in the tree house!
Members only
What if that floating sphere had come to collect him and return him to that tyrant?
I had to climb up there and check it out.
I shall bring you to my master. It shall be joyous!
Nightmare in Wax
Vampire Hunter
Collins
Amy of Darkness
What I saw in there would curl the back hairs of the browniest construction worker...

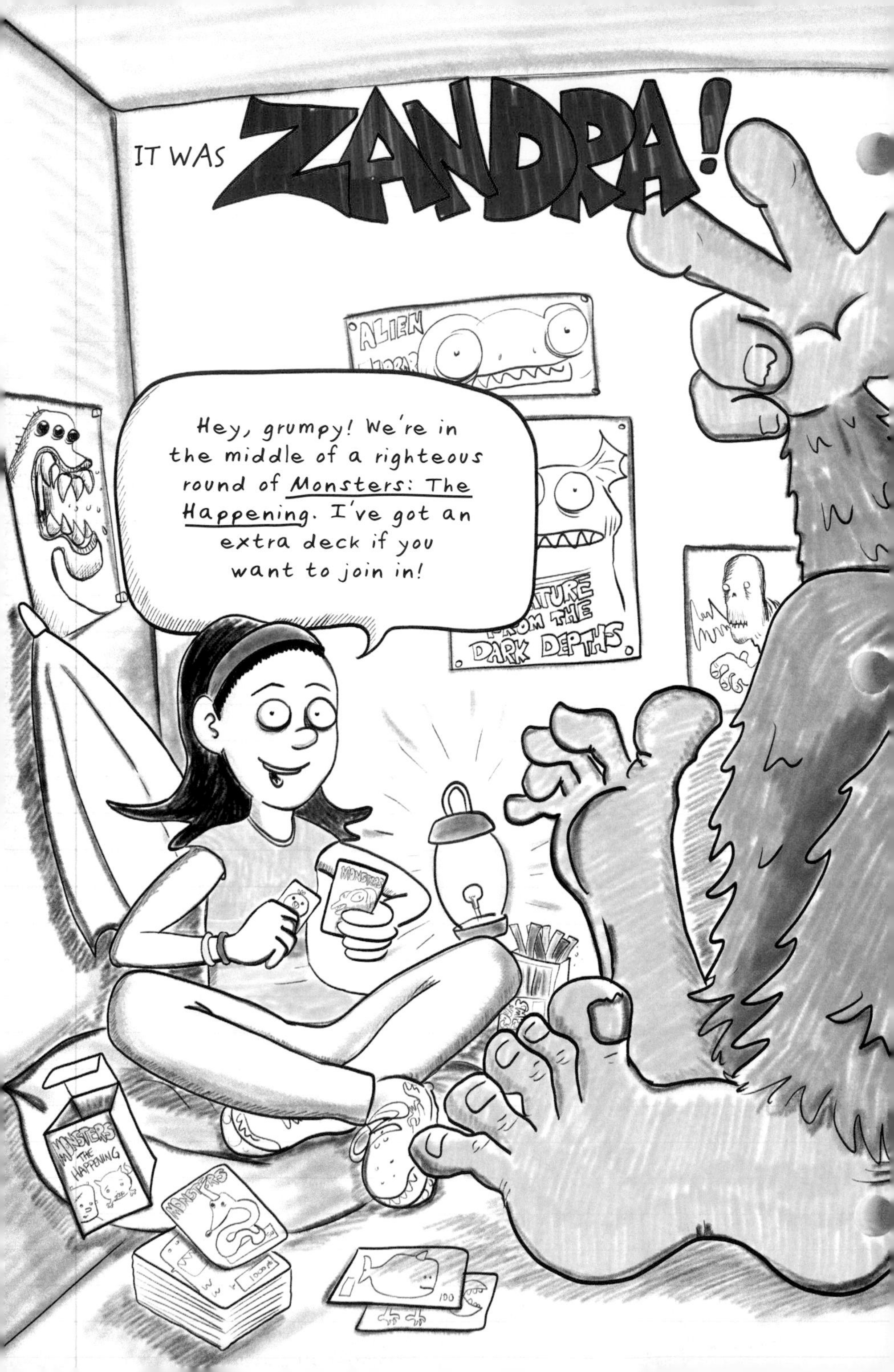
IT WAS ZANDRA!
Hey, grumpy! We're in the middle of a righteous round of Monsters: The Happening. I've got an extra deck if you want to join in!
ALIEN
FROM THE DARK DEPTHS
MONSTERS THE HAPPENING
MONSTERS

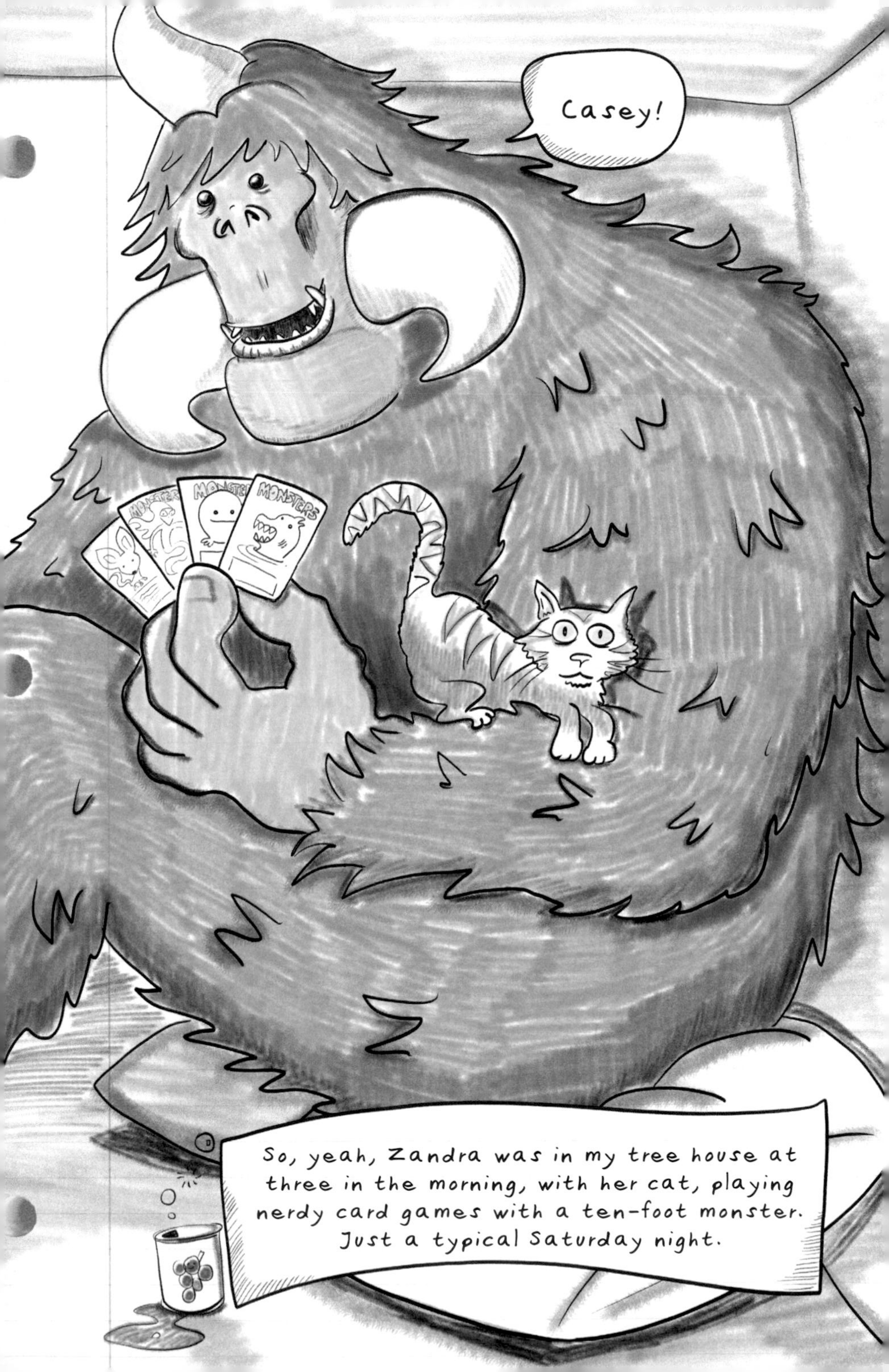
Casey!
MONSTERS
MONSTERS
MONSTERS
So, yeah, Zandra was in my tree house at three in the morning, with her cat, playing nerdy card games with a ten-foot monster. Just a typical Saturday night.

Needless to say, I had questions.

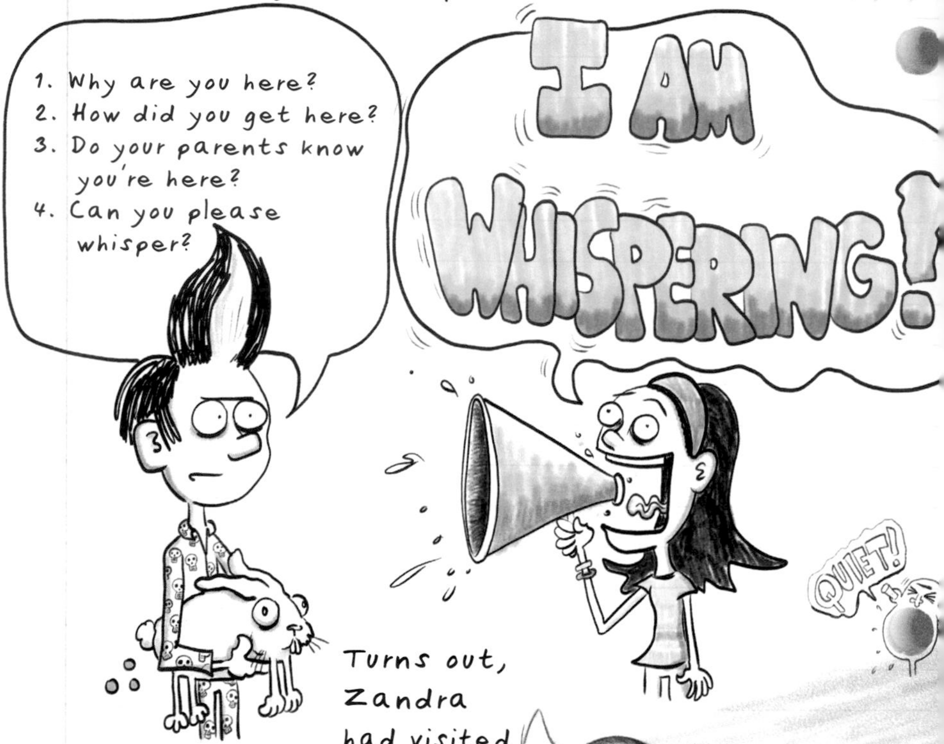
1. Why are you here?
2. How did you get here?
3. Do your parents know you're here?
4. Can you please whisper?
I AM WHISPERING!
QUIET!

Turns out, Zandra had visited him overnight before. Remember the mystery sour straw dust?

I felt pretty rotten when she told me the reason for the covert visits.

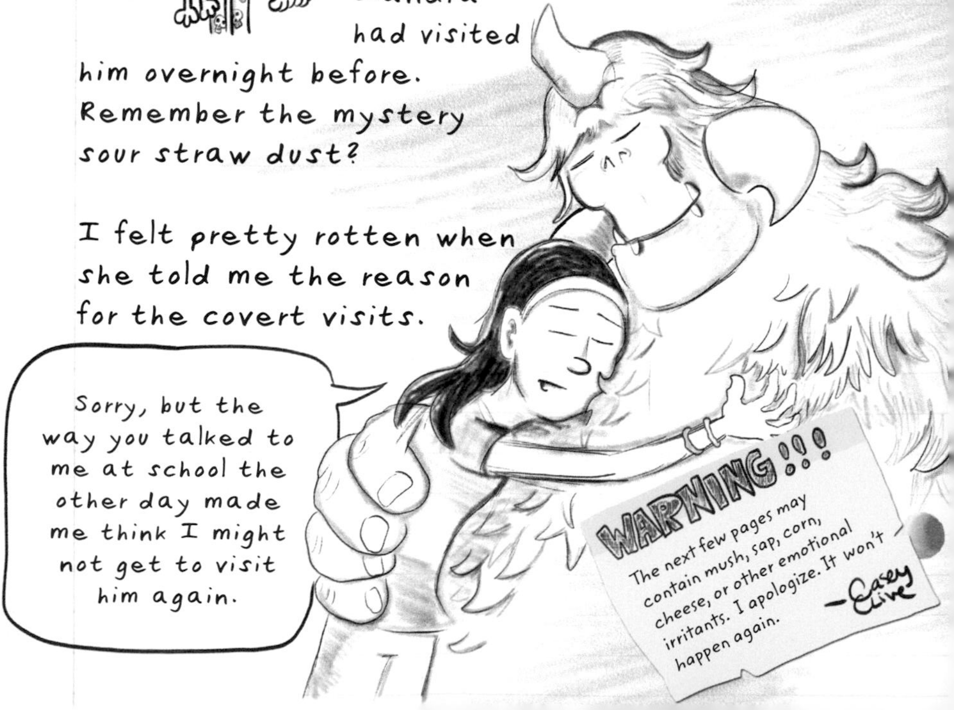
Sorry, but the way you talked to me at school the other day made me think I might not get to visit him again.
WARNING!!!
The next few pages may contain mush, sap, corn, cheese, or other emotional irritants. I apologize. It won't happen again.
—Casey Clive

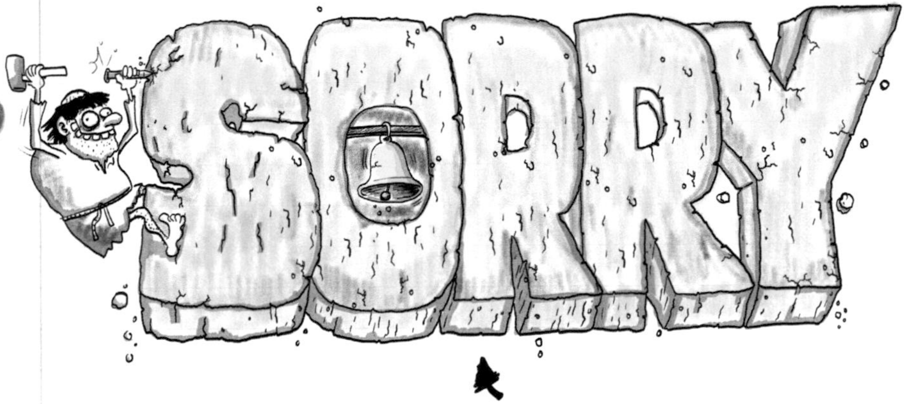
SORRY

Really huge "sorry," carved from the cold stone that is my heart.

I pretty much owned up to being a butthead and treating Zandra poorly earlier. It's just that these monsters are like my new, hairy, scaly, slimy family. They rely on me to protect them. I haven't let anyone else in on this secret in the last year. It's tough.

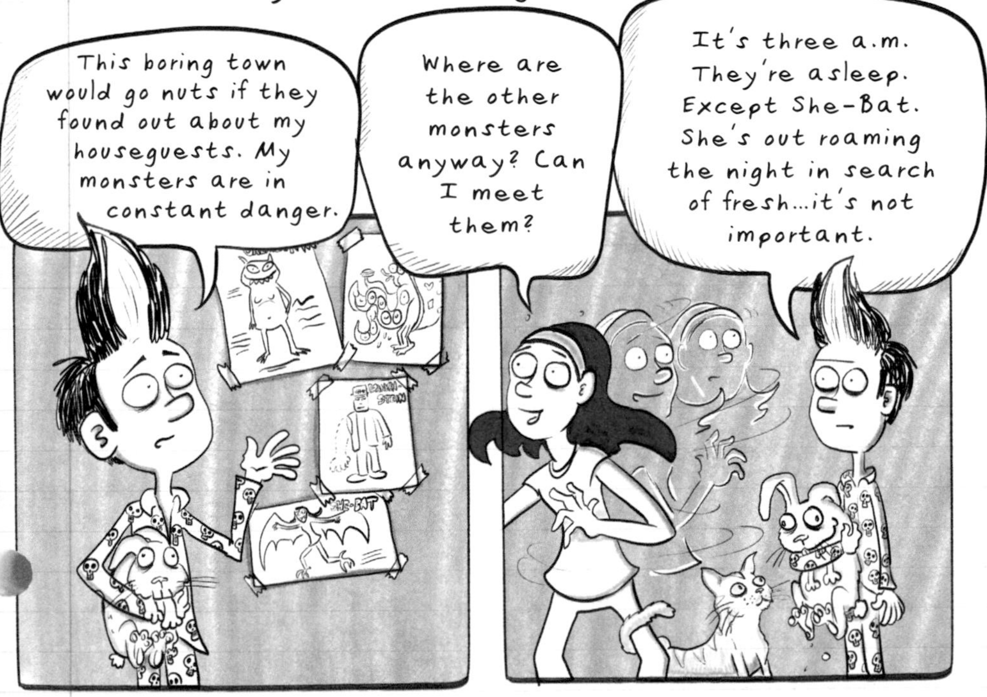
This boring town would go nuts if they found out about my houseguests. My monsters are in constant danger.
Where are the other monsters anyway? Can I meet them?
It's three a.m. They're asleep. Except She-Bat. She's out roaming the night in search of fresh...it's not important.
SHE-BAT

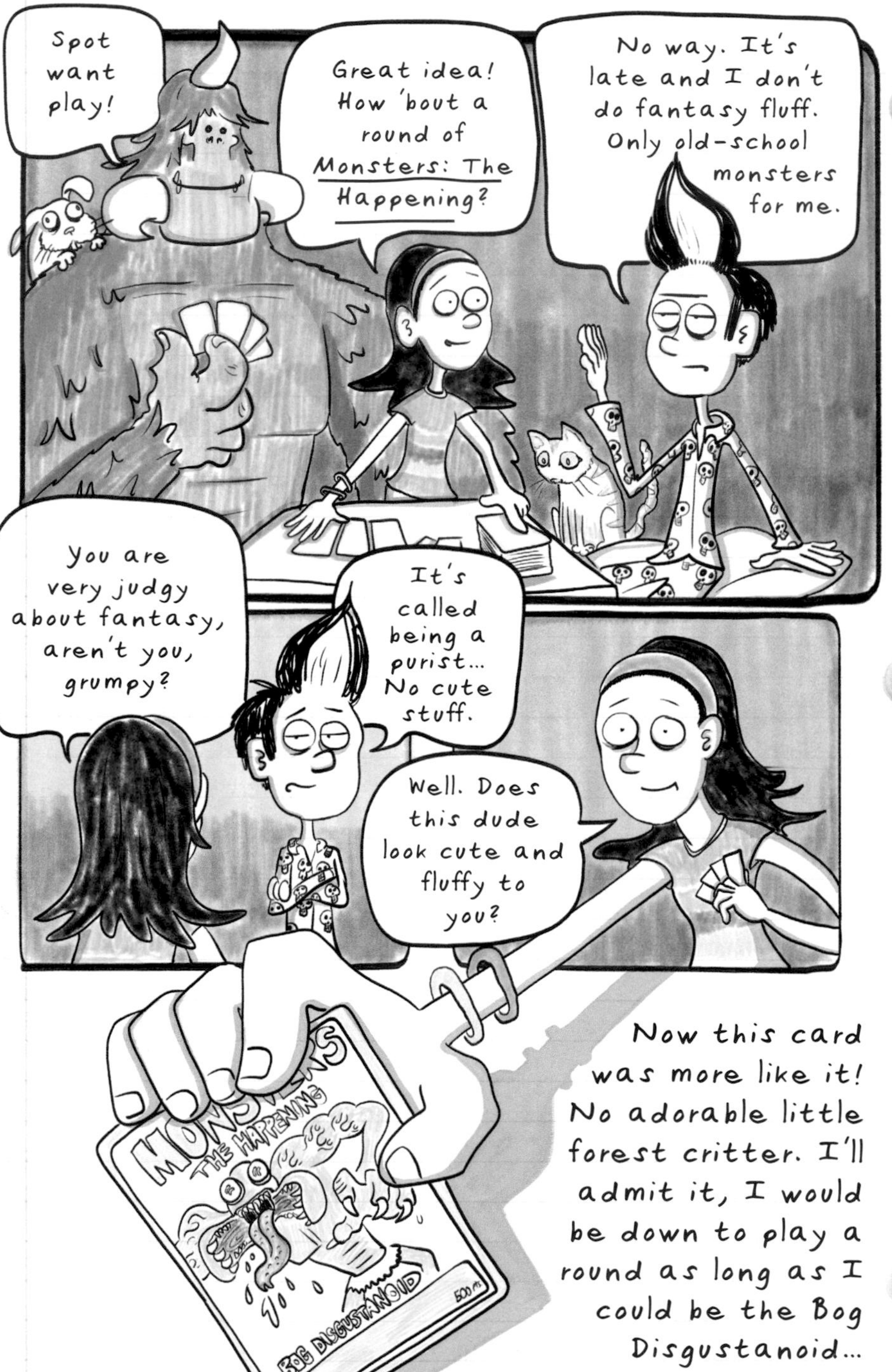
Spot want play!
Great idea! How 'bout a round of Monsters: The Happening?
No way. It's late and I don't do fantasy fluff. Only old-school monsters for me.
You are very judgy about fantasy, aren't you, grumpy?
It's called being a purist... No cute stuff.
Well. Does this dude look cute and fluffy to you?
THE HAPPENING
BOG DISGUSTANOID
Now this card was more like it! No adorable little forest critter. I'll admit it, I would be down to play a round as long as I could be the Bog Disgustanoid...

Turns out her card game had all sorts of horrific nightmare creatures with cute exteriors. Like a turtle humanoid thing that likes to pull people to a watery grave.

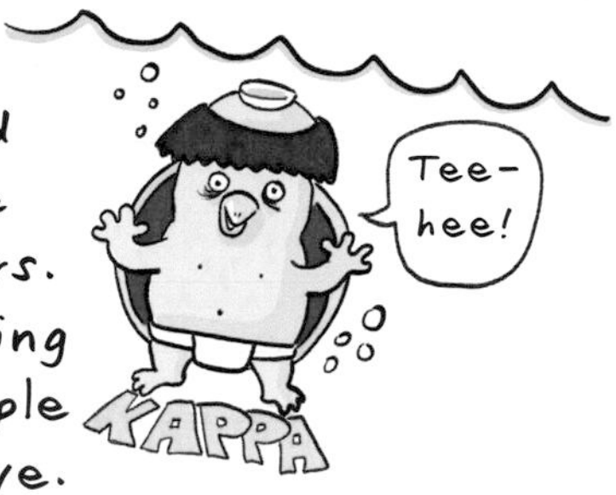
Tee-hee!
KAPPA

Or specters that wail and cry outside your house just before you meet your doom.

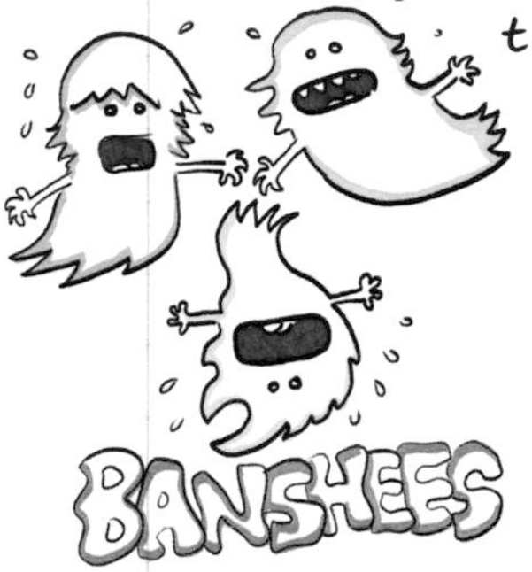
BANSHEES

Or an electro-rodent with high voltage flatulence.

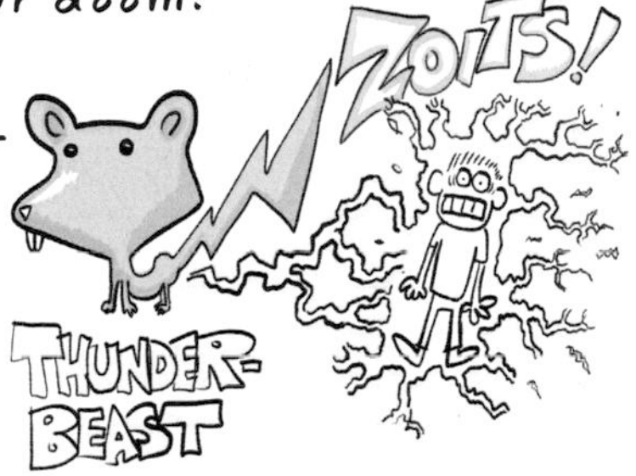
ZOITS!
THUNDER-BEAST

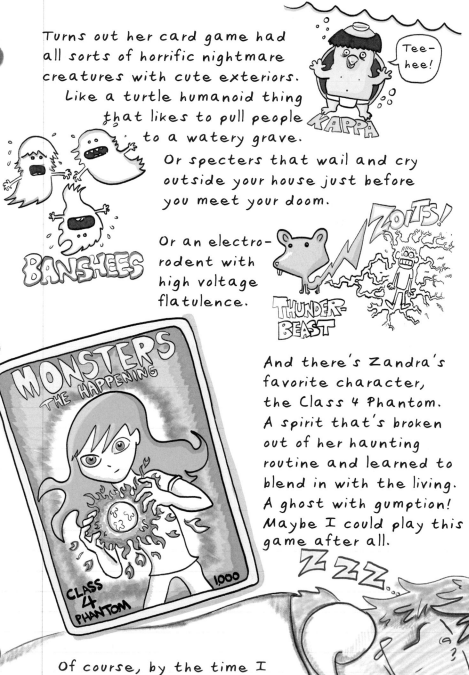

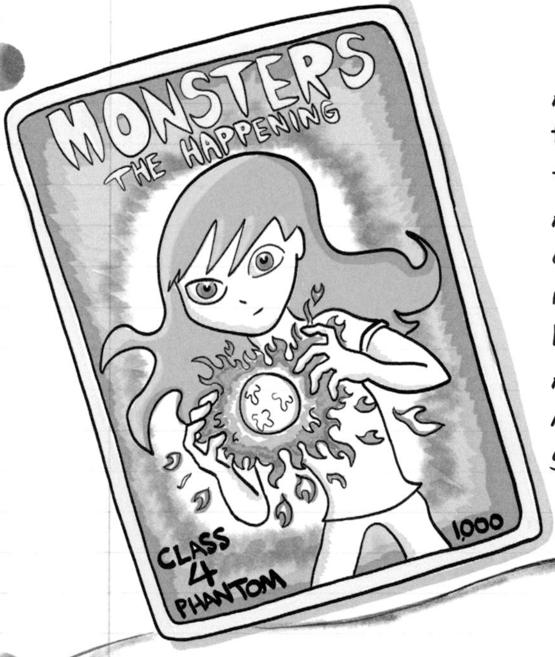
MONSTERS
THE HAPPENING
1,000
CLASS 4 PHANTOM

And there's Zandra's favorite character, the Class 4 Phantom. A spirit that's broken out of her haunting routine and learned to blend in with the living. A ghost with gumption! Maybe I could play this game after all.

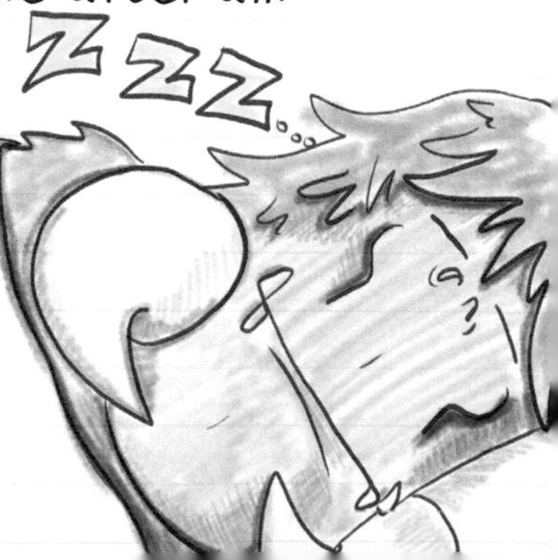
ZZZ...

Of course, by the time I picked my character, Spot had drifted off to sleep.

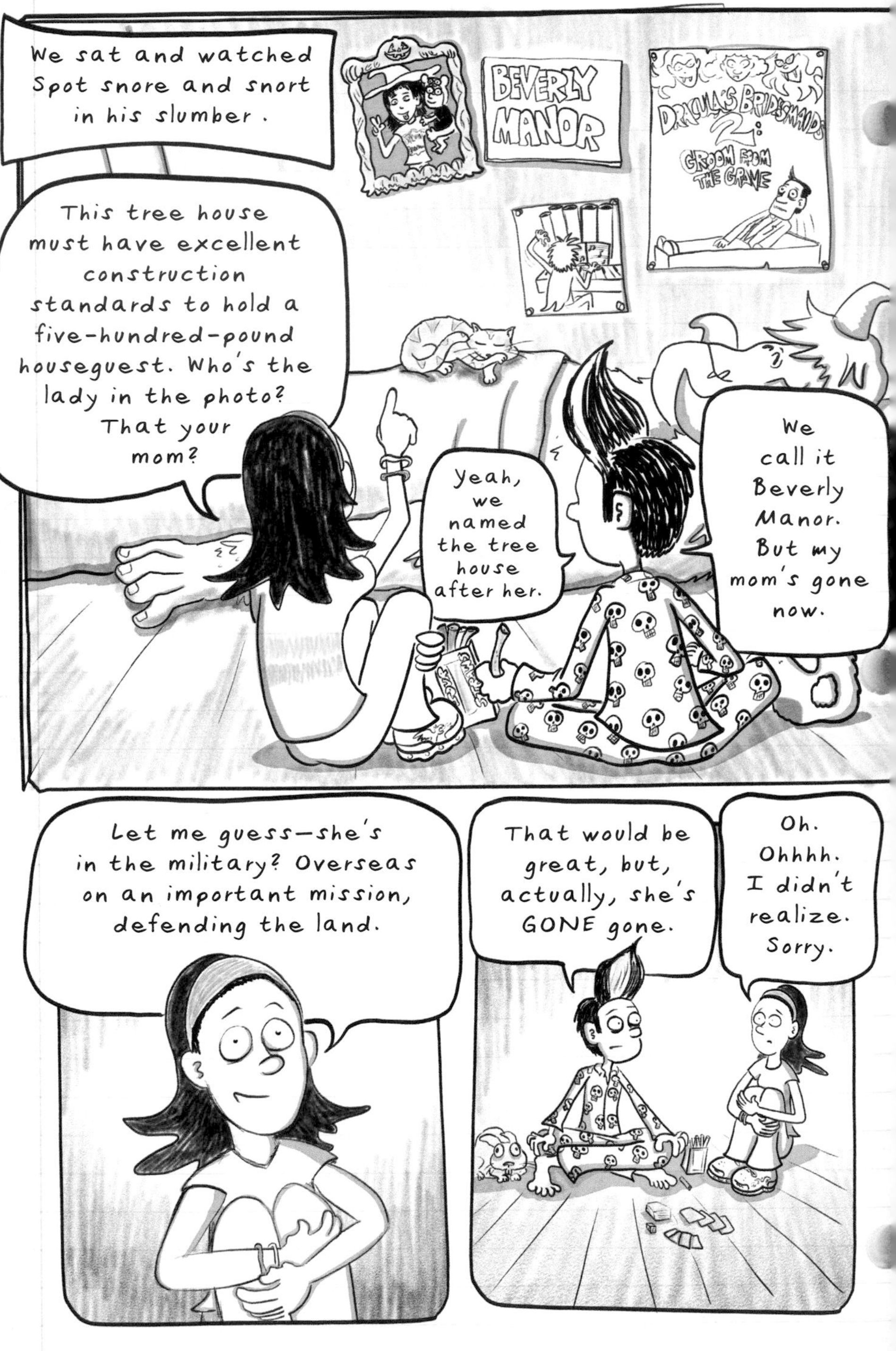
We sat and watched Spot snore and snort in his slumber.
BEVERLY MANOR
DRACULA'S BRIDESMAIDS 2: GROOM FROM THE GRAVE
This tree house must have excellent construction standards to hold a five-hundred-pound houseguest. Who's the lady in the photo? That your mom?
Yeah, we named the tree house after her.
We call it Beverly Manor. But my mom's gone now.
Let me guess—she's in the military? Overseas on an important mission, defending the land.
That would be great, but, actually, she's GONE gone.
Oh. Ohhhh. I didn't realize. Sorry.

Don't know why she said sorry. She had no way of knowing. I don't talk about Mom too much. Dad never brings it up.

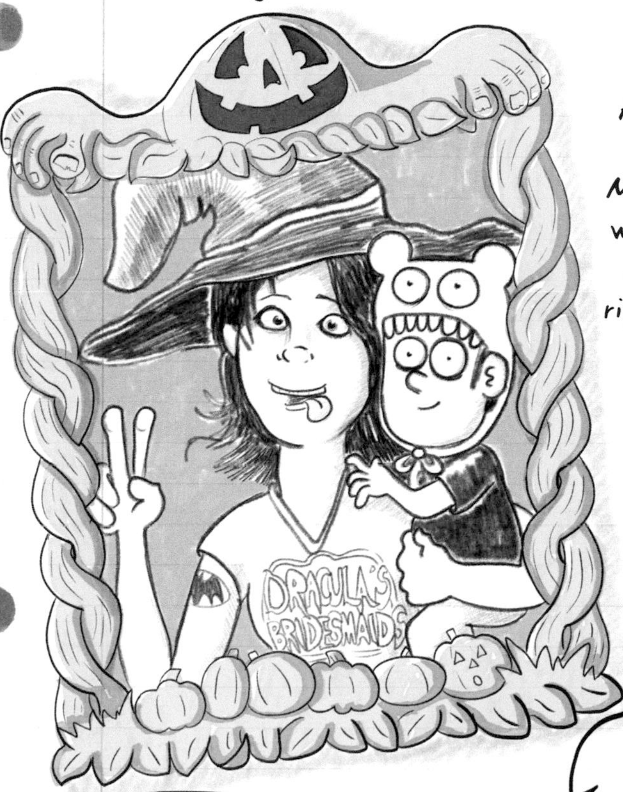
DRACULA'S
BRIDESMAIDS

A lot has happened since we lost her. Mainly my hair went white and monsters started showing up right away. She was a monster movie expert too. Wish she were here to help me take care of these maniacs.

This pic was from Halloween. I was three.

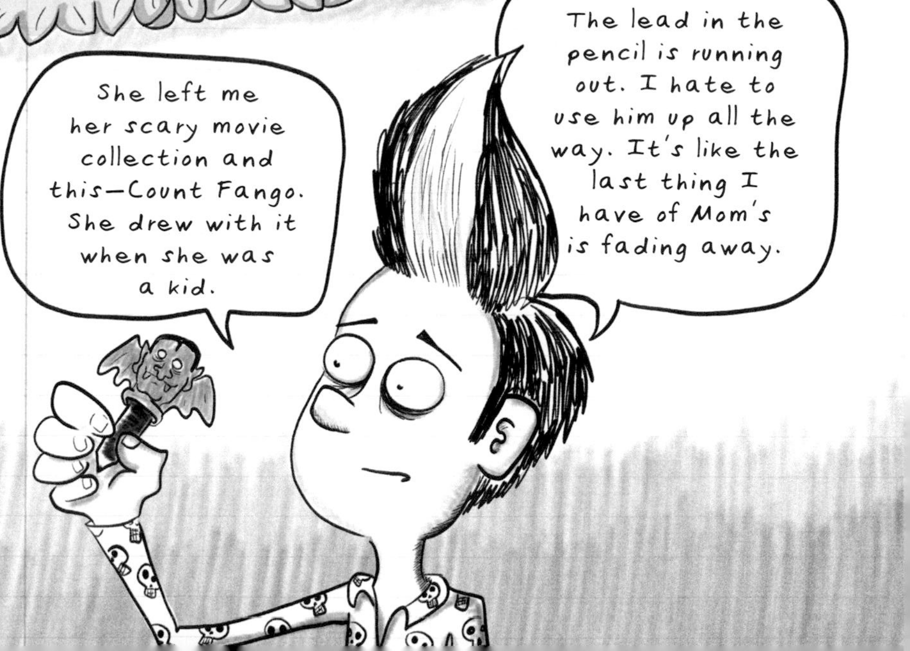
She left me her scary movie collection and this—Count Fango. She drew with it when she was a kid.
The lead in the pencil is running out. I hate to use him up all the way. It's like the last thing I have of Mom's is fading away.

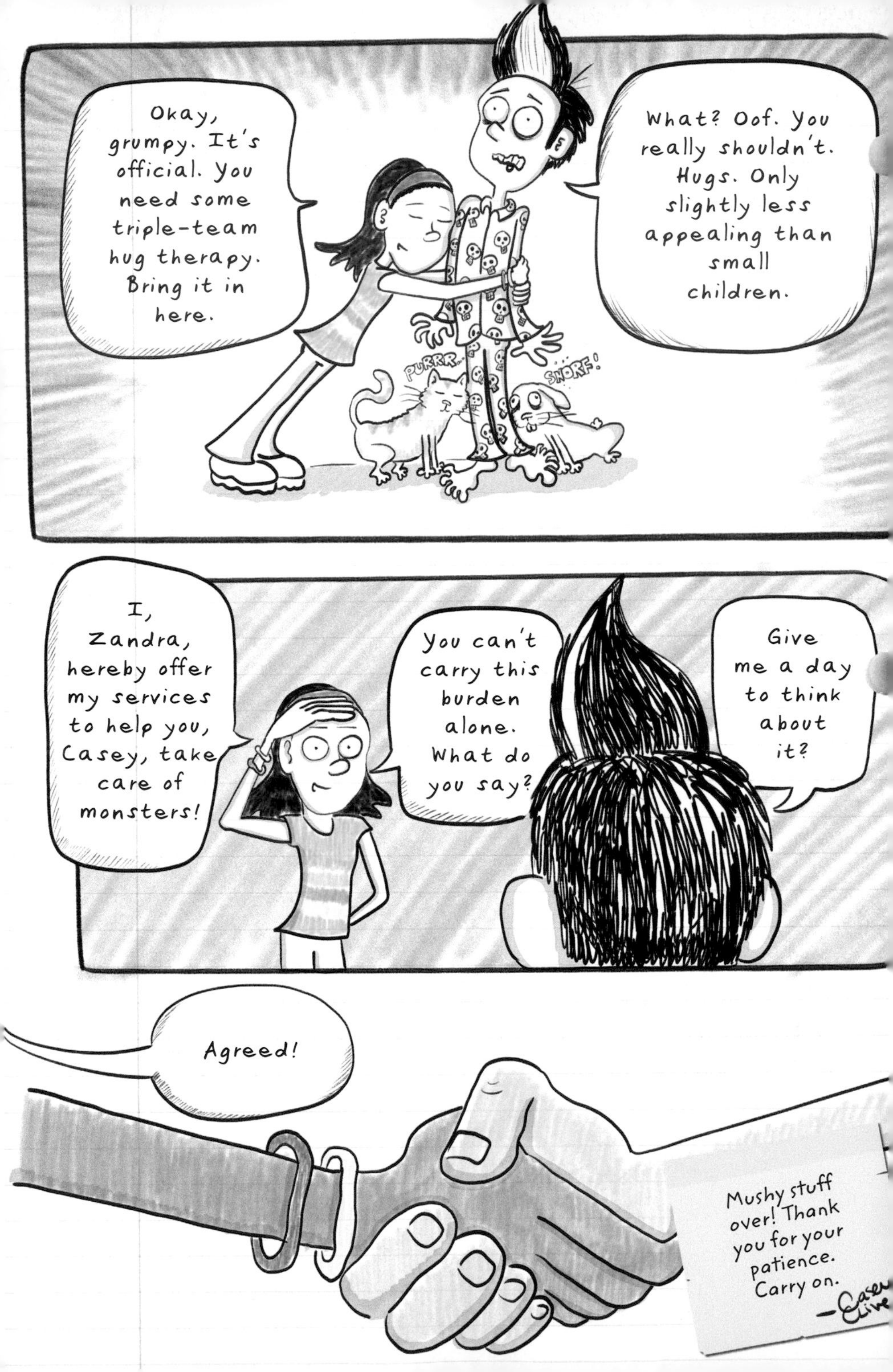
Okay, grumpy. It's official. You need some triple-team hug therapy. Bring it in here.
What? Oof. You really shouldn't. Hugs. Only slightly less appealing than small children.
PURRR...
SNORF!
I, Zandra, hereby offer my services to help you, Casey, take care of monsters!
You can't carry this burden alone. What do you say?
Give me a day to think about it?
Agreed!
Mushy stuff over! Thank you for your patience. Carry on.

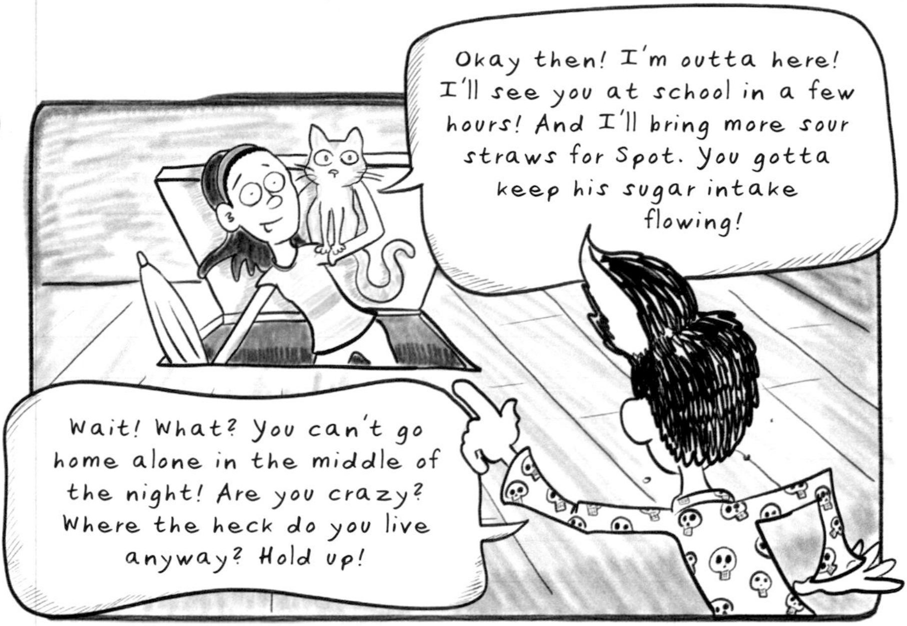
Okay then! I'm outta here! I'll see you at school in a few hours! And I'll bring more sour straws for Spot. You gotta keep his sugar intake flowing!
Wait! What? You can't go home alone in the middle of the night! Are you crazy? Where the heck do you live anyway? Hold up!

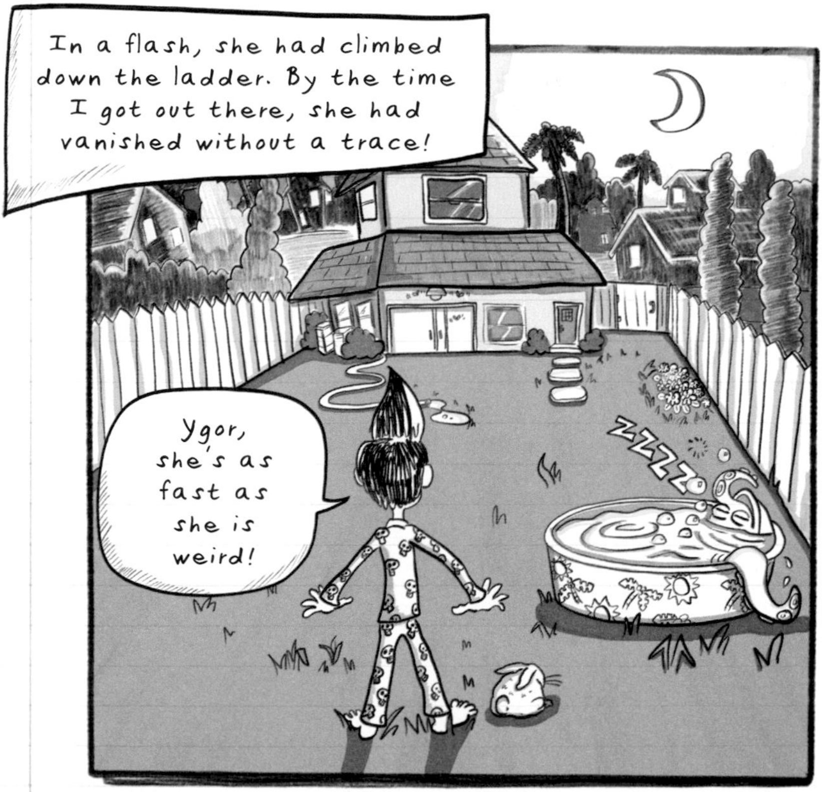
In a flash, she had climbed down the ladder. By the time I got out there, she had vanished without a trace!
ZZZZ
Ygor, she's as fast as she is weird!

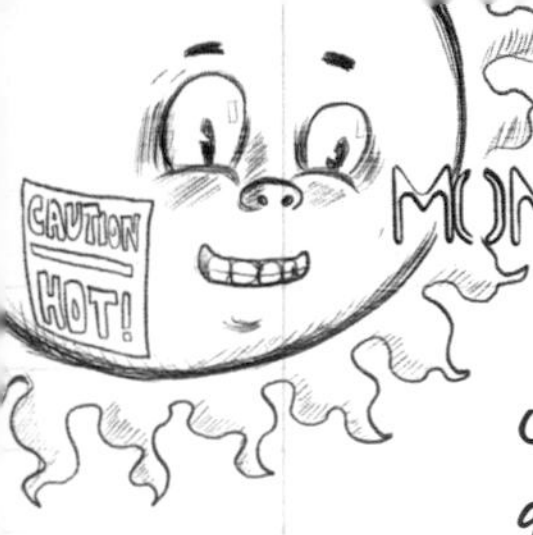

CAUTION
HOT!

MONDAY 7:25 A.M.

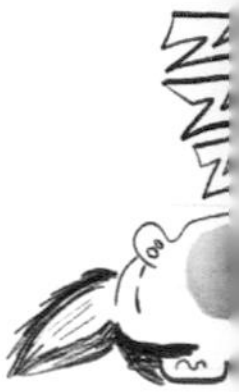

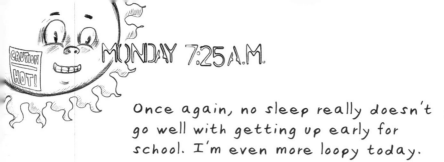

Once again, no sleep really doesn't go well with getting up early for school. I'm even more loopy today.

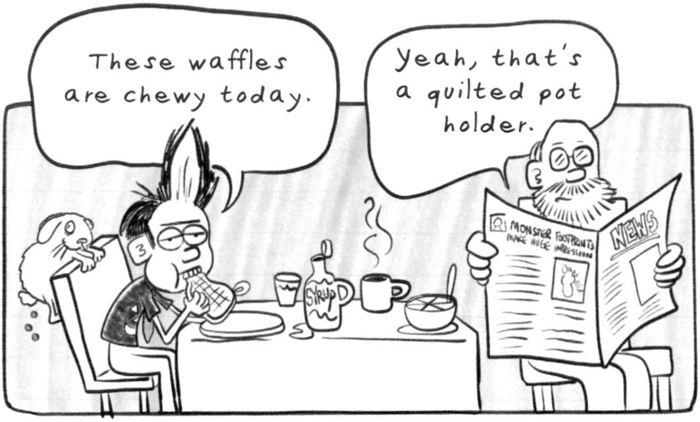

These waffles are chewy today.
Yeah, that's a quilted pot holder.
SYRUP
MONSTER FOOTPRINTS MAKE HUGE IMPRESSION
NEWS

Noticed an interesting article in Dad's paper: monster footprints at the beach!

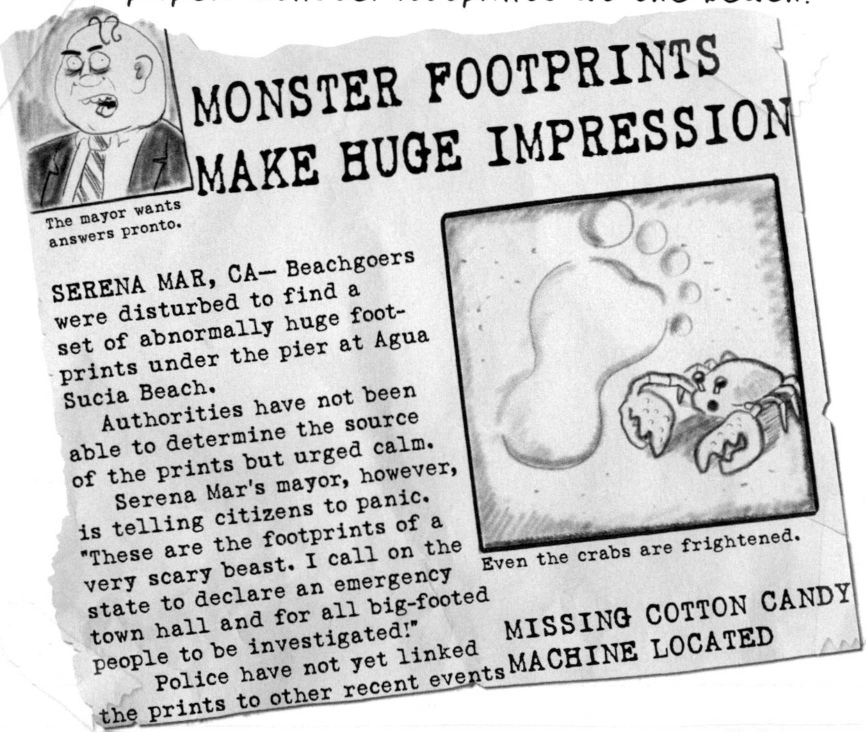

MONSTER FOOTPRINTS MAKE HUGE IMPRESSION

The mayor wants answers pronto.

SERENA MAR, CA— Beachgoers were disturbed to find a set of abnormally huge foot-prints under the pier at Agua Sucia Beach.

Authorities have not been able to determine the source of the prints but urged calm.

Serena Mar's mayor, however, is telling citizens to panic. "These are the footprints of a very scary beast. I call on the state to declare an emergency town hall and for all big-footed people to be investigated!"

Police have not yet linked the prints to other recent events

Even the crabs are frightened.

MISSING COTTON CANDY MACHINE LOCATED

Sure hope Spot doesn't create another monster panic. We've had a few around here.

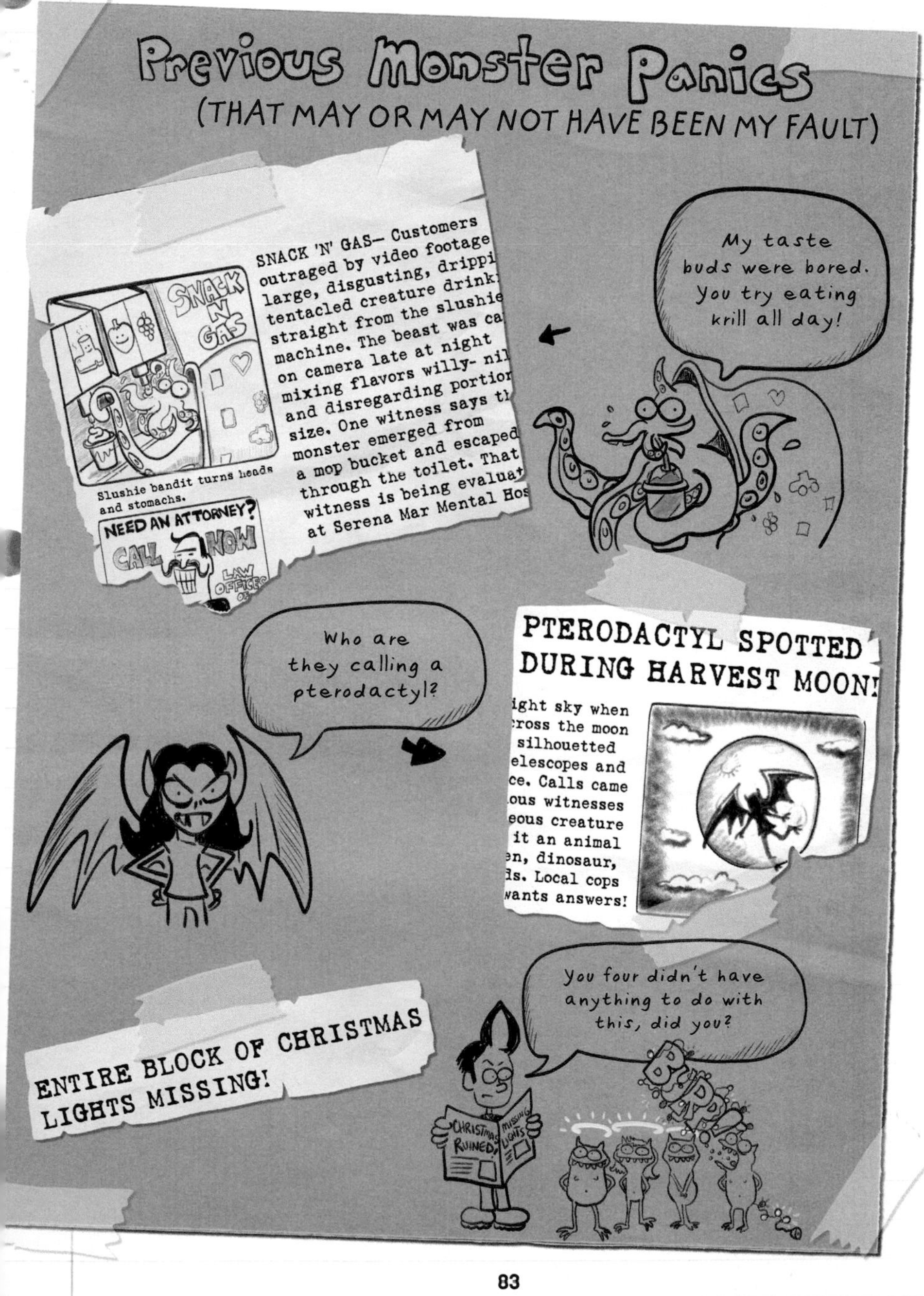
Previous Monster Panics
(THAT MAY OR MAY NOT HAVE BEEN MY FAULT)
SNACK 'N' GAS— Customers
outraged by video footage
large, disgusting, drippi
tentacled creature drink
straight from the slushie
machine. The beast was ca
on camera late at night
mixing flavors willy- nil
and disregarding portion
size. One witness says th
monster emerged from
a mop bucket and escaped
through the toilet. That
witness is being evaluat
at Serena Mar Mental Hos
SNACK N GAS
Slushie bandit turns heads and stomachs.
NEED AN ATTORNEY?
CALL NOW
LAW OFFICES OF
My taste buds were bored. You try eating krill all day!
Who are they calling a pterodactyl?
PTERODACTYL SPOTTED DURING HARVEST MOON!
ight sky when
cross the moon
silhouetted
elescopes and
ce. Calls came
ous witnesses
eous creature
it an animal
en, dinosaur,
ds. Local cops
wants answers!
ENTIRE BLOCK OF CHRISTMAS LIGHTS MISSING!
You four didn't have anything to do with this, did you?
CHRISTMAS RUINED
MISSING LIGHTS
BURP!

ART Ms. Kindle let us work on the boring Fall Festival posters during class. She had some questions for Zandra, though. Seems I'm not the only one who finds this girl mysterious.

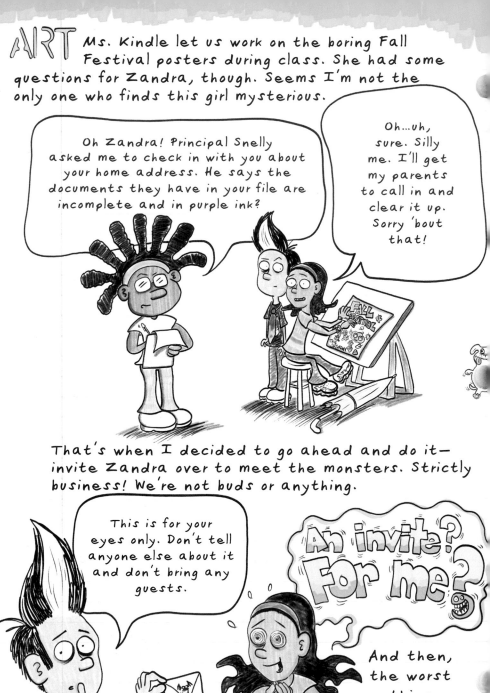

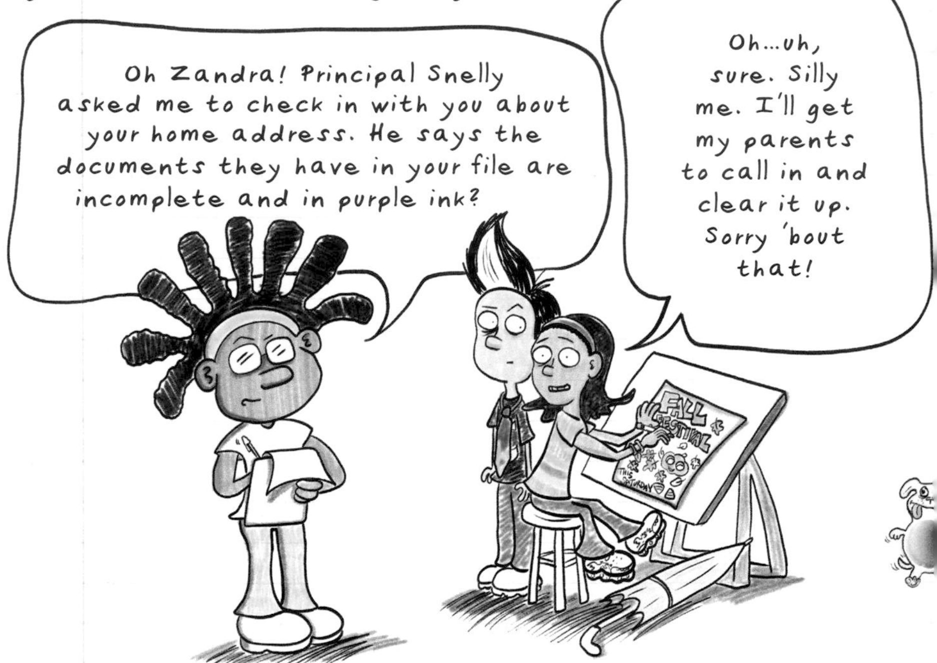
Oh Zandra! Principal Snelly asked me to check in with you about your home address. He says the documents they have in your file are incomplete and in purple ink?
Oh...uh, sure. Silly me. I'll get my parents to call in and clear it up. Sorry 'bout that!
FALL FESTIVAL

That's when I decided to go ahead and do it—invite Zandra over to meet the monsters. Strictly business! We're not buds or anything.

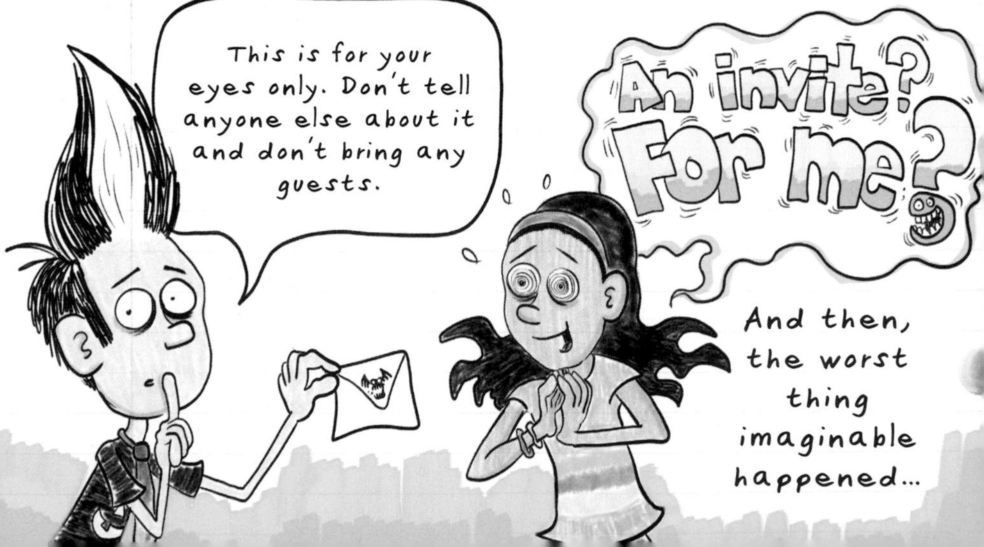
This is for your eyes only. Don't tell anyone else about it and don't bring any guests.
An invite? For me?

And then, the worst thing imaginable happened...

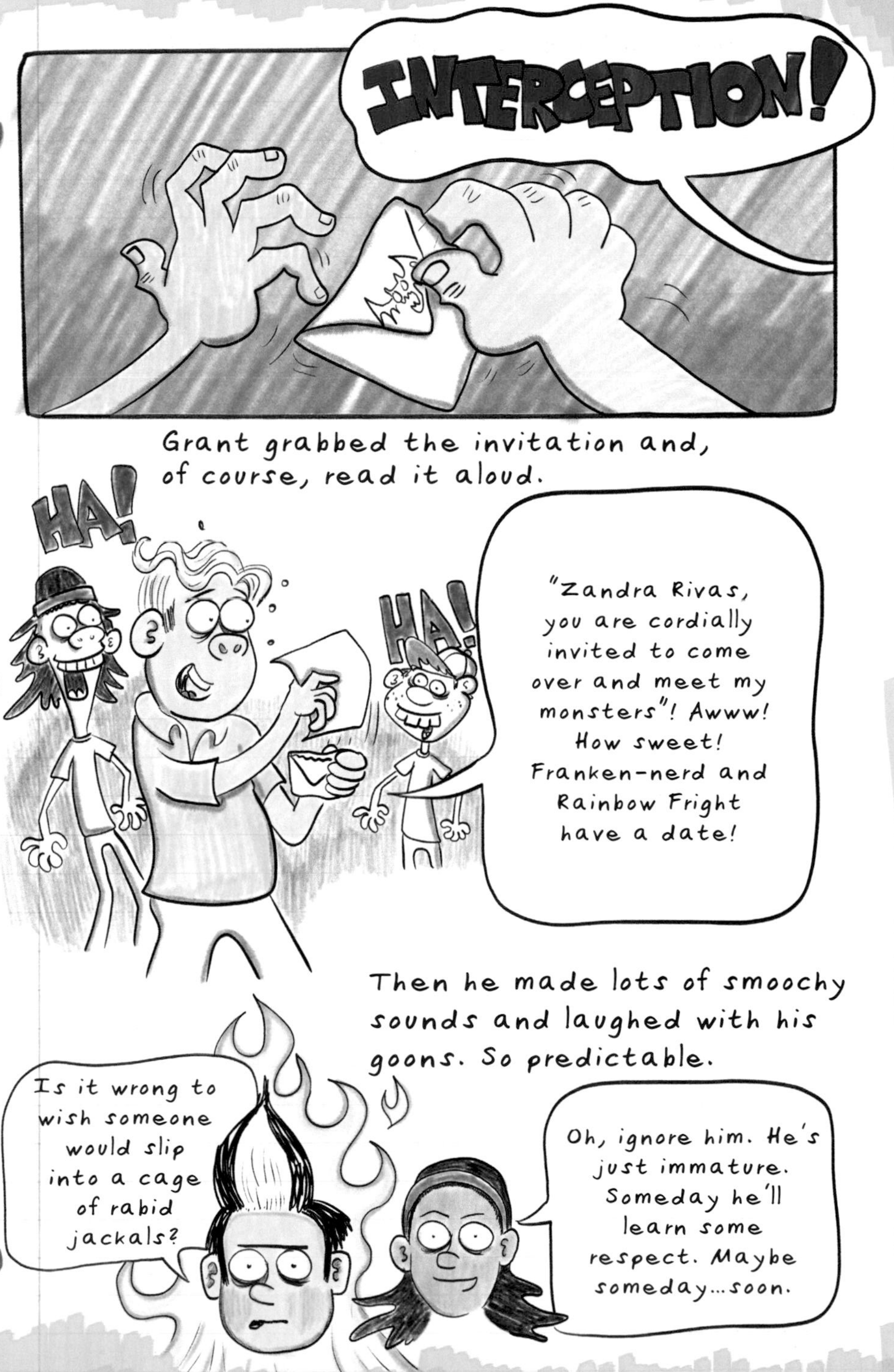
INTERCEPTION!
Grant grabbed the invitation and, of course, read it aloud.
HA!
HA!
"Zandra Rivas, you are cordially invited to come over and meet my monsters"! Awww! How sweet! Franken-nerd and Rainbow Fright have a date!
Then he made lots of smoochy sounds and laughed with his goons. So predictable.
Is it wrong to wish someone would slip into a cage of rabid jackals?
Oh, ignore him. He's just immature. Someday he'll learn some respect. Maybe someday...soon.

RECESS

Excuse the sloppiness of the next few pages.

Only got a fifteen-minute break to scribble this down.

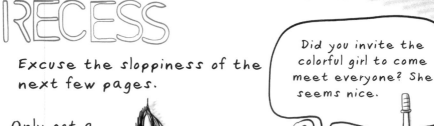

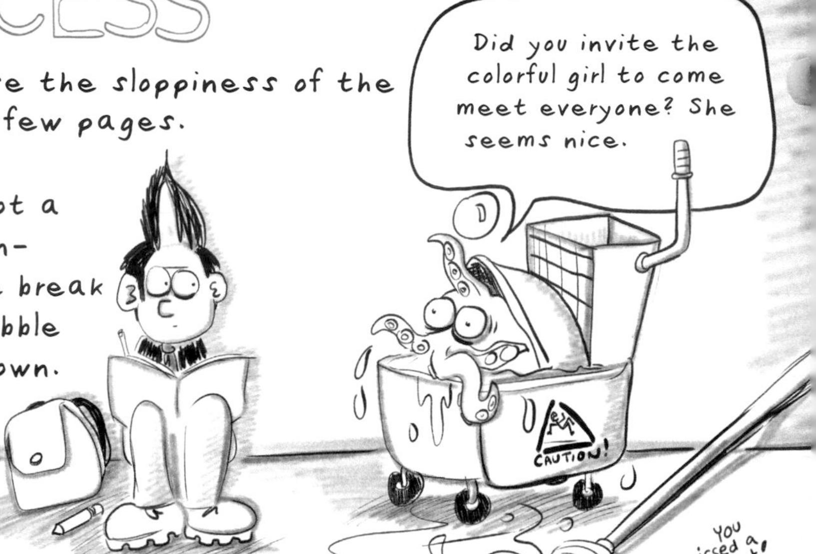
Did you invite the colorful girl to come meet everyone? She seems nice.
CAUTION!

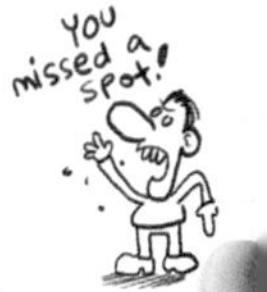
You missed a spot!

I was just doodling in the hall, minding my business. Topo was bugging me about Zandra. Then there was a scream down by the gymnasium! It sounded like a newborn piglet with a charley horse!

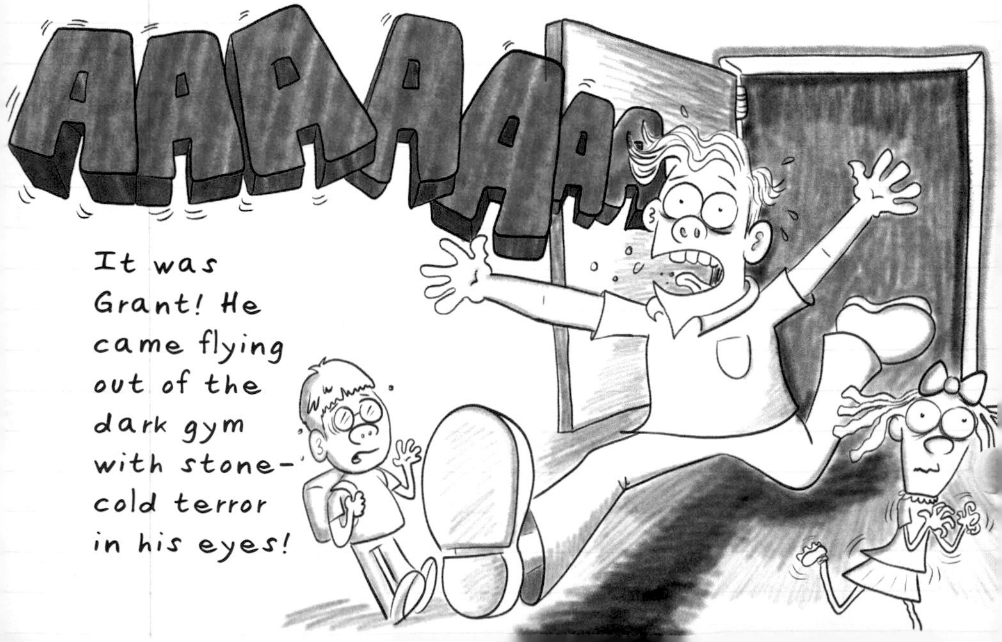
AAAAAAA

It was Grant! He came flying out of the dark gym with stone-cold terror in his eyes!

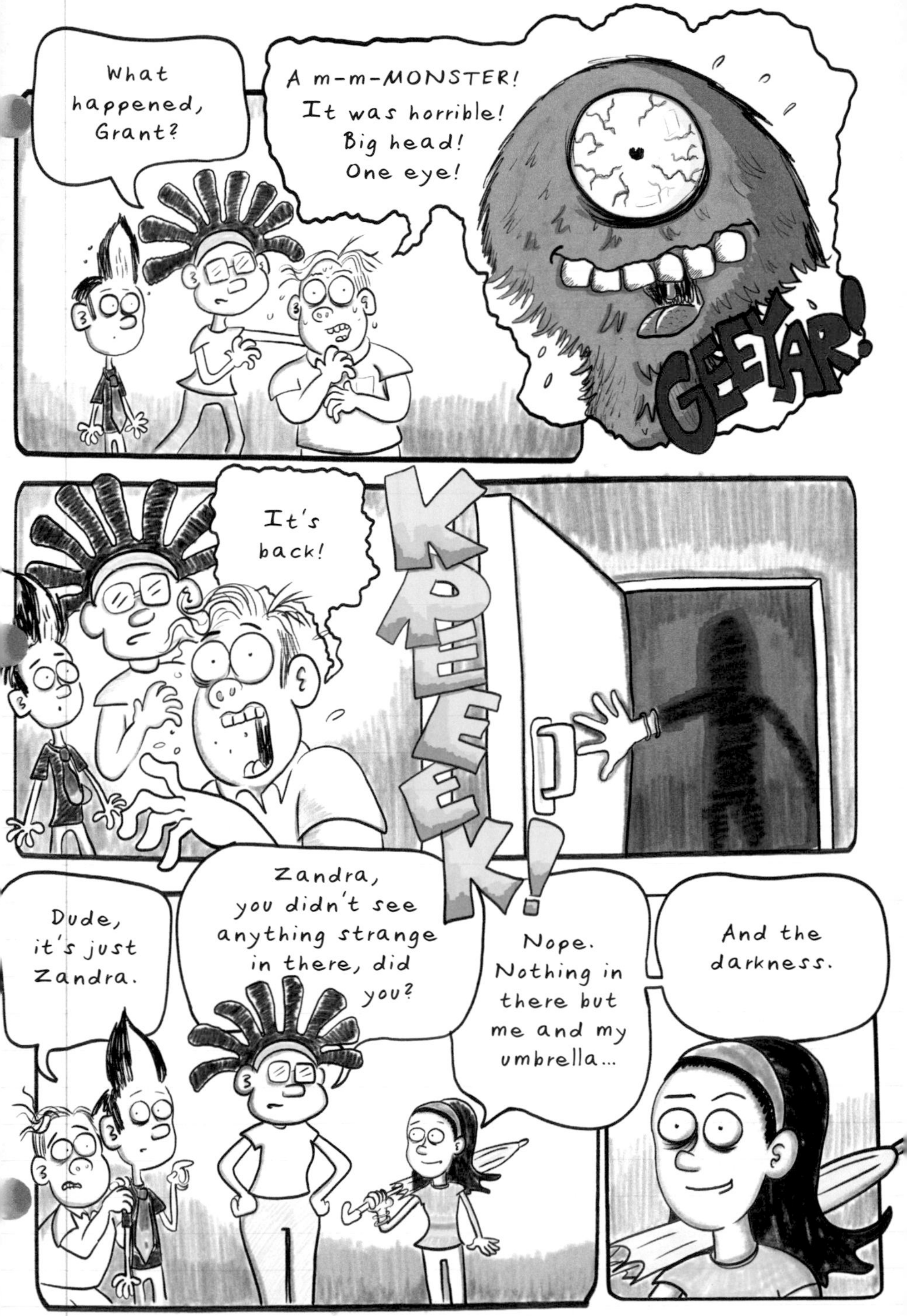

What happened, Grant?
A m-m-MONSTER! It was horrible! Big head! One eye!
GEEYAR!
It's back!
KREEEEEK!
Dude, it's just Zandra.
Zandra, you didn't see anything strange in there, did you?
Nope. Nothing in there but me and my umbrella...
And the darkness.

WED. MY HOUSE

It's Wednesday. After school. The big day. Zandra finally gets to meet the monsters.

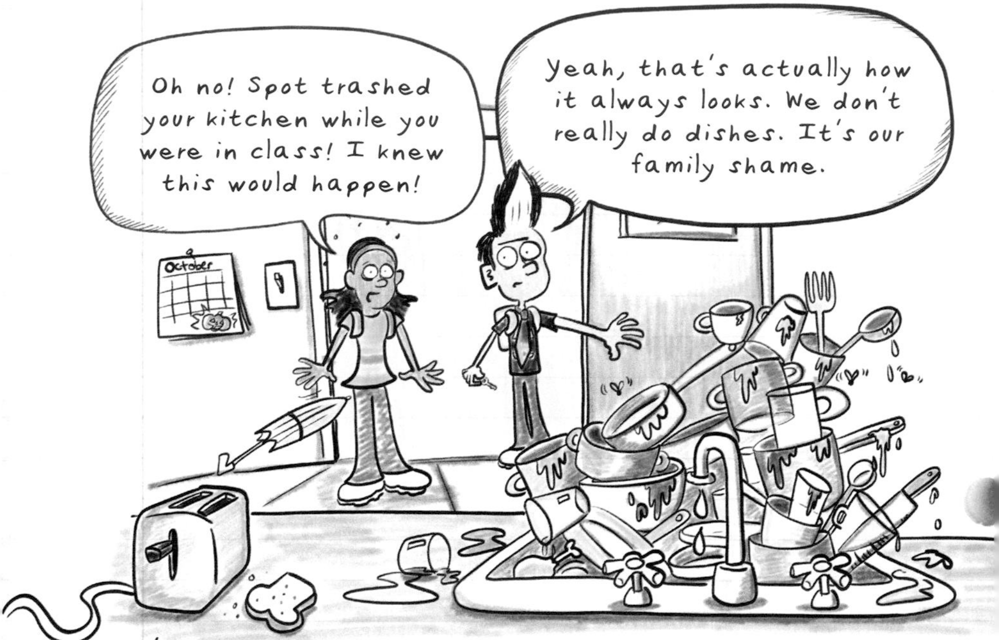

Oh no! Spot trashed your kitchen while you were in class! I knew this would happen!
Yeah, that's actually how it always looks. We don't really do dishes. It's our family shame.
October

It's true. Our kitchen always looks like we just hosted a Viking victory feast.

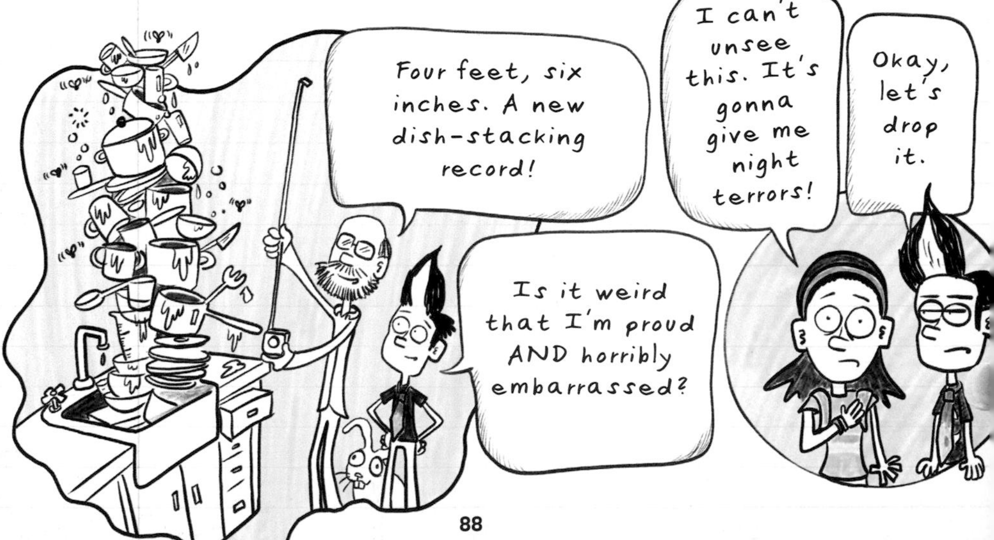

Four feet, six inches. A new dish-stacking record!
Is it weird that I'm proud AND horribly embarrassed?
I can't unsee this. It's gonna give me night terrors!
Okay, let's drop it.

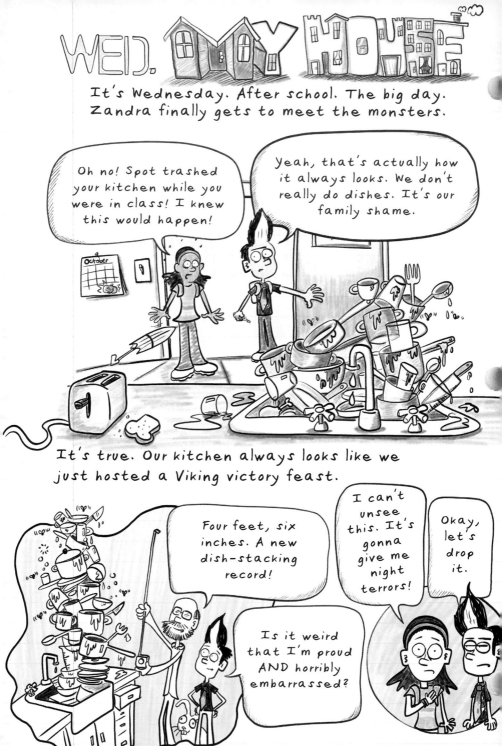

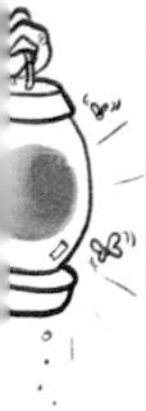

In the living room we found Topo. Zandra was excited to finally meet my cephalopod buddy.

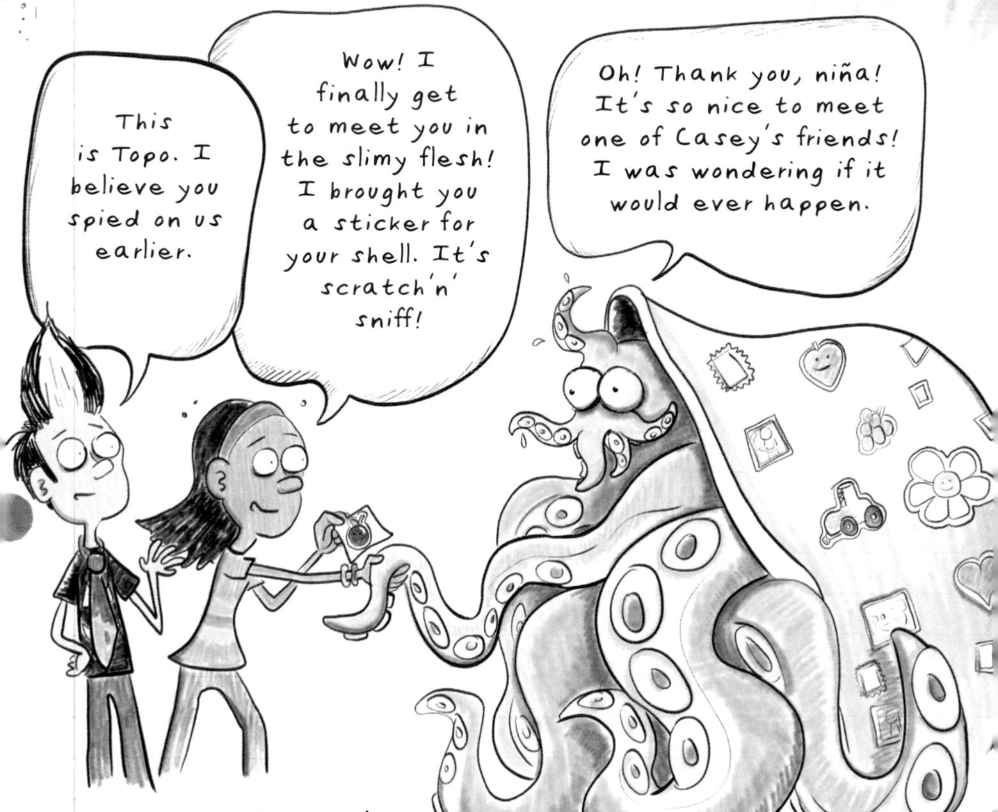
This is Topo. I believe you spied on us earlier.
Wow! I finally get to meet you in the slimy flesh! I brought you a sticker for your shell. It's scratch'n' sniff!
Oh! Thank you, niña! It's so nice to meet one of Casey's friends! I was wondering if it would ever happen.

I can tell they're gonna be bonding over stickers for eternity.

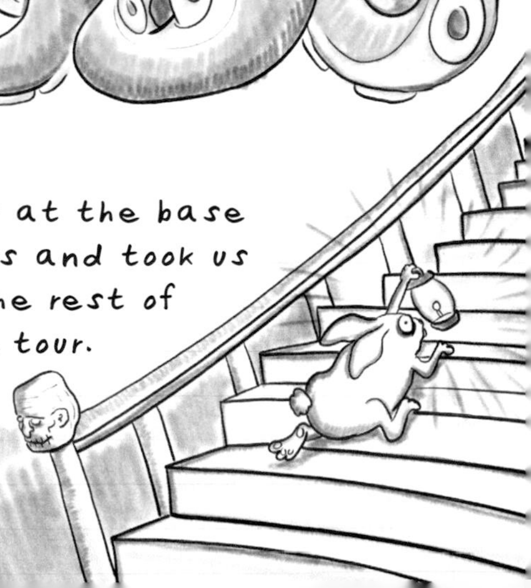

Ygor met us at the base of the stairs and took us up for the rest of the tour.

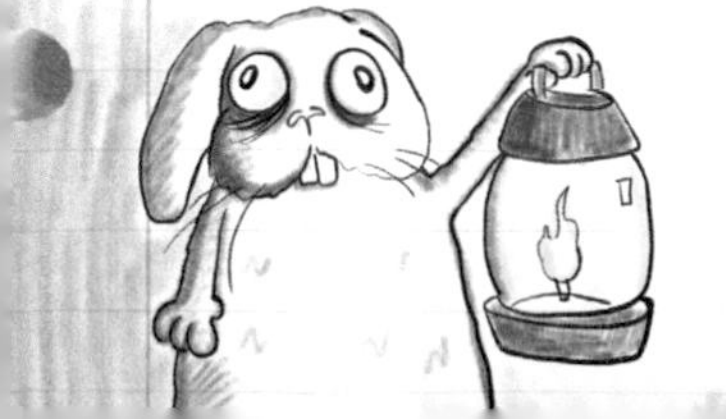

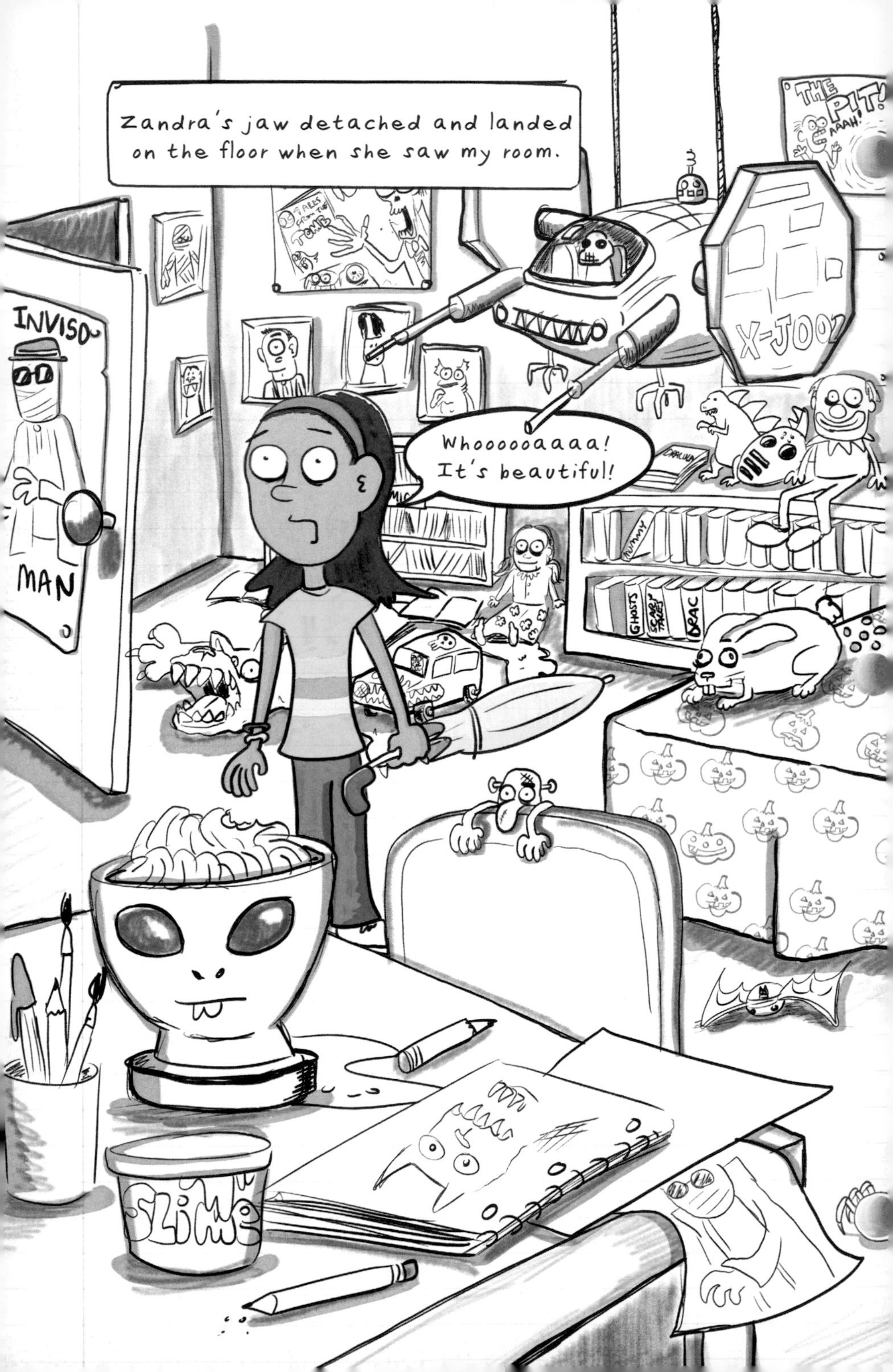
Zandra's jaw detached and landed on the floor when she saw my room.
Whoooooaaaa! It's beautiful!
INVISO MAN
THE PIT!
AAAH!
GHOSTS
DRAC
SLIME

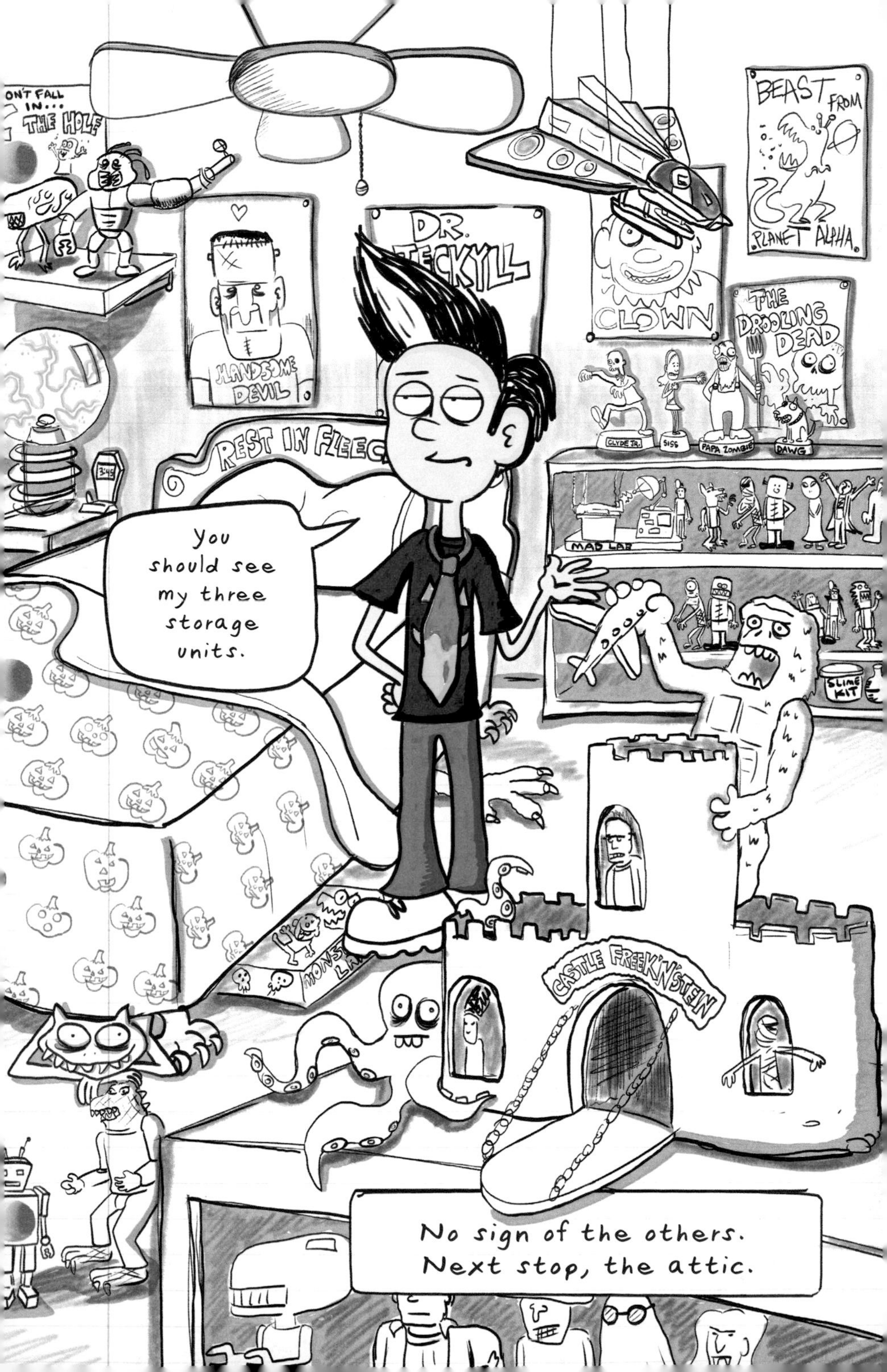

ON'T FALL IN... THE HOLE
DR. JECKYLL
BEAST FROM PLANET ALPHA
HANDSOME DEVIL
CLOWN
THE DROOLING DEAD
REST IN FLEEC
CLYDE JR.
SISS
PAPA ZOMBIE
DAWG
MAD LAB
SLIME KIT
You should see my three storage units.
CASTLE FREEK'NSTEIN
No sign of the others. Next stop, the attic.

I warned Zandra that Spot and Franky weren't getting along so good. And from the sounds coming from the attic, things had only gotten worse.

But, surprise, surprise! When we got up there, they were playing table tennis! I guess it's the perfect outlet for unbearable monster tension. Who knew?

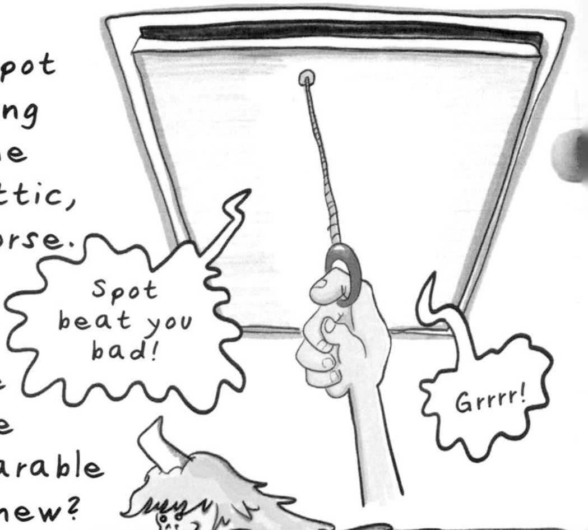

Spot beat you bad!
Grrrr!

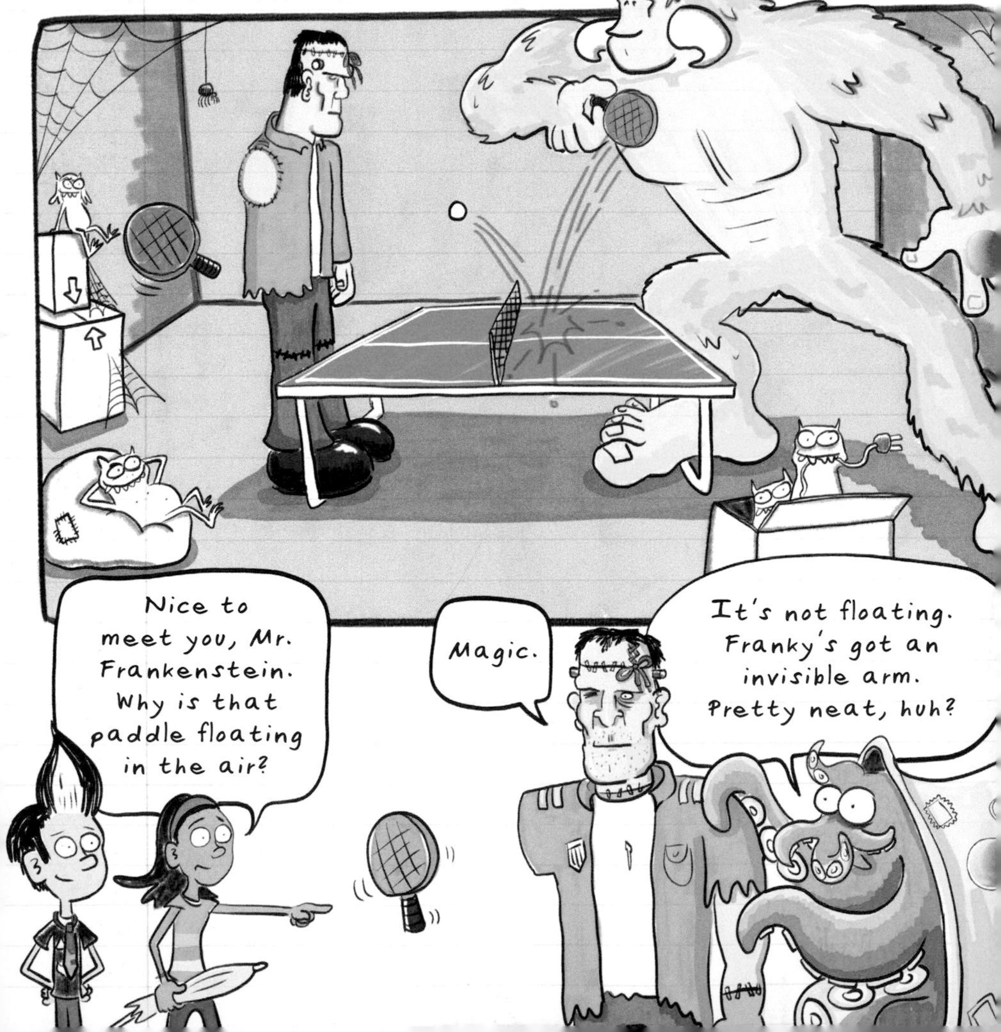

Nice to meet you, Mr. Frankenstein. Why is that paddle floating in the air?
Magic.
It's not floating. Franky's got an invisible arm. Pretty neat, huh?

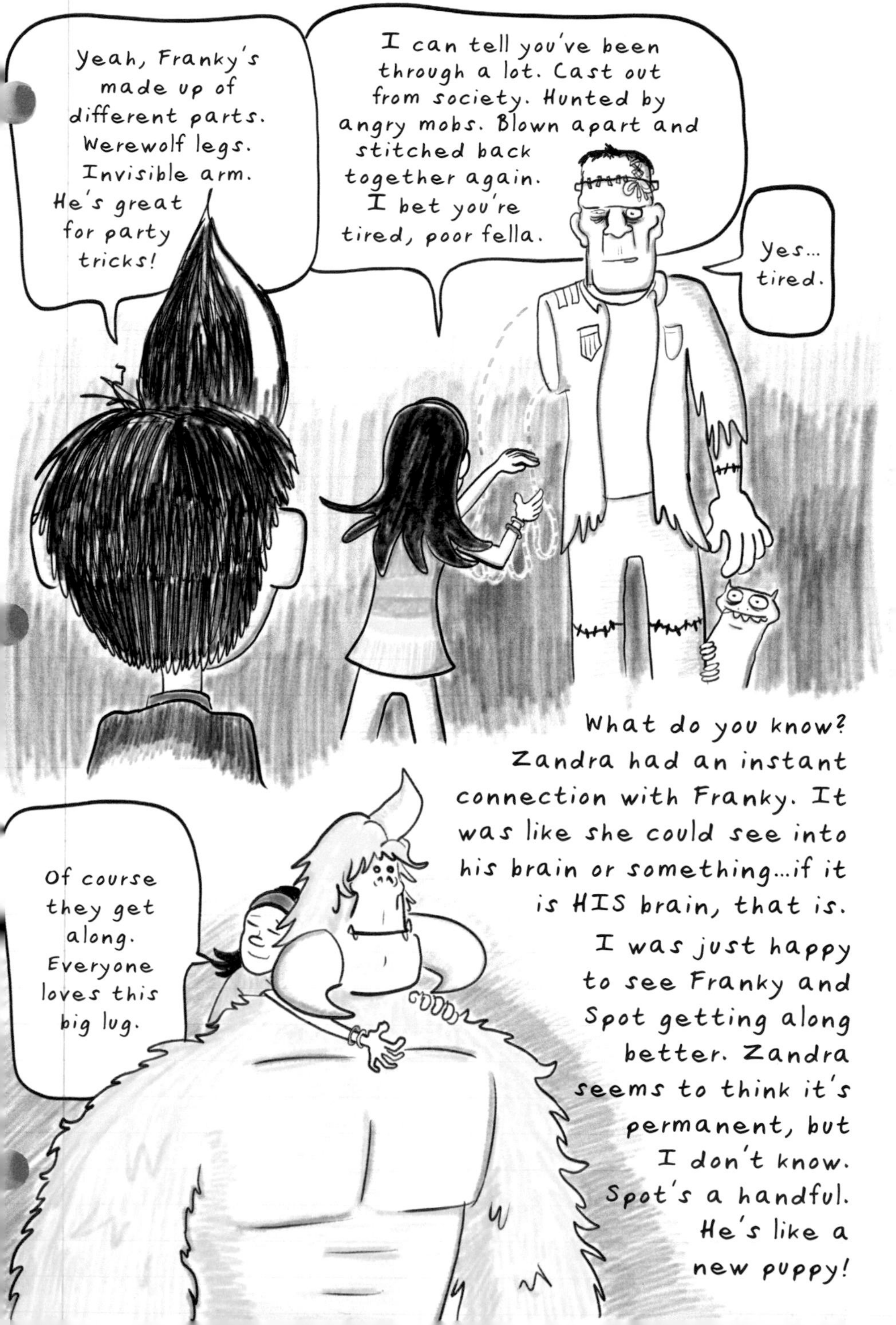
Yeah, Franky's made up of different parts. Werewolf legs. Invisible arm. He's great for party tricks!
I can tell you've been through a lot. Cast out from society. Hunted by angry mobs. Blown apart and stitched back together again. I bet you're tired, poor fella.
Yes... tired.
What do you know? Zandra had an instant connection with Franky. It was like she could see into his brain or something...if it is HIS brain, that is.
I was just happy to see Franky and Spot getting along better. Zandra seems to think it's permanent, but I don't know. Spot's a handful. He's like a new puppy!
Of course they get along. Everyone loves this big lug.

All the monsters really opened up to Zandra. She is like the monster whisperer or something.

Turns out the gremlins are at a loss with today's digital technology.

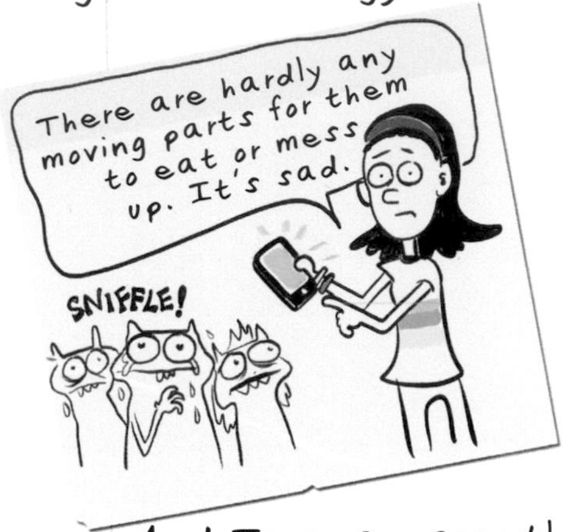
There are hardly any moving parts for them to eat or mess up. It's sad.
SNIFFLE!

And the zombie has image issues.

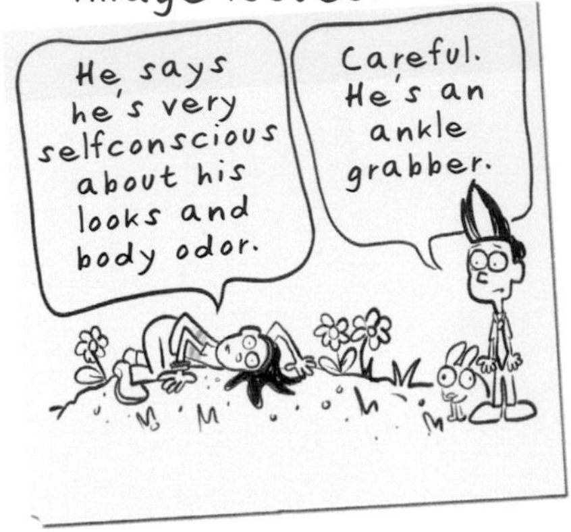
He says he's very selfconscious about his looks and body odor.
Careful. He's an ankle grabber.

And Topo, apparently, used to be official council to a royal family in the city of Atlantis? Huh?

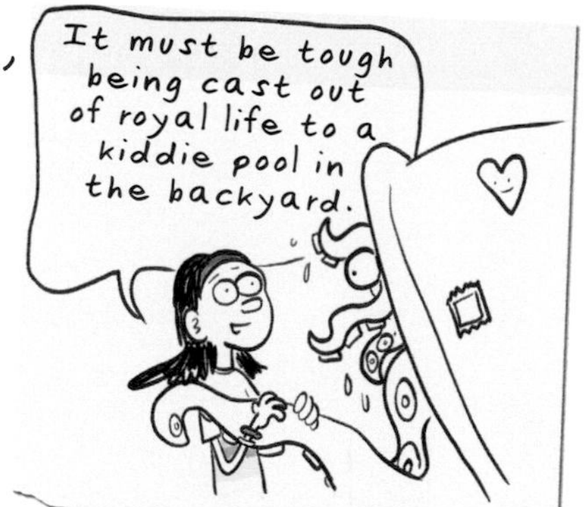
It must be tough being cast out of royal life to a kiddie pool in the backyard.

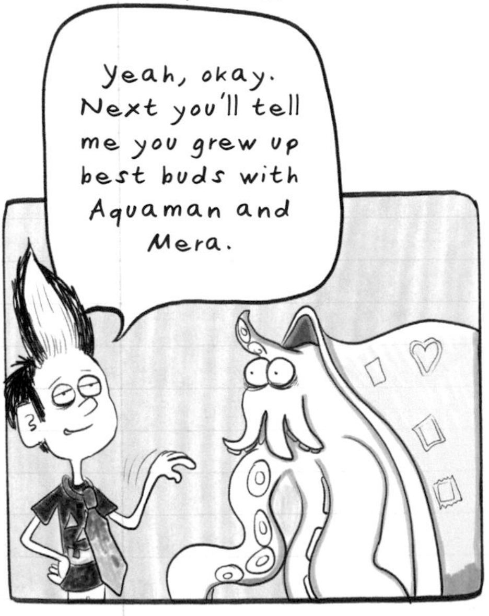
Yeah, okay. Next you'll tell me you grew up best buds with Aquaman and Mera.

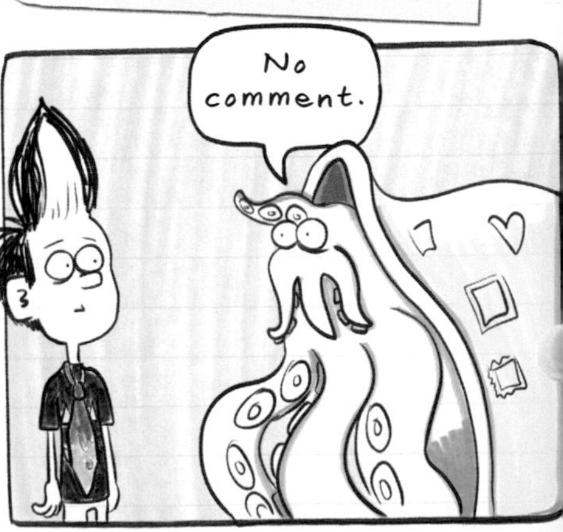
No comment.

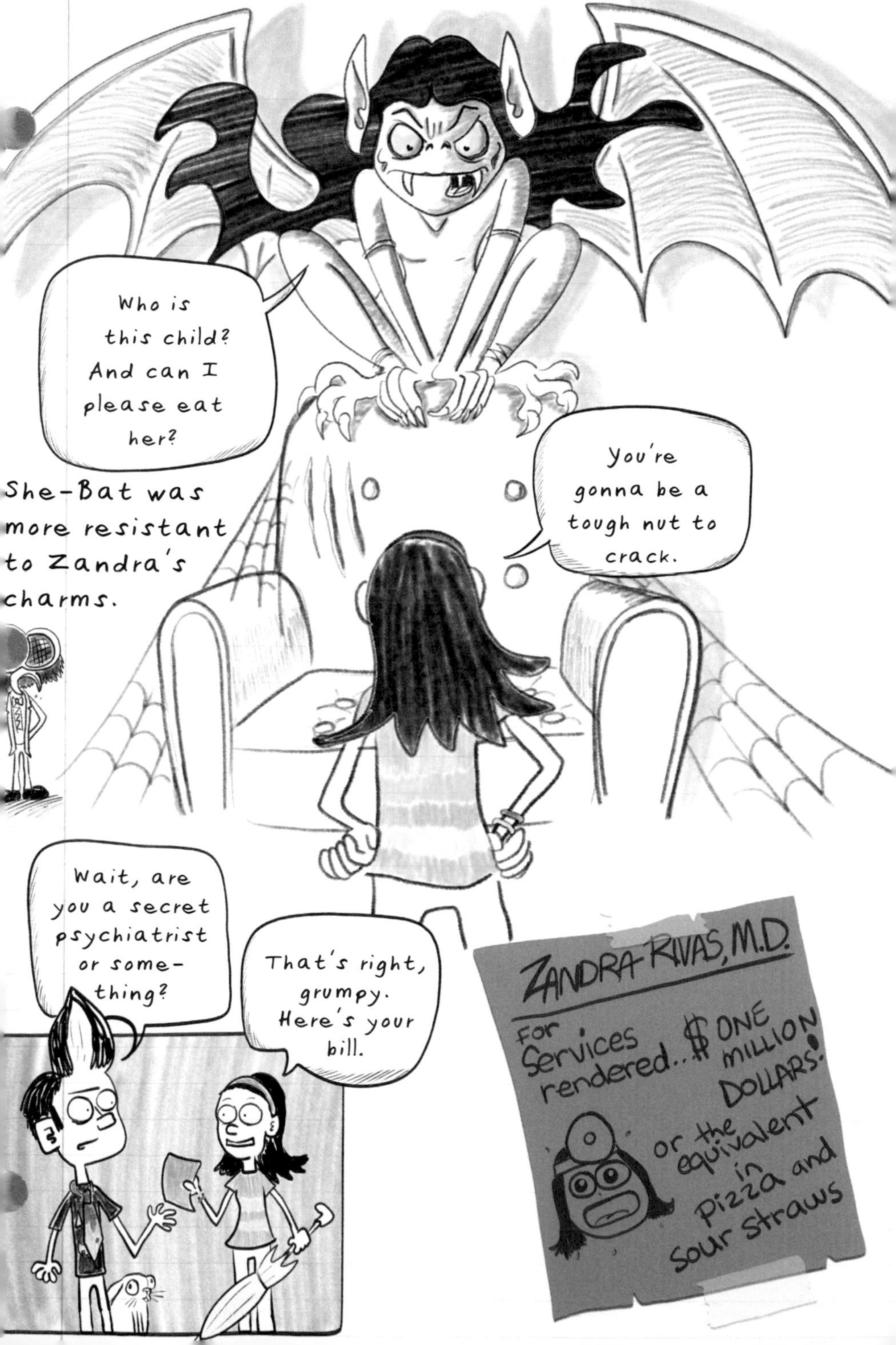
Who is this child? And can I please eat her?
She-Bat was more resistant to Zandra's charms.
You're gonna be a tough nut to crack.
Wait, are you a secret psychiatrist or some-thing?
That's right, grumpy. Here's your bill.
ZANDRA RIVAS, M.D.
For Services rendered... $ ONE MILLION DOLLARS!
or the equivalent in Pizza and Sour Straws

MIDNIGHT

Breaking news! Please ignore the crinkled paper. A monster landed on my notebook. About twenty minutes ago I wasawakened by a series of loud thumps, then a chunk of ceiling hit my ear.

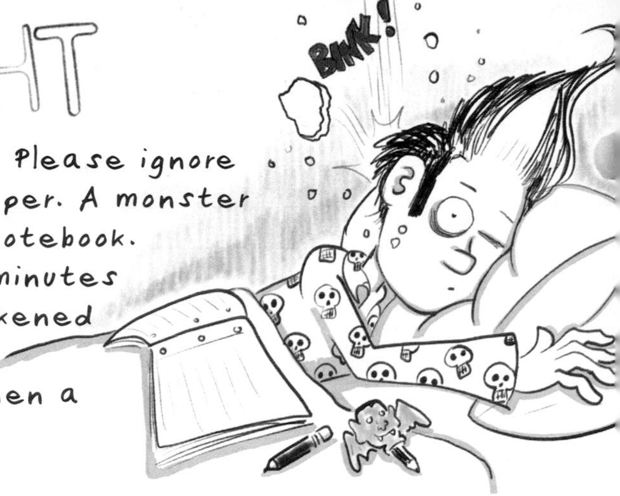

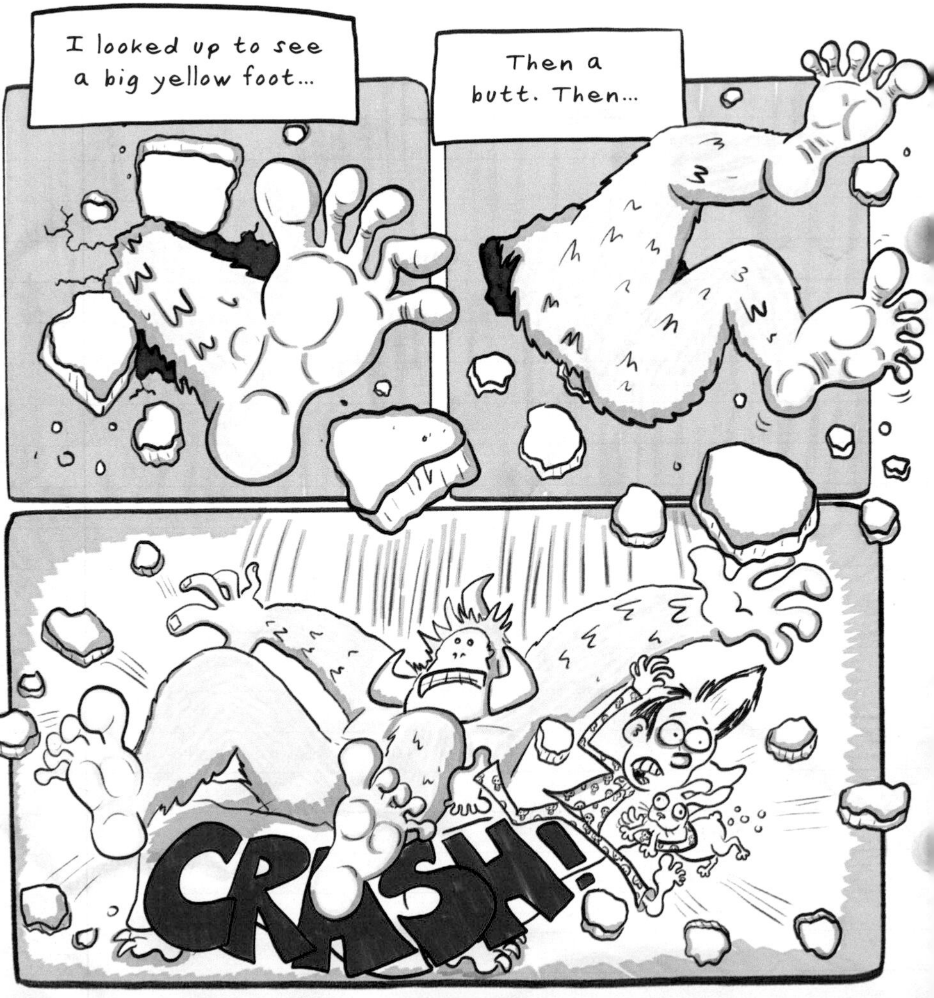
I looked up to see a big yellow foot...
Then a butt. Then...
CRASH!

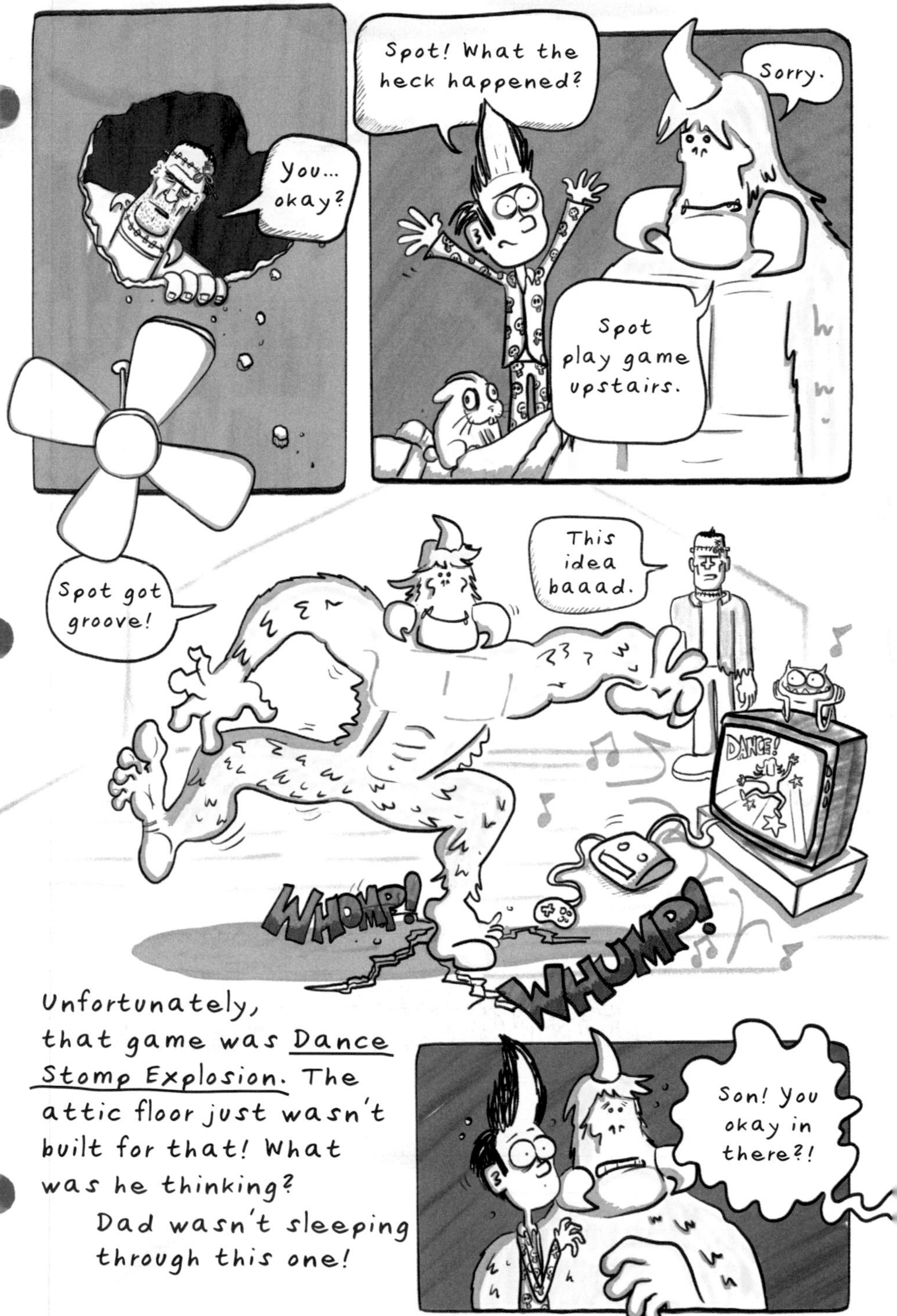
You... okay?
Spot! What the heck happened?
Sorry.
Spot play game upstairs.
Spot got groove!
This idea baaad.
DANCE!
WHOMP!
WHUMP!
Unfortunately, that game was Dance Stomp Explosion. The attic floor just wasn't built for that! What was he thinking?
Dad wasn't sleeping through this one!
Son! You okay in there?!

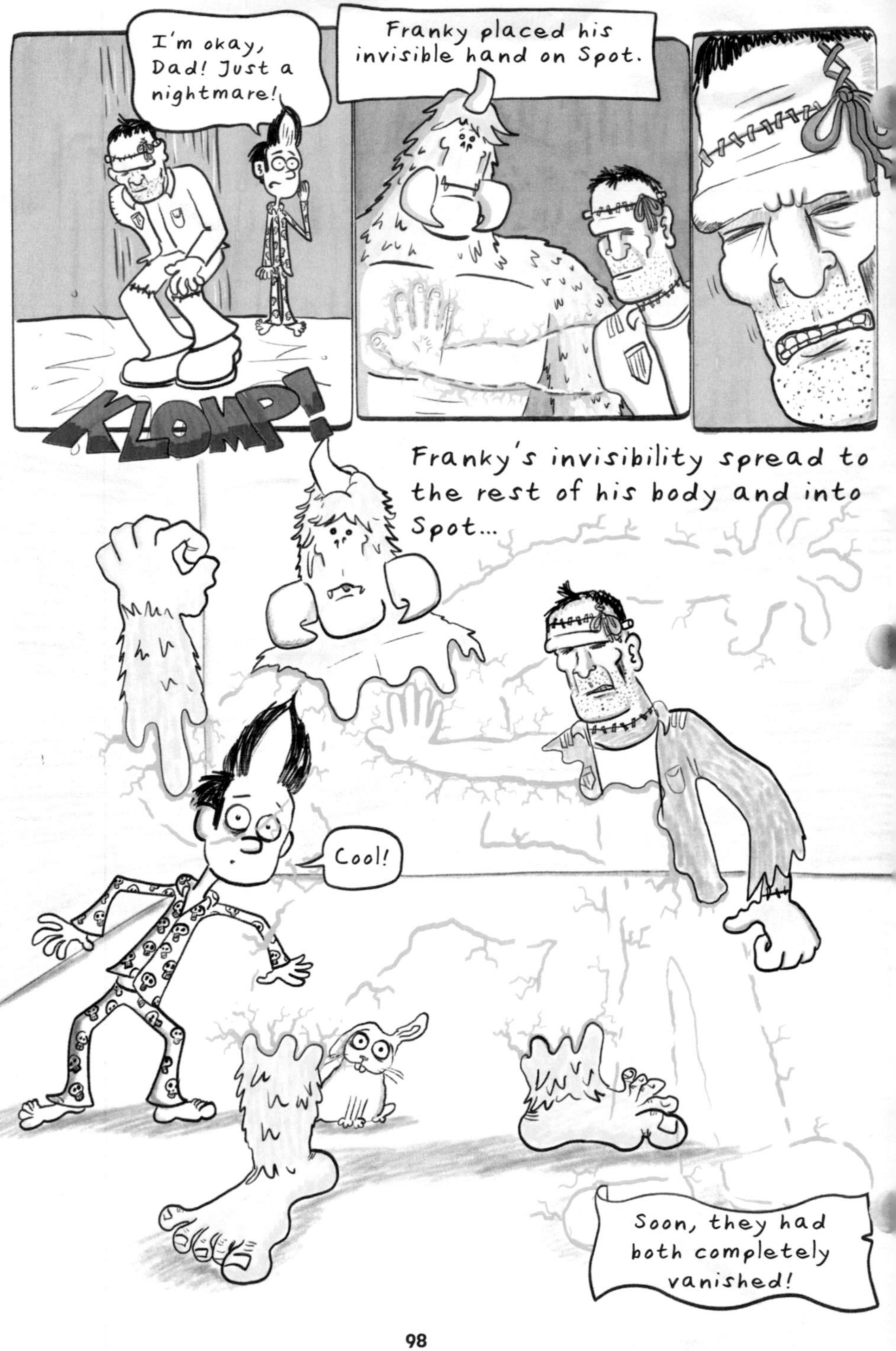

I'm okay, Dad! Just a nightmare!
KLOMP!
Franky placed his invisible hand on Spot.
Franky's invisibility spread to the rest of his body and into Spot...
Cool!
Soon, they had both completely vanished!

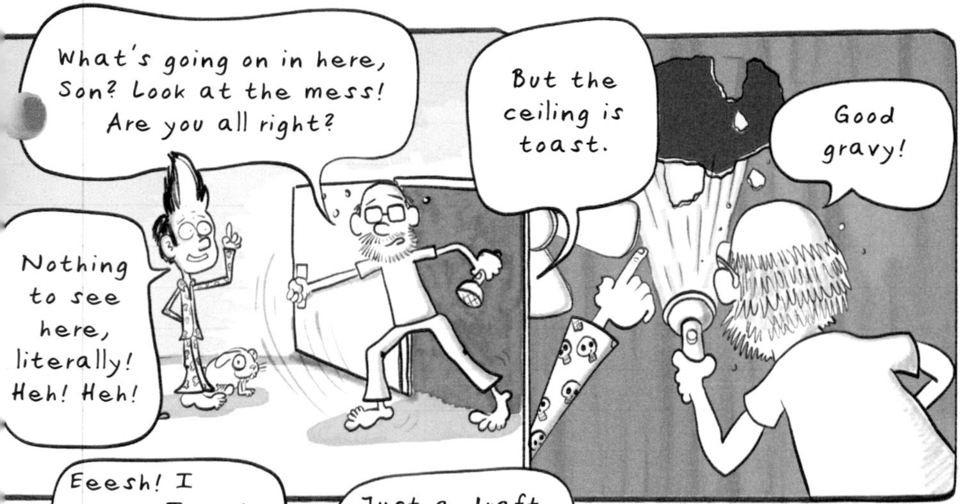
What's going on in here, Son? Look at the mess! Are you all right?
Nothing to see here, literally! Heh! Heh!
But the ceiling is toast.
Good gravy!

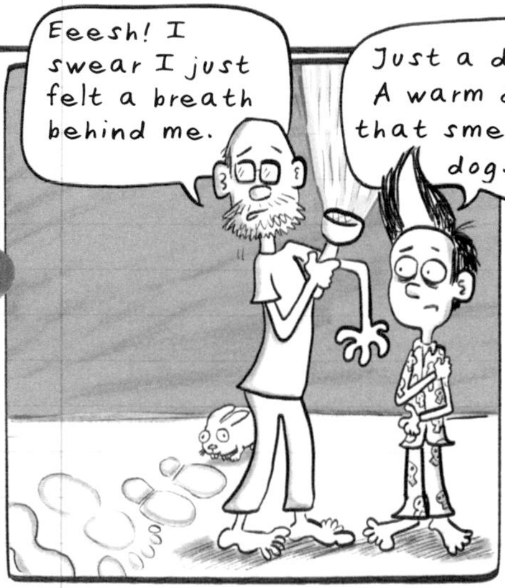
Eeesh! I swear I just felt a breath behind me.
Just a draft. A warm draft that smells like dog.

I convinced Dad to go back to bed. This could have been bad. Real. Bad. Dad could've spotted Topo in the tub, or She-Bat in the attic. I gotta move forward with relocating the monsters. Maybe I'll have a group meeting tomorrow. It's time.

BREAKFAST

Get this—Dad just told me Mom used to have imaginary monster friends when she was a kid. Her family thought she was disturbed. Interesting.

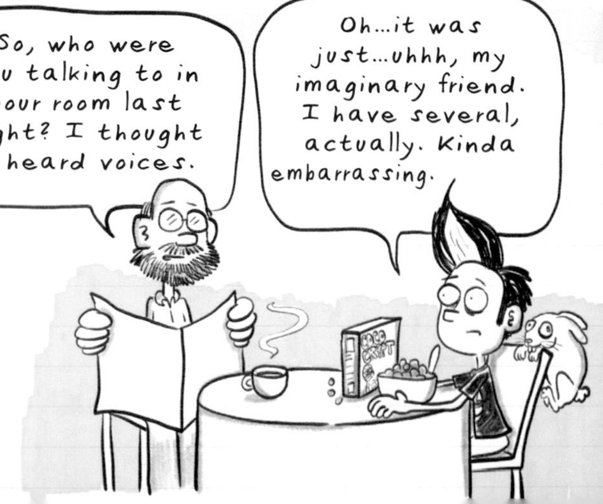
So, who were you talking to in your room last night? I thought I heard voices.
Oh...it was just...uhhh, my imaginary friend. I have several, actually. Kinda embarrassing.

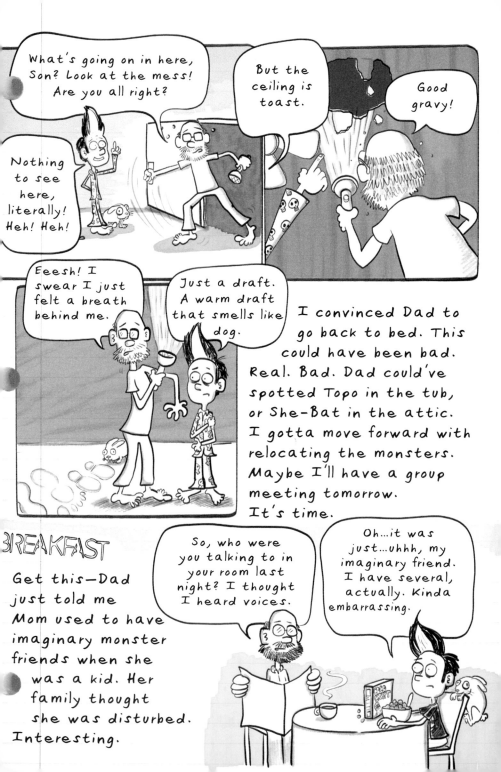

LUNCH

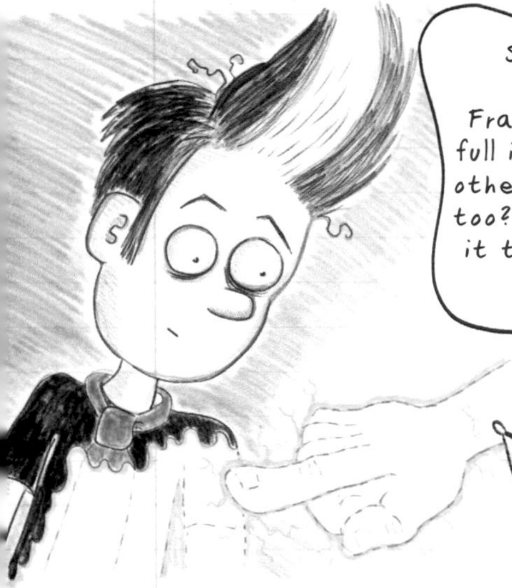

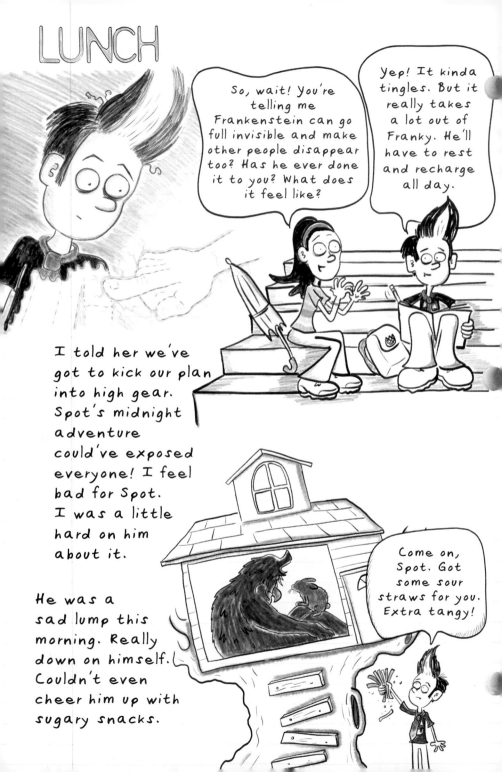

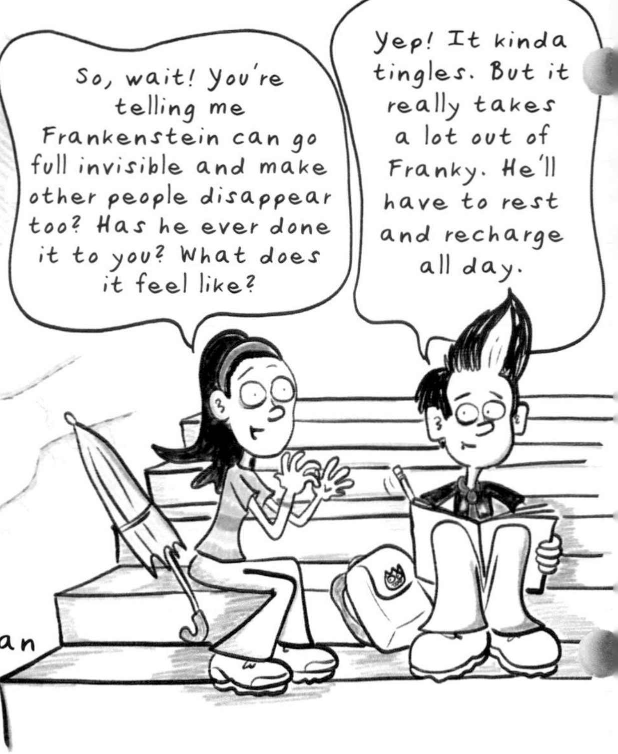
So, wait! You're telling me Frankenstein can go full invisible and make other people disappear too? Has he ever done it to you? What does it feel like?
Yep! It kinda tingles. But it really takes a lot out of Franky. He'll have to rest and recharge all day.

I told her we've got to kick our plan into high gear. Spot's midnight adventure could've exposed everyone! I feel bad for Spot. I was a little hard on him about it.

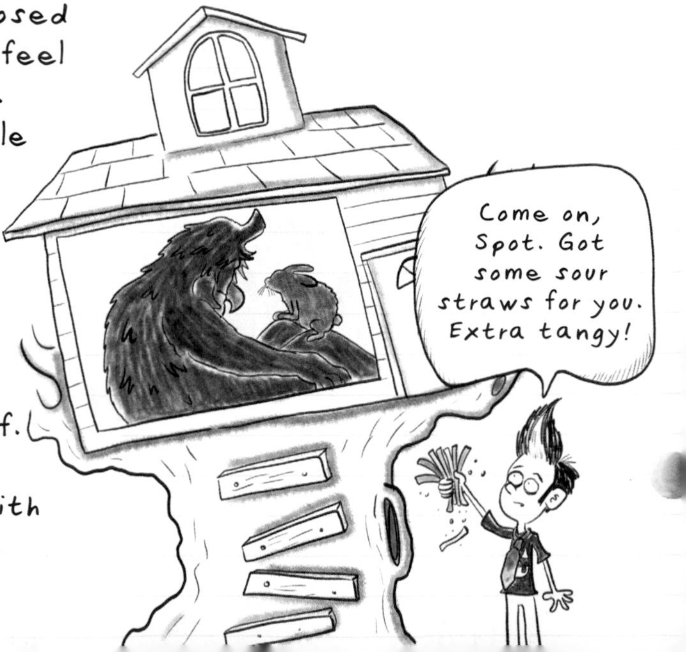
Come on, Spot. Got some sour straws for you. Extra tangy!

He was a sad lump this morning. Really down on himself. Couldn't even cheer him up with sugary snacks.

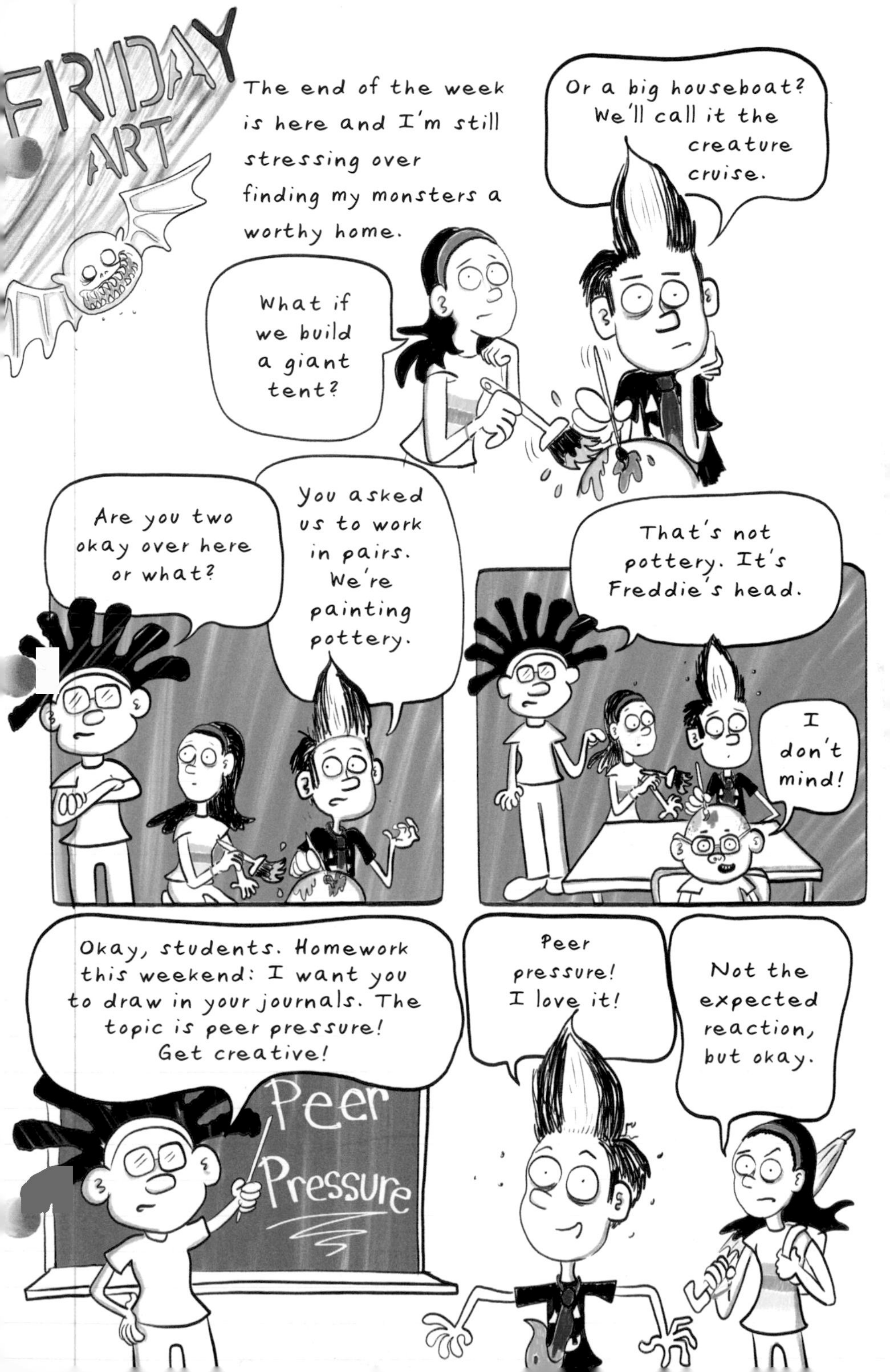
FRIDAY ART
The end of the week is here and I'm still stressing over finding my monsters a worthy home.
What if we build a giant tent?
Or a big houseboat? We'll call it the creature cruise.
Are you two okay over here or what?
You asked us to work in pairs. We're painting pottery.
That's not pottery. It's Freddie's head.
I don't mind!
Okay, students. Homework this weekend: I want you to draw in your journals. The topic is peer pressure! Get creative!
Peer Pressure
Peer pressure! I love it!
Not the expected reaction, but okay.

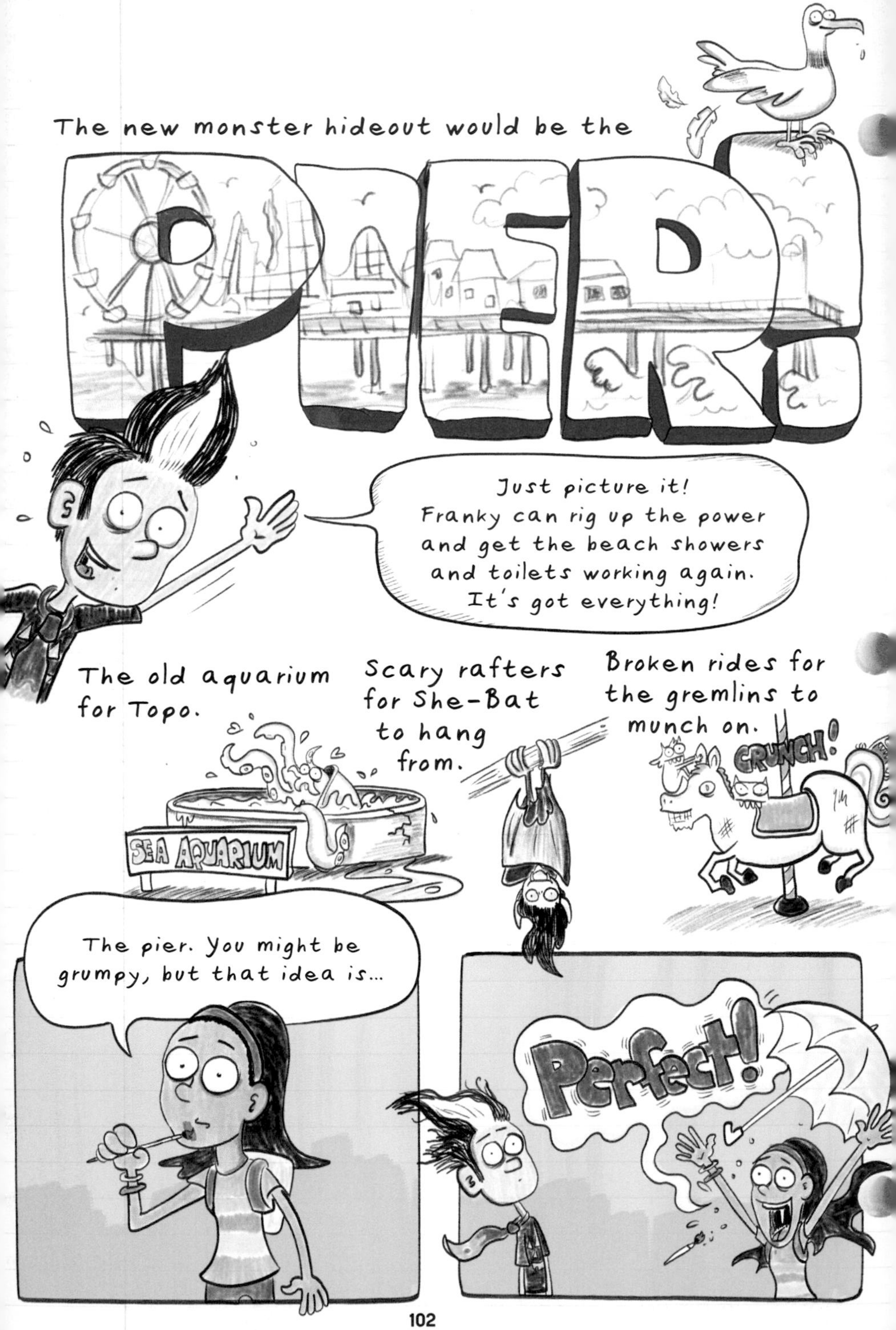
The new monster hideout would be the
PIER!
Just picture it! Franky can rig up the power and get the beach showers and toilets working again. It's got everything!
The old aquarium for Topo.
SEA AQUARIUM
Scary rafters for She-Bat to hang from.
Broken rides for the gremlins to munch on.
CRUNCH!
The pier. You might be grumpy, but that idea is...
Perfect!

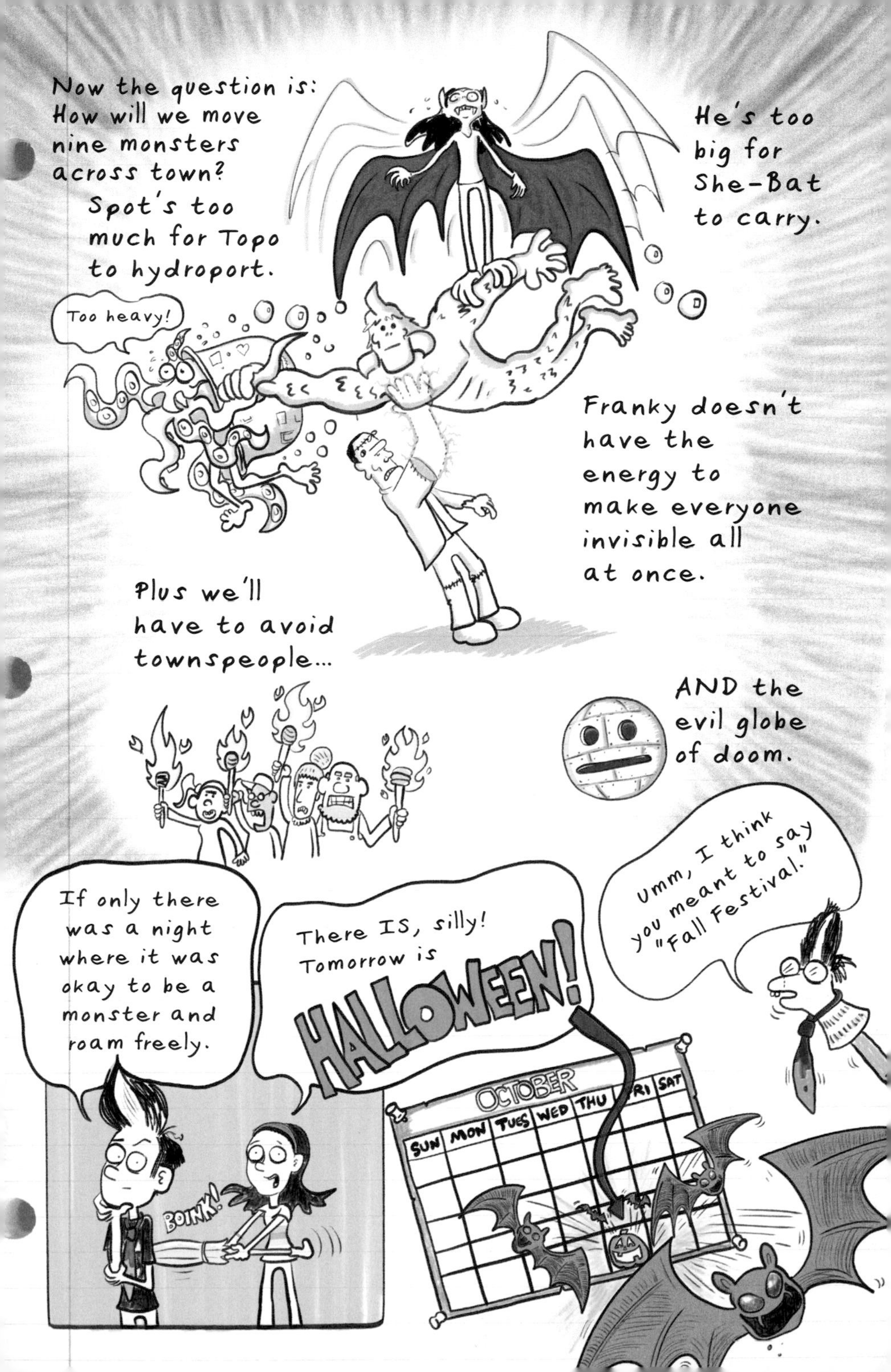
Now the question is: How will we move nine monsters across town?
He's too big for She-Bat to carry.
Spot's too much for Topo to hydroport.
Too heavy!
Franky doesn't have the energy to make everyone invisible all at once.
Plus we'll have to avoid townspeople...
AND the evil globe of doom.
If only there was a night where it was okay to be a monster and roam freely.
There IS, silly! Tomorrow is
HALLOWEEN!
Umm, I think you meant to say "Fall Festival."
OCTOBER
SUN
MON
TUES
WED
THU
FRI
SAT
BOINK!

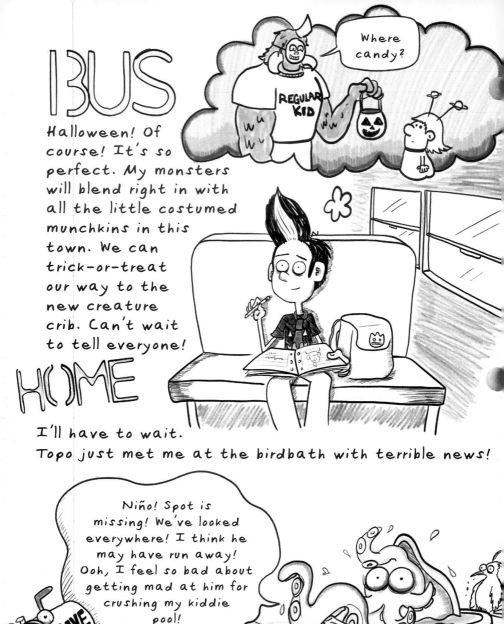

BUS

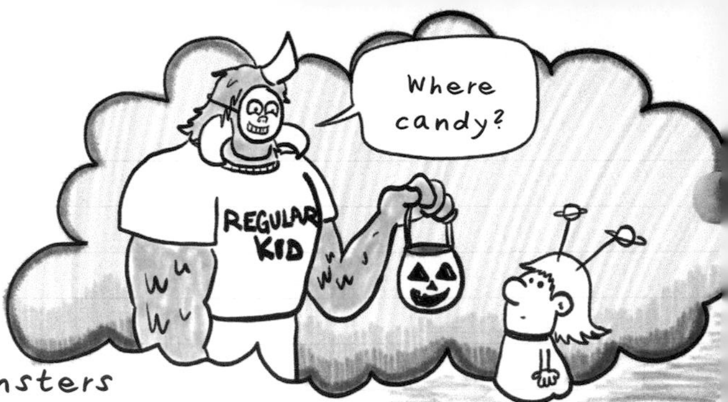
Where candy?
REGULAR KID

Halloween! Of course! It's so perfect. My monsters will blend right in with all the little costumed munchkins in this town. We can trick-or-treat our way to the new creature crib. Can't wait to tell everyone!

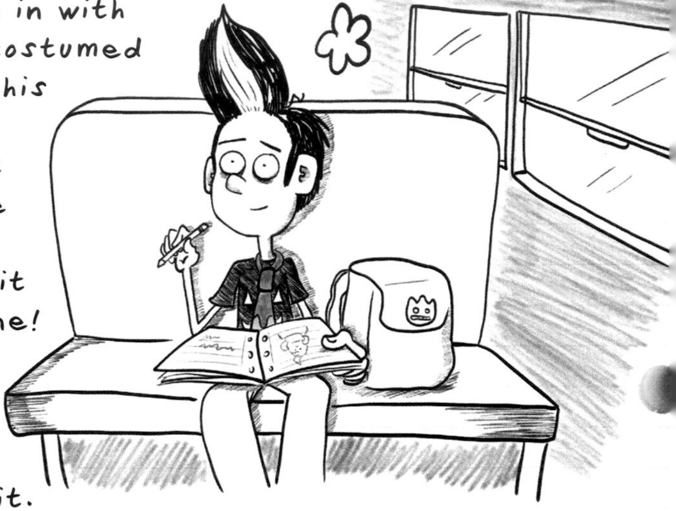

HOME

I'll have to wait.
Topo just met me at the birdbath with terrible news!

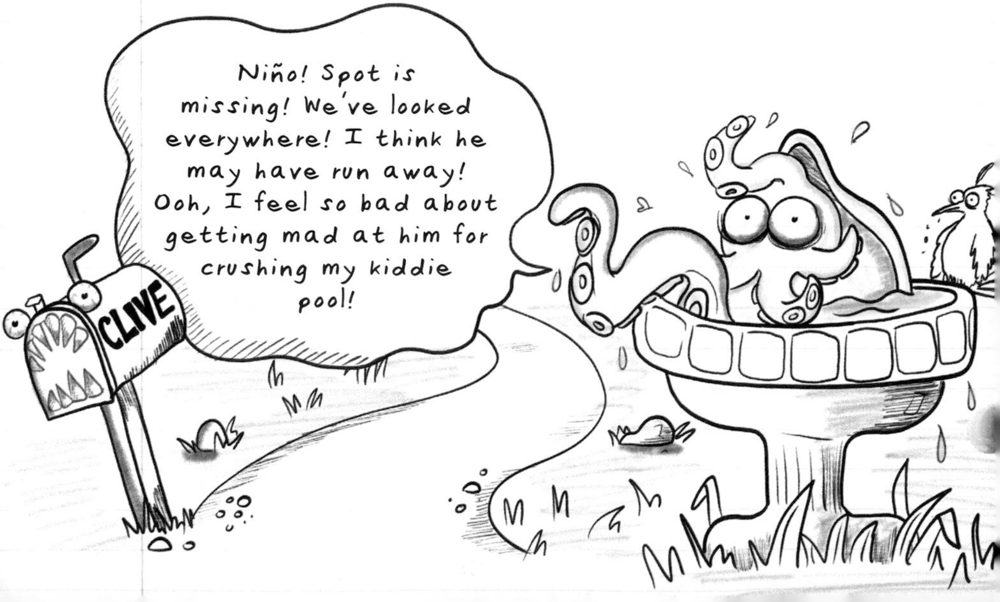
Niño! Spot is missing! We've looked everywhere! I think he may have run away! Ooh, I feel so bad about getting mad at him for crushing my kiddie pool!
CLIVE

Sure enough, Spot had left a note taped to my statue of Vlad the Impaler.

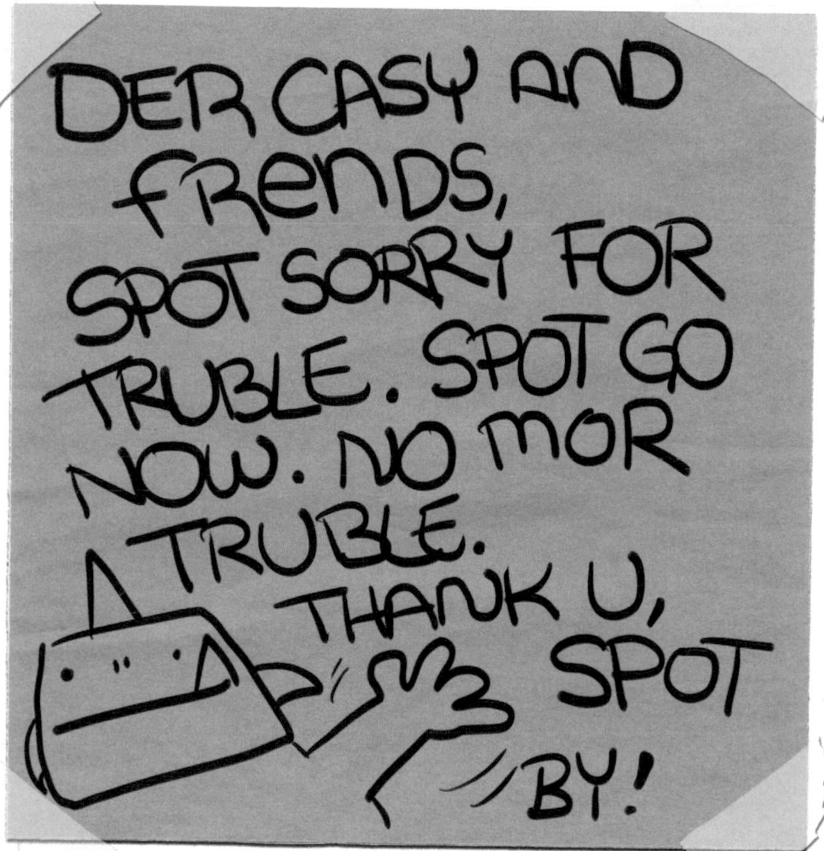
DER CASY AND FRENDS,
SPOT SORRY FOR TRUBLE. SPOT GO NOW. NO MOR TRUBLE.
THANK U,
SPOT
BY!

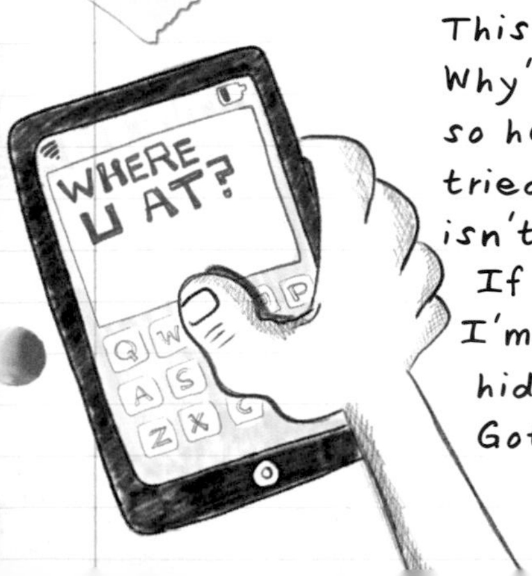
WHERE U AT?

This is my stupid fault! Why'd I have to come down on him so hard for the other night? Just tried to check with Zandra but she isn't responding to texts or calls. If Spot was going to run away, I'm sure he'd try to go back to her hideout. Why won't she answer? Gotta go. Gotta find Spot!

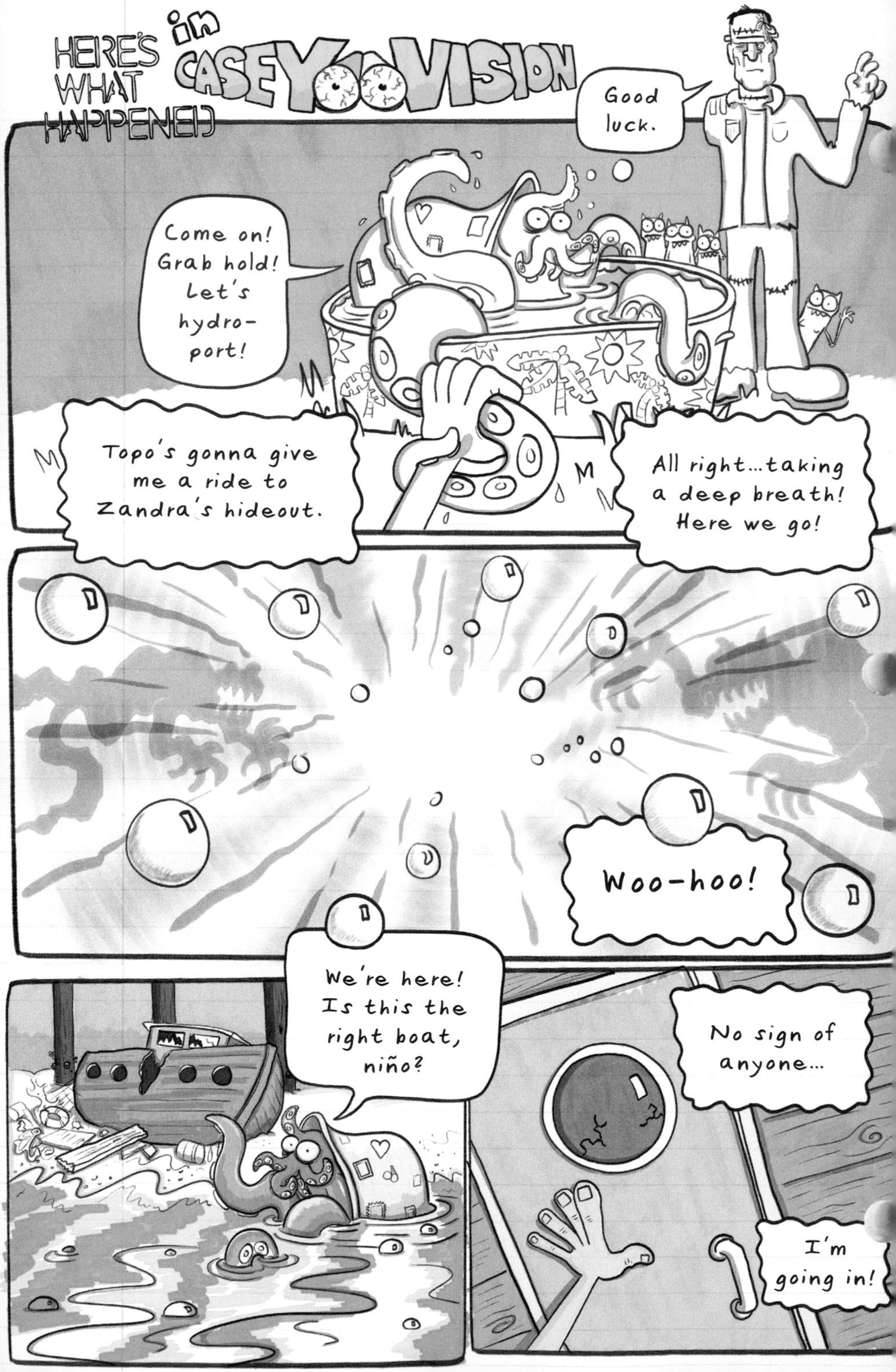
HERE'S WHAT HAPPENED in CASEY VISION
Good luck.
Come on! Grab hold! Let's hydro-port!
Topo's gonna give me a ride to Zandra's hideout.
All right...taking a deep breath! Here we go!
Woo-hoo!
We're here! Is this the right boat, niño?
No sign of anyone...
I'm going in!

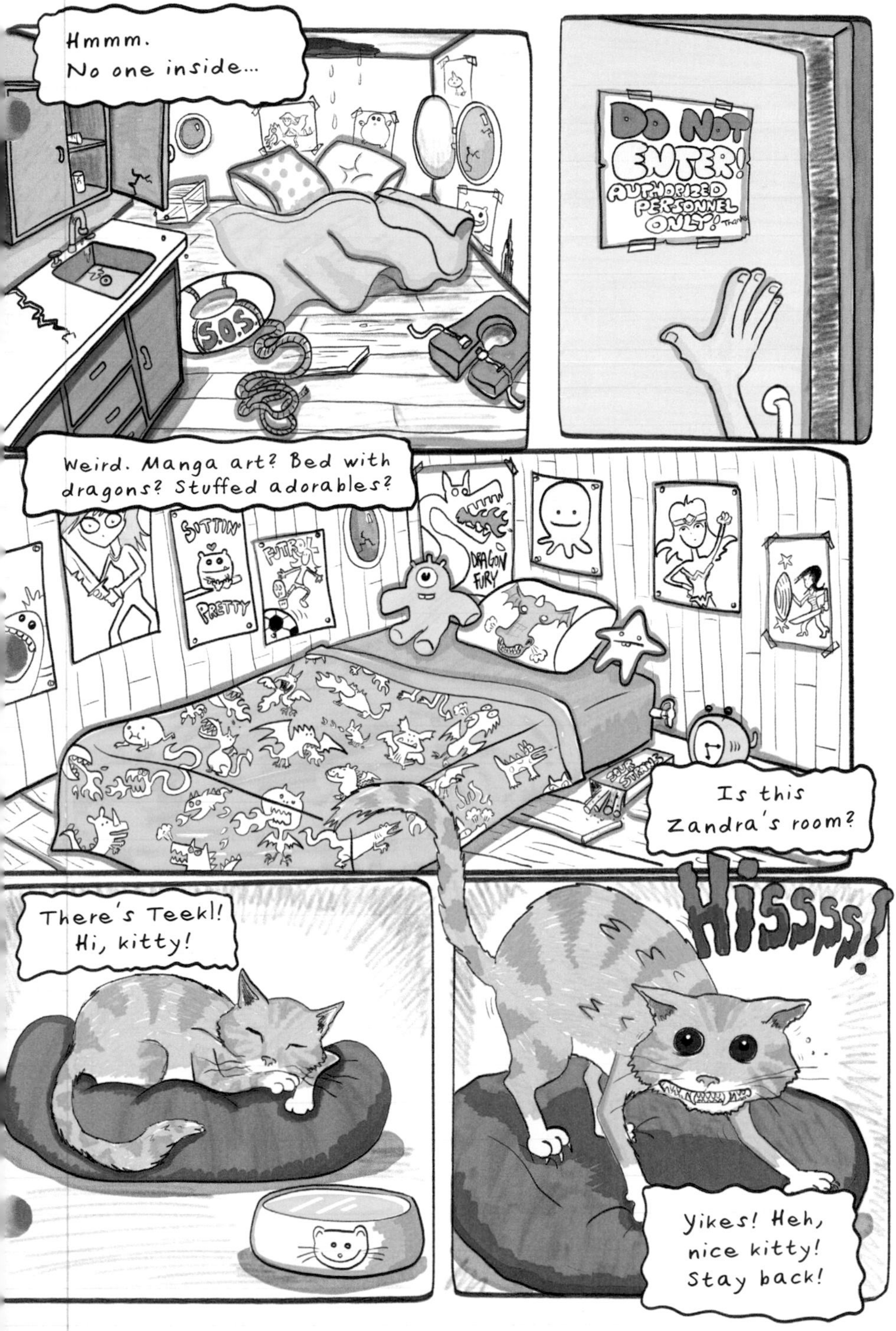
Hmmm.
No one inside...
S.O.S.
DO NOT ENTER! AUTHORIZED PERSONNEL ONLY! Thanks
Weird. Manga art? Bed with dragons? Stuffed adorables?
SITTIN' PRETTY
FUTBOL
DRAGON FURY
Is this Zandra's room?
There's Teek!! Hi, kitty!
HISSSSS!
Yikes! Heh, nice kitty! Stay back!

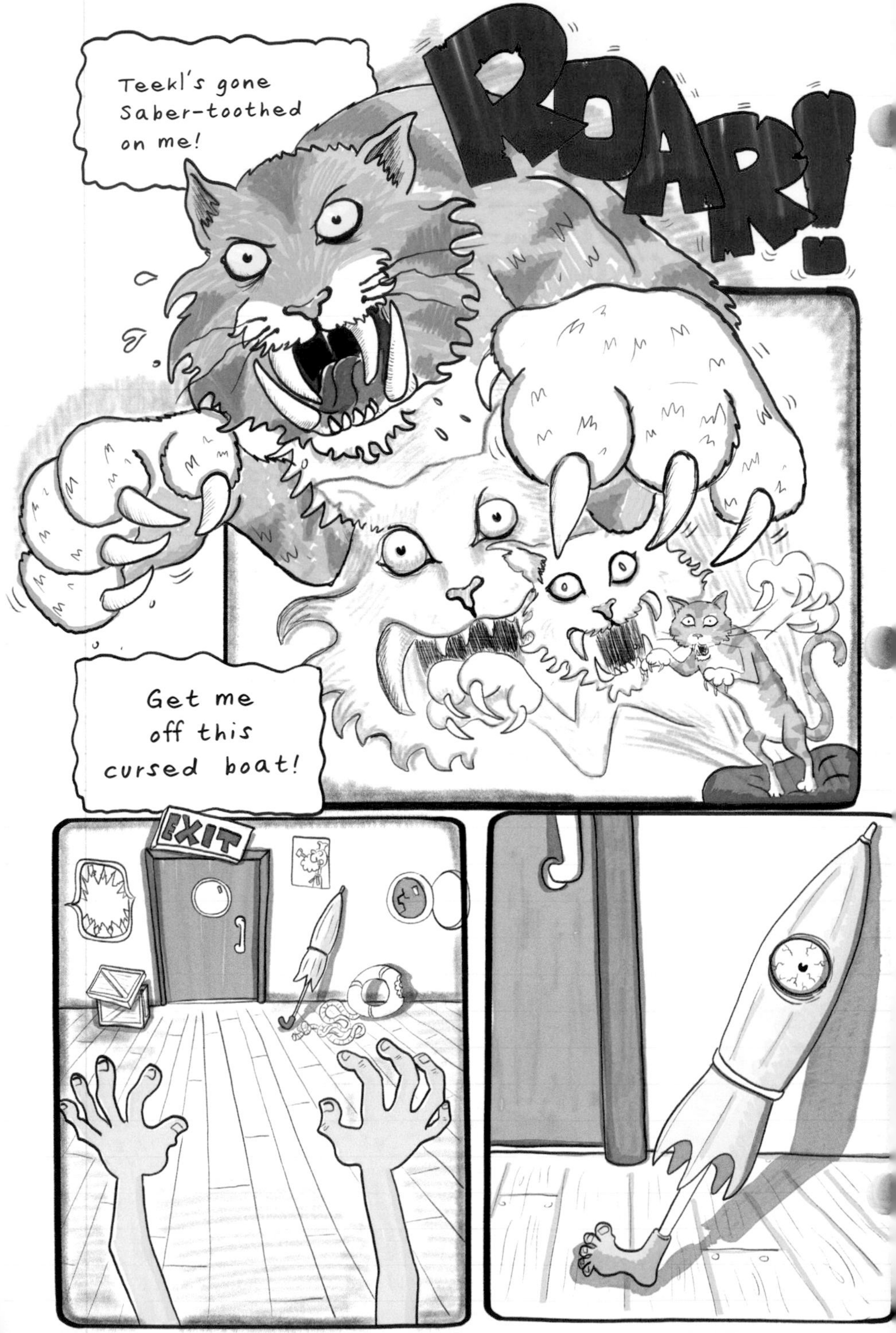
Teekl's gone Saber-toothed on me!
ROAR!
Get me off this cursed boat!
EXIT

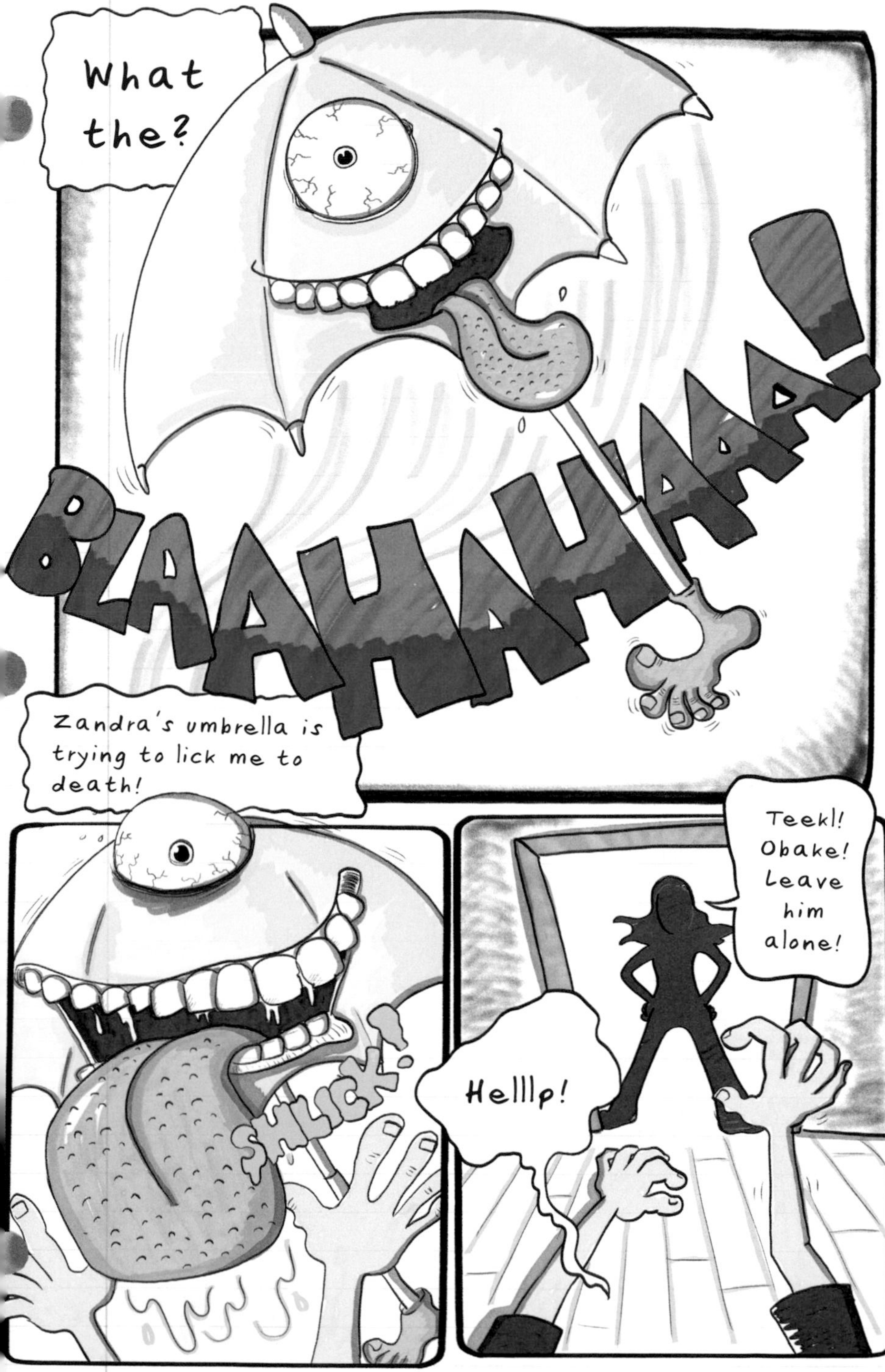

What the?
BLAAHAHAAAA!
Zandra's umbrella is trying to lick me to death!
SHLICK!
Helllp!
Teekl! Obake! Leave him alone!

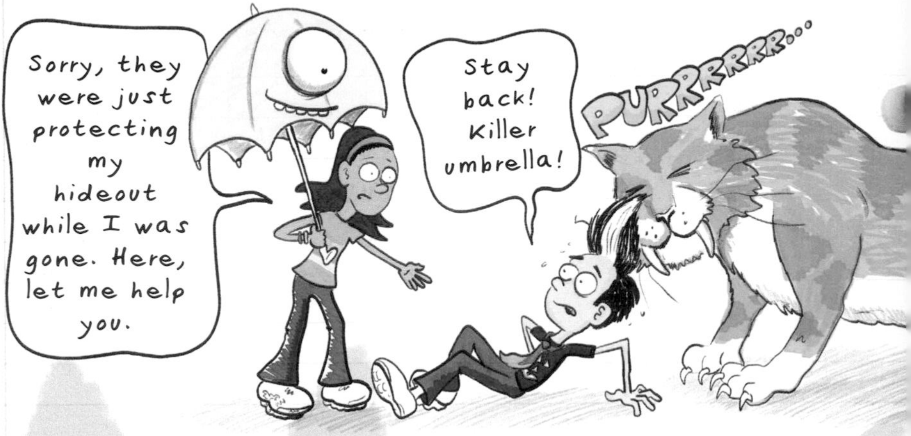
Sorry, they were just protecting my hideout while I was gone. Here, let me help you.
Stay back! Killer umbrella!
PURRRRRR...

Once I had realized I wasn't going to be eaten and had calmed down, Zandra revealed that Obake is actually an ancient yōkai monster from Japan.

Teekl is a little more of a mystery. She's a shape-shifter who maybe once belonged to a powerful sorcerer.

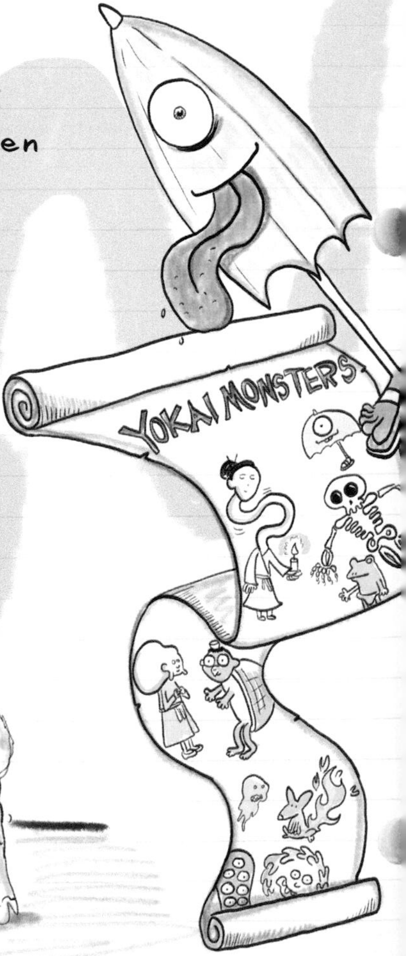
YOKAI MONSTERS

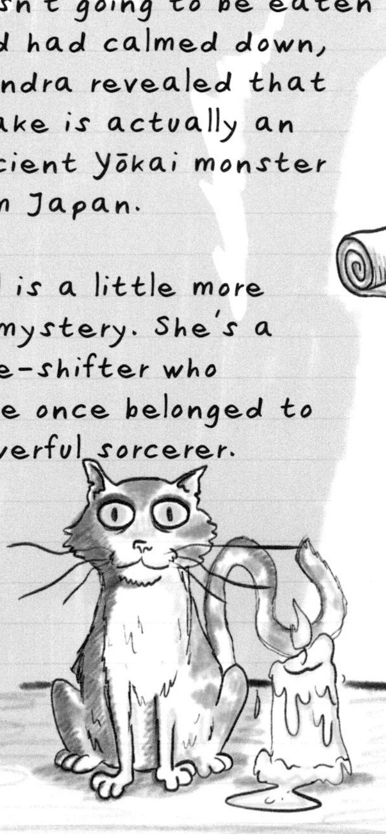

Zandra apologized for not telling me earlier that she had more monsters. I guess she didn't want to overwhelm me and she really just wanted Spot back in good health.

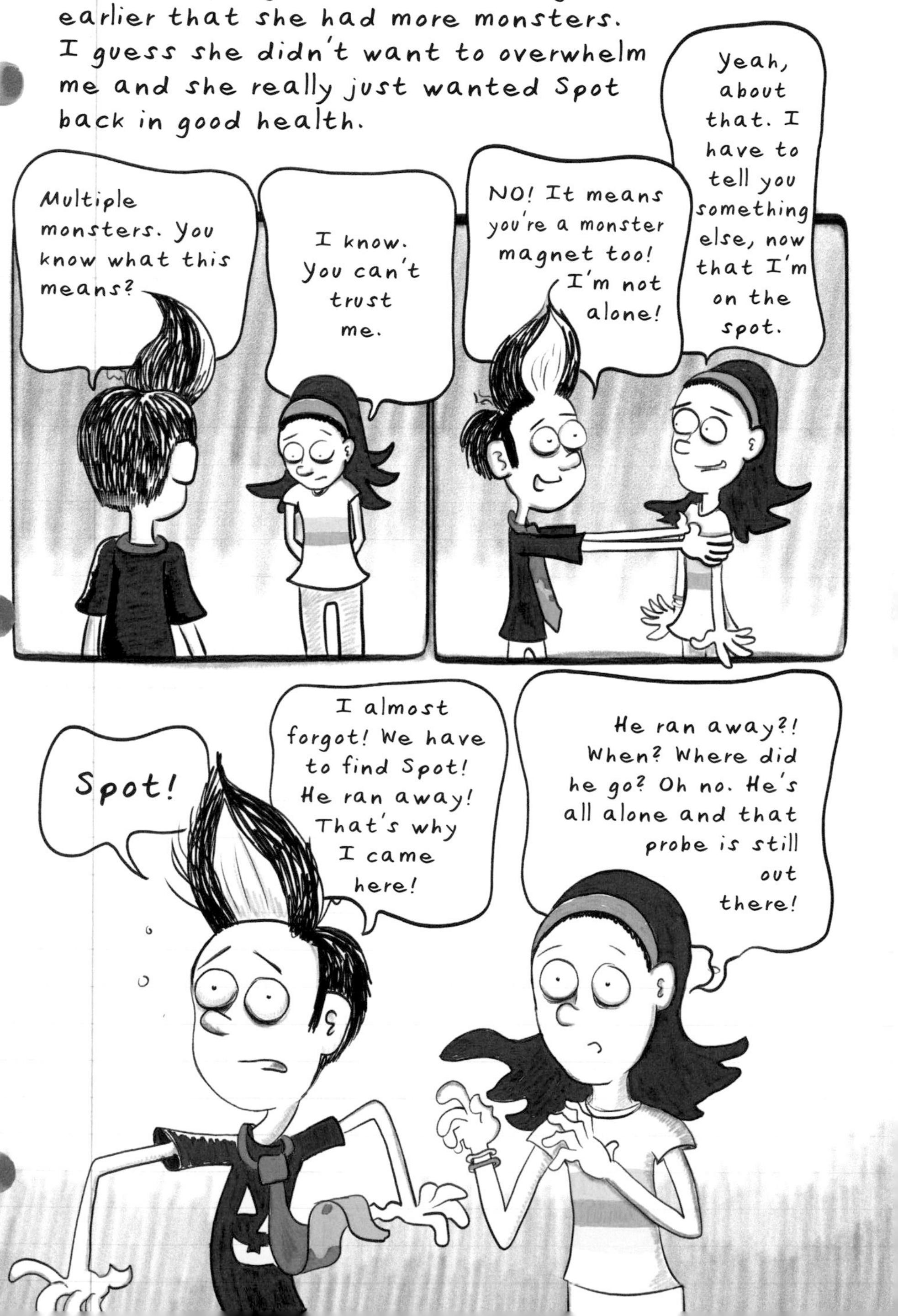
Multiple monsters. You know what this means?
I know. You can't trust me.
NO! It means you're a monster magnet too! I'm not alone!
Yeah, about that. I have to tell you something else, now that I'm on the spot.
Spot!
I almost forgot! We have to find Spot! He ran away! That's why I came here!
He ran away?! When? Where did he go? Oh no. He's all alone and that probe is still out there!

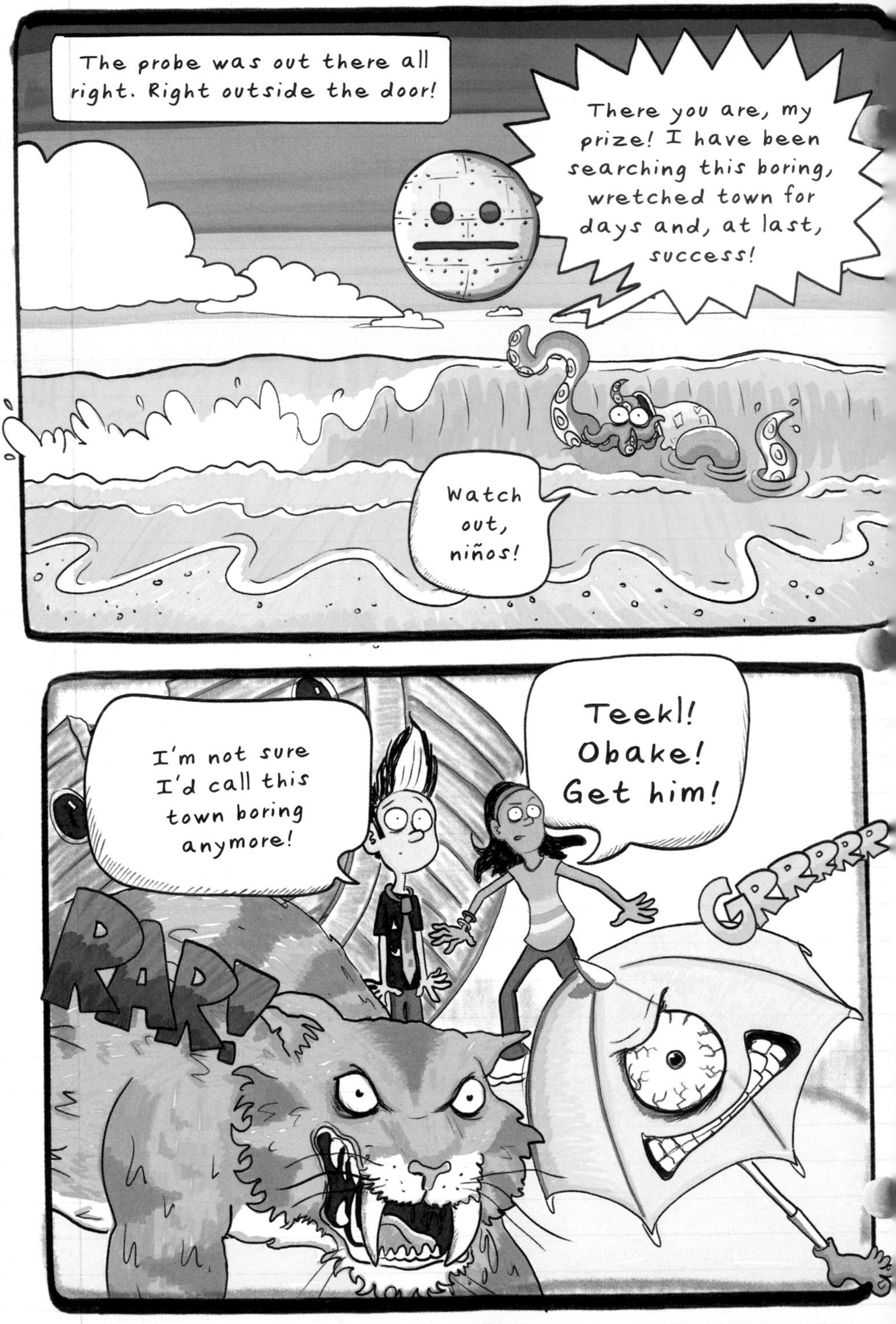
The probe was out there all right. Right outside the door!
There you are, my prize! I have been searching this boring, wretched town for days and, at last, success!
Watch out, niños!
I'm not sure I'd call this town boring anymore!
Teekl! Obake! Get him!
RAR!
GRRRRR

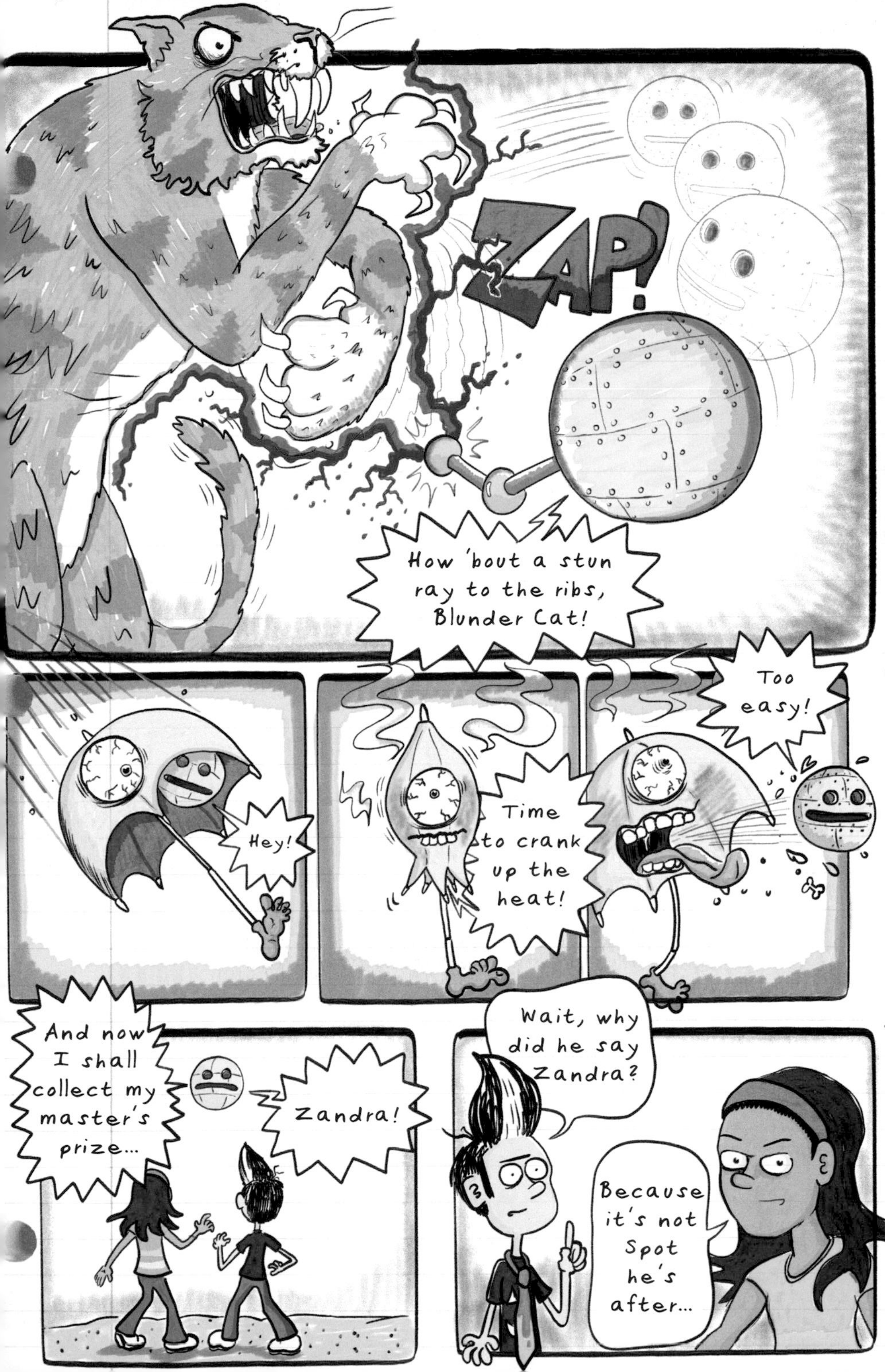
ZAP!
How 'bout a stun ray to the ribs, Blunder Cat!
Hey!
Time to crank up the heat!
Too easy!
And now I shall collect my master's prize...
Zandra!
Wait, why did he say Zandra?
Because it's not Spot he's after...

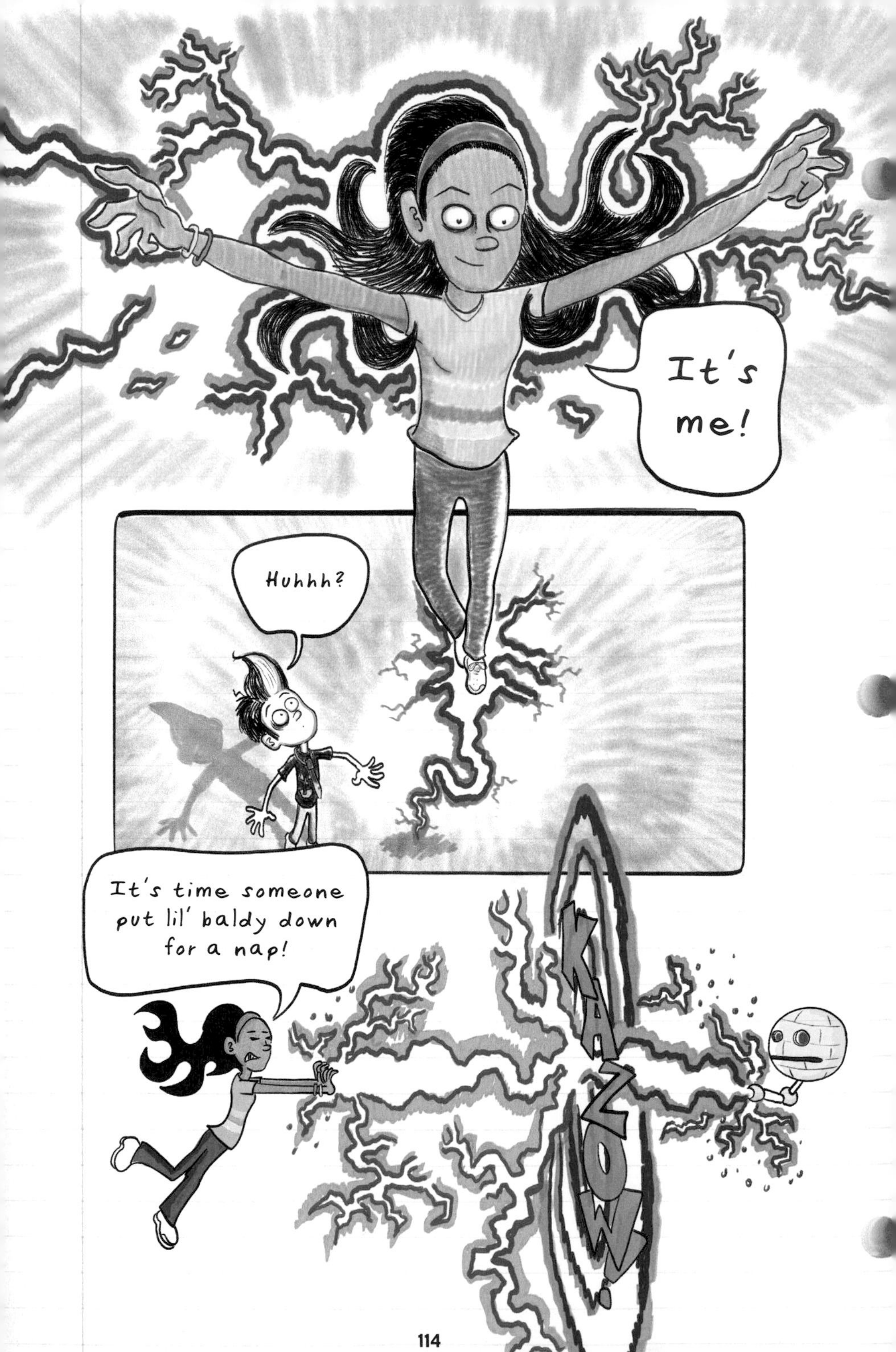
It's me!
Huhhh?
It's time someone put lil' baldy down for a nap!
KA-ZOW!

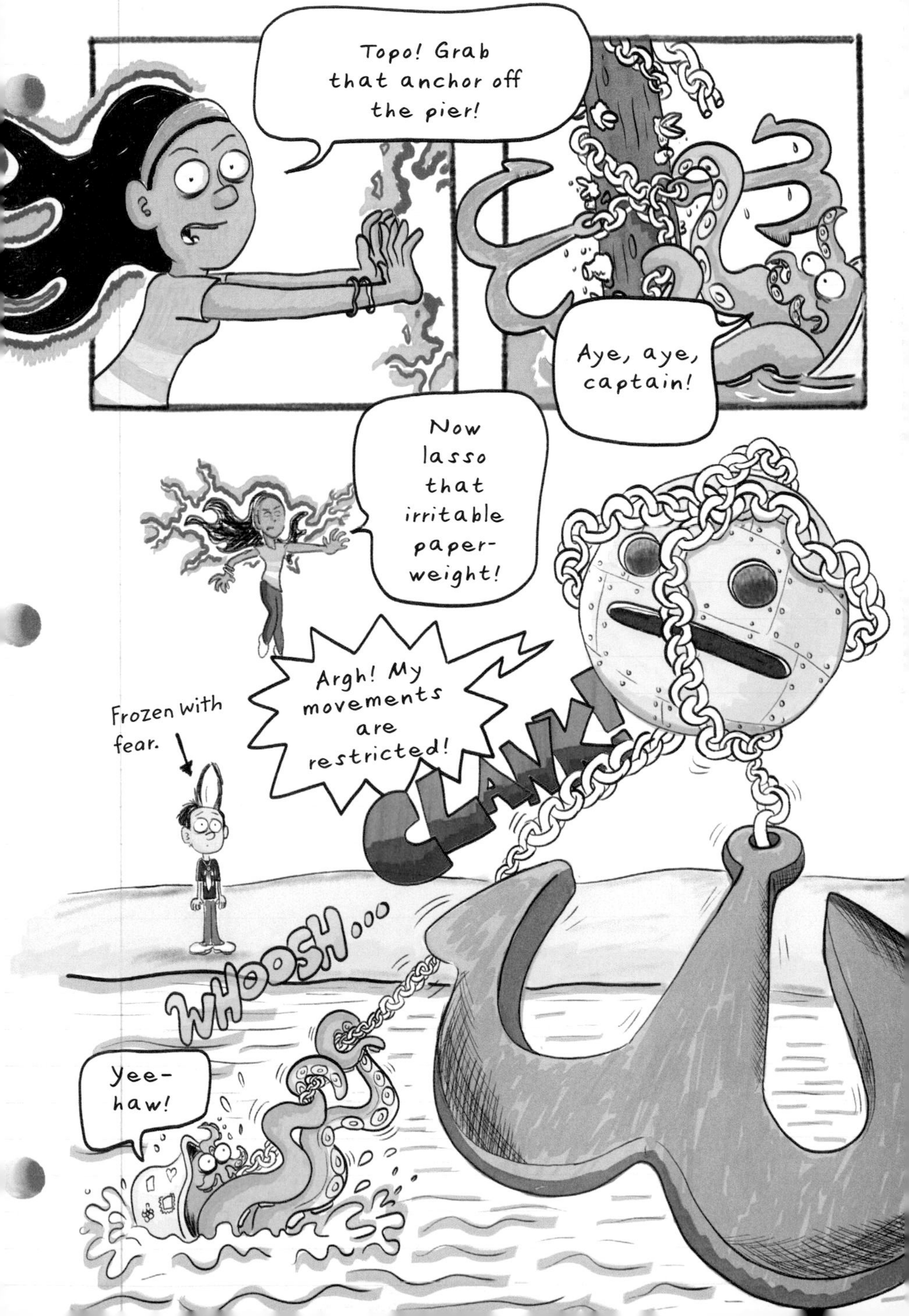

Topo! Grab that anchor off the pier!
Aye, aye, captain!
Now lasso that irritable paper-weight!
Argh! My movements are restricted!
CLANK!
Frozen with fear.
WHOOSHooo
Yee-haw!

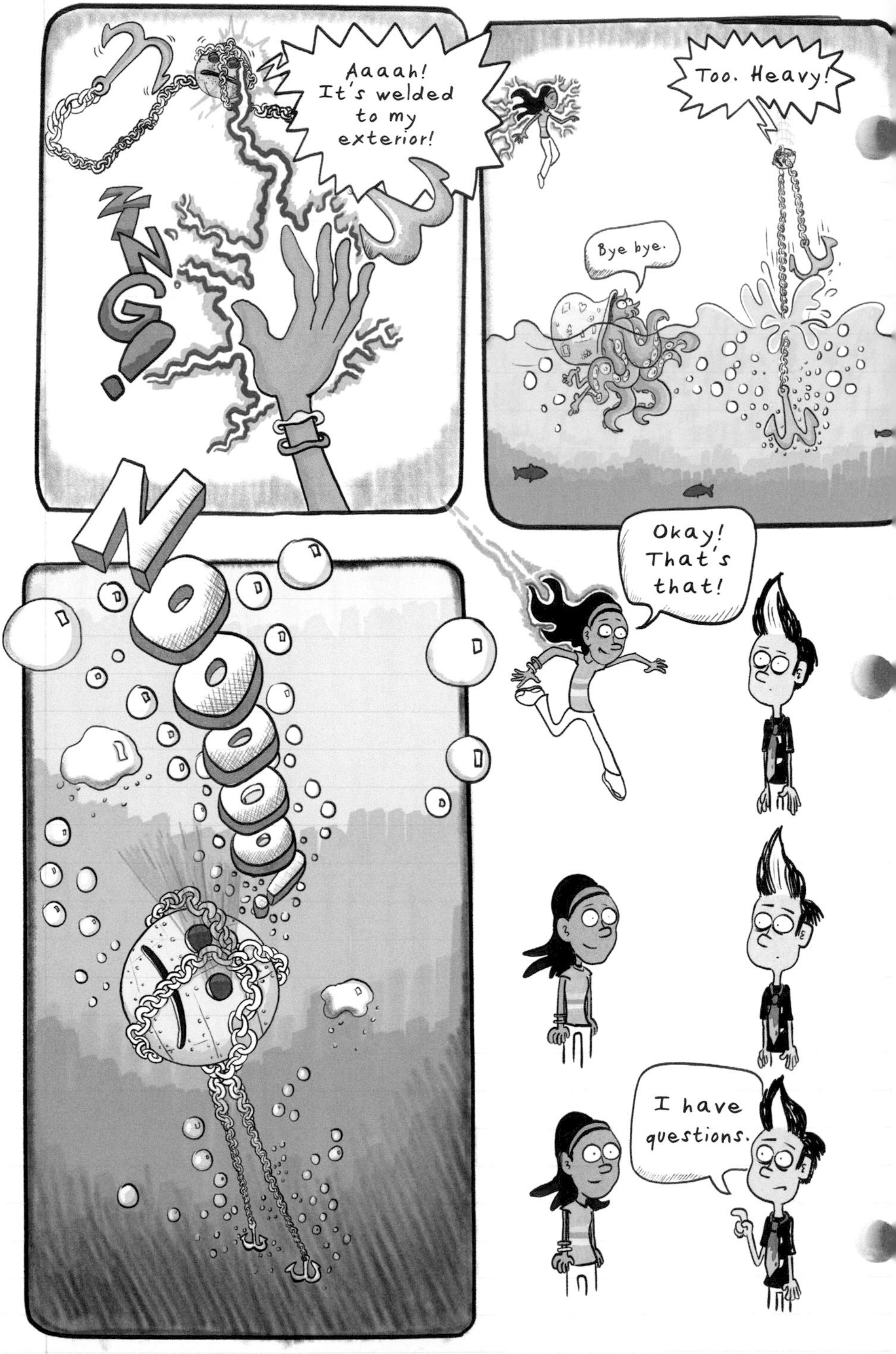

Aaaah! It's welded to my exterior!
ZING!
Too. Heavy!
Bye bye.
NOOOOOO
Okay! That's that!
I have questions.

My questions would have to wait.

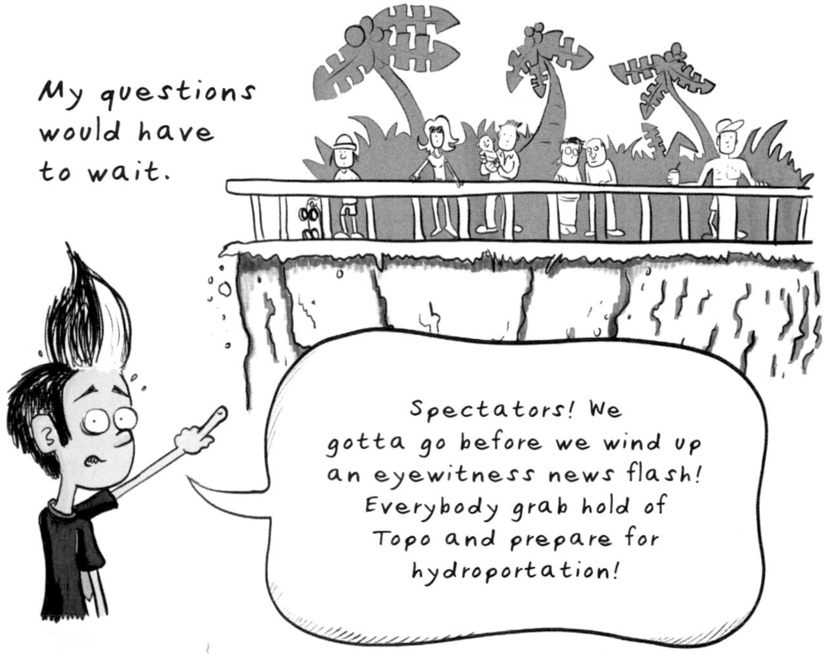
Spectators! We gotta go before we wind up an eyewitness news flash! Everybody grab hold of Topo and prepare for hydroportation!

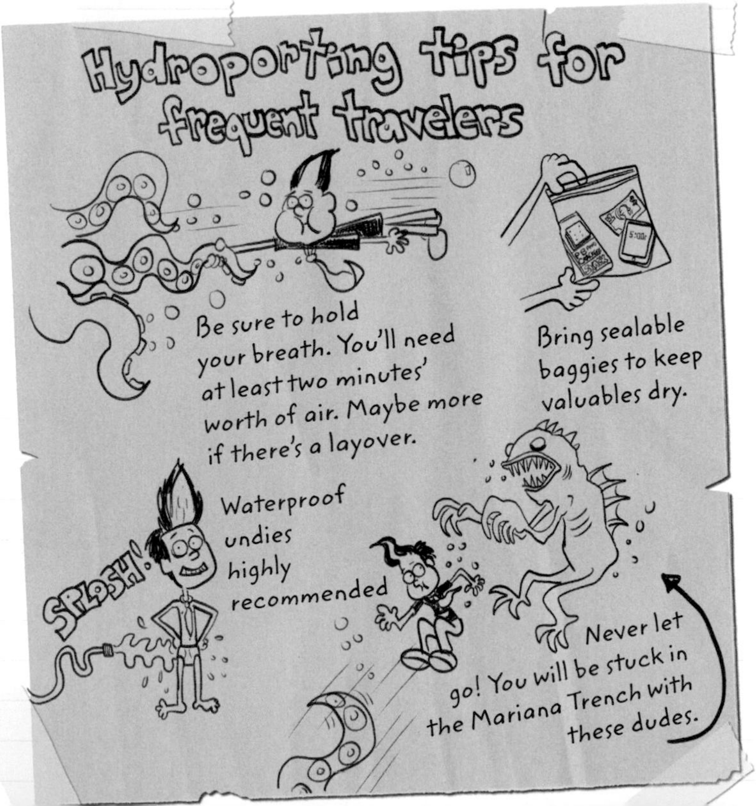
Hydroporting tips for frequent travelers
Be sure to hold your breath. You'll need at least two minutes' worth of air. Maybe more if there's a layover.
Bring sealable baggies to keep valuables dry.
Waterproof undies highly recommended
SPLOSH!
Never let go! You will be stuck in the Mariana Trench with these dudes.

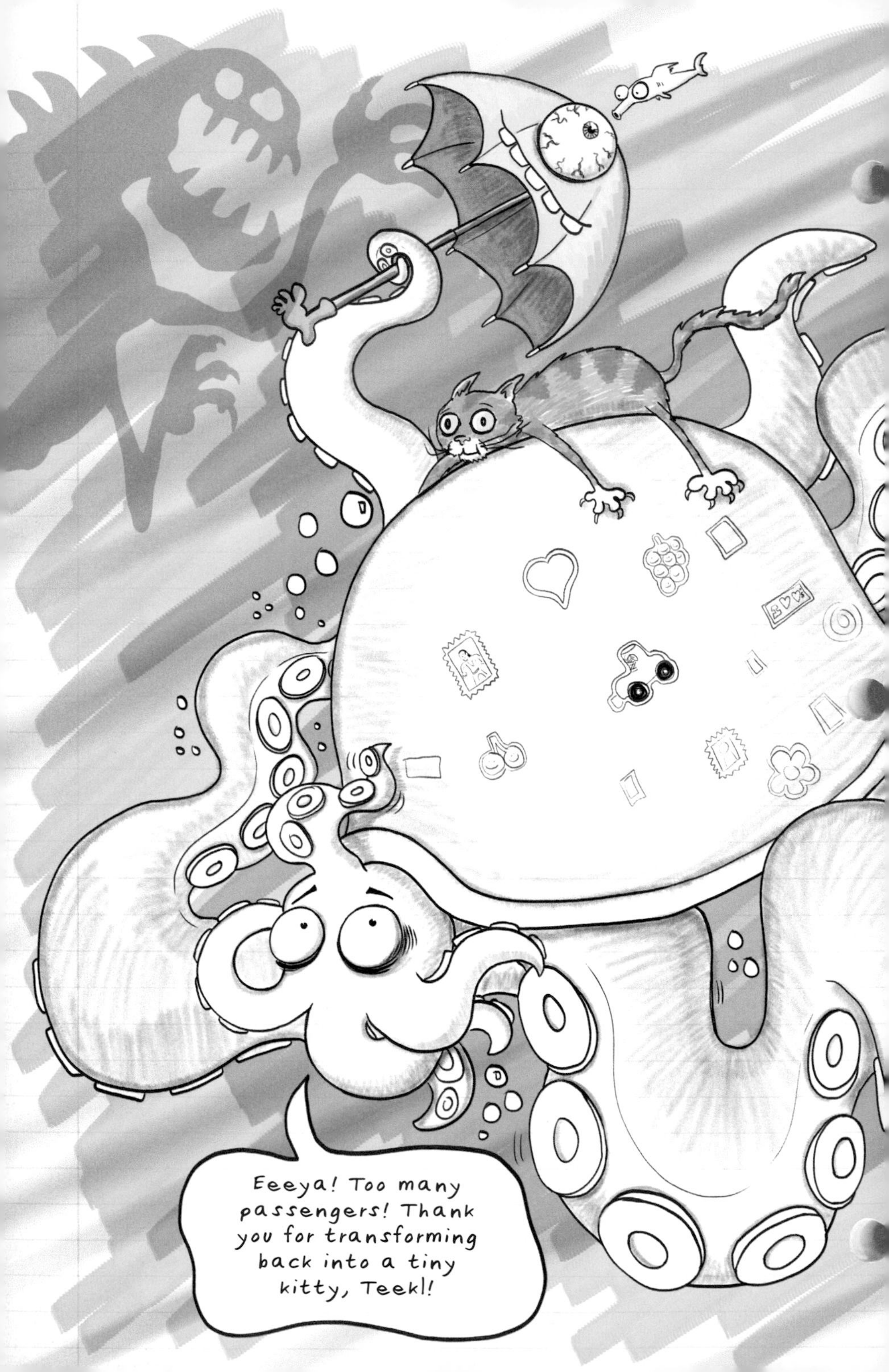
Eeeya! Too many passengers! Thank you for transforming back into a tiny kitty, Teekl!

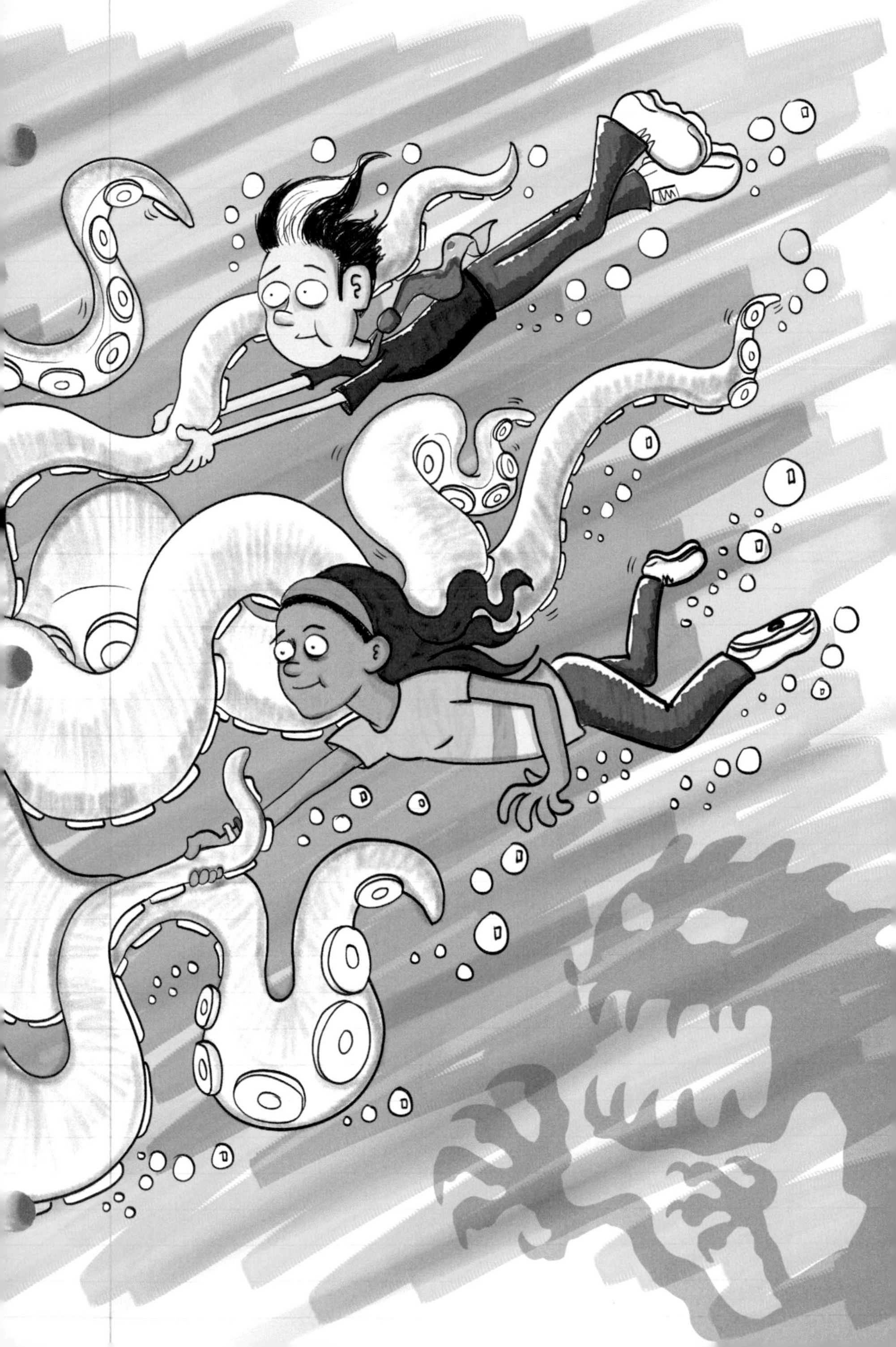

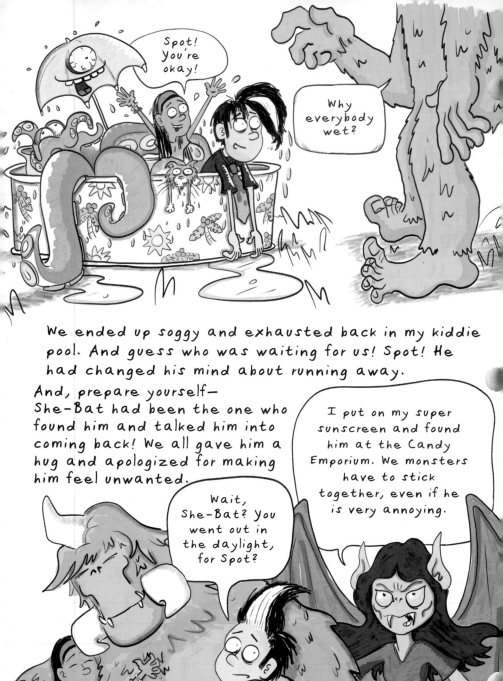

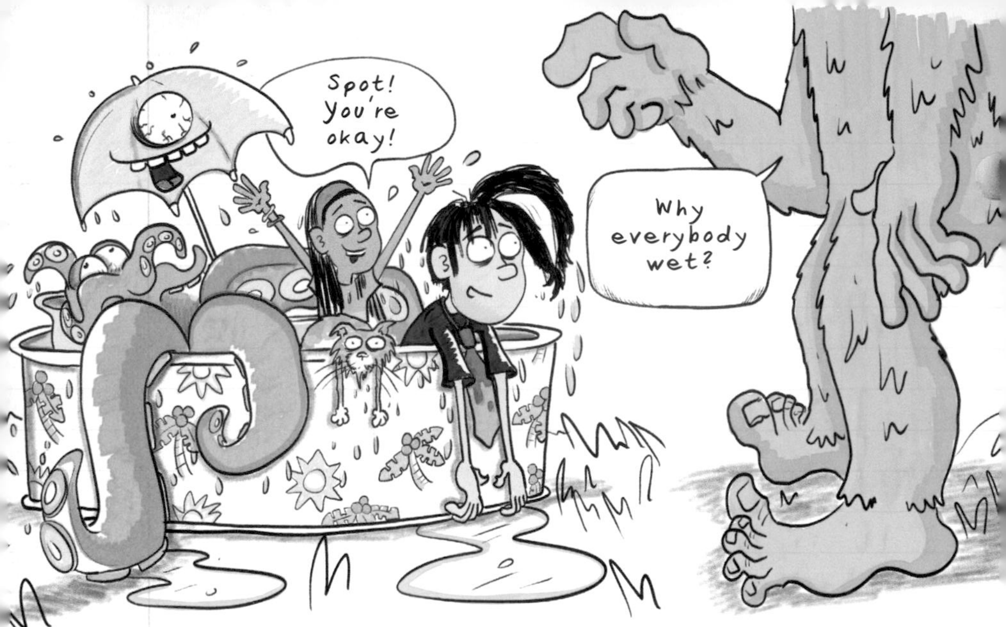
Spot! You're okay!
Why everybody wet?

We ended up soggy and exhausted back in my kiddie pool. And guess who was waiting for us! Spot! He had changed his mind about running away.

And, prepare yourself—
She-Bat had been the one who found him and talked him into coming back! We all gave him a hug and apologized for making him feel unwanted.

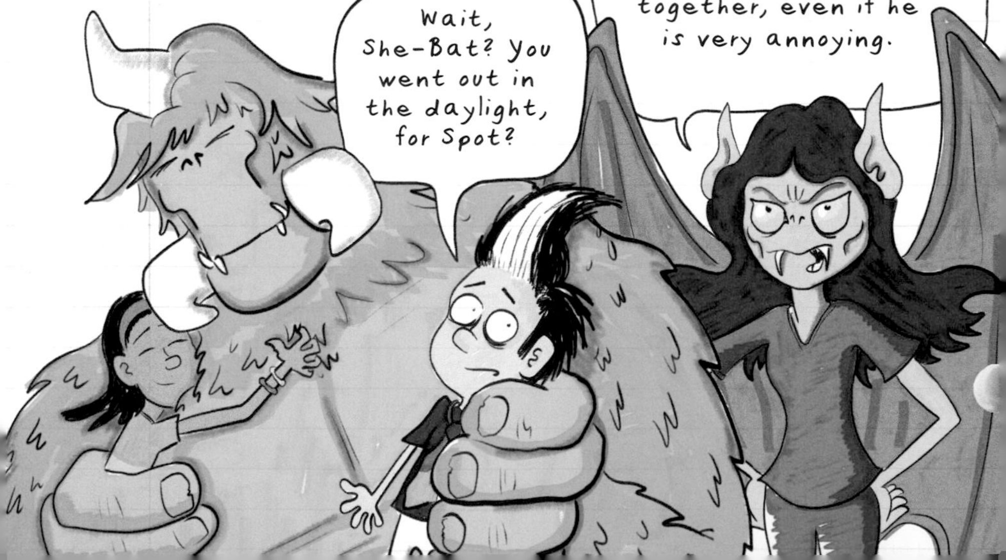
I put on my super sunscreen and found him at the Candy Emporium. We monsters have to stick together, even if he is very annoying.
Wait, She-Bat? You went out in the daylight, for Spot?

8:44 P.M.

Zandra and Teekl and Obake are staying in the tree house tonight. It's just for tonight then we move to the pier. Hope Dad doesn't wander out here.

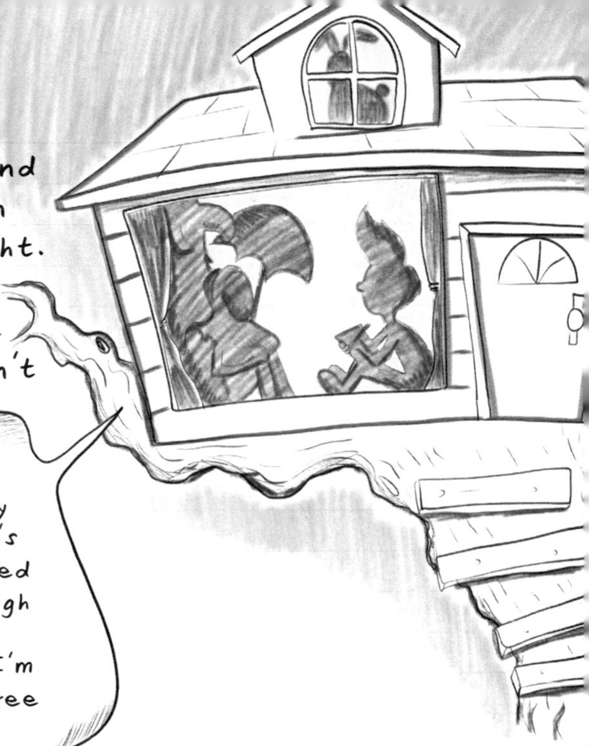
Spot and Teekl and Obake were my cellmates in Faust's awful prison. We helped each other get through it and busted out together. Someday I'm going back there to free everyone in his... collection.

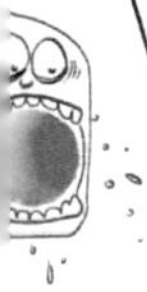

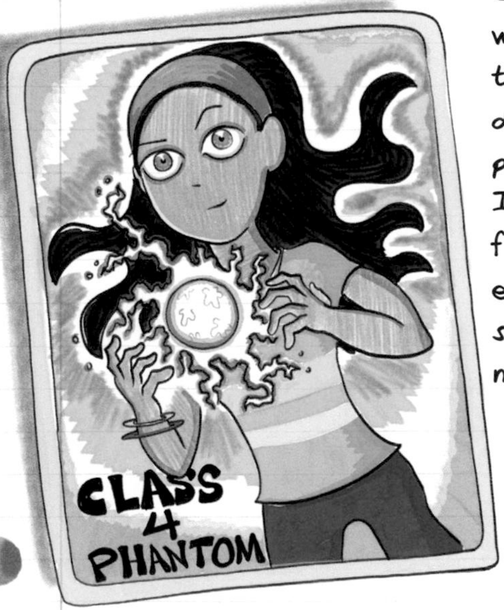
CLASS 4 PHANTOM

Turns out Zandra is a Class 4 Phantom...a ghost with gumption, just like the card in her monster deck. Not sure what her powers are exactly, but I just witnessed her flying and hurling electricity, so she sure has me beat.

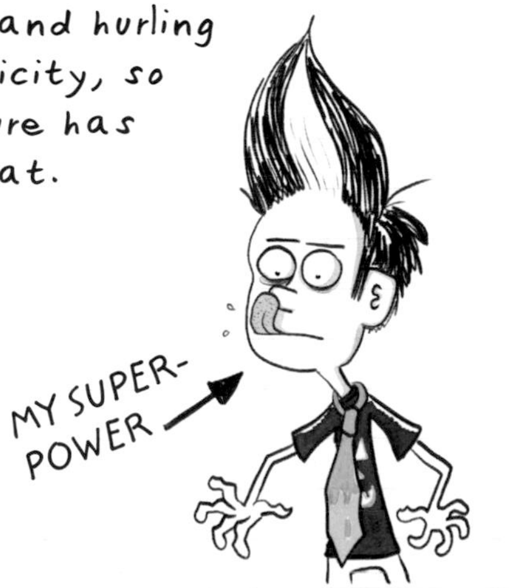
MY SUPER-POWER

This Faust dude sounds like a nightmare. Every night he would feed off the powers of his prisoners.

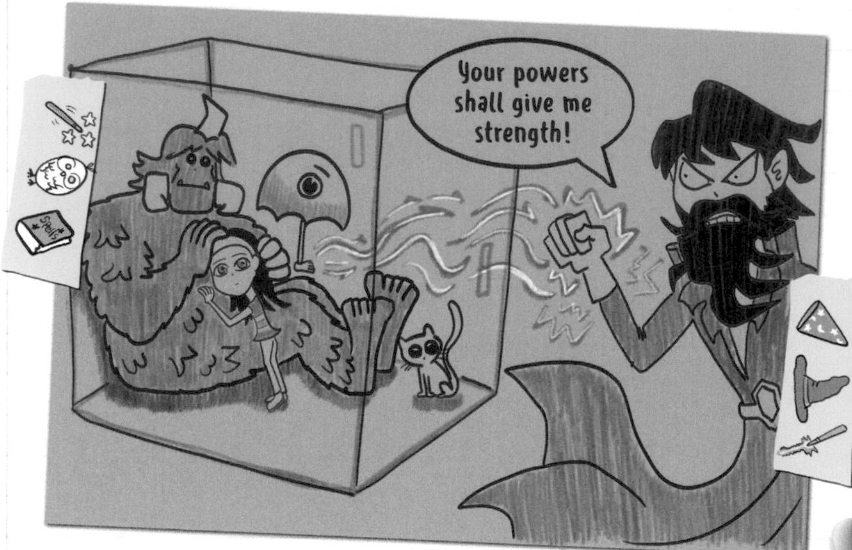
Spells
Your powers shall give me strength!

From the sound of it, he preferred Zandra's energy. No wonder he sent ol' orby out to find her. I wanted to hear more about Zandra's life and, uh, afterlife, but I could tell it was getting her down.

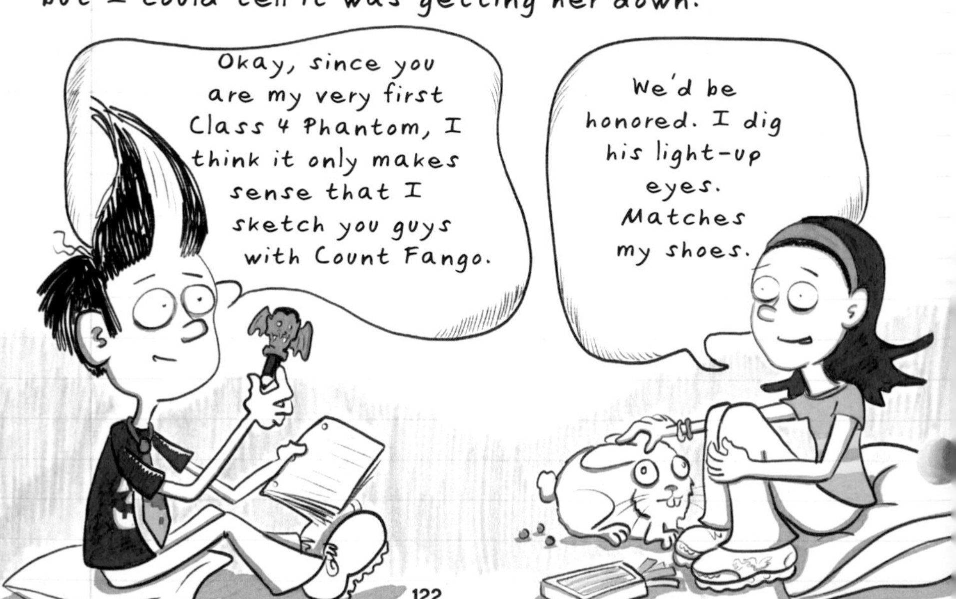
Okay, since you are my very first Class 4 Phantom, I think it only makes sense that I sketch you guys with Count Fango.
We'd be honored. I dig his light-up eyes. Matches my shoes.

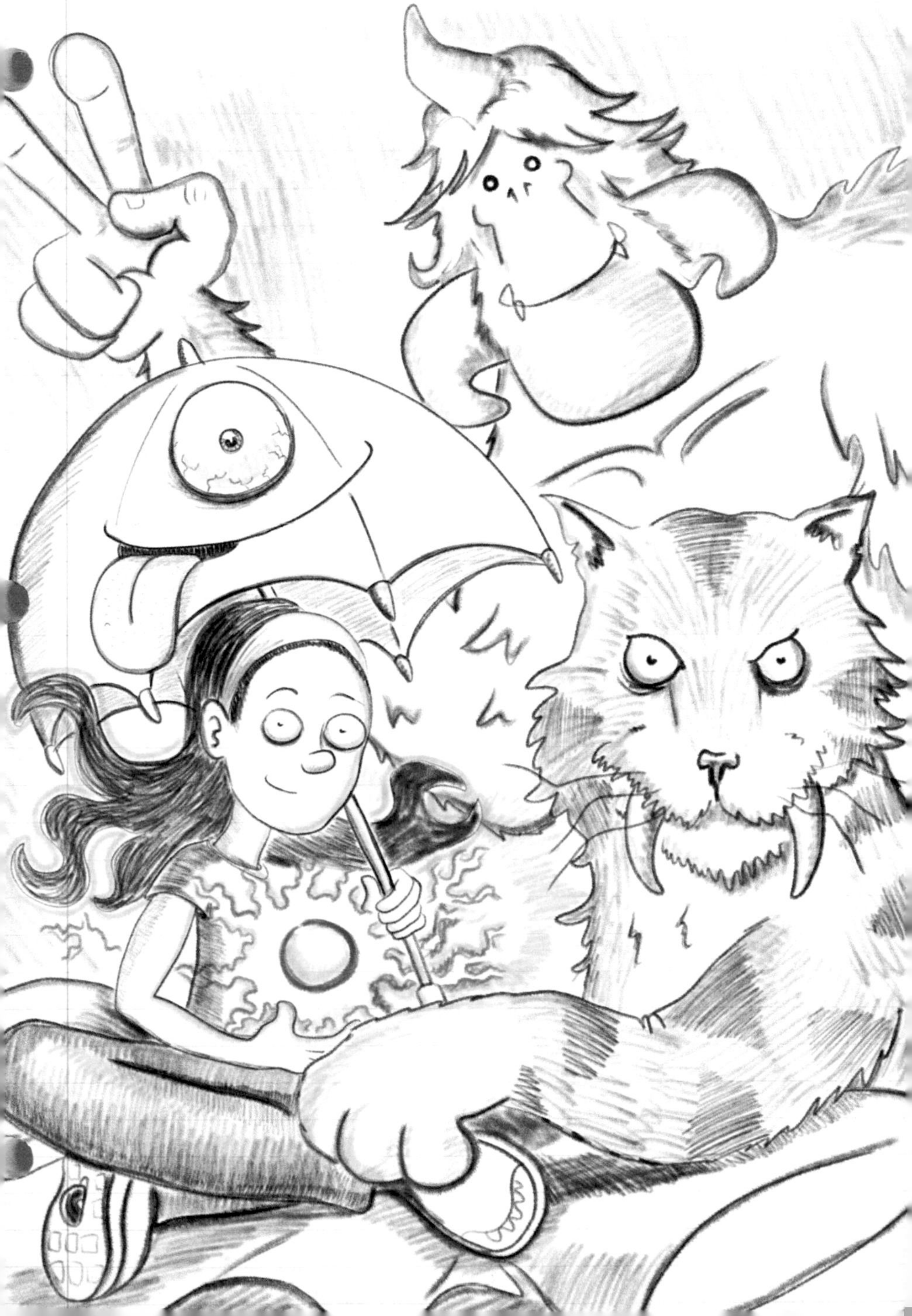

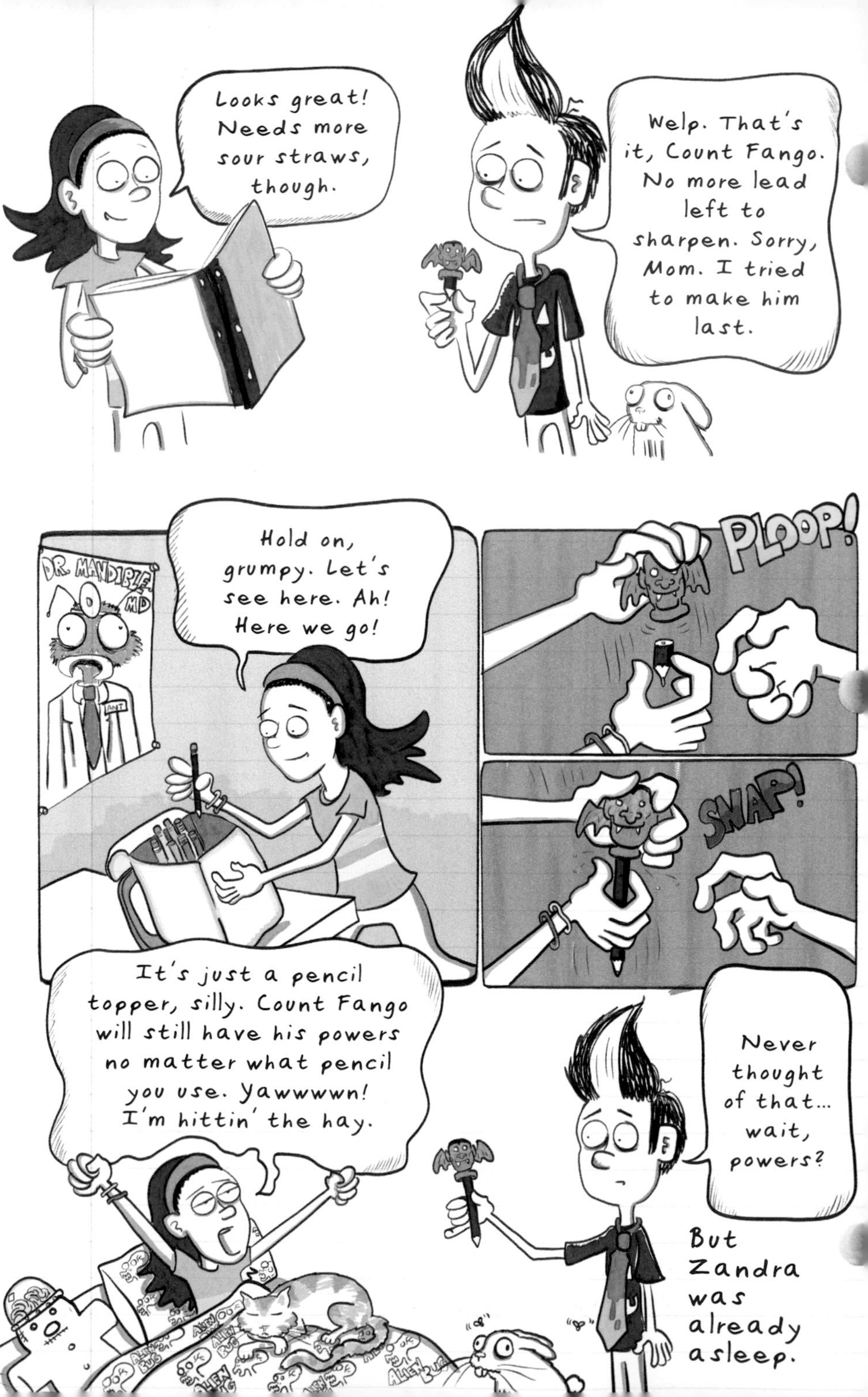
Looks great! Needs more sour straws, though.
Welp. That's it, Count Fango. No more lead left to sharpen. Sorry, Mom. I tried to make him last.
DR. MANDIBLE, MD
Hold on, grumpy. Let's see here. Ah! Here we go!
PLOOP!
SNAP!
It's just a pencil topper, silly. Count Fango will still have his powers no matter what pencil you use. Yawwwwn! I'm hittin' the hay.
Never thought of that... wait, powers?
But Zandra was already asleep.

9:30 P.M.

A lot to think about and chew on tonight. Nothing is what it seems. At least Ygor is here for me.

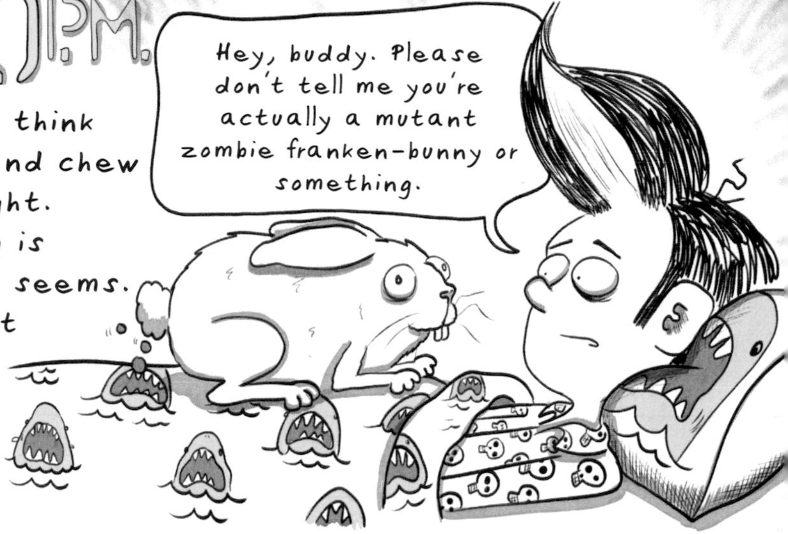
Hey, buddy. Please don't tell me you're actually a mutant zombie franken-bunny or something.

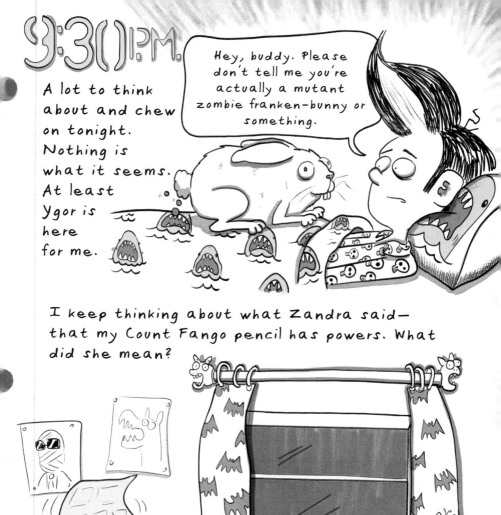

I keep thinking about what Zandra said— that my Count Fango pencil has powers. What did she mean?

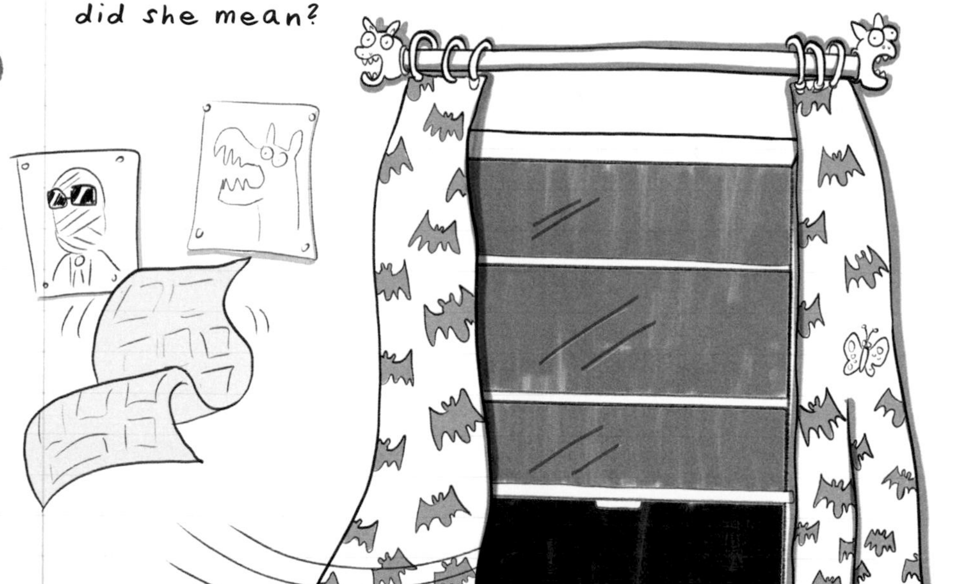

Something just blew in through the window. Another purple piece of paper.

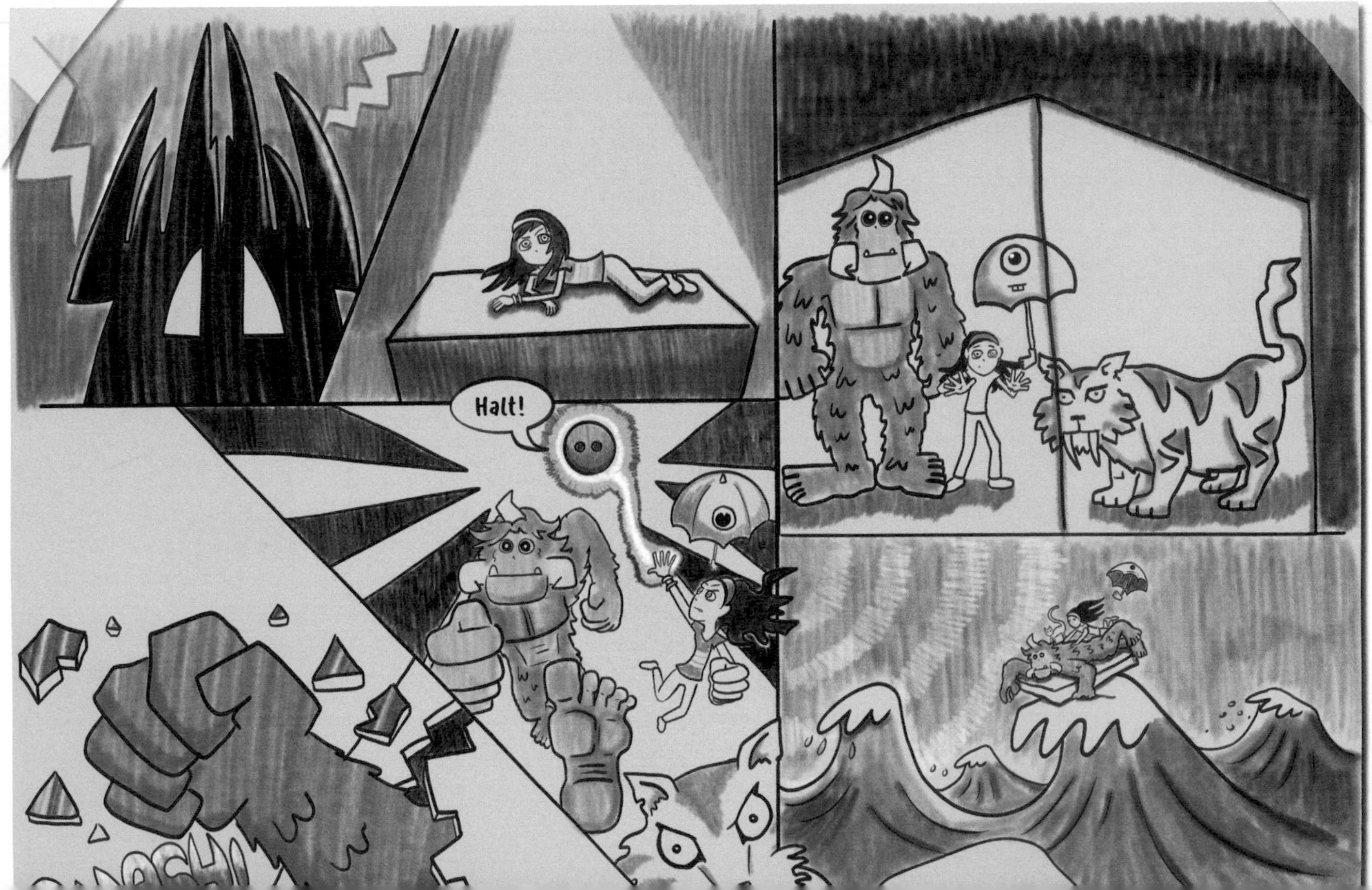
Halt!

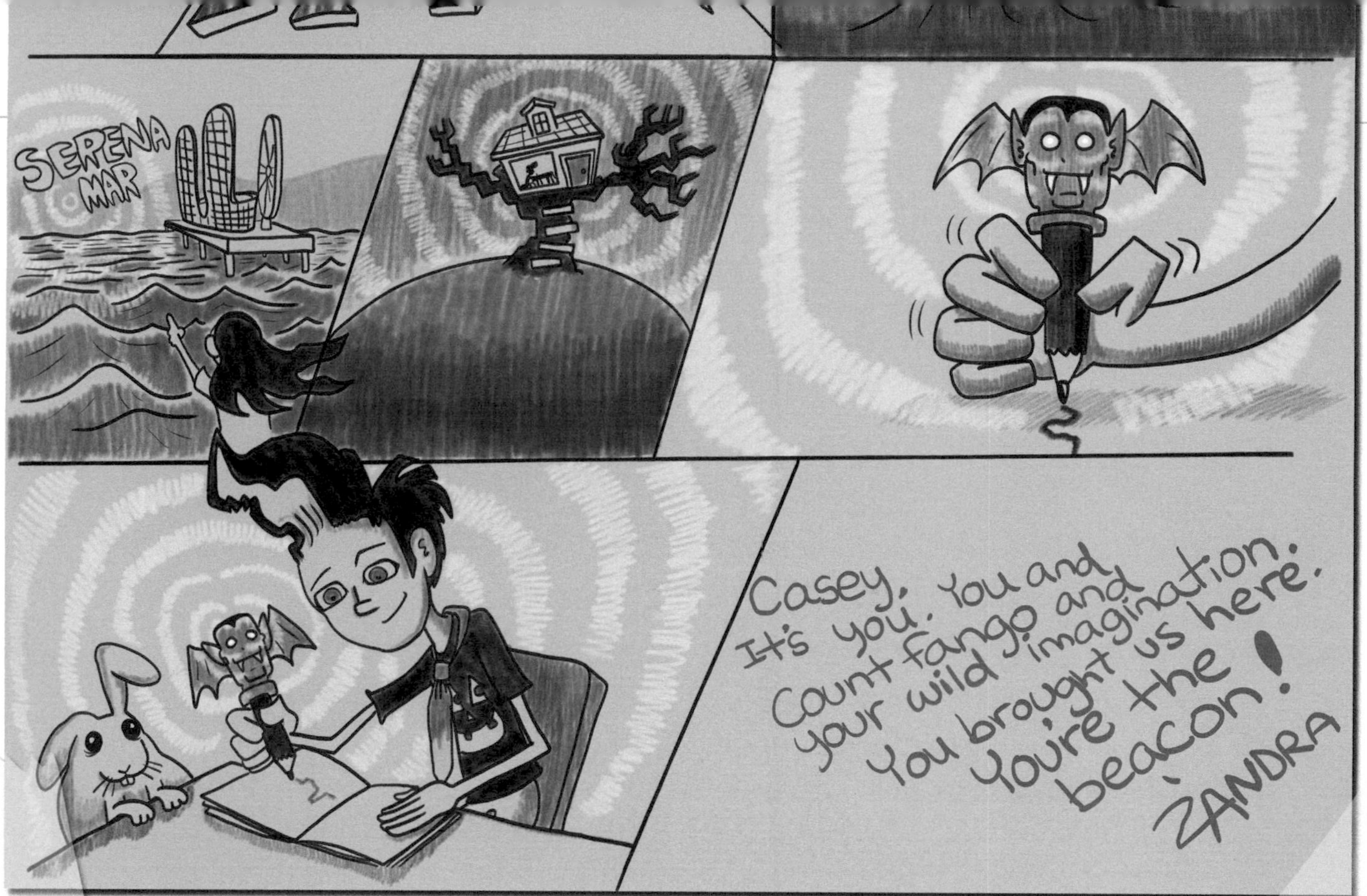
SERENA MAR
Casey, You and Count Fango and
It's you. your wild imagination.
You brought us here.
You're the beacon!
ZANDRA

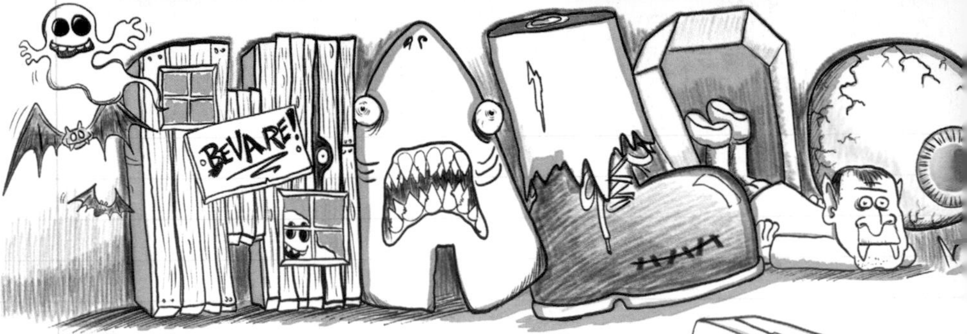
BEVARE!

8:01 A.M.

It's officially Halloween! Or, as I call it, All Hallow's Morn. Starting off the day with my traditional limited-edition Candy Corn Coco Crypt. I only eat it once a year because, honestly, it's disgusting.

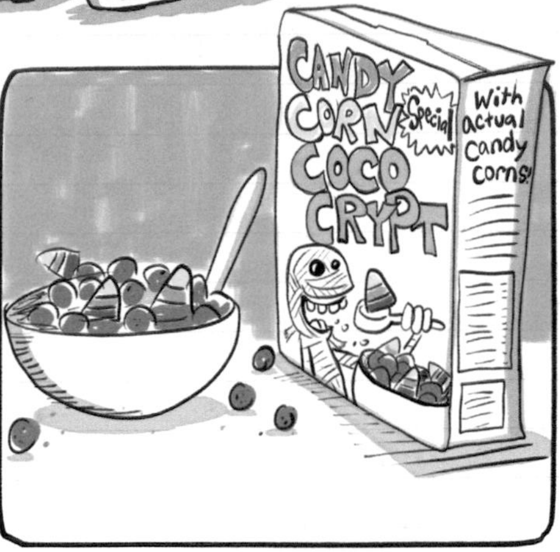
CANDY CORN COCO CRYPT
Special
With actual candy corns!

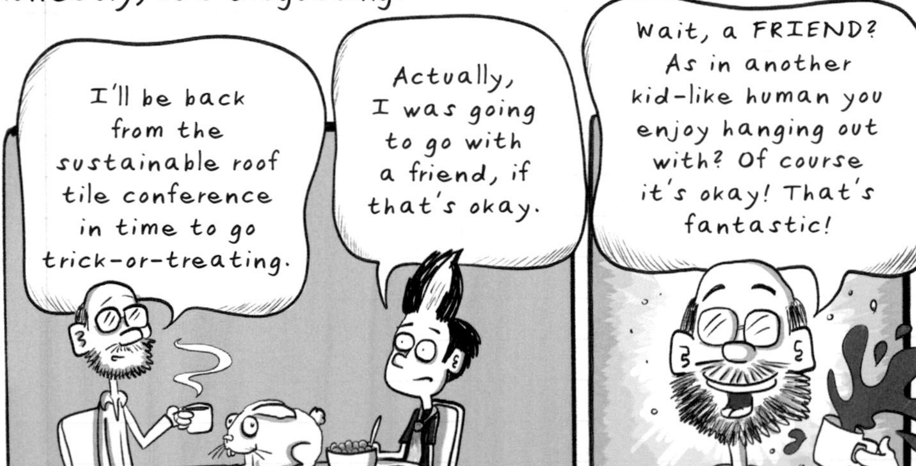
I'll be back from the sustainable roof tile conference in time to go trick-or-treating.
Actually, I was going to go with a friend, if that's okay.
Wait, a FRIEND? As in another kid-like human you enjoy hanging out with? Of course it's okay! That's fantastic!

I didn't tell him my new friend wasn't exactly human. Kid-like at least.

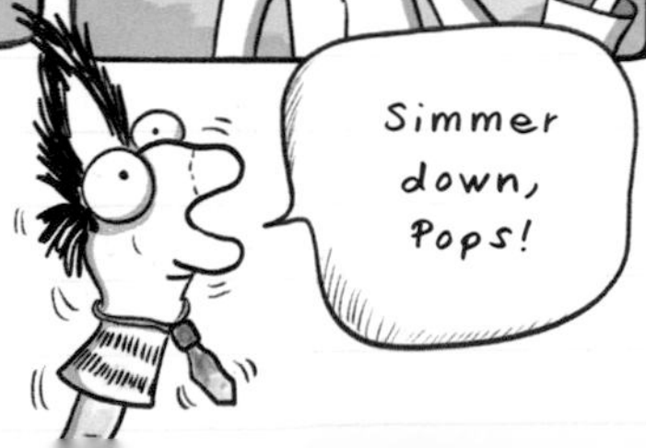
Simmer down, Pops!

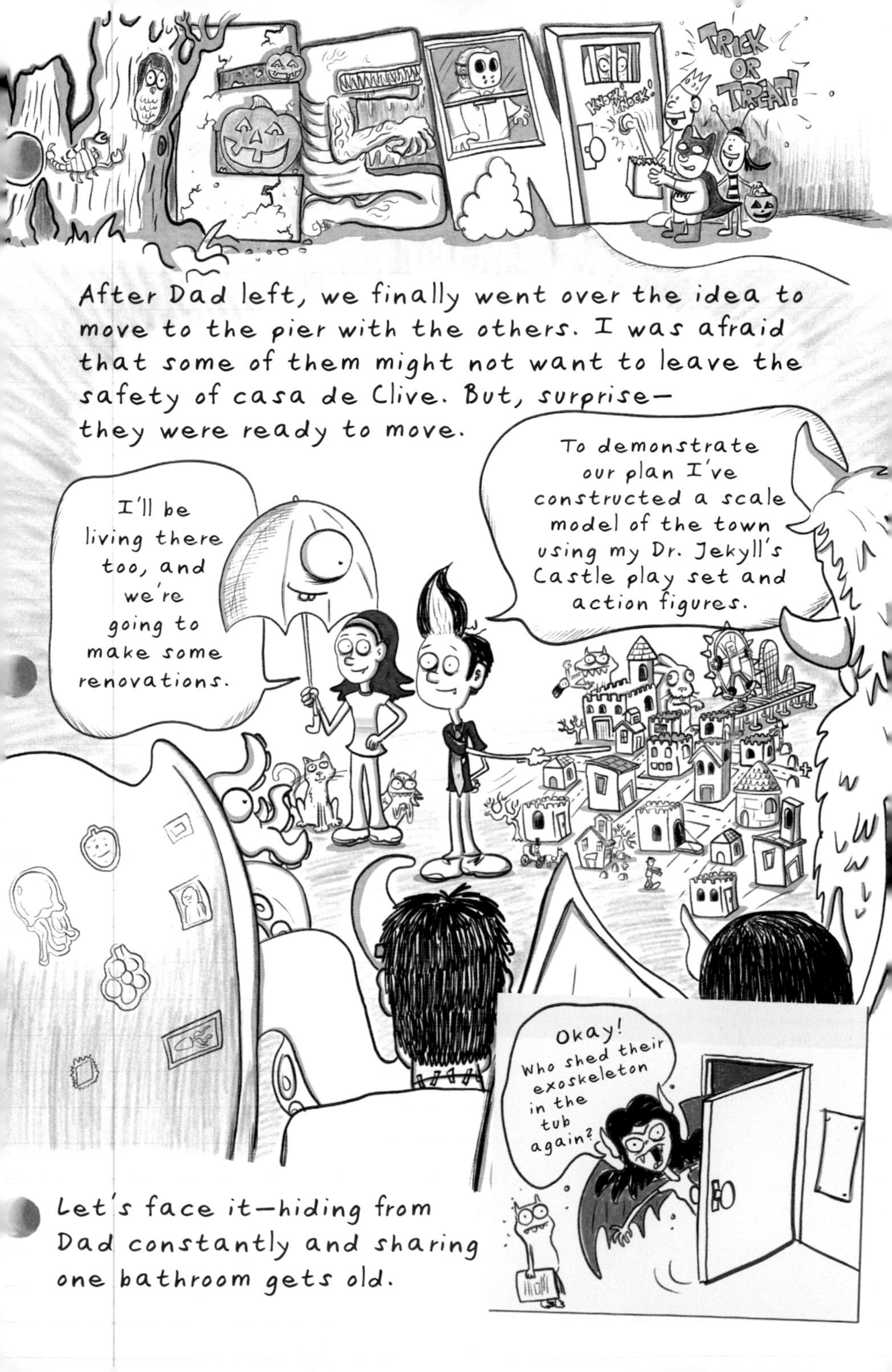
KNOCK! KNOCK!
TRICK OR TREAT!
After Dad left, we finally went over the idea to move to the pier with the others. I was afraid that some of them might not want to leave the safety of casa de Clive. But, surprise— they were ready to move.
I'll be living there too, and we're going to make some renovations.
To demonstrate our plan I've constructed a scale model of the town using my Dr. Jekyll's Castle play set and action figures.
Let's face it—hiding from Dad constantly and sharing one bathroom gets old.
Okay! Who shed their exoskeleton in the tub again?

7:35 P.M.

The sun has set. It's time to put on my finest haunting attire and get down to business. I'm keeping my costume simple this year. Just going as your common. everyday bloodsucker. (Don't tell She-Bat I said that.)

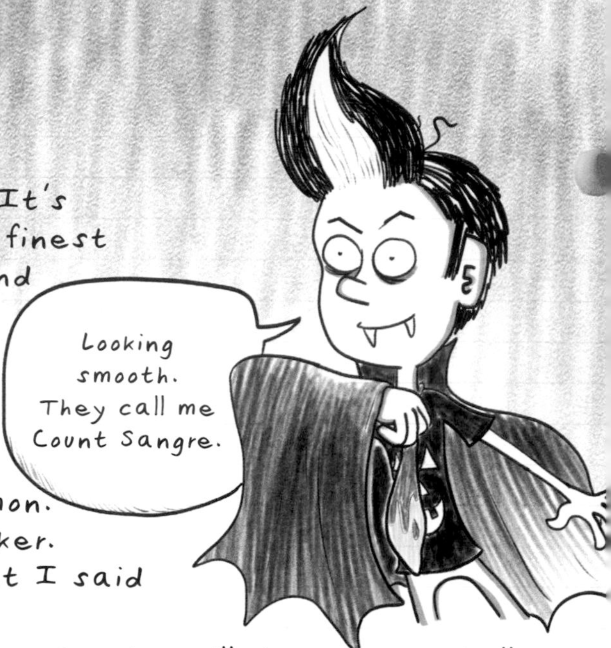
Looking smooth. They call me Count Sangre.

So, here's the plan. Zandra will ring the doorbell in ten minutes and I'll introduce her to Dad. He'll be way too excited and embarrass himself and me. He's bound to give us a curfew, but since I know he'll fall asleep on the couch after the last trick-or-treater, it'll be no big deal if we're late.

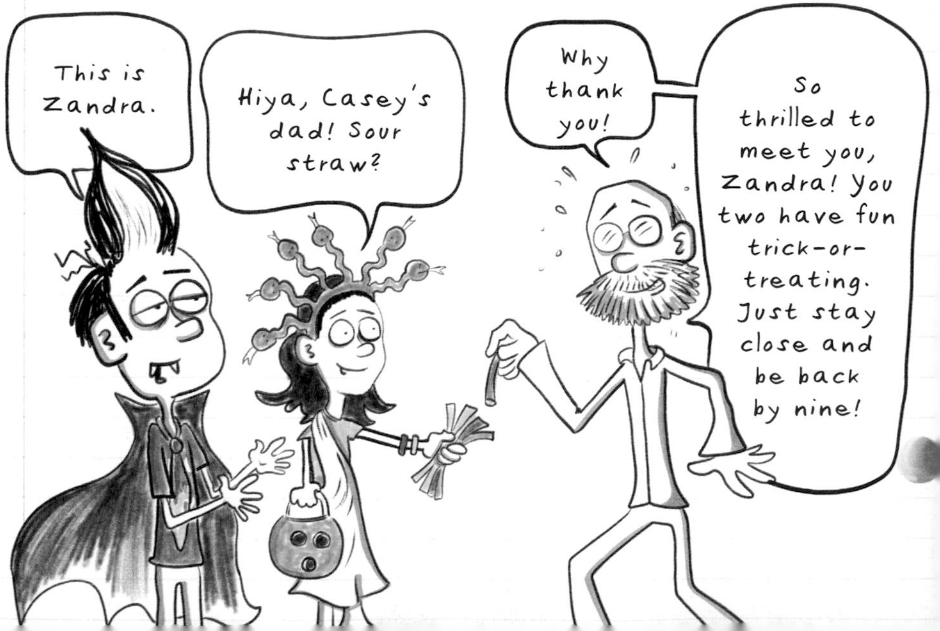
This is Zandra.
Hiya, Casey's dad! Sour straw?
Why thank you!
So thrilled to meet you, Zandra! You two have fun trick-or-treating. Just stay close and be back by nine!

Then, we'll meet up with the others around the back of the house and take off from there.

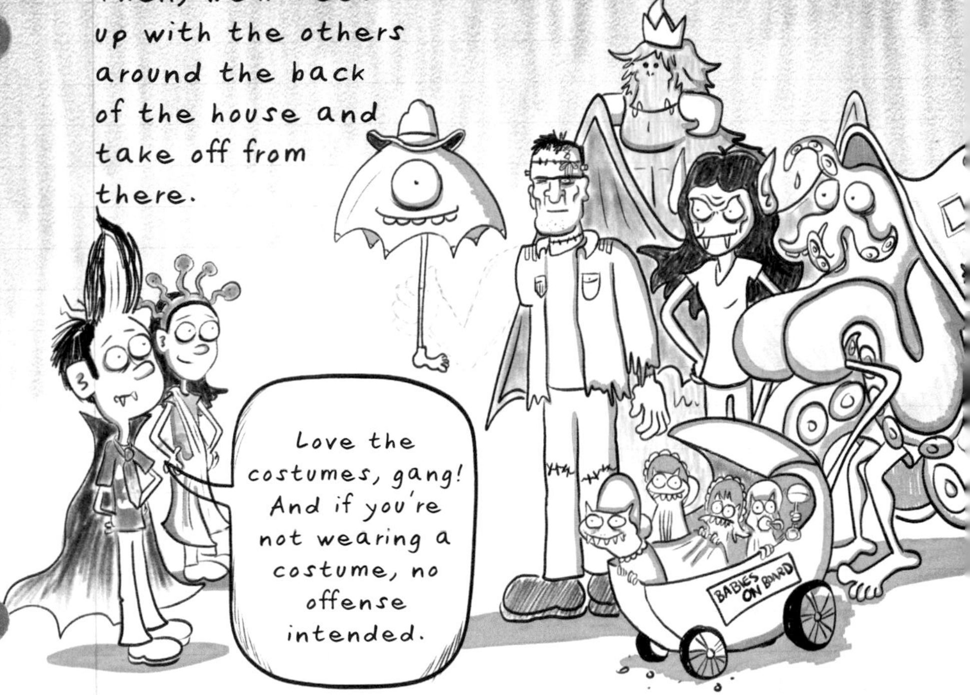
Love the costumes, gang! And if you're not wearing a costume, no offense intended.
BABIES ON BOARD

The zombie is coming too and he's dressed as an undead unicorn.

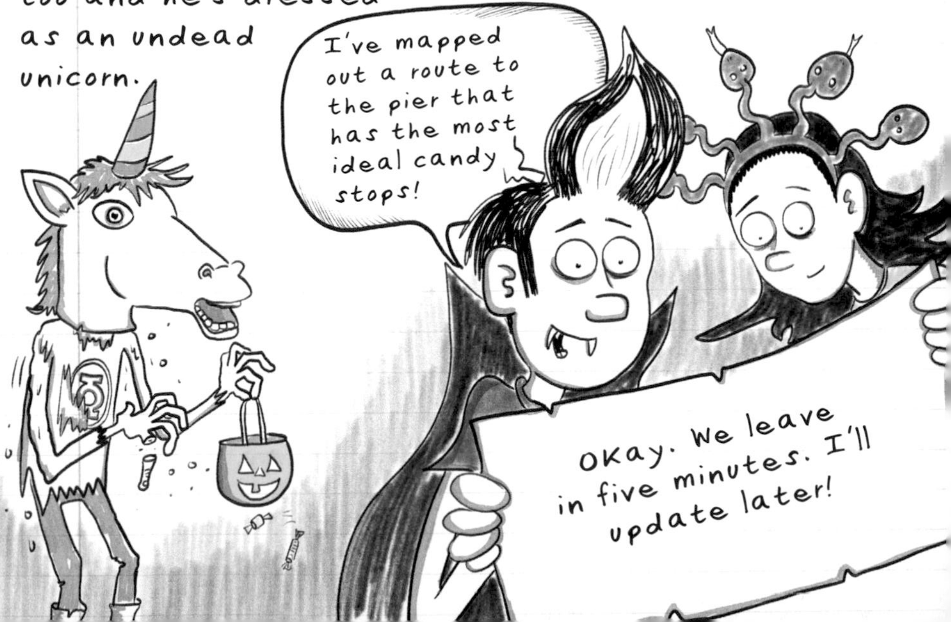
I've mapped out a route to the pier that has the most ideal candy stops!
Okay. We leave in five minutes. I'll update later!

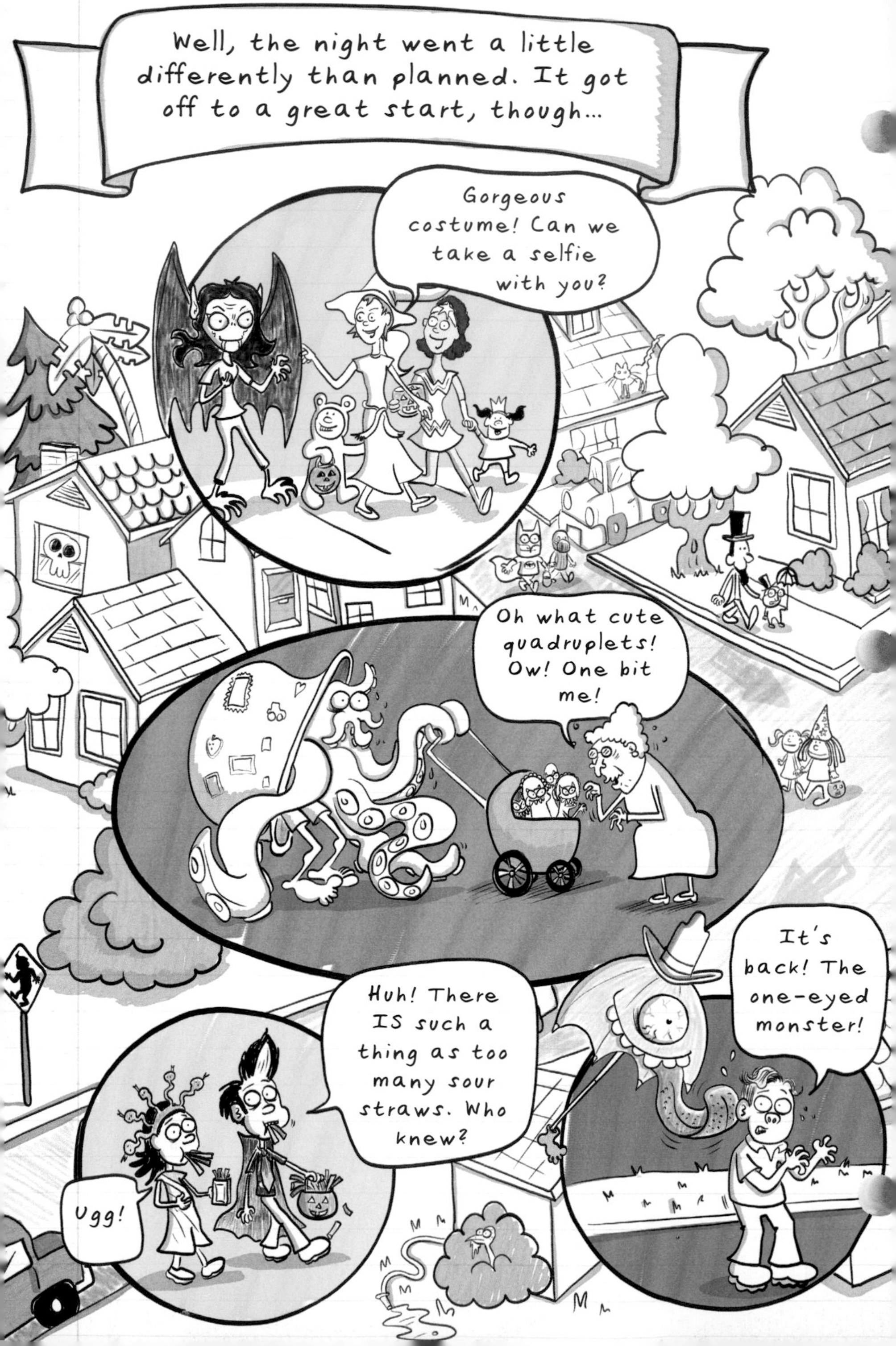
Well, the night went a little differently than planned. It got off to a great start, though...
Gorgeous costume! Can we take a selfie with you?
Oh what cute quadruplets! Ow! One bit me!
Huh! There IS such a thing as too many sour straws. Who knew?
Ugg!
It's back! The one-eyed monster!

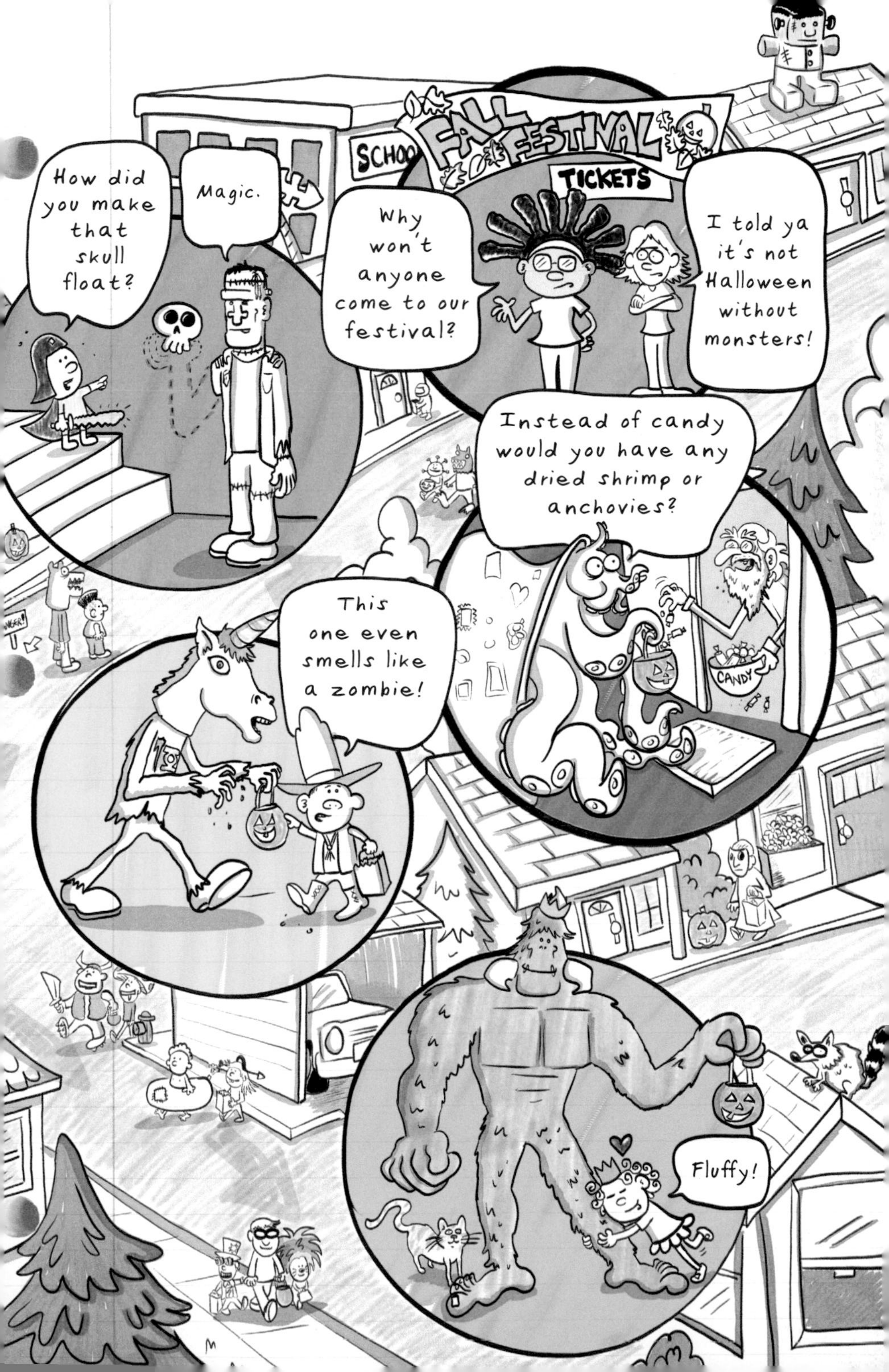
SCHOO
FALL FESTIVAL
TICKETS
How did you make that skull float?
Magic.
Why won't anyone come to our festival?
I told ya it's not Halloween without monsters!
Instead of candy would you have any dried shrimp or anchovies?
CANDY
This one even smells like a zombie!
Fluffy!

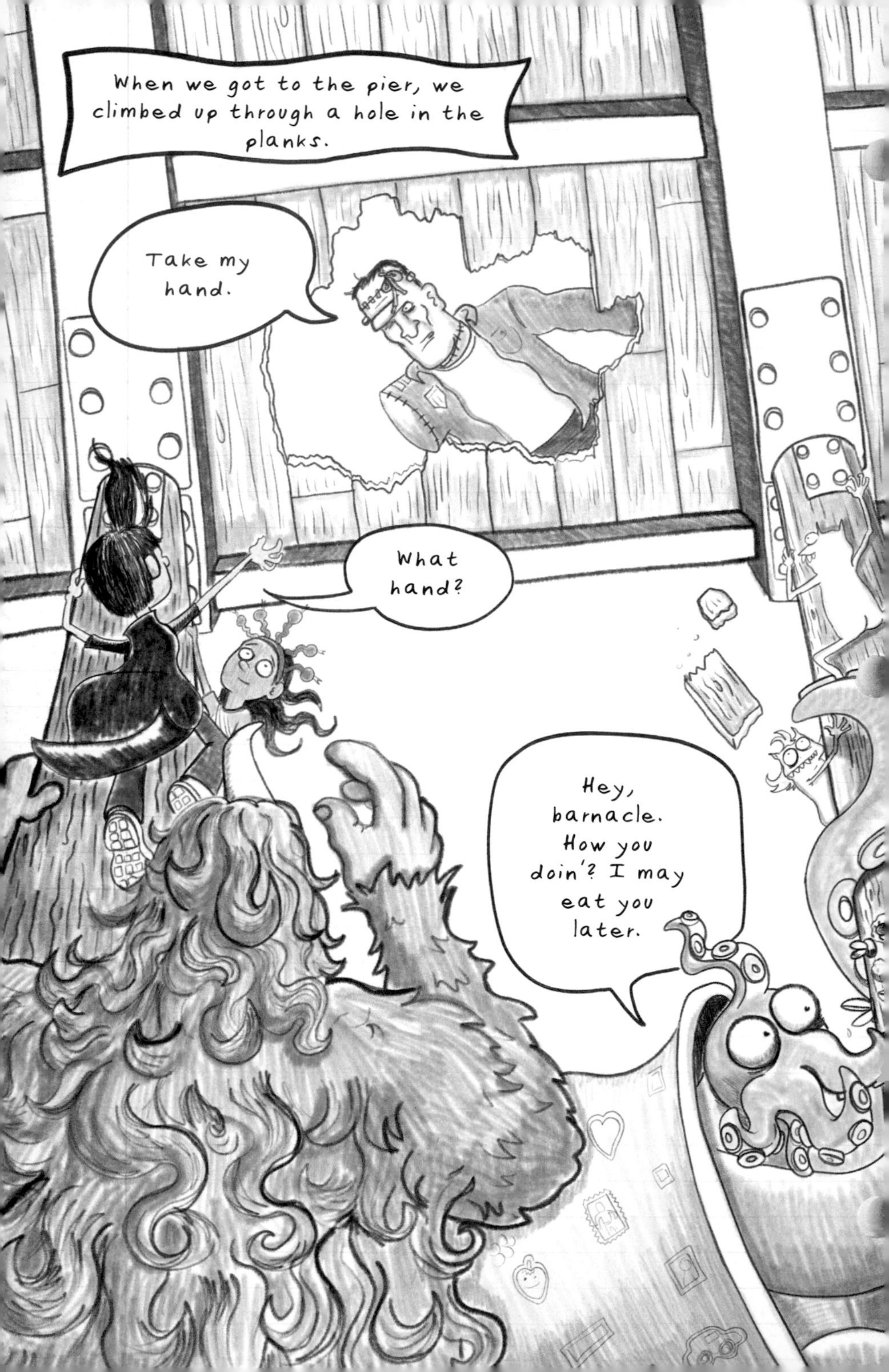
When we got to the pier, we climbed up through a hole in the planks.
Take my hand.
What hand?
Hey, barnacle. How you doin'? I may eat you later.

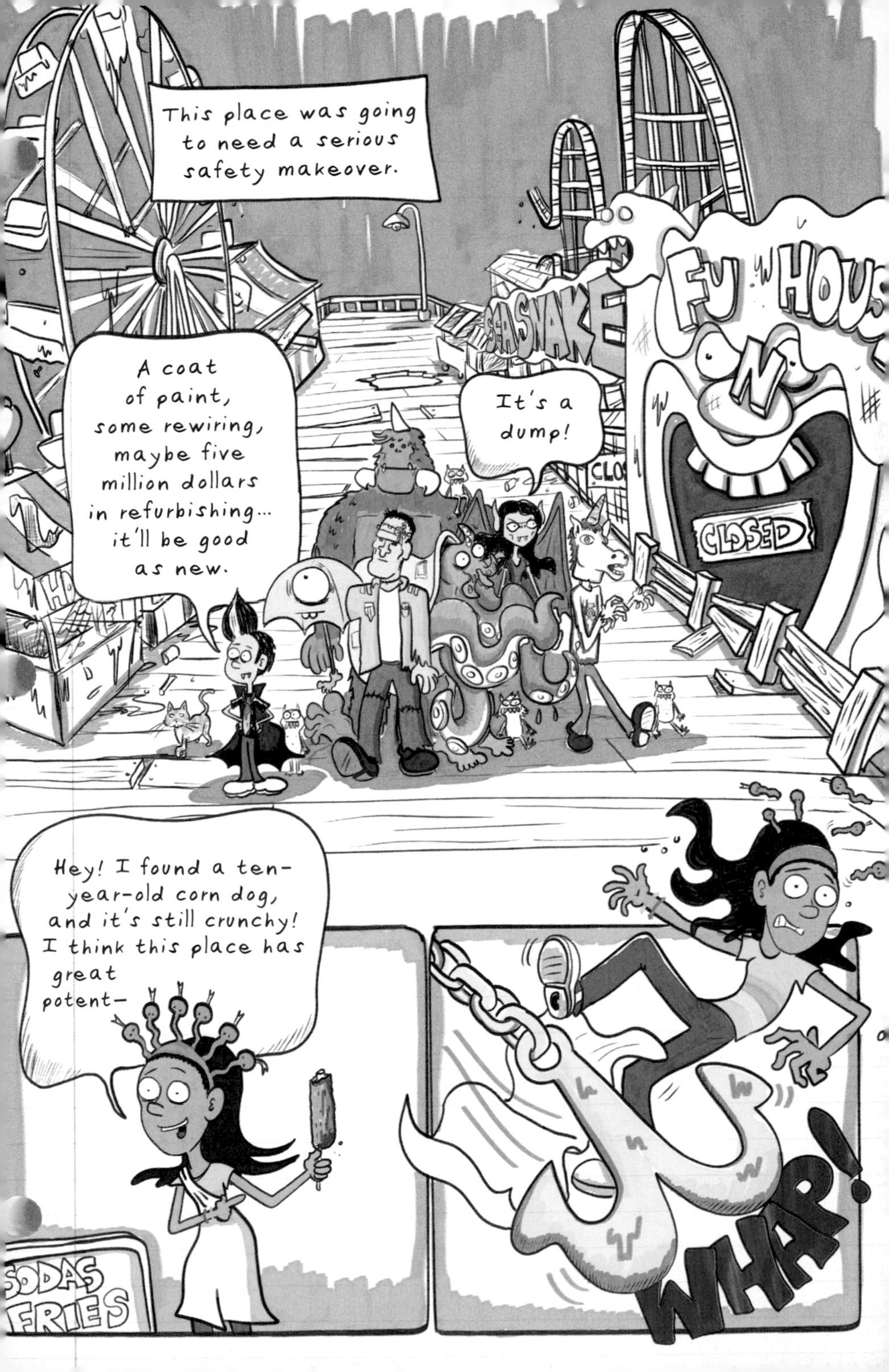
This place was going to need a serious safety makeover.
SEASNAKE
FUN HOUSE
A coat of paint, some rewiring, maybe five million dollars in refurbishing... it'll be good as new.
It's a dump!
CLOSED
Hey! I found a ten-year-old corn dog, and it's still crunchy! I think this place has great potent—
SODAS FRIES
WHAP!

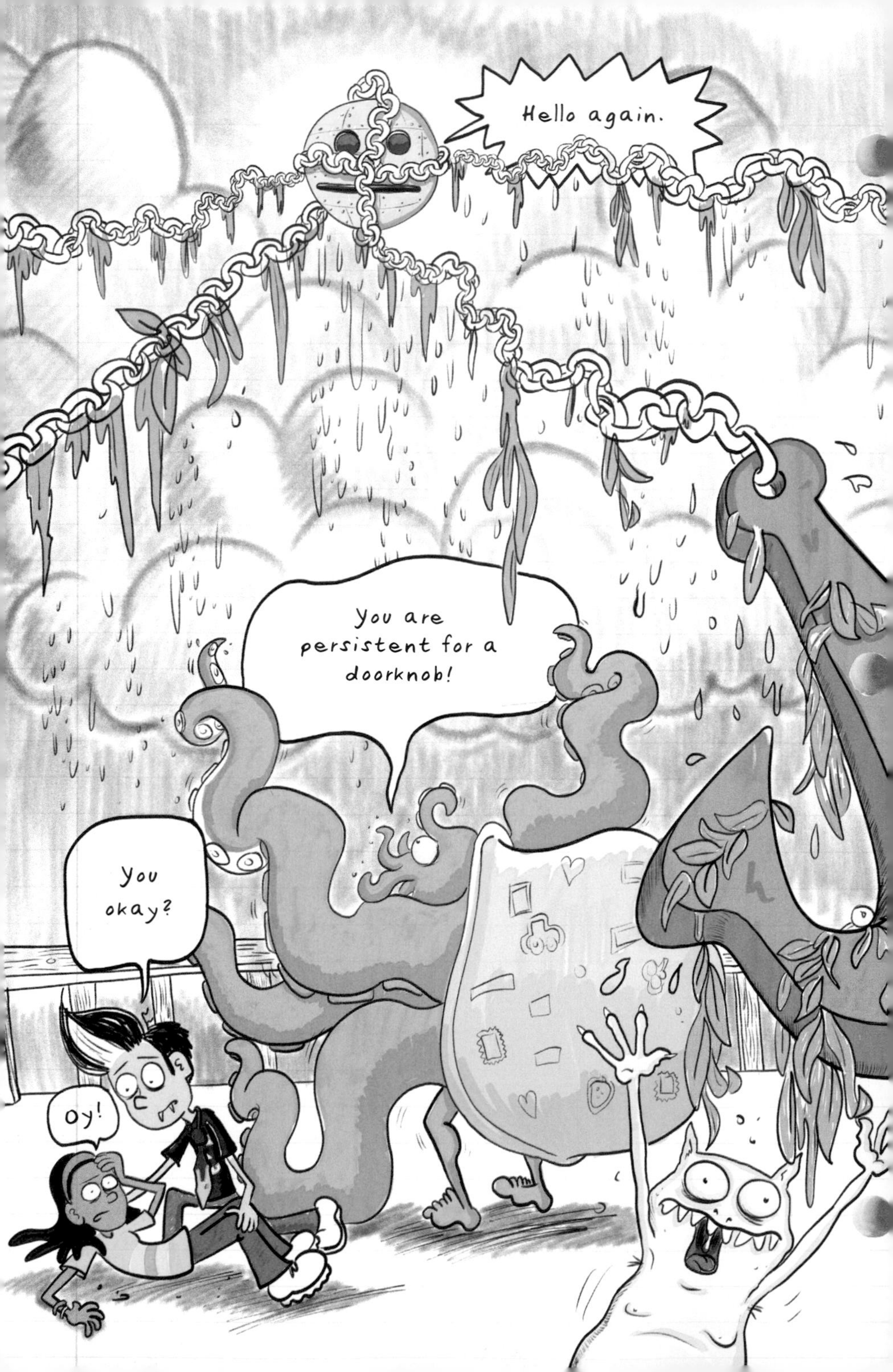
Hello again.
You are persistent for a doorknob!
You okay?
Oy!

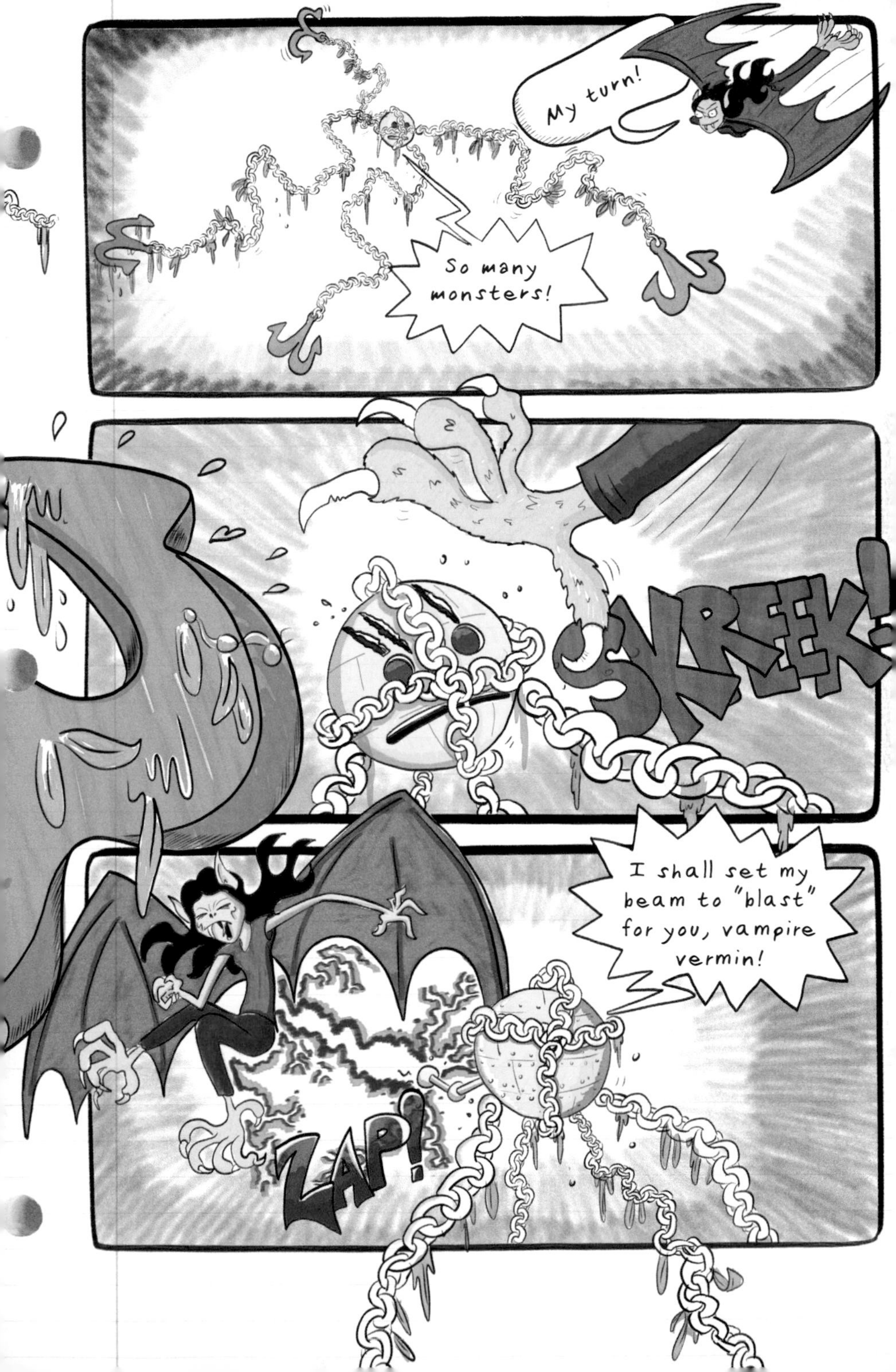
My turn!
So many monsters!
SKREEK!
I shall set my beam to "blast" for you, vampire vermin!
ZAP!

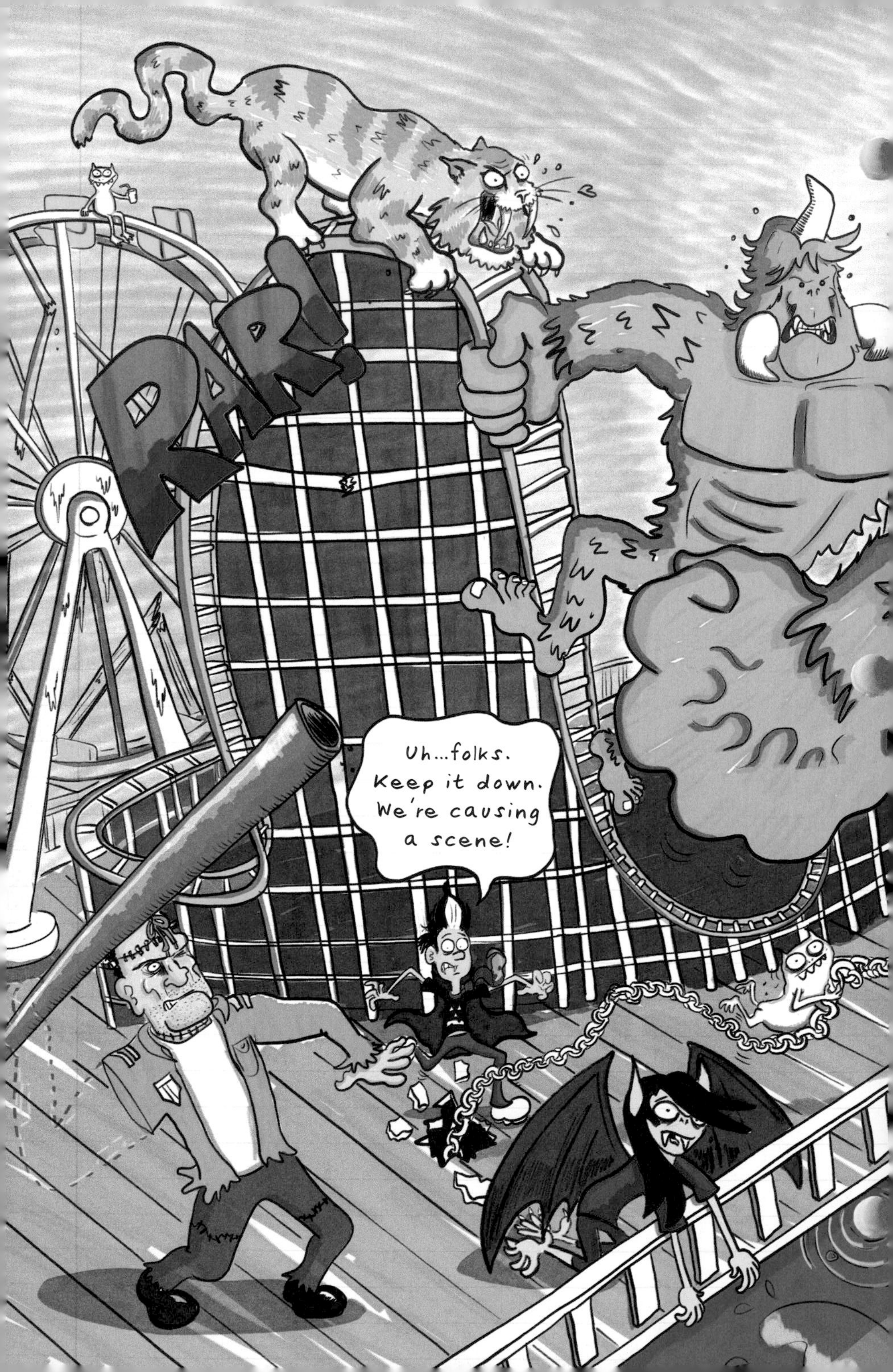
RAR!
Uh...folks. Keep it down. We're causing a scene!

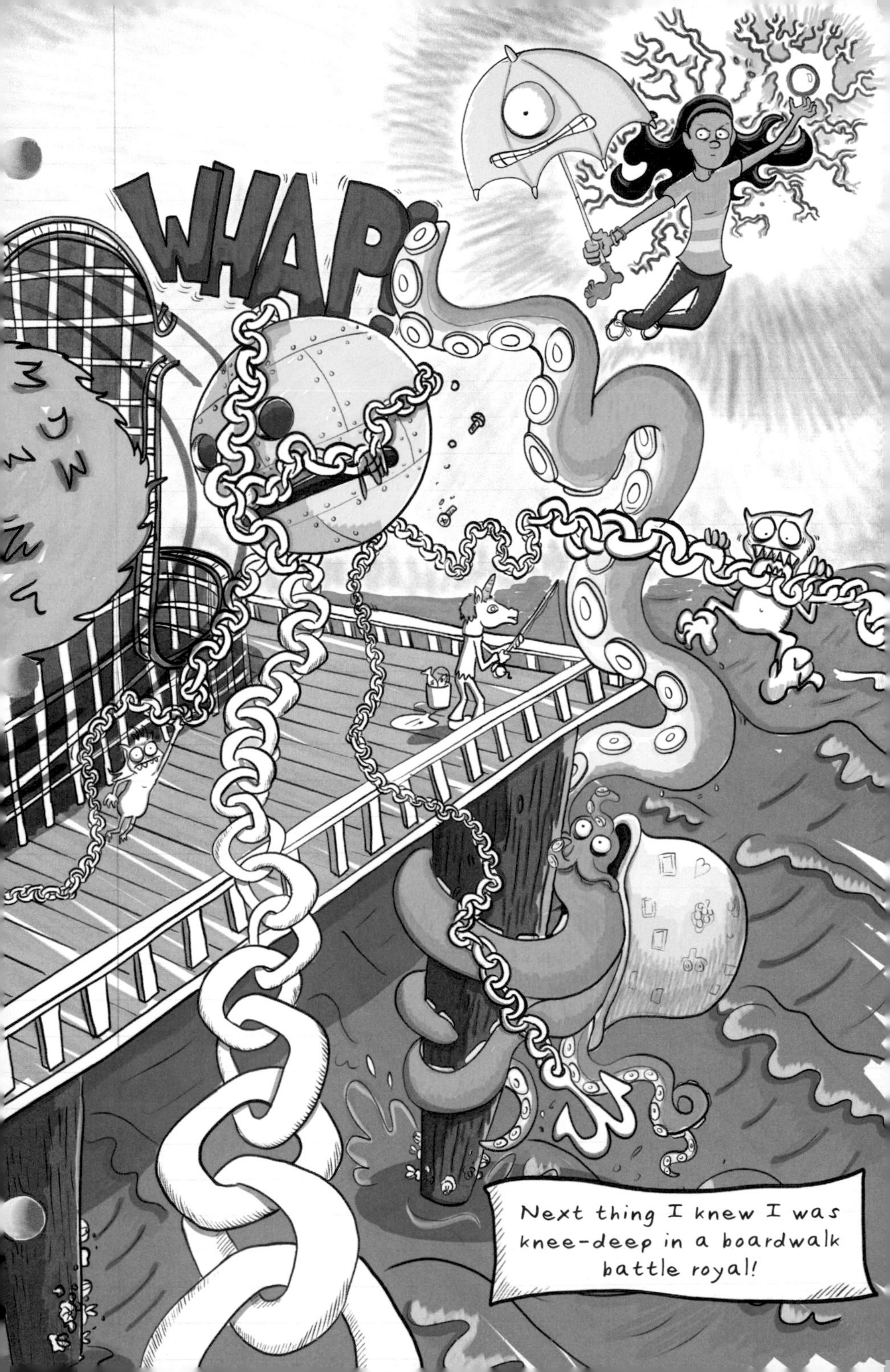
WHAP!
MWUMMWNW
Next thing I knew I was knee-deep in a boardwalk battle royal!

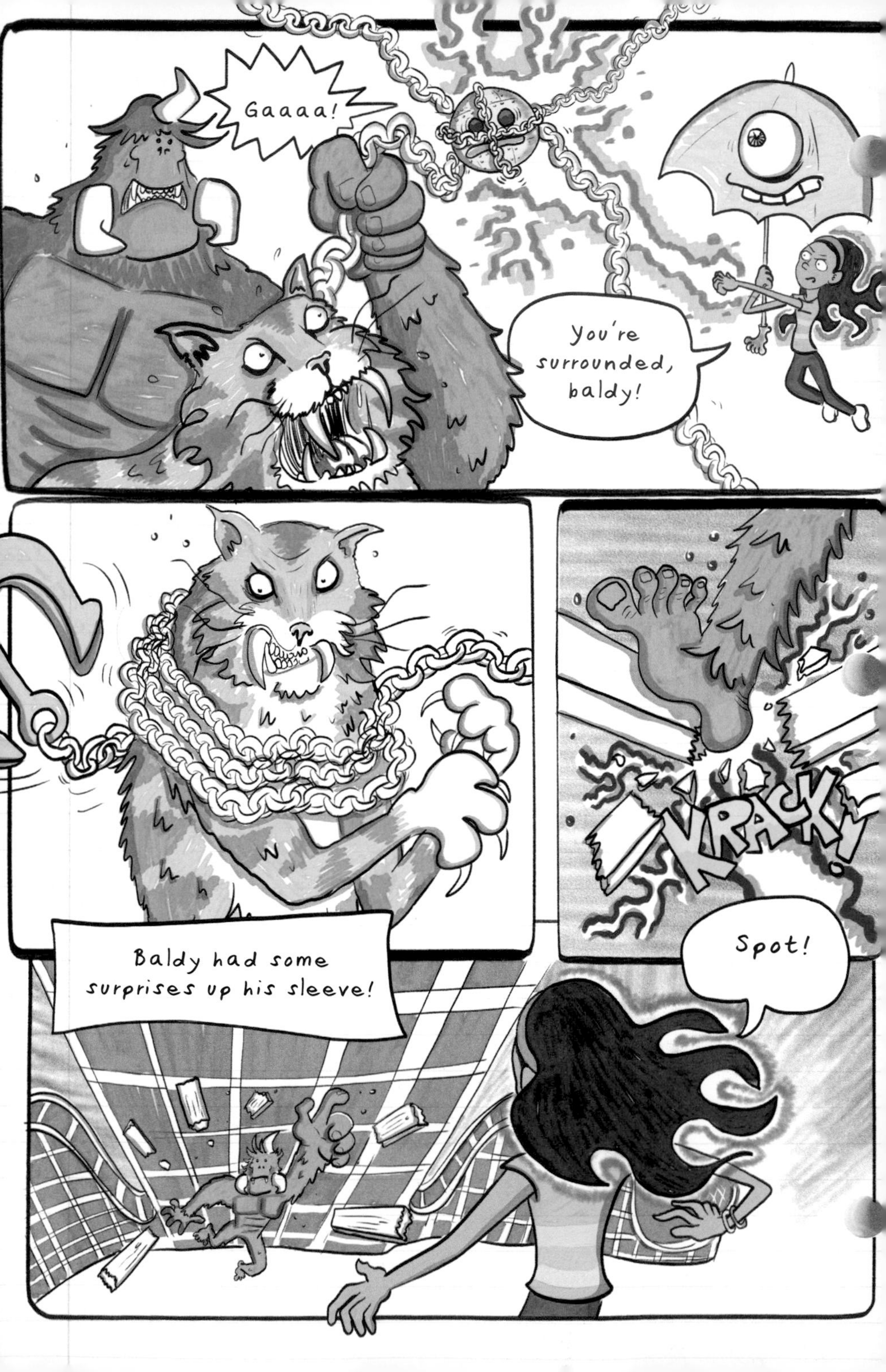
Gaaaa!
You're surrounded, baldy!
KRACK!
Baldy had some surprises up his sleeve!
Spot!

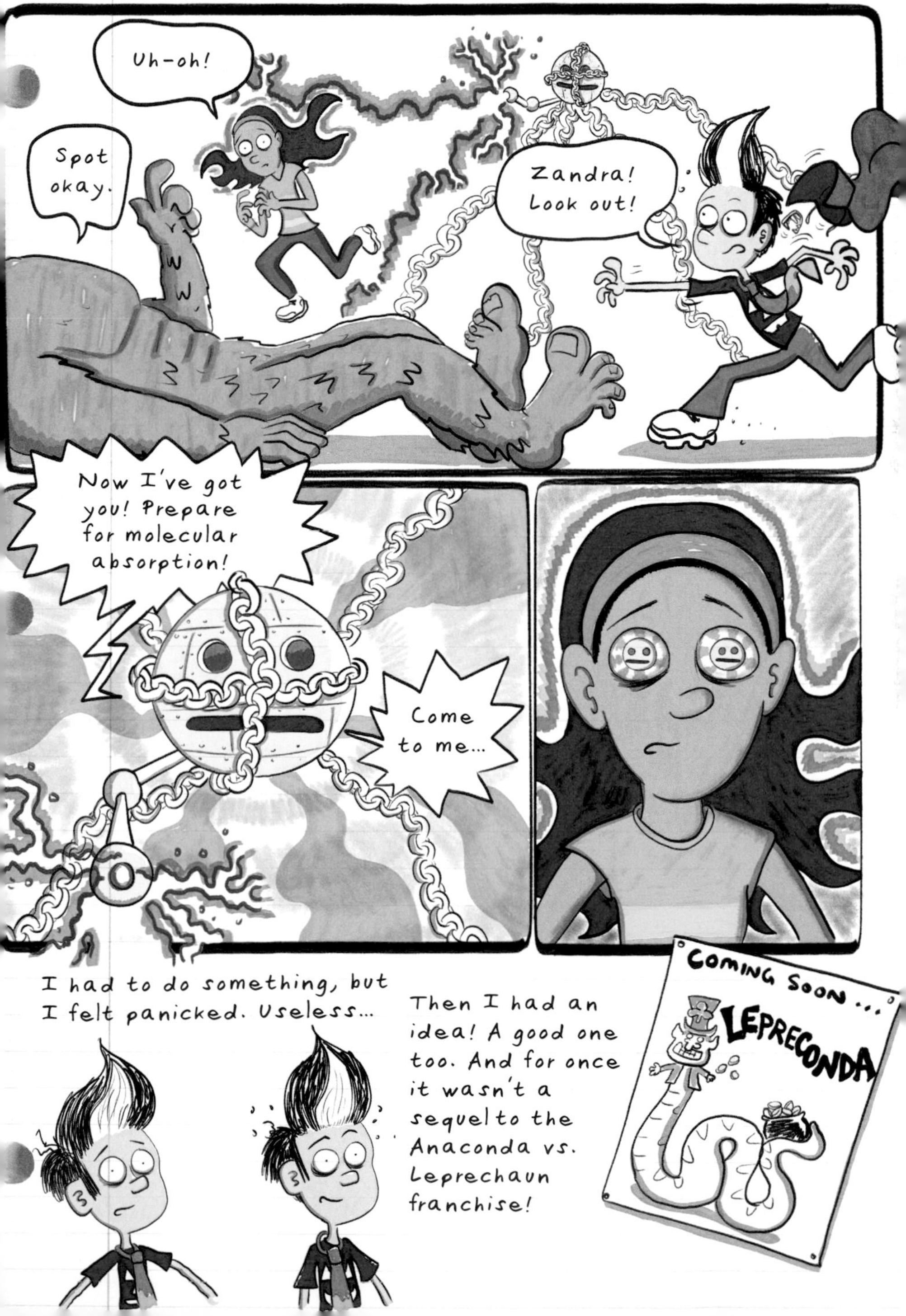
Uh-oh!
Spot okay.
Zandra! Look out!
Now I've got you! Prepare for molecular absorption!
Come to me...
I had to do something, but I felt panicked. Useless...
Then I had an idea! A good one too. And for once it wasn't a sequel to the Anaconda vs. Leprechaun franchise!
COMING SOON...
LEPRECONDA

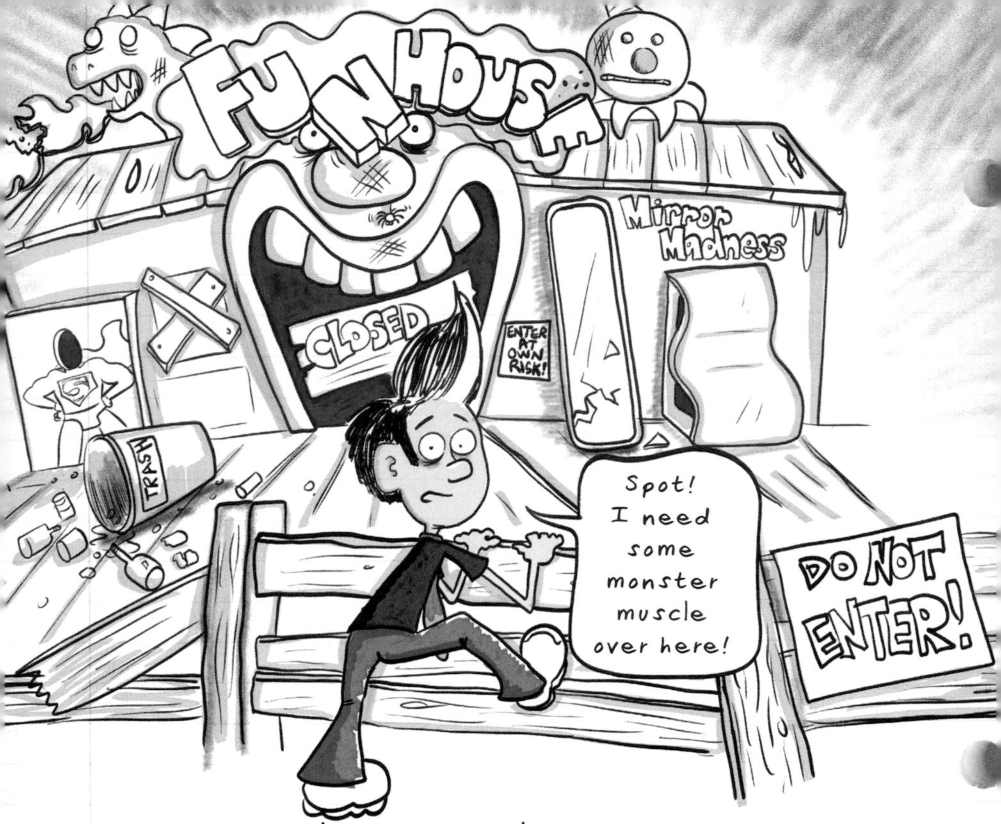
FUN HOUSE
Mirror Madness
CLOSED
ENTER AT OWN RISK!
TRASH
Spot! I need some monster muscle over here!
DO NOT ENTER!

My idea involved moving large, heavy items. I needed Spot's help! And fast! Zandra was in the grip of that thing's tractor beam!

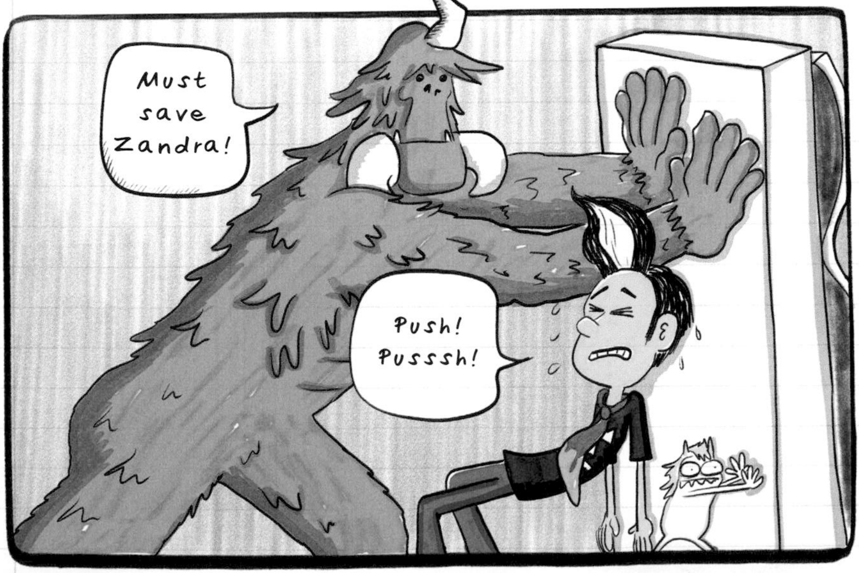
Must save Zandra!
Push! Pussssh!

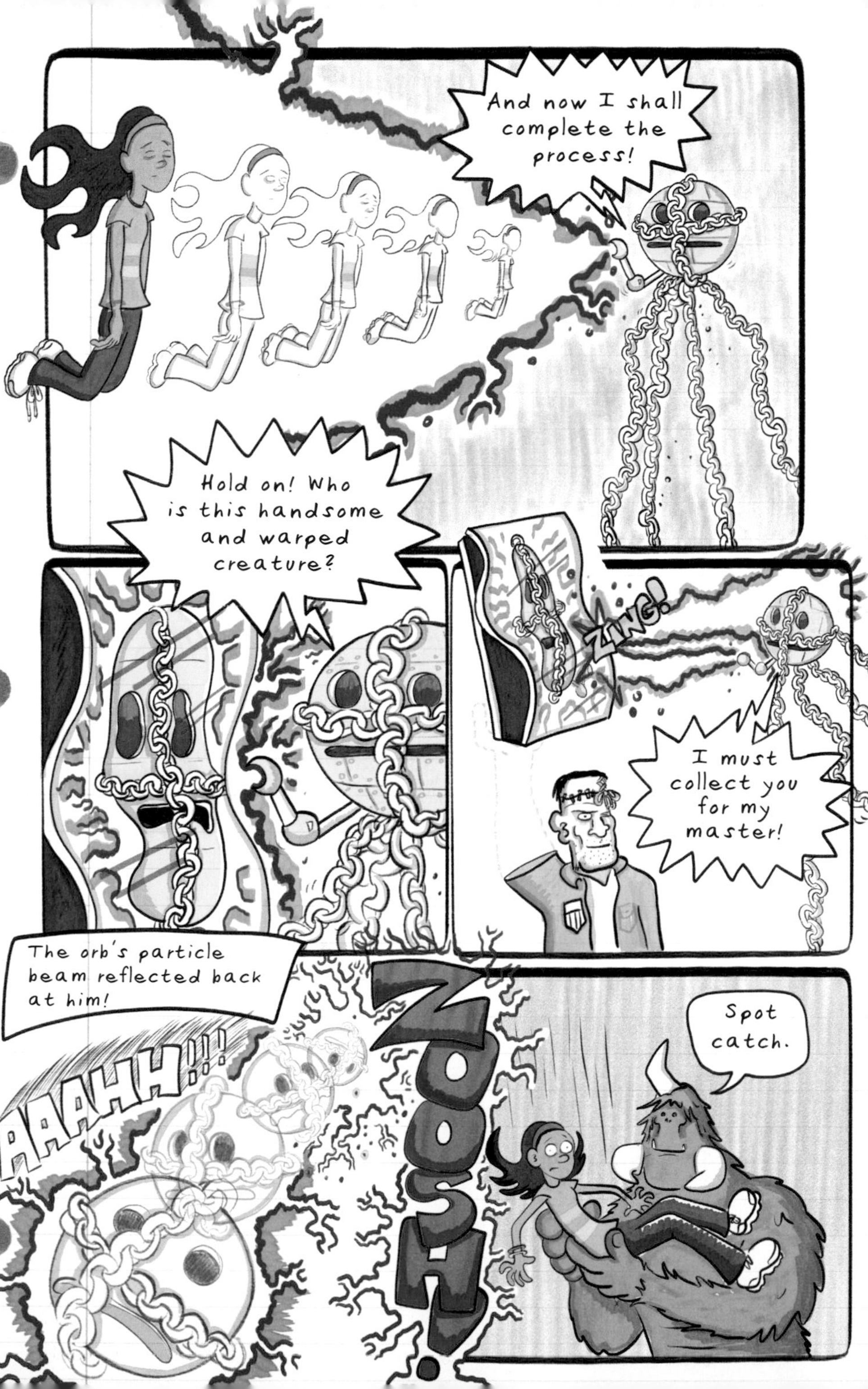
And now I shall complete the process!
Hold on! Who is this handsome and warped creature?
ZING!
I must collect you for my master!
The orb's particle beam reflected back at him!
AAAHH!!!
ZOOSH!
Spot catch.

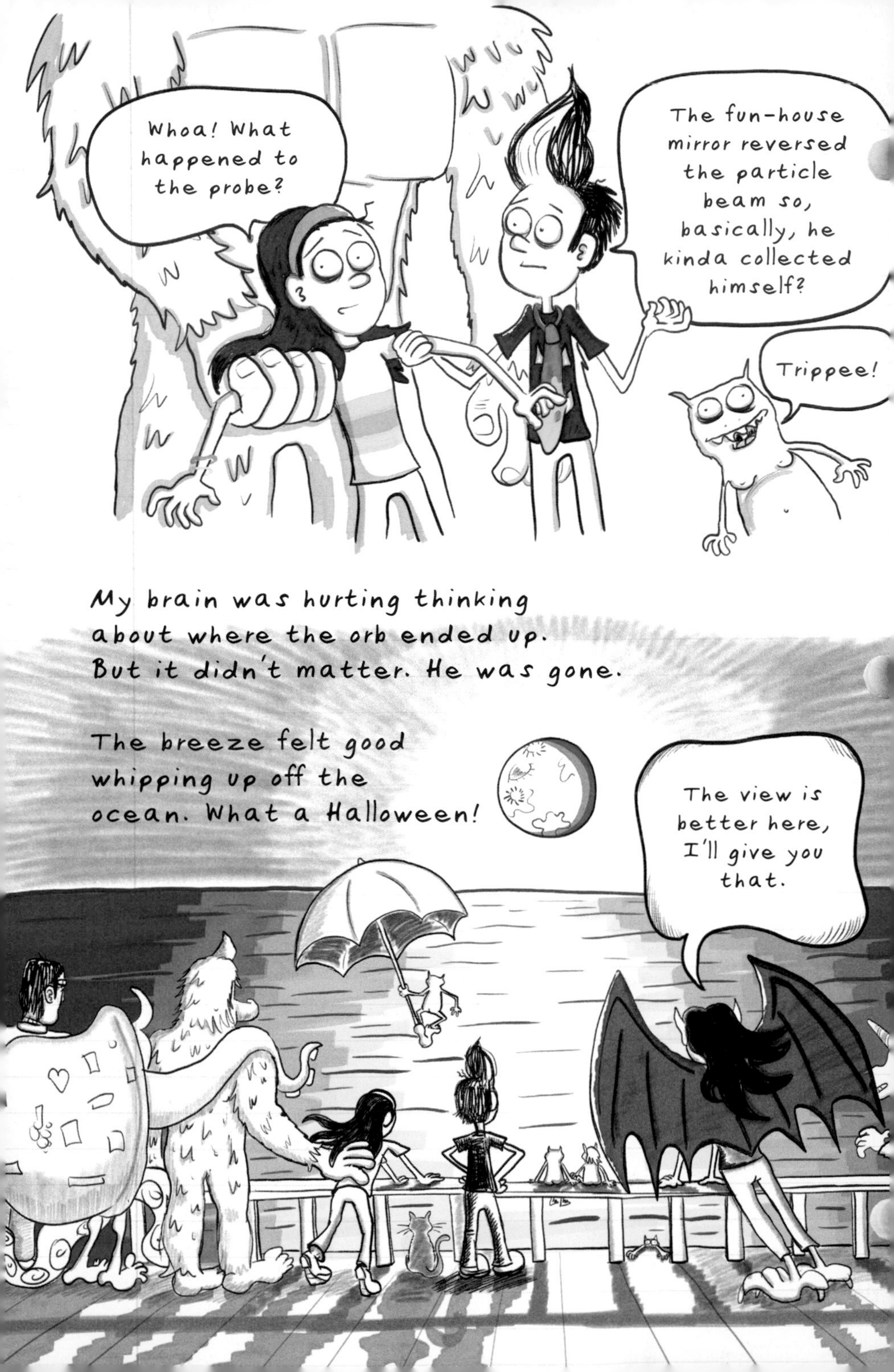
Whoa! What happened to the probe?
The fun-house mirror reversed the particle beam so, basically, he kinda collected himself?
Trippee!
My brain was hurting thinking about where the orb ended up. But it didn't matter. He was gone.
The breeze felt good whipping up off the ocean. What a Halloween!
The view is better here, I'll give you that.

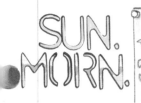

SUN. MORN.

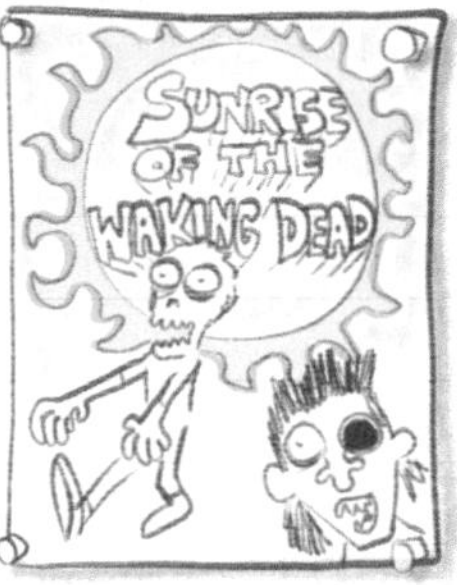
SUNRISE OF THE WAKING DEAD

t's morning
gain. And when
say morning, I
ean 12:15 p.m.
'm exhausted.

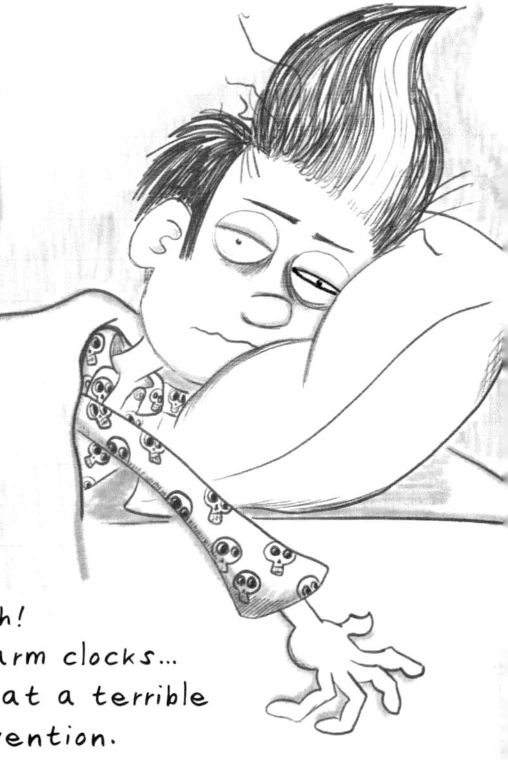

What a night. I just want to stay in bed for another twelve hours. Is that too much to ask?

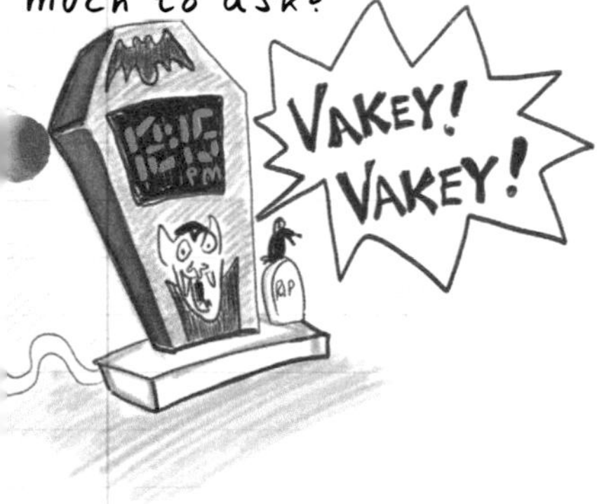
VAKEY! VAKEY!
RIP

Ugh!
Alarm clocks... what a terrible invention.

Dad is full of energy today and I can't deal with it.

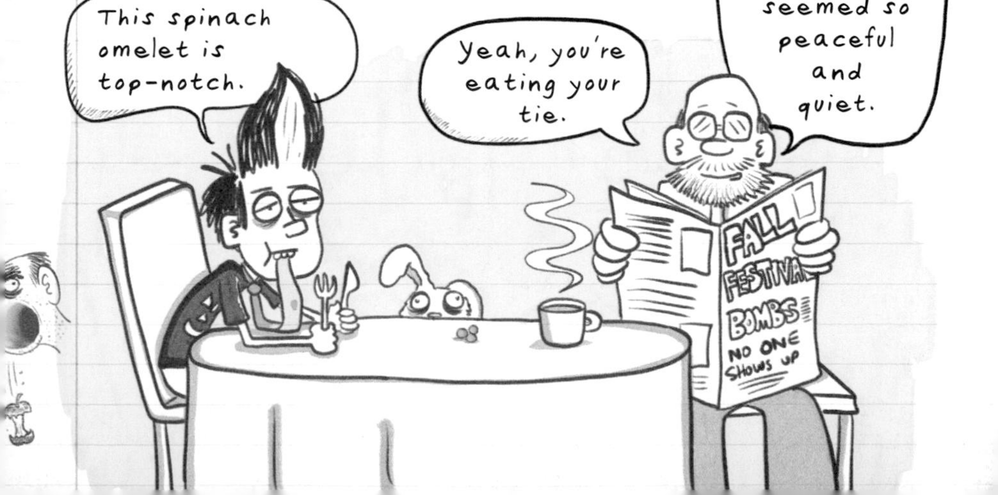
This spinach omelet is top-notch.
Yeah, you're eating your tie.
Man, I slept well last night! The house seemed so peaceful and quiet.
FALL FESTIVAL BOMBS
NO ONE SHOWS UP

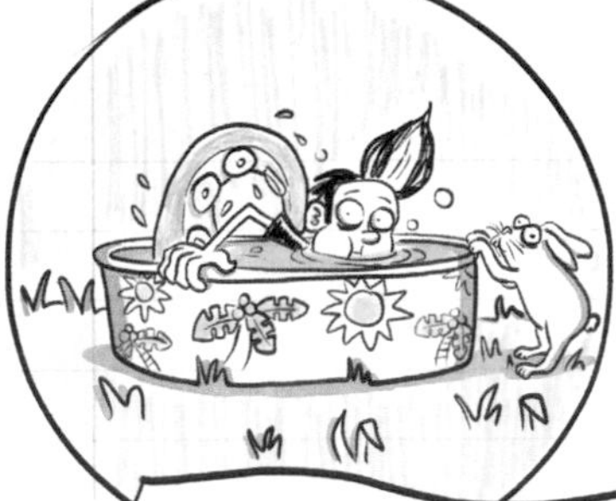

Made a quick hydroport over to the pier at lunchtime to check on the makeover progress.

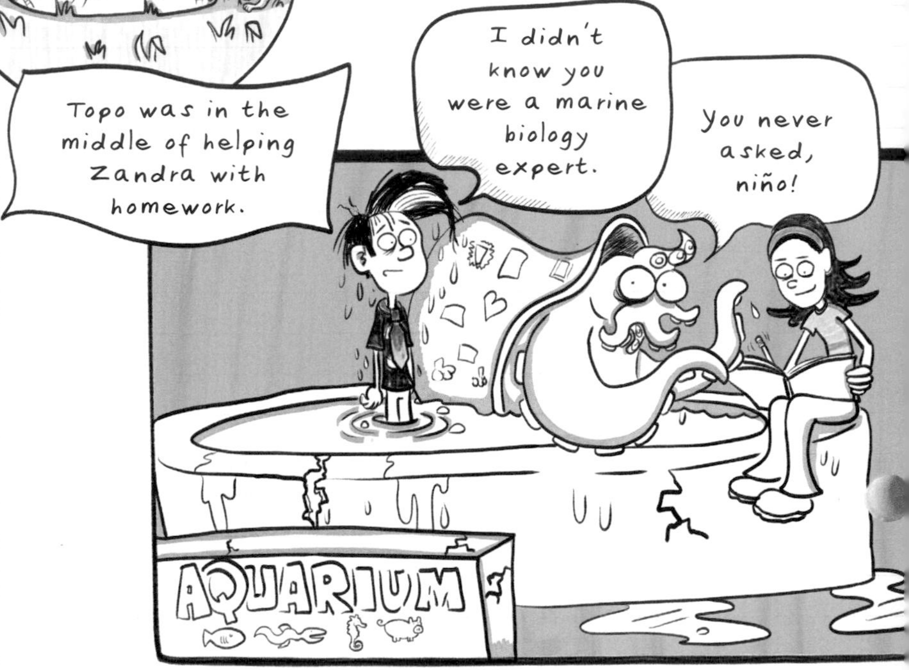
Topo was in the middle of helping Zandra with homework.
I didn't know you were a marine biology expert.
You never asked, niño!
AQUARIUM

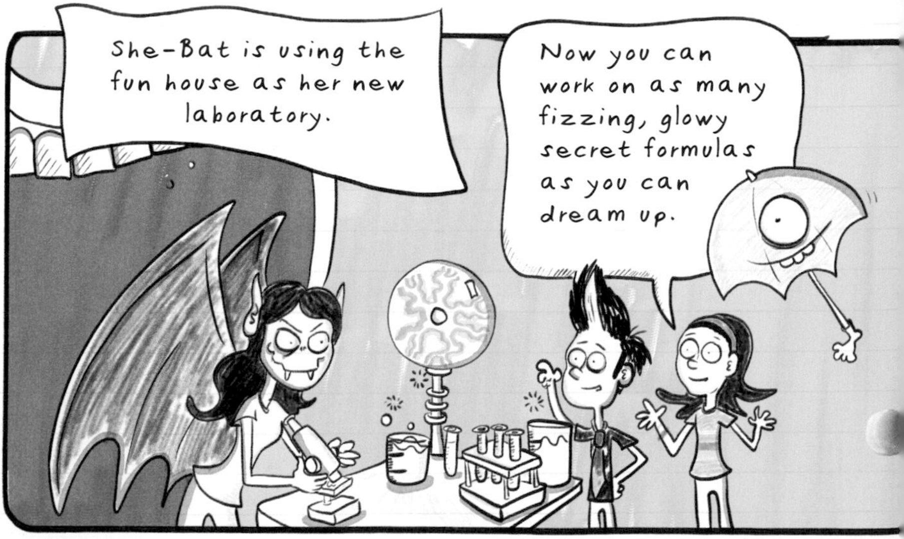
She-Bat is using the fun house as her new laboratory.
Now you can work on as many fizzing, glowy secret formulas as you can dream up.

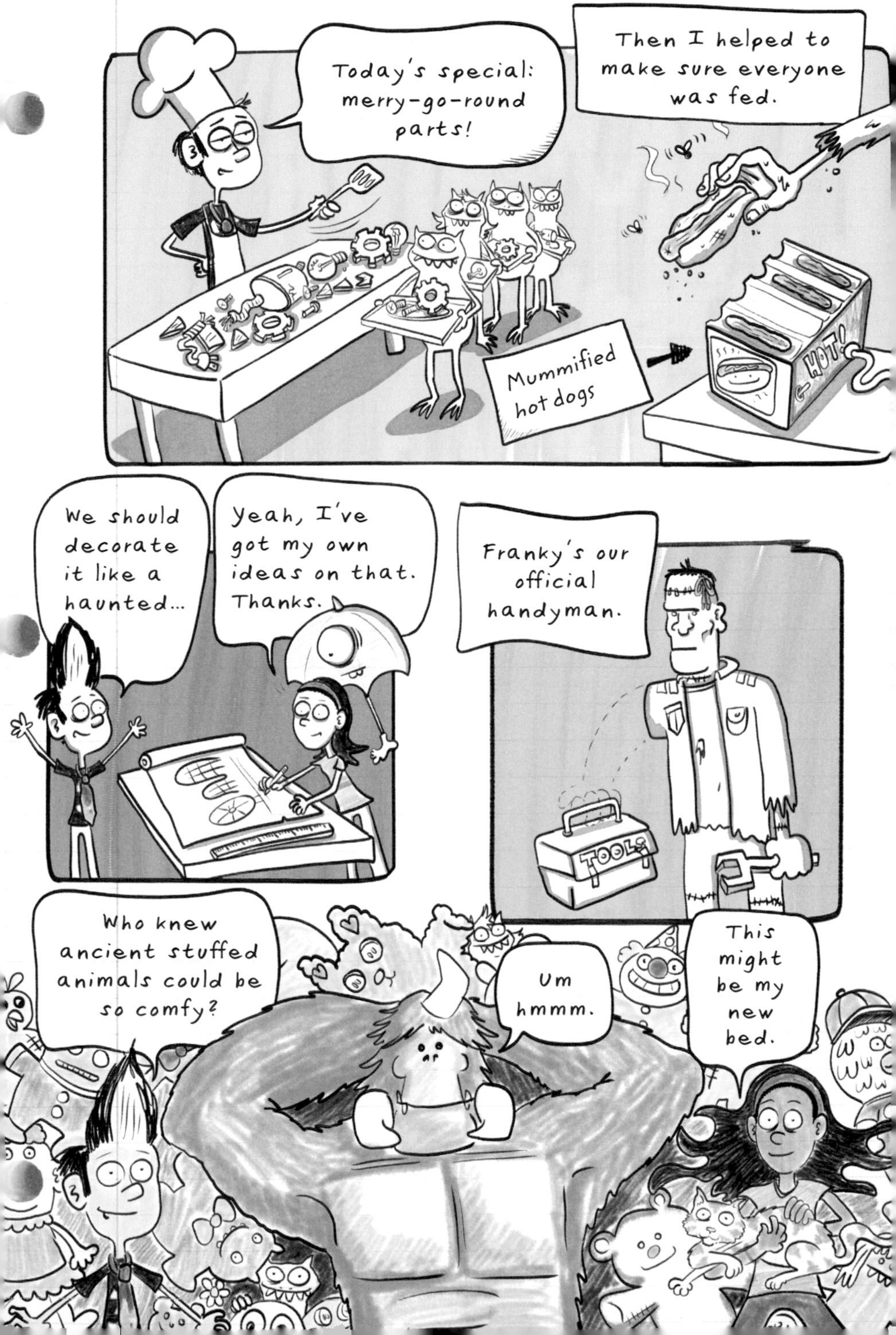
Today's special: merry-go-round parts!
Then I helped to make sure everyone was fed.
Mummified hot dogs
HOT!
We should decorate it like a haunted...
Yeah, I've got my own ideas on that. Thanks.
Franky's our official handyman.
TOOLS
Who knew ancient stuffed animals could be so comfy?
Um hmmm.
This might be my new bed.

SUNDAY 3:30

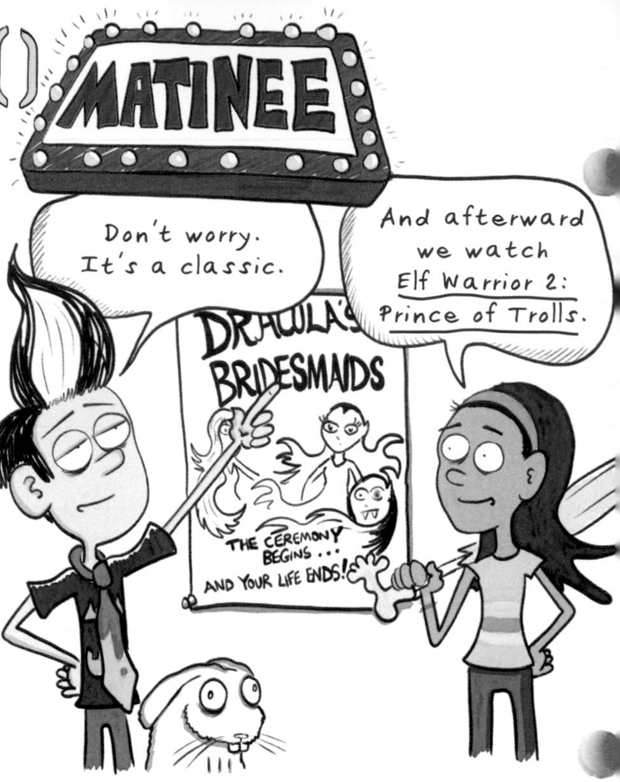
MATINEE
Don't worry. It's a classic.
And afterward we watch Elf Warrior 2: Prince of Trolls.
DRACULA'S BRIDESMAIDS
THE CEREMONY BEGINS . . .
AND YOUR LIFE ENDS!

I've invited Zandra over to watch Dracula's Bridesmaids in honor of my mom. Setting up the TV in my tree house. Dad's joining us too!

I agreed to watch one of Zandra's fantastical movies next time. It's good to compromise.

Dad threw a wrench in the works when he asked Zandra if he could speak to her folks. He just wanted to make sure she had permission to be over at our house. Makes sense. We had to get creative.

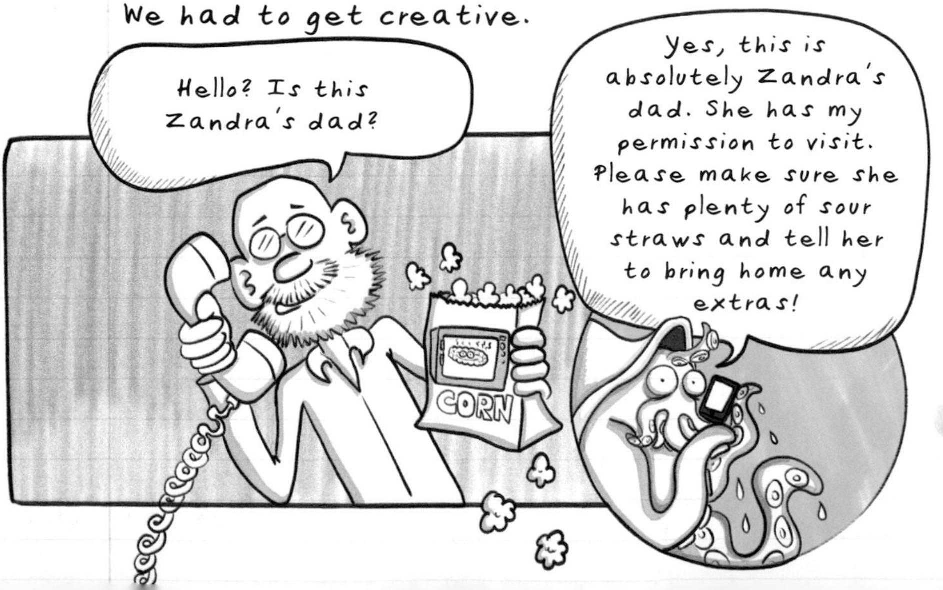
Hello? Is this Zandra's dad?
Yes, this is absolutely Zandra's dad. She has my permission to visit. Please make sure she has plenty of sour straws and tell her to bring home any extras!
CORN

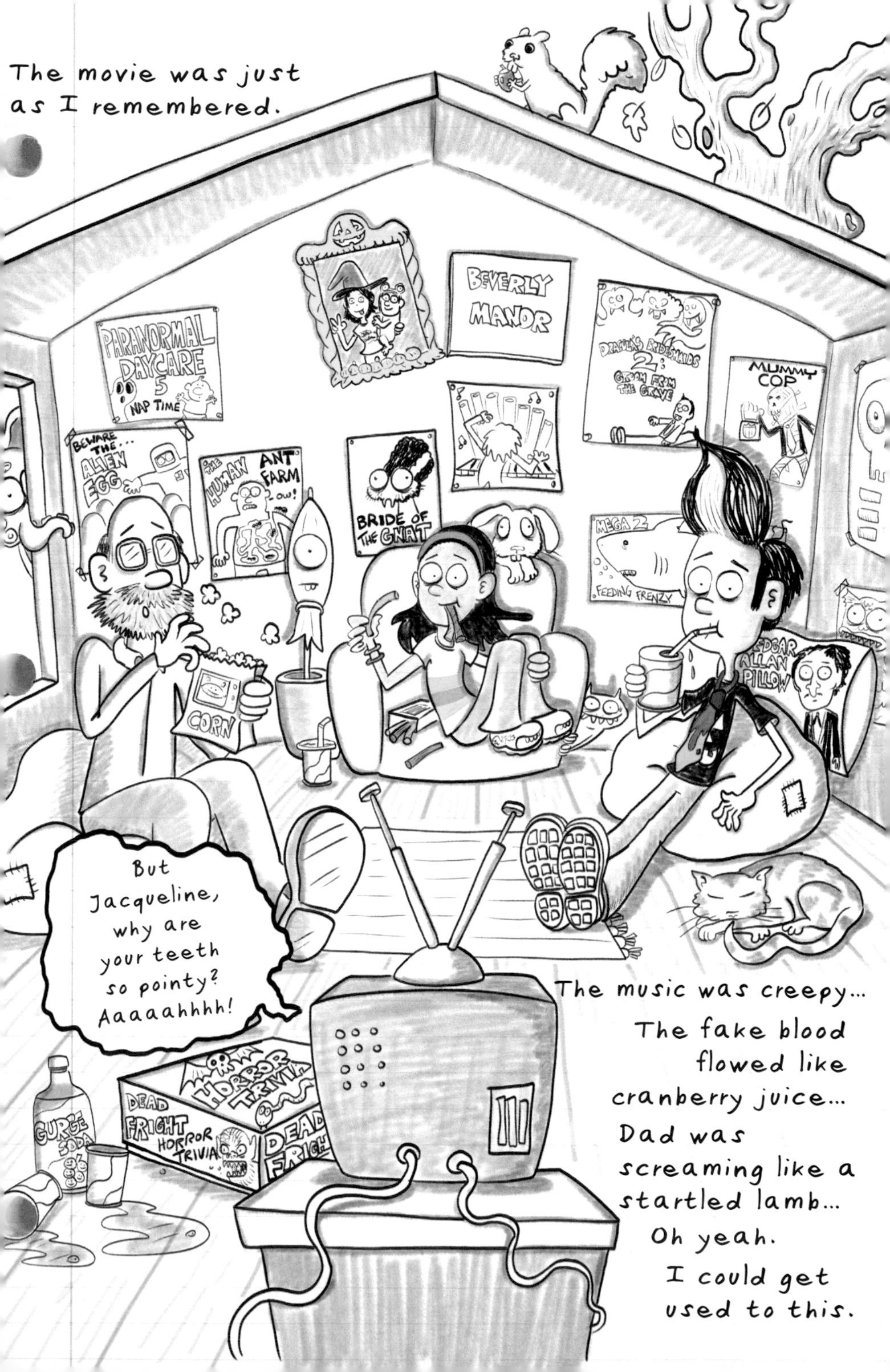
The movie was just as I remembered.
PARANORMAL DAYCARE 5 NAP TIME
BEVERLY MANOR
DRACULA'S BRIDESKIDS 2: GROOM FROM THE GRAVE
MUMMY COP
BEWARE THE... ALIEN EGG
THE HUMAN ANT FARM
OW!
BRIDE OF THE GNAT
MEGA 2 FEEDING FRENZY
EDGAR ALLAN PILLOW
CORN
But Jacqueline, why are your teeth so pointy? Aaaaahhhh!
HORROR TRIVIA
DEAD FRIGHT HORROR TRIVIA
GURGE SODA
The music was creepy...
The fake blood flowed like cranberry juice...
Dad was screaming like a startled lamb...
Oh yeah.
I could get used to this.

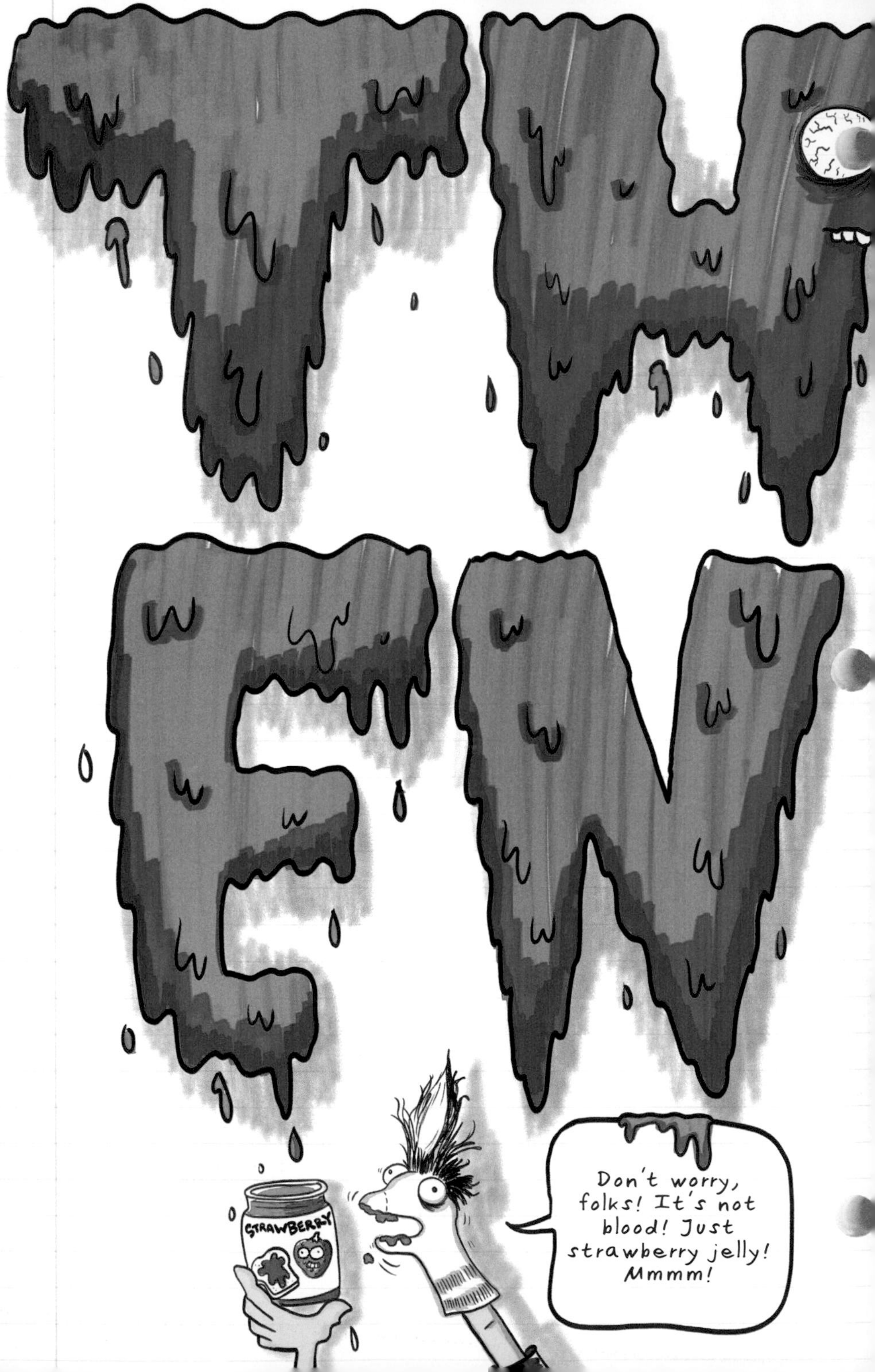
STRAWBERRY
Don't worry, folks! It's not blood! Just strawberry jelly! Mmmm!

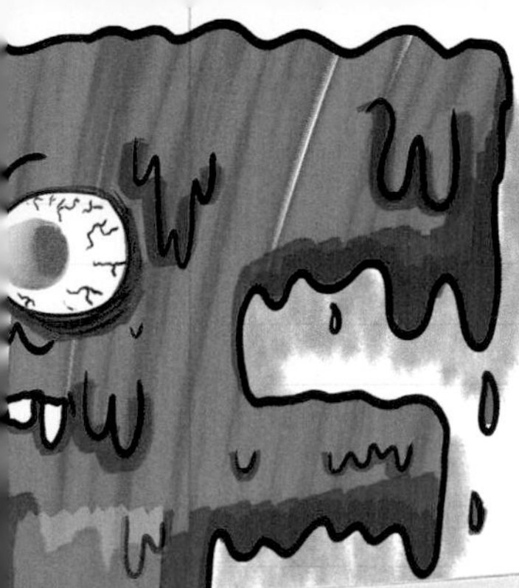

Well, Journal Number 13 is a wrap. My tale has come to its natural and most profound conclusion. Actually, I'm just running out of paper. Join me again for the next horrific chapter. I'm thinking of calling it Journal Number 14!

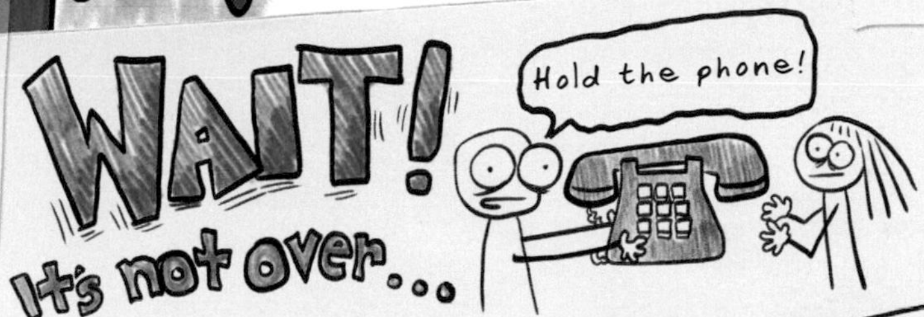

WAIT!
It's not over...
Hold the phone!

Something amazing happened today! I was hanging my new Manga Glam portrait of Frankenstein in the tree house (Yes, Zandra's been teaching me how to use colors other than twenty shades of black).

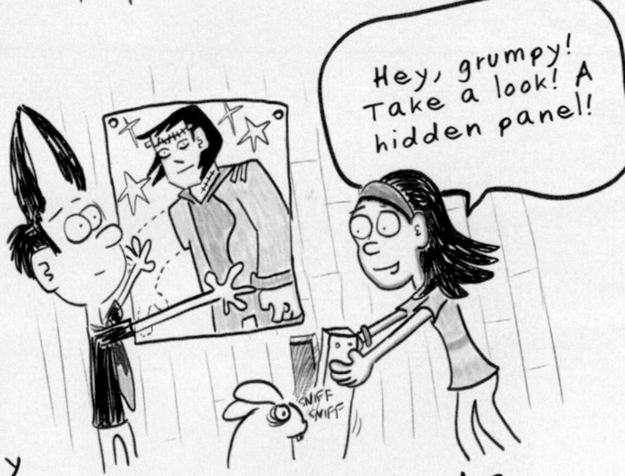

Hey, grumpy! Take a look! A hidden panel!
SNIFF SNIFF

That's when Zandra jostled a board loose. Turns out there was a secret compartment lurking in the wall!

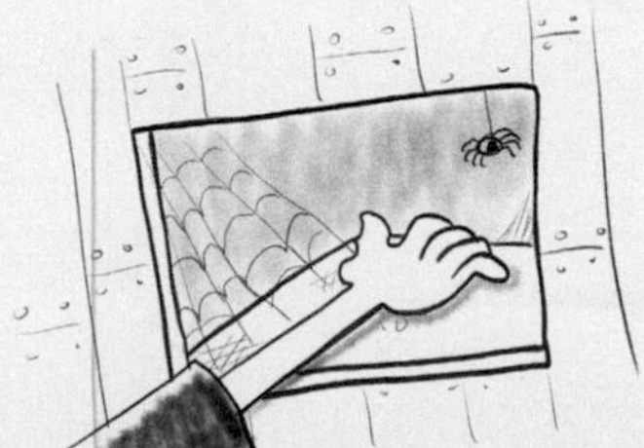

And you won't believe what was tucked away in there...

We found THIS?

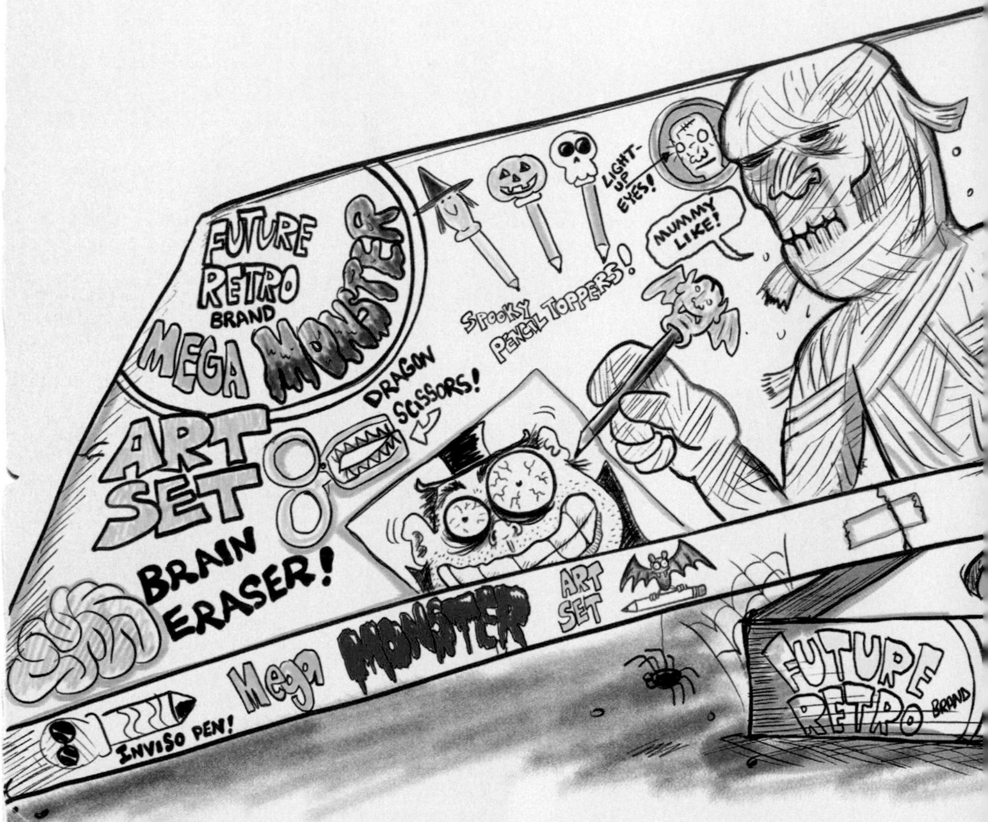
FUTURE RETRO BRAND MEGA MONSTER
ART SET
LIGHT-UP EYES!
MUMMY LIKE!
SPOOKY PENCIL TOPPERS!
DRAGON SCISSORS!
BRAIN ERASER!
Mega MONSTER
ART SET
INVISO PEN!
FUTURE RETRO BRAND

An entire
Future Retro Brand Mega Monster Art Set!
Looks like Count Fango can finally be reunited
with his monster pencil friends!

This must be Mom's from when she was a kid. I wonder if the other pencils have the same powers that Count Fango has?

Or maybe something different?

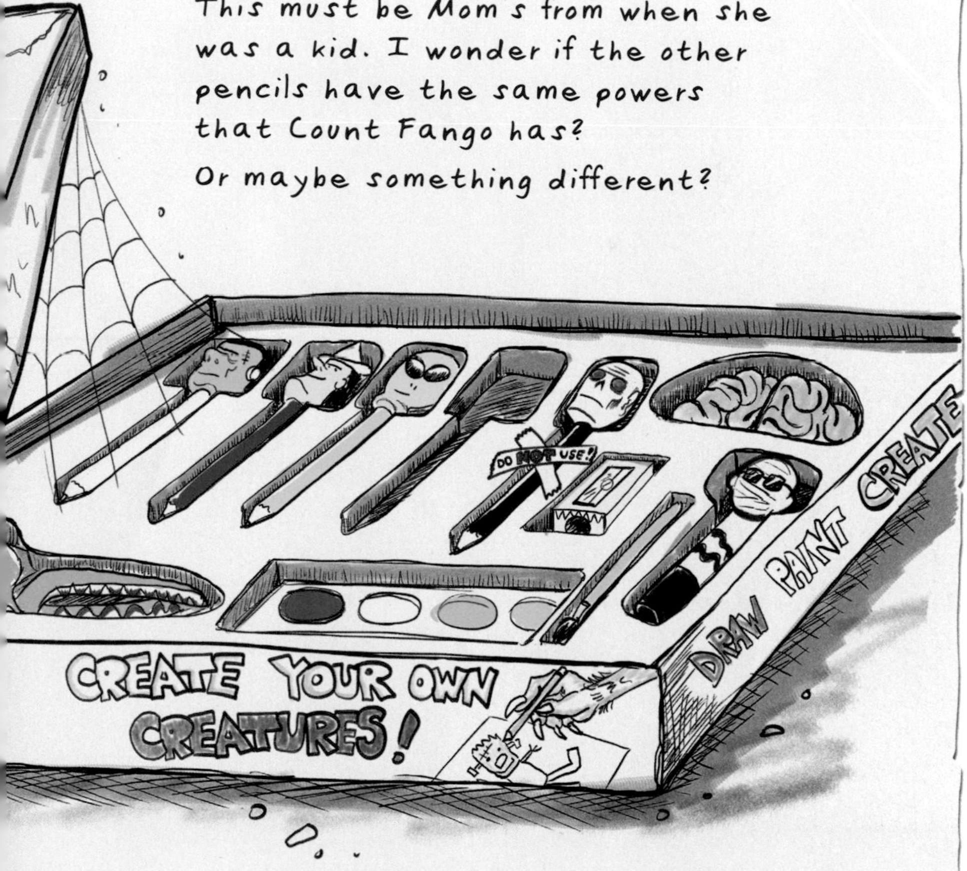
DO NOT USE!
CREATE YOUR OWN CREATURES!
DRAW PAINT CREATE

All I know is
I can't wait to try these out!

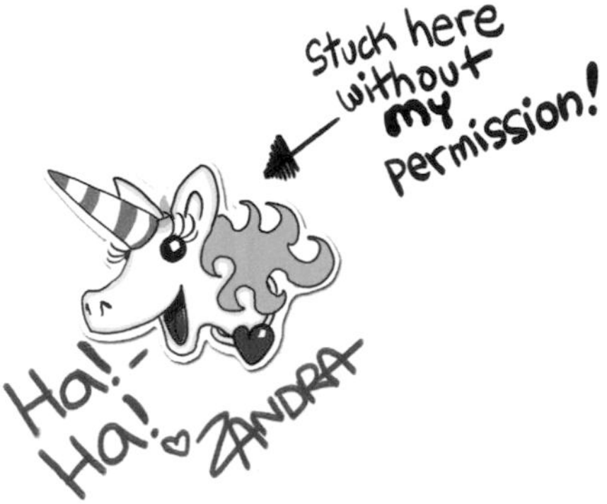
Stuck here without my permission!
Ha! Ha! ♡ ZANDRA

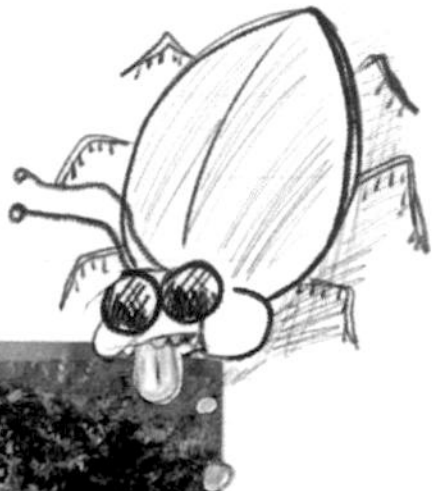

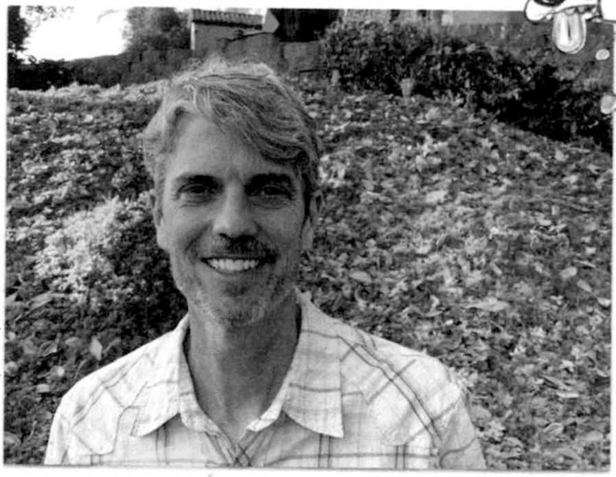

Photo by Stephen Deline

Kirk Scroggs was born and raised in Austin, Texas. In kindergarten, Kirk's teachers were so impressed with his horrifying drawings of zombies, witches, and monsters that they often called his parents and even recommended a few "experts" take a look at his work. Thankfully for Kirk's poor mother, he grew out of his monster kick and went on to study film at the University of Texas, which inspired him to move to sunny Los Angeles to pursue his dream of working retail and living in a luxury un-air-conditioned apartment. After years of reassessment, reflection, and hard work, Kirk has finally realized his true calling...drawing horrifying pictures of zombies, witches, and monsters. His first graphic novel for DC Books for Young Readers, *The Secret Spiral of Swamp Kid*, was published in 2019 to great reviews.

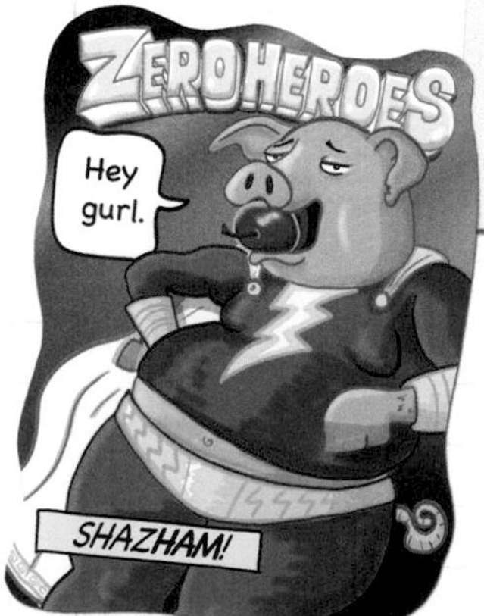
ZERO HEROES
Hey gurl.
SHAZHAM!

Have you ever wondered what's at the bottom of the sea? Why polar ice melts? Or which tools forensic scientists use to solve a crime? Well the Flash and some of his close friends are here to take readers on a journey to answer these questions and more!

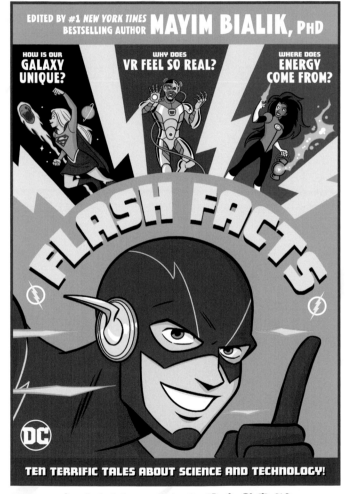

Award-winning actress and author **Mayim Bialik**, PhD, brings together an all-star cast of writers and illustrators in this anthology, including **Michael Northrop** (*Dear Justice League*), **Cecil Castelluci** (*Batgirl*), and **Kirk Scroggs** (*The Secret Spiral of Swamp Kid*)!

RUSSELL'S SPIRAL

MONDAY 4:20 P.M.

Russell here. I'm so exhausted I can barely write. Today was my first practice for the cross-country track team! Why oh why did I let Charlotte talk me into it? I swore I'd never run again after my last track fiasco!

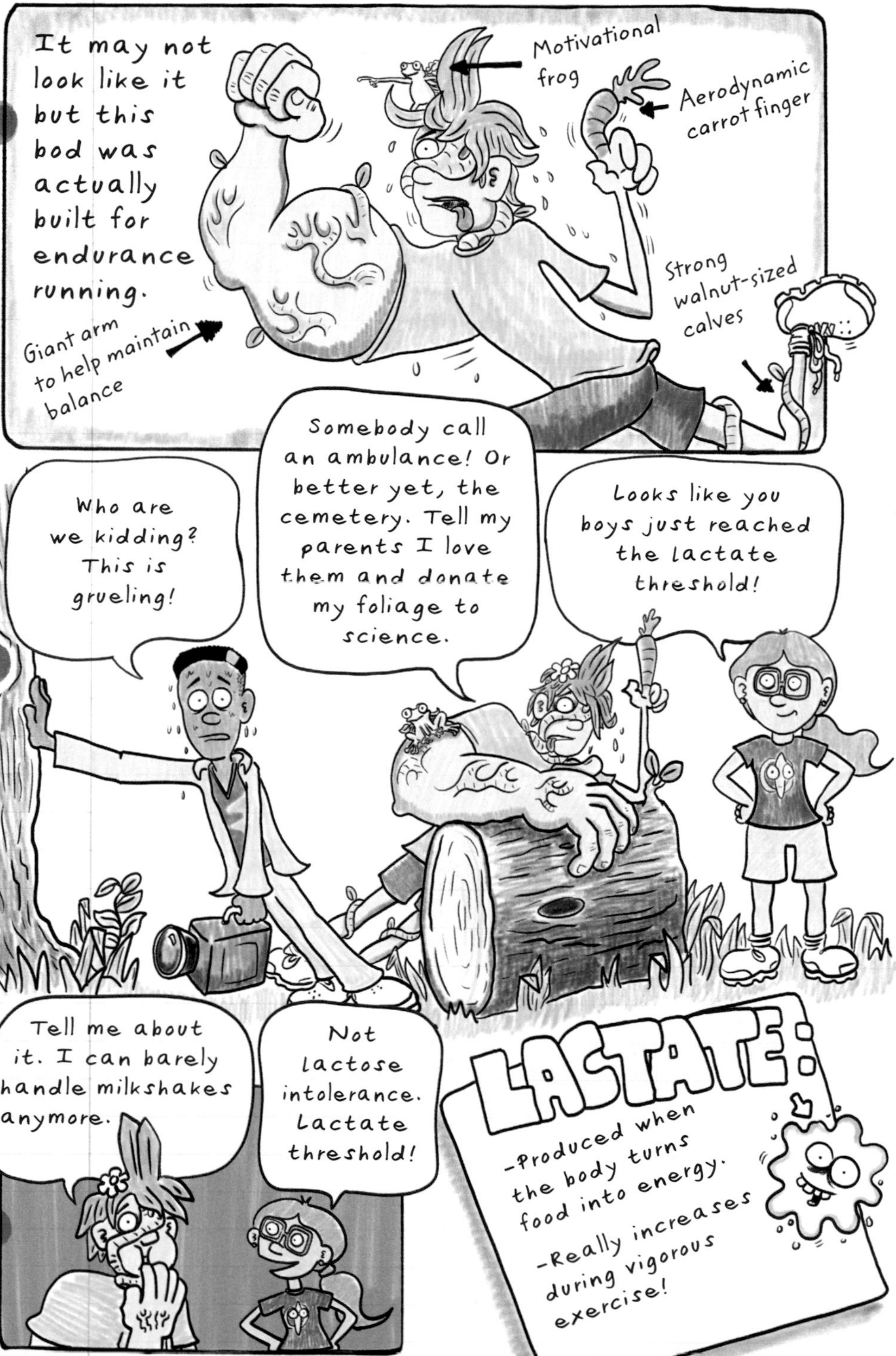
It may not look like it but this bod was actually built for endurance running.
Motivational frog
Aerodynamic carrot finger
Giant arm to help maintain balance
Strong walnut-sized calves
Who are we kidding? This is grueling!
Somebody call an ambulance! Or better yet, the cemetery. Tell my parents I love them and donate my foliage to science.
Looks like you boys just reached the lactate threshold!
Tell me about it. I can barely handle milkshakes anymore.
Not lactose intolerance. Lactate threshold!
LACTATE:
-Produced when the body turns food into energy.
-Really increases during vigorous exercise!

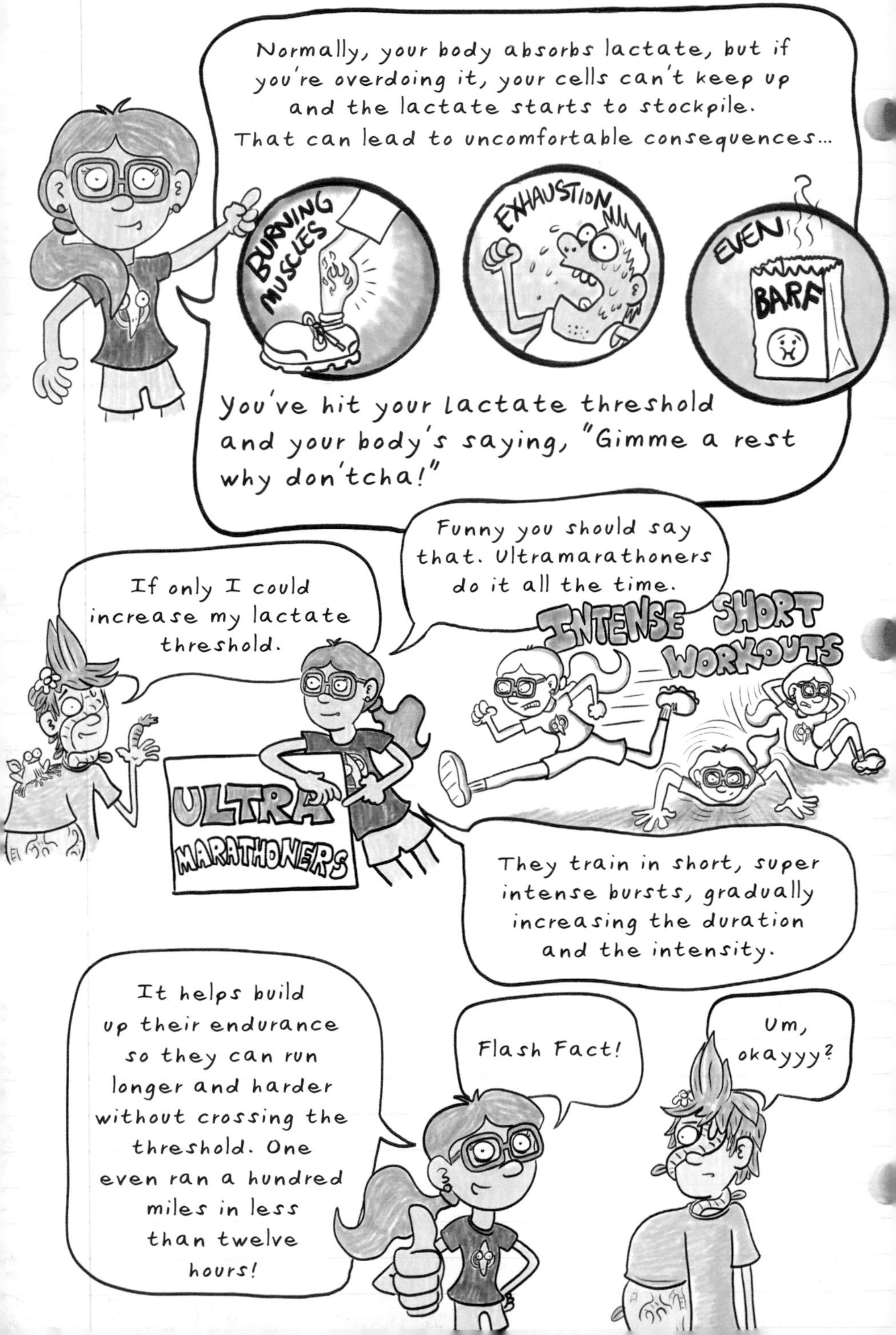
Normally, your body absorbs lactate, but if you're overdoing it, your cells can't keep up and the lactate starts to stockpile. That can lead to uncomfortable consequences...
BURNING MUSCLES
EXHAUSTION
EVEN
BARF
You've hit your lactate threshold and your body's saying, "Gimme a rest why don'tcha!"
If only I could increase my lactate threshold.
Funny you should say that. Ultramarathoners do it all the time.
ULTRA MARATHONERS
INTENSE SHORT WORKOUTS
They train in short, super intense bursts, gradually increasing the duration and the intensity.
It helps build up their endurance so they can run longer and harder without crossing the threshold. One even ran a hundred miles in less than twelve hours!
Flash Fact!
Um, okayyy?

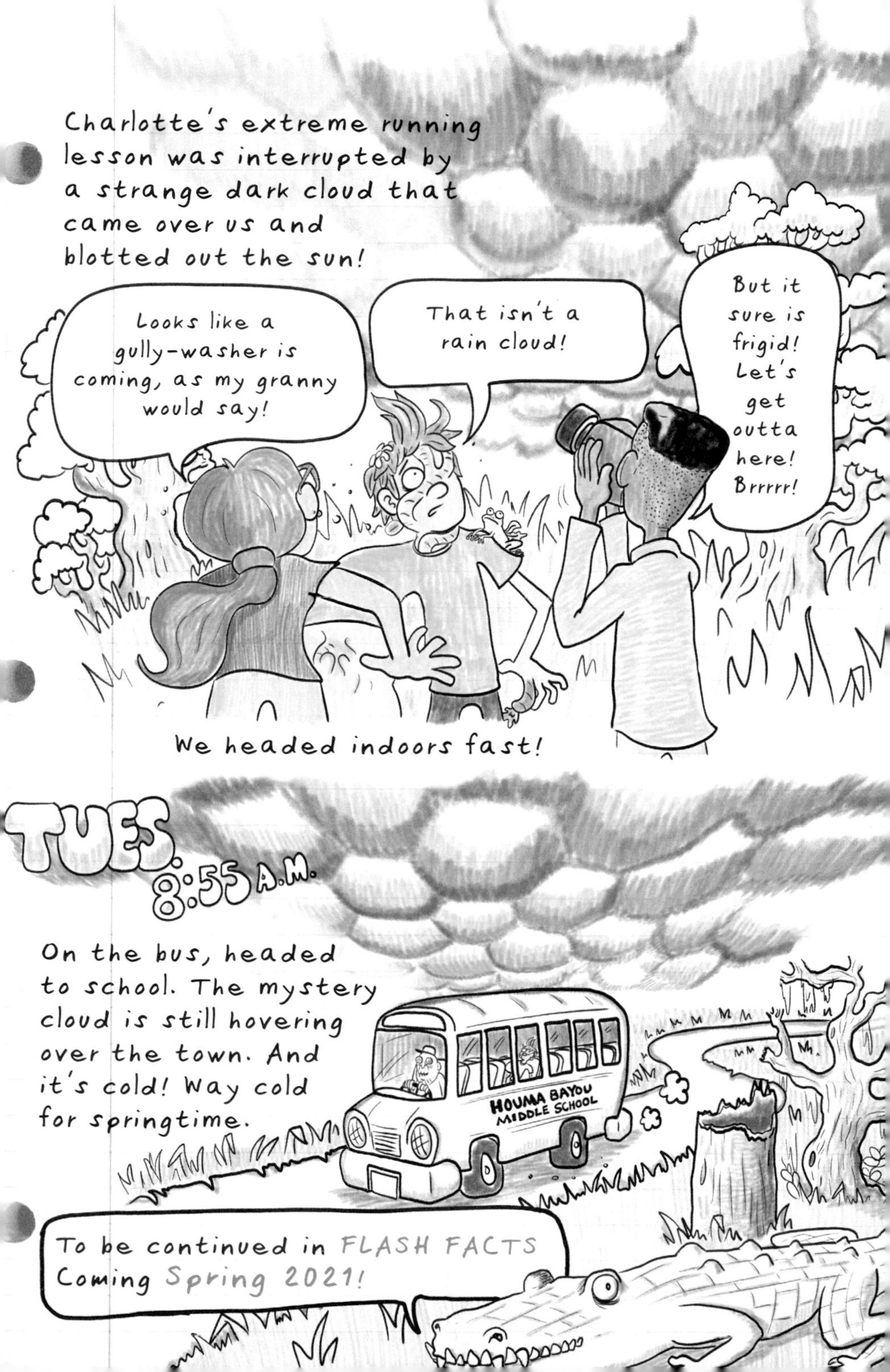
Charlotte's extreme running lesson was interrupted by a strange dark cloud that came over us and blotted out the sun!
Looks like a gully-washer is coming, as my granny would say!
That isn't a rain cloud!
But it sure is frigid! Let's get outta here! Brrrrr!
We headed indoors fast!
TUES. 8:55 A.M.
On the bus, headed to school. The mystery cloud is still hovering over the town. And it's cold! Way cold for springtime.
HOUMA BAYOU MIDDLE SCHOOL
To be continued in FLASH FACTS Coming Spring 2021!